PENGUIN BOOKS

A TIME ELSEWHERE

J.P. (Jagannath Prasad) Das is an eminent poet, playwright, fiction writer and critic. His books have been widely translated into Hindi, English and other Indian languages and his plays have been performed in many languages in different parts of India. A Ph.D. in Art History, he has authored several books on Oriya art. He was a member of the Indian Administrative Service, but left it to devote himself to full-time research and writing. He is a recipient of the Sahitya Akademi award and the Saraswati Samman. Born in 1936 in Orissa, he lives and works in New Delhi.

Educated at Ravenshaw College, Orissa and Merton College, Oxford, Jatindra Kumar Nayak teaches English at Utkal University, Orissa. He has won the Hutch-Crossword Indian Fiction Translation Award, 2004 and the Katha Translation Award, 1997.

A Time Elsewhere

J.P. DAS

Translated from the Oriya by
JATINDRA K. NAYAK

PENGUIN BOOKS

PENGUIN BOOKS
Published by the Penguin Group
Penguin Books India Pvt. Ltd, 11 Community Centre, Panchsheel Park,
New Delhi 110 017, India
Penguin Group (USA) Inc., 375 Hudson Street, New York, New York 10014,
USA
Penguin Group (Canada), 90 Eglinton Avenue East, Suite 700, Toronto, Ontario,
M4P 2Y3, Canada (a division of Pearson Penguin Canada Inc.)
Penguin Books Ltd, 80 Strand, London WC2R 0RL, England
Penguin Ireland, 25 St Stephen's Green, Dublin 2, Ireland (a division of Penguin
Books Ltd)
Penguin Group (Australia), 250 Camberwell Road, Camberwell, Victoria 3124,
Australia (a division of Pearson Australia Group Pty Ltd)
Penguin Group (NZ), 67 Apollo Drive, Rosedale, North Shore 0632,
New Zealand (a division of Pearson New Zealand Ltd)
Penguin Group (South Africa) (Pty) Ltd, 24 Sturdee Avenue, Rosebank,
Johannesburg 2196, South Africa

Penguin Books Ltd, Registered Offices: 80 Strand, London WC2R 0RL,
England

First published in Oriya as *Desh Kaal Patra* by Prachi Prakashan, India, 1992
First published by Penguin Books India 2009

Copyright © J.P. Das 2009
Translation copyright © Jatindra K. Nayak 2009

Typeset in Adobe Jenson Pro by InoSoft Systems, Noida
Printed at Chaman Offset Printers, Delhi

For two thousand years Orissa has been the Holy Land of the Hindus … it is 'the land that taketh away sin'.

—W.W. Hunter, *Orissa*

Outsiders say that Oriyas are so thick-headed that no matter how hard they try, they can never master any subject. However, closer scrutiny will show that such a view is incorrect.

—*Utkal Dipika*

The deep dark night has come to an end.

Radhanath Ray, 'Chilika'

Translator's Note

The British occupation of Orissa took place in 1803. Militarily, it was not at all an exciting event. The invading army marching into Orissa from the south met little resistance. In fact, it had no difficulty in finding collaborators on the way. A local chieftain, whose little kingdom lay on the route taken by the British army, did not come forward to help it only because he had been told that Englishmen had faces like those of pigs, and that they had such large ears that they slept on one ear and covered themselves with the other to keep warm on cold nights. In any case, the army did not need collaborators since the Marathas, then ruling Orissa, simply fled. Fourteen years later, resistance against British rule was mobilized by the dispossessed chieftains, but their rebellion was swiftly crushed. With the old military aristocracy of Orissa thus subdued and humbled, the British now set about colonizing an exhausted, defeated society.

A Time Elsewhere tells the story of the transformation of a traditional society under the impact of colonial rule. This story has of course been told time and again in the travelogues, memoirs, reports and letters written by the colonizers themselves. But in the master narratives constructed by all these, the colonized is rarely allowed to speak for himself, to have a voice. He is allowed only a bit part in the drama of colonial encounter. *A Time Elsewhere* seeks to construct an alternative narrative in which the colonized is not content to be only written about; he is seen as shaping his own destiny. The book does not only deal with the collapse of an old order; it dramatizes the emergence of a new order out of the debris of the old.

The novel begins, appropriately enough, with the events leading up to the disastrous famine of 1866. In this famine nearly a third of the entire population of Orissa perished, while a callous colonial bureaucracy, steeped in the utilitarian doctrines of J.S. Mill, refused to act or intervene. The dogmatism of the colonizer matched the fatalism of the colonized, some of whom chose to die by the wayside rather than lose their caste by going to a hospital run by the British. The 1866 famine exposed the vulnerability of a traditional social order placed under colonial rule. The contact between a militarily and technologically superior society and a community rooted in age-old custom proved disastrous for the latter. For its survival, the traditional social order of Orissa had to adapt painfully to the harsh reality of colonial rule, and to forge new techniques of survival and resistance. A newly emergent Oriya intelligentsia, themselves a product of the education system introduced by the colonial rulers, now took it upon themselves to apply these new techniques. It is not without significance that in the famine year the first printed Oriya weekly, the *Utkal Dipika* (Lamp of Orissa) was launched by Gourishankar Ray, who served as a clerk in the commissioner's office at Cuttack. What the magazine offered to the devitalized Oriya society in 1866 was the possibility of cultural resistance to British rule.

If the first half of *A Time Elsewhere* is dominated by accounts of the dismal fate of decadent feudal lords and the deeds of colonial bureaucrats, in the second half the narrator celebrates the achievements of the emergent Oriya intelligentsia, consisting of schoolteachers, minor government officials and lawyers. Refusing to be relegated to the margins of the colonizer's master narrative, they seek to step into the role of narrators themselves. Writing, therefore, assumes a special place in the lives of the Oriya intelligentsia in the nineteenth century. Fakir Mohan Senapati translates the Ramayan in order to overcome a crisis in his personal life. Pandit Harihar Das translates Homer into Sanskrit. Radhanath Ray writes poems celebrating localities and landscapes of Orissa. Pyari Mohan Acharya, expelled from school for defying British authorities, writes a history of Orissa.

But a price had to be paid for such an impressive achievement. In contesting the hegemony of the colonizer, they could not but interrogate some of the central assumptions underpinning their own society. While resisting the British, they could not at the same time avoid becoming collaborators. The pressure of the dialectic of collaboration and resistance proved too much for several members of the Oriya intelligentsia. Caught between conflicting value systems many of them experienced an acute crisis of identity. It is not to be wondered at, then, that Pandit Harihar Das loses his mind, Fakir Mohan descends into alcoholism for a time, Madhusudan Das embraces Christianity and Madhsudan Rao and Biswanath Kar reject the caste system and become Brahmo Samajis. Contact with the culture of the colonizer makes them aware of their individuality and leads them to question, and sometimes even reject, established customs, rituals and conventions. It is significant that *A Time Elsewhere* opens with the worries of a dying king without a kingdom about problems of dynastic succession and ends forty-eight years later, with Radhanath Ray, a self-made man and an established poet, experiencing a profound crisis of conscience and taking responsibility for his actions. No other conclusion could be more fitting for a narrative dealing with the decay of an old order and the emergence of a new one under the impact of colonial rule.

Constructing a counter discourse which gives a voice to the colonized is, however, only one of the achievements of *A Time Elsewhere*. The brilliant narrative strategies the author employs in writing the social and cultural history of Orissa in the latter half of the nineteenth century accounts for much of our pleasure in reading the book. Unconfined by the conventions governing the writing of scholarly history or fictionalized biography, the narrative shifts its focus constantly so that no single person or event dominates the centerstage. A picture of Orissa changing rapidly under alien rule is pieced together from fragments of biography. What gives coherence to this kaleidoscopic picture of the past and serves to unify the narrative is a vision of decay followed by regeneration.

The book is everywhere enlivened by flashes of wit and robust humour. The colonial encounter dramatized here is sometimes tragic, often funny, but never dull. We are told how Sir Cecil Beadon, the lieutenant governor, looked like a white-faced monkey to the boy-king of Puri, who is later tried for murder by a judge whom people took to be Charles Dickens's son because of his surname. The Oriya astronomer, Pathani Samanta, washes his hands after the white commissioner shakes him by the hand. And, while a controversy rages over British plans to take over the management of the Jagannath temple, people in the temple town seriously debate whether it is right to kill a flock of vicious monkeys who make life hell for them.

In translating this book I have benefited immensely from the advice and suggestions of the author, Dr J.P Das. I am deeply indebted to my friend Kamalakant Mohapatra for his encouragement and support. I express my sincere thanks to Loknath Panda for word processing the manuscript. I thank the Sikshasandhan team for their cooperation. I feel sincerely grateful to Basant Kumar Pal, who has painstakingly proofread the translation.

Jatindra K. Nayak

Bhubaneshwar
01 September 2009

one

Puri, December 1859

Jackals suddenly began howling in chorus, as if they were determined to take over the town of Puri. Their howling and the chilly morning breeze roused Birakeshari from sleep. He had dozed off in the small hours of the morning after tossing and turning all night in a fever. Lying in bed, he fixed his eyes on the lamp that burned feebly; it appeared even feebler against the first light of the day. In the darkness of the night the lamp had seemed intimately bound up with his life; as if life would come to an end when the lamp petered out. But his chief queen, Suryamani, had stayed up all night and not only kept him alive; she had also kept the lamp burning. She now lay fast asleep in a chair beside his sickbed.

Throughout the night, fear and anxieties had oppressed him. But now Birakeshari's mind was calm and untroubled. He took solace from the thought that not only was he the raja of Khurda or Puri, by the grace of Lord Jagannath, he was raja of all of Orissa. He began silently to repeat his royal title, which had taken him long to commit to memory: Illustrious Hero, Lord of Elephants, Sovereign of Bengal, Supreme Monarch of Utkal-Karnata-Nine forts, Terrible as Bhairav, Protector of the Pious, Master of Warriors, Mighty Lord with a Thousand Arms in Battle, Comet of the Kshatriya Race, the Great Emperor

Sri Sri Sri Birakeshari Dev. But rehearsing the title failed to bring him any solace. What possible relief could one, who had been king for only four years and was dying at the age of twenty-five, expect?

The thoughts which had filled his mind through the night came crowding back. His childhood had been dominated by fear and illness. Although he had wanted to study, his poor health did not permit him to go very far. And he had been subjected to harsh discipline by his father, Ramachandra Dev. Ramachandra had died four years earlier but it seemed as if he still kept a close watch over Birakeshari's every action. His father had never allowed Birakeshari to step out of the palace; his entire life was spent within its four walls, among the people who lived there and the people who visited it. Birakeshari stepped out on to the streets of Puri for the first time when he accompanied his father's bier. It remained for him a memorable occasion.

Birakeshari recalled his father with some anger mingled with a little fear. Ramachandra Dev had ascended the throne at the age of fourteen and had remained king for nearly forty years. He was a deeply religious man and intensely devoted to Lord Jagannath. In the morning, he would not touch even water before the first offerings were made to Lord Jagannath at the temple. The bitterness which Birakeshari felt towards his father spilled over into his attitude towards Lord Jagannath. Although he went through all the rituals and observed all the rules, Birakeshari never felt really close to the god. All night, every time he tried to think of the deity, Birakeshari succeeded only in remembering his father. It was as if Ramachandra stood between him and Lord Jagannath, and this was yet another of Birakeshari's many grievances against his father. Whenever he thought about his father, the solid, well built figure of Ramachandra would appear before him, and Birakeshari would remember the many occasions when his father had tried to discipline him.

When Birakeshari was a child, Ramachandra would take him to a heap of stones lying near the palace wall and show him the stone sculptures. These had been brought there from the temple at Konark and Ramachandra planned to use them to repair the temple of Lord Jagannath. So profound was his devotion to Lord Jagannath that he did not hesitate to pull portions of the Konark temple down in order to repair the Jagannath temple. After getting permission from the district magistrate of Puri, he set about dismantling the Konark temple and bringing sculptures and stones over to Puri with such zeal and vigour that the Asiatic Society had to intervene and get the magistrate to withdraw permission.

By this time, however, Ramachandra Dev's men had brought quite a few sculptures from the Konark temple to Puri. Ramachandra would point to these and tell Birakeshari, 'If Commissioner Ricketts had not stopped me, I would have brought half of the stones of Konark temple to Puri.' One wish of his, however, remained unfulfilled. When the figures were thrown down from a height, many of them were damaged. But Ramachandra had instructed his men to ensure that the *Navagraha* slab of stone with the images of the nine planetary gods carved on it remained absolutely intact. The masons had lowered the slab with immense care. Ramachandra had wanted to install the planetary gods in the Puri temple premises. But in this he had not been successful, and he always told this to Birakesari with some regret.

Ramachandra also used to tell Birakeshari of his many grievances against the sahibs. They had always harassed and levied fines on him whenever things went wrong in the temple. A few years ago, an accident inside the temple had claimed the lives of some pilgrims. Birakeshari recalled that this incident made life very difficult for Ramachandra for a long time. The sahibs made life no less difficult for Birakeshari himself after he became the king. From time to time, various orders were issued to him by the district magistrate of Puri, Mr Mactier. If he ever protested, the magistrate would simply not listen and if he protested too much, the magistrate would tell him that the order came from Cuttack from the commissioner, Cockburn. It was as if Cockburn were god almighty, against whom there existed no court of appeal.

Once, a document had come to Birakeshari for his signature. This said that the government would discontinue the money grant to the temple and offered him some land in Khurda in lieu of it. His attorneys advised Birakeshari against putting his signature to such a document, for doing so would amount to admitting that all the lands in Khurda belonged to the government, not to the raja. When Birakeshari refused to sign the document, the magistrate sent word that the money grant for the temple would be stopped from 1 October 1858, and that Birakeshari would also be removed from the post of superintendent of the temple. But when Birakeshari still refused to sign the document, Cockburn, now terribly annoyed, wrote to the magistrate of Puri to bring the raja to the collectorate and force him to add his signature. In the end, Birakeshari signed the document against his will. From that day onward he held Cockburn in awe. Even though he had never set eyes on Cockburn, the very thought of him brought back memories of Ramachandra to Birakeshari.

Birakeshari now turned to look at Suryamani as if he wanted respite from these unpleasant reflections. A deep sadness came over him at the sight of Suryamani lying fast asleep. All his life he had been in poor health; he had given her no happiness at all. The grief of being childless always occupied her thoughts. Suryamani was quiet, innocent, simple and free of guile. How would she cope with such vast responsibilities all by herself after his death? Had his uncle, Padmanabh Ray, been a good man,

Birakeshari could have entrusted Suryamani to his care and stopped worrying. But Padmanabh was a wicked, villainous man, always involved in some intrigue or the other. Ramachandra had been completely dependent on him. Padmanabh was in charge of managing the raja's landed property and he was creating a lot of trouble. His conduct as superintendent of the Satyabadi temple and his management of its funds were not above board. Moreover, he had had such an unholy influence on Ramachandra that Suryamani could not bear even to look at him.

Since he had no issue of his own, Birakeshari had decided to adopt the prince of Khemandi. Although some other kings had sent in proposals offering their sons for adoption, Birakeshari had made up his mind to adopt the second son of the king of Khemandi, for the reports he had received about this royal family were extremely favourable. The raja of Khemandi had come to Puri with his four-year-old son a few days earlier and was staying in a rented house by the seashore. Whenever Birakeshari spoke of organizing the ceremony of adoption, Suryamani would change the subject, for, though unexpressed, she was convinced that this ceremony was somehow tied up with Birakeshari's life. So the ceremony was delayed and the raja of Khemandi kept waiting in Puri. As far as possible, the whole matter was kept a close secret for fear that Padmanabh might create mischief if he got wind of it.

Suddenly, Birakeshari was racked by a fit of coughing, and Suryamani woke up. She felt his forehead and found that there was no temperature and his face was looking fresher. Birakeshari said to her, 'Make arrangements for the ceremony today.' Suryamani was going to demur, but the look in Birakeshari's eyes dissuaded her. She now realized she could no longer put the ceremony off. Knowing that the raja was awake, the maidservant, Nanima, entered the room and informed Suryamani that the rajguru, the palace priest, had arrived. It was one of his chief tasks to perform the worship of the deities in the palace every morning. When Birakeshari was taken ill, a *salagram* had been brought over from the Jagannath temple and installed in a room adjoining his bed-chamber. Birakeshari was carried there every day and worship was offered. At the end of today's worship, when Birakeshari was brought back to his room and laid on the bed, he seemed more worn out than ever before. Even in this condition, he told the court priest about the adoption ceremony and gave Suryamani instructions to send for Dewan Mahadev Lal.

Since Queen Suryamani now spent nearly all her time in the raja's bedchamber, male servants of the royal household were forbidden access to the room. If someone was to be called over, Nanima would be informed and then she would send for him through one of the palace servants. Because of this arrangement, the servants of the palace had become powerful—they were the only links between the palace and the outside world. Presently, Mahadev Lal arrived. Ever since Birakeshari had taken to his bed, Mahadev Lal had come to the palace nearly every morning and stayed on until late into the night. After the queen left the room, he came in and stood beside Birakeshari's bed. Birakeshari could speak only with great difficulty. He said to Mahadev, 'We will hold the ceremony this very day. Make arrangements. And request the magistrate to come to me. I want to talk to him about the adoption.'

It was a Sunday morning. The magistrate of Puri, J.B. Mactier, was smoking a cigar after breakfast, sitting on the veranda of his bungalow by the sea. Seated at his feet, a sepoy was busy cleaning a gun. At one end of the veranda, Seristadar Purushottam Patanayak, his record keeper, sat cross-legged beside a heap of files. There was a palanquin outside and its bearers sat near it, waiting. At this time, another palanquin arrived and Mahadev Lal emerged. When Mactier saw him, he looked up at the wall clock and knew his departure for his tour would be delayed.

From the day he had taken up post in Puri, Mactier had always felt it would have been better if he had been posted in Cuttack. Cuttack was an important station for the sahibs. And in Puri there was always some problem or the other relating to the temple and the raja. True, the raja had been granted a monthly pension of two thousand rupees, and landed property had been specially allotted to the temple for meeting with its expenses. But there was no end to troubles, big or small. The temple priests were a constant source of nuisance; they were always harassing the pilgrims. On occasion, even terrible mishaps had occurred. In 1853, during the Swing Festival, some pilgrims died in a stampede on account of the irresponsibility of these temple priests. Then, the temple priests, the head constables and the police officer who had been in charge of the festival had been fined and jailed. A warning had also been issued to the raja, Ramachandra Dev. On another occasion, Ramachandra had prevented a king from Ganjam from offering worship at the temple for three months to extort money from him. For this offence, he was made to pay a fine of one hundred rupees.

Natives could not meet the sahibs whenever they wanted, but Mahadev Lal enjoyed some privilege in this matter. Many sahibs knew that he was a relation of Deputy Collector Ram Prasad Ray. When Mactier sahib was supervising settlement work at Kujang, Ram Prasad had assisted him, and Mahadev had had an opportunity of making his acquaintance. After Mactier came to Puri, Mahadev called upon him from time to time to express his dismay at the the king's mismanagement of his affairs. Now Mahadev took off his shoes and went up to the veranda. He saluted the magistrate and informed him that the raja's condition was critical and that he wanted to see the magistrate.

This was nothing unusual. That the raja was suffering from a terminal illness was known to all. Now and then word was sent by the inspector of police, Puri, that the raja was about to die; but he had rallied every time. Mactier said, 'But this is no news.' Mahadev answered, 'No sir, it seems he will not be able to leave his sickbed this time.'

Had he been in a different mood he would have told Mahadev that he had no time. But yesterday's mail had brought him not one but two letters from his dear wife. The letters were sweet and loving. That morning Mactier had read them a second time and this had put him in very good spirits. He said, 'You go on ahead. I will follow you on horseback.' As he descended the stairs and made his way towards the syce who was waiting with his horse, he told Mahadev, 'Take Dr Kendall with you on your way back.'

When he entered Birakeshari's bedchamber he could see that the raja's condition was indeed very serious. Birakeshari lay listlessly on his bed and did not open his eyes even after Mactier entered the room. Only the sound of his breathing, which was barely audible, indicated that he was still alive. A servant tried to rouse Birakeshari but Mactier asked him not to and took a chair by the sickbed. A little while later, Mahadev Lal and the civil surgeon, Dr Kendall arrived. Kendall went straight up to Birakeshari, removed the blanket and felt his chest and pulse. Replacing the blanket, he looked across at the magistrate and shook his head to indicate that there was no hope.

At this moment Birakeshari opened his eyes. Mactier got up from the chair and went close to him. Recognizing him, Birakeshari made an effort to rise but Mactier put a hand on Birakeshari's shoulder and asked him not to. Mactier said, 'Everything is all right. You will get well.' Birakeshari said something in reply but the sound of his breathing rendered the words so indistinct, they became unintelligible. He made another attempt to speak. Mactier put his ear to his lips but still could not make sense of what he said. Mahadev explained, 'The king is saying that he will adopt the king of Khemandi's son as his heir.'

These words made Mactier suddenly grow cautious. In his career as a civil servant he had learnt a very important lesson: nothing natives do is ever simple or straightforward. What a native says, what he does and what his real intention is, are always an impenetrable mystery. What Mahadev Lal said made him think of Act 10 of the year 1840. Since there was always some complication involving the king and the temple, the magistrate had to have recourse to this Act and Mactier had committed it to memory. The Act made no provision for adopting an heir. Since he now found himself in an awkward situation, Mactier said, 'You send in an application on this subject; we'll see.'

Suryamani came into the room as soon as the magistrate and the others left. Birakeshari had again dropped off to sleep. Suryamani knew what she had to do now. She sat down in a chair by his bed and laid her hand on his as if she expected support for all her actions from this man lying before her like a lifeless object. She called Nanima over and said, 'Send word to Sibadas Babaji that he should come immediately. And tell the dewan and the court pandit to make arrangements for the adoption ceremony.'

There was, however, no need to send someone over to the rajguru for he had been waiting in the adjoining room for a long time. He was not at all happy about holding the ceremony in such a hurry. Before the heir was adopted, the court priest should have taken a Brahmin to Khemandi and performed the rite of welcoming. After this, the raja of Khemandi could have brought his son to Puri. Now all these rituals would have to be observed in Puri in the house rented by the raja of Khemandi.

Mahadev Lal had a lot of things to do. Legal documents would have to be prepared for the adoption; merely holding a ceremony would not be enough. He promptly set to work. He got an attorney to write out the adoption document, which was then signed by Birakeshari. Since he could not write properly, his thumb impression was also taken. In addition to this document, a will was prepared which stipulated that Suryamani would inherit all his immovable and movable property and remain responsible for the management of the temple. The will also included a clause stipulating that in the event of the death of the prince of Khemandi, Suryamani could adopt another son. A platform for the ceremony was constructed and other necessary arrangements made. Invitations were sent out to the mahants of the mutts and other personages in the town. A feast for Brahmins was also arranged. While doing all this Mahadev had to make sure that Padmanabh Ray was kept absolutely in the dark about the ceremony.

By evening, everything had gone off without a hitch. Although Birakeshari was required to be present when oblations were offered to the holy fire, it was decided that he should not be disturbed in view of his serious condition. He was brought in only at the time of the *havan*, when the offerings were made, and he took part in the rites of oath-taking, receiving and giving, and the pledging. Birakeshari and Khemandi's son, whom everyone now called Jenamani, the young prince, together made an offering of flowers. After this, Birakeshari was taken back to his bed.

It was about 9 p.m. when the holy man, Sibadas, arrived at the palace. Thoroughly worn out by the stressful events of the day, Birakeshari had fallen into a deep sleep. Suryamani stayed near him, like a shadow. She stood up when Sibadas came in. She felt no reservations about speaking to Sibadas because he was a holy man. He was famous for his nostrums and was often asked to come to the palace. Today, he went straight up to Birakeshari and felt his pulse, chanted some mantras with his eyes closed and said to Suryamani, 'Let the king have his last glimpse of Lord Jagannath.' He then advised against any more medicines and left.

Taking the raja to the temple was no simple matter, for it involved several precise rules and procedures. First, it had to be cleared of people. After everyone was informed about the raja's visit, Birakeshari and Suryamani set out for the temple in two separate palanquins accompanied by umbrellas, gongs and trumpets. Temple officials, *mudiratha* and *paricha*, stood waiting at the Lion Gate to receive them. While the queen's palanquin was carried up to the *Kalpabata*, Birakeshari was borne on a litter from the Lion Gate. After the chief priest called out 'O Lord', as was the ritual to be observed on such an occasion, worship was offered to the deity. However, Birakeshari was in no state to go through the last part of his visit to the temple, which required him to walk around the jewelled throne.

The news of the raja's visit to the temple had by now spread to some parts of the town. It was a winter night; the roads were deserted and most people had gone to bed. However, on the verandas of a few houses along the route which the king was to take on his way back, water-filled pitchers had been set and lamps had been lit. Of all this, of course, Birakeshari was totally unaware, for he lay unconscious in the palanquin.

Back in the palace, he was made to lie down on the bed and when he opened his eyes, he saw Suryamani and tried to say something. But the words stuck in his throat. When Suryamani brought her face closer to his, he said with great difficulty, 'I leave the young prince in your care. Never chastise him!' Suryamani was suddenly reminded of something; she left Birakeshari's side and ran into the next room. Sibadas had given her some holy water from the river Ganga. But by the time she returned with it, Birakeshari had passed away.

When the wailing began, Mahadev Lal, who was waiting outside, decided his next course of action. He got a torch lit and made straight for the magistrate's bungalow in a palanquin. He must first be told of the raja's death. But this could not be done, for Mahadev was told at the gate that the magistrate had already left on a tour of Fatepur after returning from the palace.

Fatepur, December 1859

Fatepur is a small, rather insignificant village near Chilka lake. However, it could boast of the salt works of the fort of Malud and a large, capacious field which was very convenient for sahibs to set up camp. Although this village lay far away from the centres of administration and was not widely known, it was important to the sahibs for historical reasons. In 1803, when the British began their expedition from Ganjam to conquer and annex Orissa, they had to pass through Fatepur. Orissa was under Maratha rule at the time and Fateh Muhammad was the *jagirdar* of Malud and other *praganas* around Chilka. A month before their invasion of Orissa, the British had signed an agreement with him which stipulated that he would send his brother Waj Muhammad to help them during their expedition to Cuttack and that he himself would extend to them all possible help when they passed through areas near Chilka and would supply them with provisions.

A contingent of British soldiers led by Colonel Harcourt set off from Ganjam and reached Mithakua in Malud on 15 September. They not only faced no resistance on the way, they received cooperation from the local people who were fed up with the tyrannical Marathas. The raja of Parikud, who was a local zamindar, could have helped the British the way Fateh Muhammad did, but strange notions about the British led him to keep his distance. He had been told that the invaders were grotesque monsters: they had faces like pigs and huge drooping ears in which they wrapped their bodies at night as it was very cold in their country. Convinced that the British were like the demons from Lanka, the raja hid himself in his palace. The British marched towards Puri from Mithakua, passing through Manikapatna, without facing the least resistance on the way. Brahmins from the Jagannath temple gave them a warm reception. The army set up camp at Puri on 18 September. The Marathas ran away, scared, and Puri came under British occupation without any difficulty. After spending a week in Puri the soldiers marched towards Cuttack.

Thus the sahibs and the officers came to have a special relationship with places like Fatepur and Mithakua near the Chilka lake, and magistrates and the police officers in Puri came to camp here from time to time. Land disputes in this area provided them with a convenient pretext. They would discover more reasons for visiting these villages particularly in the winter months, the best time of the year for bird shooting on Chilka lake.

Mactier had set up camp here two days earlier. Whenever he came from Puri, he was accompanied by an army of attendants which included sixteen palanquin bearers and six men to carry loads on *bahangis*, rods balanced on the shoulder with bags hanging from both ends. There were elephants and bullock carts for the babus accompanying him. No matter how early Mactier started from Puri, it always took him at least two days to reach his destination.

The magistrate's campsite looked like a small village. The pleasures of hunting apart, Fatepur also provided a lot of opportunities for enjoyment. It had another great advantage too: the raja of Parikud and the jagirdar of Malud vied with each other to make the sahib's stay a pleasant one. During Maratha rule, Parikud had enjoyed pre-eminence; but with the coming of the British, Malud assumed greater importance. Both the raja and the jagirdar were no longer as prosperous as they used to be, but they seemed to forget this when it came to entertaining the sahib.

The raja and the jagirdar would send over baskets of fruits and sweets as soon as the sahibs arrived. Each tried to make sure he sent the bigger basket, although the sahib was not at all interested in either sweets or fruits. Those were shared by the servants. Elaborate arrangements for the sahib's food and entertainment were made by both. Firecrackers, fruits, foreign liquor and food were brought from Cuttack, and prostitutes were brought over from Rambha. Marquees were put up in open spaces. The revelries concluded late at night with fireworks. Vasts sums of money were spent in entertaining guests in this manner.

In another respect, the situations of Malud and Parikud were similar: the two were embroiled in land disputes. A relative of the raja of Parikud laid claim to the zamindari, and the matter now lay in the law courts. In Malud, the jagirdar's stepmother had filed a lawsuit demanding that the jagir be made over to her son-in-law. The present jagirdar of Malud, Jamaluddin, who was Fateh Muhammad's grandson, often met the magistrate, bringing with him papers related to this case. There was one particular document which he treasured: the charter bearing Colonel Harcourt's signature which had granted Fateh Muhammad and his descendants rent-free land. Jamaluddin would show this document to the magistrate again and again while narrating his woes.

Before Mactier could attend to any official business in Fatepur, he received the news of the death of the raja of Puri. The seristadar, Purushottam Pattanayak, arrived from Puri bearing a sheaf of papers related to this matter. The daroga of Puri mentioned in his report that the raja had passed away on 11 September, and on 12 September, his widow had placed the son of the raja of Khemandi on the throne, naming him Divyasingh Dev. The deputy collector had also sent a long letter on the same subject. After the raja died, his keys had been handed over to the queen, Suryamani Dei, by the deputy collector. The letter contained advice on how to manage temple affairs under the present circumstances. Among the letters was a petition from the rani saying that she had adopted and enthroned Divyasingh, and praying that she be placed in charge of the affairs of the temple and the royal property till Divyasingh came of age.

Putting all other affairs aside, Mactier set to work replying to all these letters. First, he must endorse whatever action the deputy collector had taken. So Mactier wrote out a *robkari* order. In a long letter, he informed the commissioner of the passing away of the raja of Puri and of all the arrangements made so far. However, since the management of Puri temple was a complicated matter, he decided to write on this only after careful deliberation. That afternoon, after giving the subject much thought, he wrote out the following letter to the commissioner.

From:
J.B. Mactier Esquire, Offg. Magistrate of Pooree

To:
The Commissioner of Cuttack Division,
Cuttack

Sir,

I have the honour to forward a copy of an Urgee received by me this morning reporting the death of Bir Kishore Deb, Superintendent of the Temple.

2. He is stated to have adopted the second son of the raja of Kimendy under the name of Dibya Singh, a boy of 4 years of age.

3. As the adopted son is too young to manage the affairs of the Temple I have the honour to request that for securing the peace of the town, immediate measures be adopted as to the choice of a successor—the Act X of 1840 not providing for the contingency which had occurred.

4. The party who may perhaps be considered the only one entitled to the office is the Raja's cousin Padlab Rai whose father Gopinath Rai was a brother to the deceased Raja's grandfather Mokund Deb, however his conduct with regard to the management of the Sutbadei Endowment and the fact that he is prepared to contest the adoption does not point him out as in any way the fittest person who could be chosen, and as far as I can ascertain the native feeling, it would be a choice by no means agreeable to them.

5. There are two other persons well qualified for the post and both personally known to myself: Gopinath Bidyadhar, Zemindar of Killah Rorung, the lineal descendant of the Buxshee of the Rajas of Khordah; and Radhasham Narrindra, Zemindar Cuttack. They would, I believe, both perform their duties conscientiously; but, I would give a preference to the latter, he is an older man, has a perfect knowledge of business as the state of his own Zemindari shows, is universally respected by both European and Native for his probity and I believe would be selected by every unprejudiced native in preference to any one else, as his Superintendence would be guarantee for the due administration of the Funds of the Temple and his personal influence for the due adhesion to all police regulations at the time of the festivals.

6. I have as a temporary measure directed the Pooree *Daroga* to see that none of the temple property is removed.

7. As some time will elapse before the orders of Government are received and as it is most desirable there should be no delay in appointing a successor to the Superintendent, perhaps it is within your competency to place some one in temporary charge in anticipation of Government sanction.

I have the honour to be,
Sir,
Your most obedient servant,
J.B. Mactier,
Offg. Magistrate

Pooree Magistracy
Camp Fatepur
13 December 1859

This letter was immediately dispatched with a *dak* runner. As an afterthought, Mactier got a copy of the letter made, gave it to Purushottam Pattanayak, and asked him to go to Cuttack and obtain the commissioner's orders.

The dak runners were under orders to cover six miles per hour. There were also specific instructions as to how long they could rest after travelling for a certain number of hours. But the runners travelled at their own convenience, and the letters usually reached late. Mactier's letters reached Commissioner Cockburn three days later. Purushottam Pattanayak had arrived there by then.

Cuttack, December 1859

G.F. Cockburn, the commissioner, was a stern, short-tempered, conservative and principled officer. He had come to Cuttack as commissioner three years earlier and took his job very seriously. Trevor, who was secretary, board of revenue, in Calcutta, had served in Orissa earlier and was a friend of Cockburn's. For this reason, proposals forwarded by the Cuttack commissioner had no difficulty in getting approved by the board.

Cockburn was in the habit of taking out old files now and then and browsing through them. He had now at hand a file on the Konark temple which contained many old records. Cockburn had once travelled to Konark from Puri. The road was in bad shape and he had had to face many difficulties on the way. When at last he reached the ruined temple, the erotic sculptures upset him terribly. Rather than find out who had built this temple and why, he only wondered why this glaring obscenity had not yet been pulled down.

Browsing through the old records he learnt that if Commissioner Ricketts had not stopped Ramachandra then, the latter would have levelled the temple to the ground. Officers like

Ricketts had not only stopped the demolition, they had thought of conserving the temple. Fortunately, none of their proposals could be put into effect and the obscene pagoda disintegrated on its own. A year earlier, when the magistrate of Puri sent him a proposal for repairing the Konark temple, Cockburn in his reply said that rather than mourn the collapse of the black pagoda, one should rejoice over it. The beastly statues carved on the body of the temple deserved to crumble and there was no justification for spending even a rupee on preserving whatever remained.

From the old records Cockburn also learnt that the government of Bengal had wanted the Navagraha slab to be sent to Calcutta. However, no steps had been taken in this direction so far. The stone slab lay on the ground after it had been dislodged at the order of the raja of Puri. Cockburn now decided that even if he were not able to pull the temple down and send its stones to Calcutta, he would certainly send this stone slab there, although there were no obscene carvings on it.

He would have started writing on this matter immediately had he not received a letter from the magistrate of Puri marked urgent. The magistrate's suggestion that Gopinath Bidyadhar succeed the dead raja was utterly ridiculous. Gopinath's father, Buxi Jagabandhu, had given the British no end of trouble. After Jagabandhu's death everyone had forgotten all about his family. So, to appoint Gopinath as the temple superintendent would be inviting trouble.

Setting all other work aside, Cockburn consulted old records, interpreted the rules and wrote out a long letter addressed to the board of revenue. The gist of the letter was that it would be improper on the part of the government to interfere with the management of the temple. According to the terms of the will, the management of the temple should be left in the rani's care. The rani should apply for a certificate to the civil court for possession of the estates of the temple known as *satais hazari mahal* and the rent-free land in Khurda. The rest of the landed property should remain under the Court of Wards. The adopted heir would remain under the queen's guardianship for the time being and study at the Wards' Institute in Calcutta.

When the day's work was done, Cockburn left the cutcherry, office, in his coach. Then his new clerk, Gourishankar Ray, also left office. The first thing Gourishankar would do now was to go to the collector's office and seek out Bichitranand Das. The two would walk home from office together every evening. Although Bichitranand was ten years older than Gourishankar, and had joined the cutcherry fifteen years ago, he was the latter's close friend. This was because Gourishankar was learned, full of self-confidence and possessed a keen intelligence. Today, they were joined by Purushottam Pattanayak.

Outside the cutcherry premises, Bichitranand asked Gourishankar, 'Tell me, Mr Know-it-all, what decisions have been taken about Puri?'

Gourishankar said, 'To my mind, there is something wrong about adopting the son of the raja of Khemandi.'

Bichitranand asked, 'Why do you think so? The raja of Khemandi is a very good man.'

Gourishankar went on, 'We have to go back a hundred years to get to the root of the matter.' Bichitranand sensed that this was the beginning of a long lecture. He said, 'So, do we sit here and listen to you tell us all about it?'

Purushottam said that he could not wait since he had to make arrangements to go back to Fatepur. Gourishankar told him, 'Please sit down. Fateh Muhammad has something to do with the story I am going to narrate.'

They all made themselves comfortable on the lawn in front of the cutcherry and Gourishankar began:

In 1760, the raja of Khemandi, Jagannath Narayan Deb, attacked Khurda. Birakeshari Dev the First, was the ruler of Khurda at the time. To save himself from the raja of Khemandi, he sought the help of the Maratha *subedar*, Shiv Bhatta Sathe. Help was offered on condition that he would give one lakh rupees to Shiv Bhatta. The Marathas defeated and repulsed the raja of Khemandi, but Birakeshari could not pay the cash to the Marathas; instead, he mortgaged to them four praganas of Khurda.

In 1803, before the British invaded Orissa, they had sought the assistance of the raja of Khurda. The *vakil* of Raja Mukund Dev the Second, who was a minor at the time, went to Ganjam to talk to Colonel Harcourt. The raja was willing to help the British in their fight against the Marathas on condition that the British paid him one lakh rupees and restored the four mortgaged praganas to Khurda. Harcourt agreed to pay this sum but made it clear that he had no intention of returning the praganas. He gave the vakil ten thousand rupees by way of advance.

During the British invasion of Orissa, the Marathas fled without offering any resistance so the raja of Khurda's help was not needed. When the British began ruling Orissa, Mukund Dev's prime minister, Jayi Rajguru, met the commissioner of Cuttack and asked for the rest of the money. The commissioner gave him forty thousand rupees and told him that the rest, fifty thousand rupees, would be given after a treaty was signed.

Mukund Dev got the balance after signing the treaty, but he could not get back the four praganas. In order to retrieve these, he initiated secret negotiations with the Marathas. He sent the following message to the *peshwa* of Nagpur: I follow whoever is stronger. If Your Majesty proves to be more powerful, I am willing to be your vassal, for one should tilt the umbrella according to the direction of the rain!

But nothing came of this. In the end, the raja of Khurda attacked a few villages in Pipili which was under British authority. The British swiftly dethroned him and declared that Khurda was now placed under British rule. Anticipating trouble from the *paiks* of Banpur, which was under the rule of the raja of Khurda,

Harcourt made Fateh Muhammad's brother, Waj Muhammad, the amil of Banpur pragana. In December, Harcourt occupied the raja's fort in Barunei. The raja, however, escaped. In January 1805, Waj Muhammad captured the raja and received a reward of three thousand rupees from the British. The British imprisoned Mukund Dev first in fort Barabati, and later in Midnapur. Mukund Dev sent the British authorities a petition claiming that not he, but his prime minister, Jayi Rajguru, was responsible for all the trouble. It was Jayi Rajguru, the raja submitted, who imprisoned him in Khurda and instigated the paiks.

The British released Mukund Dev in 1807 but they did not allow him to return to Khurda. He now had to make Puri his place of residence. Since that time, although he had no dominion to rule over, he had come to be known as the raja of Puri.

Bichitranand remarked, 'The raja did not do Jayi Rajguru justice by saying such things against him.'

Gourishankar said, 'The story repeated itself during the paik uprising. Buxi Jagabandhu was trying to bring the raja from Puri to Khurda but, in the end, it was the raja of Puri who forced Buxi to apologize to the British, surrender, and accept a pension. In 1825, the same Waj Muhammad persuaded Buxi Jagabandhu to come to the magistrate of Cuttack. This time he received a reward of one thousand rupees for his pains.'

After Gourishankar's account of the recent history of Orissa came to an end, they all got up to leave. Although Bichitranand and Gourishankar pressed Purushottam to accompany them, he refused, for he was in a great hurry. Besides, Purushottam was not at all interested in drinking or in attending a dancing girls' *bai naach* party in Telenga Bazaar.

Konark, February 1860

Seated on a block of stone in a sandy clearing in the middle of the forest, G. Raynor, executive engineer, Puri division, checked the figures in his notebook. He had received a letter from Commissioner Cockburn, and had come there to find out how the Navagraha stone could be transported to Calcutta.

His Bengali overseer stood beside him, staring. Wiping the sweat off his forehead with a handkerchief, Raynor made many calculations in his head. The following details were mentioned on the first page of his notebook: the Nabagraha stone: 361.5 cubic feet; weight 61,997.25 cwts or 26.67 tons or about 723 maunds.

He had left Puri when it was still dark and had reached Konark around noon. Raynor had no interest in anything except his work. Someone else in his position would have chosen to pass through the jungle and make for the temple which stood close by. But Raynor had gone straight to the Navagraha stone and had been sitting beside it since he arrived. He measured it and figured out its weight by making various calculations.

The task proved more difficult than he had thought. The place posed peculiar difficulties as well. There was no good road from Puri to Konark and the area around the temple was overgrown with trees, creepers and bushes. Here and there rose hillocks of shifting sands. People avoided the place for fear of wild beasts. In order to carry the stone to the seashore from the sandy clearing, a road had to be laid. Wooden planks would be placed on the road and the big stone would then be dragged to the seashore on rollers by means of a rope, and kept steady by labourers. For this operation, the following would be required:

1) Twelve 4-inch planks, eight sal wood logs for rollers, fifty hand spikes, twenty-five crowbars, and six 2-inch-thick ropes (a hundred feet long) and fifty men.
2) The raft to convey it to the ship might be made of a sufficiently strong platform resting on and attached to a

number of water barrels of a total capacity of 6500 gallons or more.

Raynor calculated that the labour and materials to move the stone to the coast would cost about 225 rupees. Having gone through these figures, Raynor turned the page. The next page bore only a large question mark. He did not have a way to raise such a big stone on to the ship with the usual tackle. Even if they managed to get the stone on to the ship, there was the possibility that it would cause the vessel to list to one side and sink. A little while earlier, Raynor had taken the measurements of the broken iron beam—it was one square foot thick. The Navagraha stone had fallen on it and had broken it in three places.

Raynor decided that he would give the matter more thought after returning to Puri. He closed his notebook, looked up and saw six fierce looking men standing before him. He hurriedly rose to his feet and discovered that his overseer was now nowhere to be seen. Looking closely at the visitors, he realized that these men, who wore sacred threads across their dark shoulders and vermilion marks on their foreheads, were Brahmins. They were looking at the Navagraha stone and talking angrily among themselves. Raynor turned his eyes to the stone and found it smeared with vermilion paste in places.

Raynor sensed danger Leaving the Brahmins to argue with each other, Raynor hurried towards his palanquin, which had been kept by the road outside the jungle. Nervously peering over his shoulders, Raynor found that he was not being pursued by the priests. He decided that he would teach the Bengali overseer a lesson, and in replying to Cockburn's letter he would not forget to add that local people might create trouble when the Navagraha stone was moved.

Jagannath Sadak, June 1860

Natha Khuntia called out to the pilgrims loudly and roused them from sleep before it became light. They had reached a rest-house near Bhubaneswar rather late the night before and were all fast asleep. Natha kicked one or two of them and said, 'You bitches, if you don't start early, you will certainly miss the Car Festival.' Now everyone hurriedly got up. Although they all seemed half dead with fatigue, they nevertheless made ready to begin another day's journey. Their faces, however, looked a little cheerful, for today their ordeal would come to an end.

Like thousands of other pilgrims, Natha's party had started its journey along the Jagannath road ten days ago. There were twenty-eight members in the party and all were women. Having averaged thirty miles a day, their feet were blistered and bandaged with pieces of rag. Luckily for them, no one had fallen ill, if any one had she would have been abandoned along the way. It was only the hope of setting their eyes on Lord Jagannath that had sustained the party during this arduous, but otherwise uneventful, journey.

It was, of course, not unusual that such terrible things should happen to pilgrims travelling to Puri. Every year, in the month of Chaitra, Natha Khuntia would make a trip to Kanchanpur and its neighbouring villages in Burdwan. In Puri, he normally wore only a cotton towel, leaving the rest of his body bare. But when he set out to collect pilgrims, he chose an entirely different outfit. He would shave clean the front half of his head and tie back the rest of his hair into a pendulous knot. He would wear a *chapkan*, a short jacket, a short dhoti and a skull cap on his head. He would carry a palm leaf umbrella and a bundle, and stuff the side of his mouth with a *paan*. Dressed in this outlandish costume, this panda from Puri presented quite a sight in the villages of Bengal.

Natha Khuntia had visited these parts in order to collect pilgrims for years, and he was intimately familiar with the mind and character of the people. He spoke with them in chaste Bengali and won their confidence by offering to them a little dry *nirmalya*, which he brought from Puri. Since he was from the land of Lord Jagannath, elderly women in the villages regarded him as an incarnation of god. Natha Khuntia received their veneration blithely, without embarrassment or hesitation.

He would choose to visit a village in the morning, for he knew that the menfolk would be at work in their fields at this hour of the day. In the village of Kanchanpur, he would head straight for the house of Gobinda Samanta who was a well known figure there. Gobinda's mother, Sundari, an old widow, would receive him warmly. Her sister-in-law, Aduri, had become a *Vaishnavi* and made frequent pilgrimages to Puri. Aduri always told her of Lord Jagannath and this made Sundari desperately want to go to Puri. But Gobinda would not let her, for his grandmother had died of cholera while returning from Puri after witnessing the Car Festival.

Gobinda Samanta's house would be thronged by women from houses nearby whenever Natha Khuntia arrived there. Sundari would serve him delicacies and, sitting on the veranda, Natha would impress women with exaggerated accounts of the greatness and glory of Lord Jagannath in Puri. He would tell them that the area within ten kosas of Puri was hallowed; that even one who had murdered a Brahmin could be absolved of his sin by rolling on the sands of Puri; that the goddess Lakshmi herself cooked the *mahaprasad* in the temple: the cooks would put out the rice, lentils and vegetables in the kitchen in the evening and in the morning, they would find the mahaprasad ready; the ponds in Puri were filled with nectar, he would tell them; one dip in one of these would lead unfailingly to salvation, and so on. When they heard these stories, the women reverentially touched the ground with their foreheads, treating Natha Khuntia as Lord Jagannath's deputy whose very presence temporarily transformed Gobinda Samanta's courtyard into the main street of Puri.

Some of these women resolved to go on a pilgrimage to Puri, but they found that the men in their households would not be persuaded. Gobinda tried to dissuade his mother from the pilgrimage for she was very old and would not be able to travel such a long distance on foot. Besides, one had to take into account other dangers during this journey to Jagannath—rogues, tricksters, thieves and cholera. However, these did not deter Sundari and the other women, for the pilgrimage offered them a way out of the oppressive monotony of their lives.

The night before they were to start their journey, Sundari put her clothes, some rice and a brass tumbler in a large rattan basket. She tied a few currency notes in a knot in her sari's end and tucked it into her waistfold. That night, she could not get any sleep. In the morning, when Natha Khuntia loudly chanted, 'Jai Jagannath,' she came out carrying her basket. Sundari saw many like her gathered on the outskirts of the village, ready for the journey. They were all women, and most of them were widows. Among those who were not widows, two had quarrelled with their husbands; one was going without telling her husband; the husband of the other had left her and she was staying with her parents.

Natha Khuntia led his party of pilgrims out of the village with loud shouts of 'Jai Jagannath.' At first their movements were awkward; soon, however, they learnt to walk in step. Natha Khuntia talked to them and sang devotional songs and thus cheered them up.

But when the party reached Ulubedia, Natha Khuntia's behaviour did a complete turnaround. He had been speaking in chaste Bengali but now he spoke nothing but Oriya. The women, whom he had called 'mothers' so far, he now addressed as bitches and sluts. He also walked faster and the rest of the party had to run from time to time to keep up with him. One of the women had to carry his bundle. He would go to sleep as soon as the party reached a resting place and the women, dead tired from having walked thirty miles, had to buy rice, lentils, etc., cook for him and feed him. He would choose to lie down among the women who had to squeeze themselves into the narrow space of the rest-house. He would ask a young woman to press his legs. When she got tired, he would say to her, 'You go to sleep. Tell another girl to take your place.' If no rest-house could be found for the party after a day's journey, he would join some other party and make himself comfortable, leaving the women to spend the night in the open or under a tree. In the beginning, the women found this unbearable and often broke down and cried but in a couple of days they got used to everything.

When the party arrived at Midnapore, they found the place crowded with thousands of pilgrims like them who had come from Bengal, Bihar and the north. Some of them had left home months ago. A few travelled in bullock carts and palanquins but most of the pilgrims journeyed on foot. Roasted by the sun, soaked by the rain, their feet covered with blisters, they were all on their way to have a glimpse of Lord Jagannath.

As the party approached Narayangarh, Natha Khuntia said to the women, 'This place is infested with bandits. Give me all your money, I will keep it in safe custody.' But, rather than hand their money over to him, the women tucked it deeper into the waist-folds of their saris. Natha said to himself, 'Do what you want, you bitches. I know how to make you fork out your money. Wait until you reach Puri.' Natha knew well that these helpless women had no alternative but to rely on him during the perilous journey.

The road to Jagannath was frightening for several reasons. The pilgrims encountered snakes, stray dogs and jackals. Dak runners on their routes, and village *chowkidars* too, scared them, for these people often demanded money from the pilgrims. The sight of horsemen made them incoherent with fear for, in the villages at the time, people were still afraid of the Marathas. The women looked upon Natha Khuntia as their sole saviour.

The road, which was named Jagannath Sadak after Lord Jagannath, was in a terrible condition. After occupying Orissa, the British had started building it but the work remained incomplete. Work was taken up again when Raja Sukhamoy Ray of Calcutta donated one and a half lakh rupees. However, the lack of maintenance meant that the road was full of potholes and dust. After the rains, a deep layer of mud covered it and the surface was rutted with the marks of cart wheels.

The condition of the rest-houses was even worse. Very often one could not get a place to stay, and if one reached late, the shops were closed. The shopkeepers sold provisions at a very high price. There were rumours that they, in league with the bandits, sometimes mixed poison with the rations. The boatmen harassed the pilgrims while ferrying them across rivers.

When cholera epidemics broke out, hundreds of pilgrims died on the road. If pilgrims came down with an attack of cholera, fellow pilgrims would leave them to their fate and move on. The victims had to die a lonely, lingering death by the wayside. Every morning, a government hearse would remove the corpses.

Luckily, there had been no cholera epidemic this year and Natha Khuntia's party had faced no danger or difficulties during their journey. However, on the way, they had come across an old woman lying under a tree by the roadside, crying. She had fallen and fractured her bones. When the party stopped to see her, Natha told them, 'Move on. Lord Jagannath will make sure the old woman reaches Puri.' On another occasion, when they saw a corpse being devoured by a jackal, Natha said, 'Lord Jagannath took pity on this poor fellow. He had a comfortable journey to heaven.'

Although Puri was now closer, the women were so tired, they felt little excitement at the prospect of seeing Lord Jagannath. Many of them were limping now. The only thing that gave them any relief at all was that no one had been left behind. Even Sundari, the oldest among them, had managed to keep up. As Puri came closer, Natha walked more briskly.

Suddenly, beyond a bend in the road, the crown of the temple became visible. The cry of 'Haribol' filled the air. They all threw themselves down on the dusty road and made obeisance to the temple. Natha separated his party from the crowd and gave them a short lecture: 'From here the road takes you straight into paradise. You will now be cleansed of all your sins, you will attain salvation. But you must bear one thing in mind: Keep everything that happens to you in this sacred place a closely guarded secret. If you pass it on to anyone else, you'll lose all the merit you have earned.'

When they got into town, they found it packed with people who had assembled there for the Car Festival. Natha got them to take a bath in the Narendra tank and took them to Balia Guru's lodging-house. At long last, the women seemed a little cheerful. It was only the blessed who got the opportunity to come to Puri and see Lord Jagannath!

On the day of the Car Festival, Natha Khuntia came dressed in a clean dhoti and his forehead adorned with *chita* and *tilak* and took the women to the temple in the morning. He made them offer some money at every shrine inside the temple. The women were lashed by the temple guards, abused by the priests and pinched and molested in the crowd, yet when they came out they nevertheless looked happy and contented. Natha Khuntia, too, was glad that he had made some money. He would get his share from the temple priests and the owner of the lodging-house. He had already got enough from the women. There was something else that gave him much pleasure. A young woman called Arati in the party had grown devoted to him and obeyed him ungrudgingly. He thought he would ask her to stay back when the party returned home. He would have a talk with that Muslim fellow from Patna. If the price he offered was not attractive, Natha would send her to the other fellow in Telenga Bazaar. Either way, he stood to benefit from the transaction.

Everyone now stood before the chariots and waited to pull them. Suddenly there was a commotion. Natha said, 'Look at the maharaja. Look at him.' They all looked up at Lord Jagannath's chariot, but they could not see the maharaja there. A small boy, four or five years old, wearing a brocaded dress, stood beside the priests and other temple attendants. He held a broom fitted with a gold handle and was crying. People around him were trying to pacify him but he would not be calmed. Seeing that his pilgrims were looking this way and that, Natha said, 'Why are you gaping like this? Fix your eyes on the chariot and pay homage. The little boy you see on the chariot is our god, Maharaja Divyasingh Dev.'

Puri, March 1863

During the first few days he spent in Puri with his father, Divyasingh was quite happy. It was his first visit to the place, and the sea was a great novelty for him. He even found the *yajna*, which had been organized for his adoption, a pleasant experience, for his parents were with him and he was asleep most of the time. He was not upset either when he was taken into the temple by the rajguru in a new palanquin complete with a new fan and fly whisk. Inside the temple, he was treated with every mark of respect due to a king. Divyasingh found the temple rituals quite funny and amusing. On his way back from the temple, he fell asleep.

When Divyasingh woke, he found himself in an unfamiliar place. The place was very noisy, for Birakeshari had died and arrangements were being made for his cremation. Luckily for Divyasingh, his father was by his side, and he went back to sleep in the midst of all the bustle.

The next morning, Divyasingh's father took him in his arms and kissed him goodbye, promising to return soon. By afternoon, the prince began missing his father and started crying. The servants tried their best to console the boy, but in vain. He only said that he wanted to go back to his father. That night, he refused to eat and cried himself to sleep. The scene repeated itself the next day. Divyasingh would not listen to anyone and when he flung away the food that had been given him, Suryamani was informed. She herself had been crying, mourning her husband's death. She took the child on her lap but he only cried louder and kept repeating that he wanted to go to his father. Suryamani spoke to him sweetly but he refused her overtures. When she tried to hold him in her arms, he tried to break free and run away. Weighed down by her own grief, Suryamani found Divyasingh's tantrums too much to handle. She gave up and went to her room, leaving Divyasingh in the care of a maidservant.

Now, fed up with Divyasingh, the servants began bullying him, and he howled even more than before. In the end, the servants shut him up in a room. When Divyasingh kept banging at the door, one of the servants opened it and said, 'I'll break your head if you go on crying.' This silenced the boy. He was disciplined in this way by the servants until Suryamani could compose herself and come out of her room. The raja of Khemandi did try to meet his son while he was still in Puri but the servants would not let him into the palace. They had no instructions from Suryamani regarding this. So the raja waited for a few days and at last went back to his kingdom without being able to meet his son.

In the meantime, Padmanabh Ray sent a petition saying that he should be placed in charge of the royal estate because Suryamani, being a woman, would not be able to look after it properly. The raja of Khemandi too, claimed that as Divyasingh's father he should have the right to manage the estate. When Suryamani got to know this, she forbade the raja from entering her palace.

Acting on the commissioner's instructions, Suryamani applied to the Civil Court and obtained the right to run the royal estate. However, since she never stirred out of the palace, and also because she knew nothing about matters relating to the management of landed property, her affairs were thrown into utter confusion. All power now came to be concentrated in the hands of servants.

Suryamani's other serious problem was Divyasingh himself. No matter how hard she tried, she could not get him to like her. He would never agree to come near her and talked back to her rudely even when she spoke to him with great affection. One day, when he was being very difficult, Suryamani slapped him. Divyasingh landed two blows on her and bit her hand for good measure. Suryamani broke down and tearfully asked her late husband, 'You had asked me not to discipline him. Tell me how to cope with this unruly child.'

Suryamani could not bring Divyasingh under control. Whenever he threw his tantrums, Suryamani sent him out with the servants. A teacher was engaged but Divyasingh refused his tutorship. Divyasingh grew up in the care of the palace servants. He began spending more and more time in their quarters, mostly avoiding that part of the palace where Suryamani lived. He began speaking the coarse language of the servants and picked up the habit of drinking intoxicating *bhang* in their company. The servants, too, found that the best way of quietening Divyasingh whenever he got out of hand was to get him to drink bhang.

This news spread from Puri to Khemandi. The raja of Khemandi, though no longer interested in the royal estate of Puri, was still concerned about his son. When he had word sent to Suryamani, he was told that he now had no rights over Divyasingh. And there was no question of his being allowed to meet the prince. However, not giving up hope, the raja of Khemandi went to the palace every day. One day, as he was coming back after being yet again refused permission by Suryamani, he saw Divyasingh coming of the palace. When he went forward to embrace his son, Divyasingh said, 'Who are you, you son of a bitch?' The raja's attendant told him, 'Your Highness, he is your father'. Divyasingh pushed the raja's hand away and said, 'Get lost. I have no father.'

There was another matter relating to the management of the Puri temple which kept worrying Collector Barlow. The government wanted to get a document signed by the raja of Puri but Suryamani was always evasive about this matter. Barlow had received several reminders from the new commissioner, R.N. Shore, who had replaced Cockburn. This document was concerned with the relationship of the British government with the Jagannath temple. Christian missionaries were constantly complaining that by involving itself in the affairs of the temple, the government was encouraging idolatry. In this context, the government had drafted a document which contained the following arrangements.

For many years the government had taken several steps towards completely severing its connection with the Jagannath temple. After the occupation of Orissa in 1803, the government had gradually brought the landed property of the temple under their control, and gave the temple an annual rent of 53,000 rupees for meeting its expenses. This amount was raised by imposing a tax on pilgrims. The pilgrim tax was abolished in 1840 but the Government continued to extend financial assistance to the temple.

In 1843, the landed property of the temple, satais hazari mahal, was handed over to the raja of Puri and the money grant was reduced. In 1845, and again in 1856, the grant was reduced further. In 1858, the government decided to discontinue financial assistance to the temple but to endow it with landed property which would generate the same amount of money. The document containing this agreement had been signed by Mactier, the collector, and Birakeshari Dev, superintendent of the temple, on 3 April 1858.

The purpose behind the new document was to transfer all the landed property of the temple to the raja in his capacity as superintendent of the temple. The government would make no inquiries regarding the produce of this landed property. After this document was signed, the government would discontinue its grant to the temple and would not be directly involved in its management, its income and expenses, and other such matters. As its superintendent, the raja of Puri would remain in sole charge of the affairs of the temple.

Suryamani was postponing putting her signature on this document. After sending her several notices and messengers, Barlow finally went to the palace in person on 30 March and got the document signed by her. From this day onwards, the government ceased to have any connection with the temple.

Balasore, May 1864

Radhanath had an early bath, finished his puja, put on his clothes and got ready to start work as the third teacher at Balasore Zilla School. His thin, ailing figure made the sixteen-year-old Radhanath look like a mere schoolboy. But he was confident of giving a good account of himself as teacher, for he was the first student in Balasore district to have cleared the entrance examination.

While Radhanath was combing his hair in front of a mirror, his father called him from the next room and the thought of getting a scolding from his father made Radhanath shudder. He approached his father nervously and stood before him, head lowered. His father, Sundar Narayan, looked him up and down. Even at home, Sundar Narayan behaved as if he was the *sadar kanungo*, the severe revenue officer. There was nothing wrong with Radhanath's clothes so he could not fault him on that account. He now had to look for some other fault.

'Have you got your appointment letter in your pocket?'

Radhanath took it out and showed it to his father.

'And the handkerchief?'

Radhanath took it out of his pocket. Failing in all his attempts at finding fault, Sundar Narayan fired his last shot. 'What is the time?'

Radhanath should have looked at the wall clock before replying to his father. He said, nervously, 'About nine.'

Sundar Narayan was waiting for just such a reply. He glared at Radhanath and said, 'Make sure what you say is absolutely correct and carefully thought over. You are no longer an irresponsible student. Try to become a good teacher.'

Radhanath felt depressed when he came away from his father and the excitement of starting a new job ebbed. The saddest thing about his life was the iron discipline imposed on him by his father. What complicated matters was the fact that his father loved him dearly, and to think ill of his father made him deeply ashamed of himself.

Radhanath's mother passed away when he was young. Since then, his father's affection for him as well as his desire to impose harsh discipline on him had grown more intense. If he was slightly late from school, his father would go out to fetch him, scolding him all the way. For fear of displeasing Sundar Narayan, no friend of Radhanath's dared visit his house. Radhanath had spent his entire childhood friendless and scared.

When Radhanath, having passed out of Soro Vernacular School, gained admission in Balasore Zilla School, Sundar Narayan would accompany him there every day for the first few days. Their way lay through a colony of prostitutes. As they passed through it, Sundar Narayan used to keep a close watch on his son and this made Radhanath feel acutely embarrassed. Sundar Narayan said that the road here was slippery, and one should look straight ahead.

Radhanath's classmate, Jadu Katia, who was much older, occasionally talked to him about his visits to prostitutes. Whether he was telling the truth was another matter; but whenever Radhanath asked for more details, he would say, 'I won't tell you anything. You may tell your father and I will get punished.' Now and then, while passing through the prostitutes' quarter, Radhanath disobeyed his father's injunction and looked around. The women whom he saw in the houses on either side of the path were no different from the women he came across elsewhere. Nor was the path muddy or waterlogged. So the warning about having a fall on the slippery path of life did not make sense to him.

When Radhanath met the headmaster of the school, Gangadhar Acharya, the latter was pleased to see him. Gangadhar said, 'Why do you remain standing? Please sit down. From today you are a colleague of mine.'

After Radhanath signed his joining report, Gangadhar said, 'I wish you had passed the F.A. exam from Calcutta and joined as second master here.'

This was what Radhanath, too, had wanted to do. His father had taken a great deal of trouble sending him to Calcutta with his uncle Jahnabi. Calcutta had seemed like a magical place. The special atmosphere of Presidency College, the discussions regarding great men such as Ishwar Chandra Vidyasagar, Keshab Chandra Sen and, above all else, the poetry of Michael Madhusudan Dutt, were all a source of great excitement. But unfortunately for him, Radhanath's health gave way and he had to leave Calcuttta after two months.

That day, after his first class, he found Jadu Katia waiting for him on the veranda. Jadu continued to be a student, for he had failed his examinations several times. He said, 'How did the class go? Usually the students heckle a new teacher. I, for one, have given new teachers a very bad time. Only Gourishankar Ray made me stand on a bench. You should aim to become a teacher like him.' Gourishankar had taught at the school as the fourth teacher. Radhanath had come under the spell of his powerful personality and ardently wished to become like him.

On the way home, Radhanath ran into the headmaster of the Mission School, Fakir Mohan Senapati. Fakir Mohan had come looking for him. Fakir Mohan was five years senior to Radhanath and they had studied in different schools. However, when Pandit Sadasib Nanda joined the zilla school, they both studied Sanskrit with him. Being more intelligent, Radhanath had finished the *Raghuvamsha* and had read five cantos from the *Kumarasambhavam* while Fakir Mohan struggled with five cantos of *Raghuvamsha*. Put off by such an unequal competition, Fakir Mohan changed his tutor and went to take lessons from another pandit.

When Radhanath sat for his entrance examination, Fakir Mohan was a teacher at Barabati school. His monthly salary, to start with, was only two and a half rupees. This had been later raised to four rupees. When the post of the headmaster of the Mission School fell vacant the following year, the secretary of the school, Reverend Miller, appointed Fakir Mohan at a salary of ten rupees per month. On meeting Radhanath, Fakir Mohan said, 'It is good that you have joined as the third teacher. What is your monthly salary?'

Radhanath said, 'Thirty rupees.'

Fakir Mohan said, 'That's good money. I wish someone would give me a job like that.'

They walked together for a while. Then Fakir Mohan invited Radhanath to go with him to Gadgadia pond ghat and have a chat. But Radhanath, unwilling to risk his father's displeasure, went home.

Puri, February 1865

No one had ever seen a scholar like him in Puri. At a time when not wearing one's dhoti in the accepted way was enough to make one an outcaste in Brahmin villages, when Brahmins would not even touch paper, and when receiving an English education was a public acknowledgement of conversion to Christianity, Pandit Harihar Das used to wear trousers, a coat and shoes like the sahibs and ride a horse. Yet no one dared criticize him to his face for his outlandish dress and manners because his position as a Sanskrit scholar was unassailable. He had studied in Sanskrit colleges in Nabadwip and Calcutta and could speak Sanskrit fluently. Although he was only twenty-three, even old and experienced scholars did not dare engage him in debate. Besides Sanskrit, Harihar had also mastered Greek and Latin.

Another reason why ordinary people respected him, and feared him a little, was that he socialized freely with the sahibs in Puri. He was not intimidated by them and considered himself their equal. The sahibs came to his house to take lessons in Sanskrit.

Harihar Das's life was dominated by a single aim: to spread modern education along with Sanskrit in Orissa. To this end, he had set up a school in his own village, Sriramachandrapur. Here students used paper and pen instead of palm leaves and stylus; they also read printed books. Conservative Brahmins did not send their children to this school so the school had only non-Brahmin students. When he was in Puri, Harihar occasionally taught the pupils himself and distributed among them the new books he had brought from Calcutta.

Harihar often had to visit places outside Orissa. He had to do this to collect funds to support himself, to buy books, and to run the school. Harihar earned money by performing priestly duties or as gifts from native chieftains, whom he impressed with his knowledge of Sanskrit. Although he received warm appreciation from kings outside Orissa, the response to him at home was far from enthusiastic. This was because Pandit Harihar did not believe in god and was a confirmed atheist.

In spite of this, many people stayed in touch with him. Boxwell, the magistrate, who took Sanskrit lessons from him, was a very good friend. When kings from outside Orissa came to Puri to have a *darshan* of Jagannath, they sent word to Harihar. Anyone who wanted to get something written in English also came to him for help.

A twelve-year-old boy made a point of calling on Harihar every day during his stay in Puri. He was Madhu, son of Bhagirathi Rao, a police *jamadar*. At the time, Bhagirathi was attached to the police station in Bhubaneswar, and Madhu stayed with his father's friend Balaramji and in Puri studied in the Zilla School. Madhu's mother had died when he was only five. After his mother's death, Madhu had become extremely pious. He would get up very early and chant mantras and not even touch food or water until he had offered worship to the image of Lord Banambar Mahadev near Pathuria Sahi in Puri.

Balaramji made a living by supplying flour to the temple. There were several grinding stones in his house to make flour and these were worked by women who came very early every day. In the morning, Balaramji's house in Khundheibent Sahi would be filled with the grating sound of grinding stones. To escape this, Madhu wandered about in the streets by the seashore. Sitting on the sands, he would fix his gaze on the boundless sea for hours on end. Sometimes, he would lie down on the beach and gaze into the evening sky. A bright star would make him think of his dead mother.

Madhu often saw his mother in his dreams. When he woke up in the morning, he could remember nothing at all but still the dream would make him feel happy all day long.

There was one dream which would not lose itself in the mists of oblivion like the others. He could recall it vividly in the morning: while taking a stroll on the seashore he came across a gigantic figure which strode ahead, chanting 'Om'. As he chanted, a bright light illuminated everything around. This being beckoned to Madhu to follow him. Madhu followed him for a distance but the figure vanished as it reached the outskirts of the city.

The next day Madhu found Harihar walking in front of him on the road. He had no doubt that Harihar was the person he had seen in his dream. Madhu tried to dispel this thought from his mind by reminding himself of Harihar's atheism, but he failed to separate the being he saw in his dream from Harihar, whom he was now seeing in the flesh.

Madhu had another problem to worry about. Although no one had told him about it, he knew that plans were afoot to get him married to Balramji's second daughter, Champa. Madhu used to mix freely with Champa at home, but these days the very sight of her made him feel deeply self-conscious and his face reddened. As far as possible, he now avoided her.

That day, when Madhu arrived at Harihar's residence, he was teaching English to a few boys on his veranda. After he finished teaching, he said to Madhu, 'Let's go. I'll take you to Boxwell today'. Madhu was not unfamiliar with Boxwell's name because

Boxwell had organized a competition for the boys of Puri Zilla School. Every year, the students would be asked twenty questions on four different topics. The student who could answer all of them correctly received a cash prize of one hundred rupees. Madhu had won this prize for three consecutive years.

Harihar's visit to Boxwell had a definite objective: he was very keen to set up a Sanskrit school in Puri where, in addition to Sanskrit literature and philosophy, languages such as English, Greek and Latin and subjects such as history, mathematics and astrology would be taught. During his tour of north India, he had received assurance of financial assistance from the king of Balrampur. For this project, he needed Boxwell's help.

When Harihar and Madhu reached Boxwell's bungalow, they found him working on files in his office. He was happy to see Harihar and he also inquired about Madhu's studies. The proposed school was discussed at length. When the subject of teaching Greek and Latin came up, Boxwell said to Harihar, 'I don't know much about these. There is one John Beames who is collector of Purnea. He is an authority on philology. You may correspond with him.'

When Harihar got up to leave, Boxwell asked him to wait a little, went inside the house, and came out with a book written in Greek. Giving it to Harihar, he said, 'I have not read this. I present it to you. Have a look.' The book was *Oedipus Rex*, a play by Sophocles. On their way back, Harihar started reading the book even as he walked. He said to Madhu, 'It is a good book. I will translate it into Oriya.'

Cuttack, June 1865

Bichitranand Das had in the meantime risen to become the commissioner's seristadar, his chief assistant. He often had to accompany the sahib on his tours. However, during the time he spent in Cuttack, he would meet Gourishankar in the evenings. Bichitranand's garden house in Tulsipur was a meeting place for the important people of the town and for the rajas who were visiting Cuttack. Rajas who came to meet the commissioner would never leave Cuttack without calling on Bichitranand. While having drinks in the evening and attending musical parties at the house of Chota Tara, the dancing girl of in Telenga Bazaar, Bichitranand and Gourishankar would discuss various matters relating to Orissa.

Their discussions these days centred on the setting up of a printing press in Cuttack. Of course, there was the Mission Press and it had been in existence for a long time. But, for the natives, there was not a single printing press in all of Orissa. When *Prabodh Chandrika*, a magazine brought out by William Lacey folded up in 1859, the idea of publishing a magazine had occurred to Bichitranand. The only expert on printing in Orissa at the time was Brooks sahib of the Mission Press. He had learnt printing as a child and after having worked with the Calcutta Mission Press for many years, had come to Cuttack about twenty-five years ago. Bichitranand and Gourishankar met him at the Mission Press, found out from him about printing machines and saw how a press functioned. But, when they ascertained from Calcutta how much a printing machine would cost, they realized that it would not be possible for them to arrange for so much money.

At this time, an opportunity presented itself to Bichitranand. The raja of Dhenkanal, Bhagirathi Mahendra, often came to meet the commissioner to sort out his many problems and took the opportunity to call on Bichitranand. Looking at him—he was grossly obese—no one would have suspected that he was such a huge a patron of learning. But every evening he would preside over a meeting of scholars. Pandits from Kashi, Nabadwip and Orissa came to these meetings and discussed not only Oriya and

Sankrit poetry, but also philosophy. Bichitranand explained to him the need for setting up a printing press and the raja agreed to provide financial support.

Bichitranand and Gourishankar met every educated and well-to-do person in Cuttack and sought their support as well. In 1864, the Cuttack Printing Company was registered. Bhagirathi Mahendra bought twenty-five shares paying 1050 rupees. The founding capital of the company was 7500 rupees. Everyone who mattered in Cuttack was among its shareholders. By the end of that year, Bhagirathi paid the promised money and from the others, half of the first instalment was collected. The company began its operations with Gourishankar Ray as its secretary and treasurer.

The first task of the company was to acquire a cheap machine from Calcutta. But when they made enquiries in Calcutta they learnt that a printing machine was available but Oriya type was not; they could have only English type. At last an old machine and English letters were procured after a great deal of searching. Since the company did not have its own premises, they were kept on the veranda of deputy magistrate Jagmohan Ray's house in Alamchand Bazaar. But there was no one in Cuttack who knew how to operate the machine. Moreover, there was no need for books in English, so the machine lay idle.

In June, while in Puri, Bichitranand came to know that a Bengali gentleman there had a lithograph press. He had brought it to print books in Bengali but it lay unused for he had no work in Puri. Bichitranand promptly purchased the machine, paying two hundred rupees and brought it to Cuttack by bullock cart. It now stood in Jagmohan Ray's sitting room, and the directors of the company who had come to a hurriedly convened meeting were subjecting it to a thorough and rigorous scrutiny.

At the meeting were present, besides Bichitranand and Gourishankar, the zamindar of Kendrapara, Radhashyam Narendra, and his brother Gourishyam Jena, zamindars Golakchandra Bose, Banamali Singh and Jagmohan Ray. Although a hand-pulled *punkha* moved squeakily overhead, everyone fanned himself with a *bena*-root fan. The *chaprasi*, Sheikh Jamir, was collecting empty sharbat glasses from the guests.

All eyes were focussd on Gourishankar for no one could figure out how printed words could be made to appear on paper using the machine lying in front of them. Gourishankar gave an account of everything he had done to set up the press: he had gone to the East India Irrigation Company in Jobra to see how their lithograph press—the only one of its kind in all of Cuttack at the time—worked. First someone who had a good hand would write on a stone slab. After the writing was done, ink would be spread on it and a printed page obtained by pressing a sheet of paper against it. To get all this done, an experienced man was needed. Gourishankar had talked to the printer at the Irrigation Company and he had agreed to come and operate the machine of the Cuttack Printing Company from July.

After listening to Gourishankar's report, all the members present applauded him for his efforts and decided to appoint someone to receive training from the printer of the Irrigation Company. Bhagirathi Sathia was appointed printer at a monthly salary of twelve rupees, and Bhagabat Das was employed as a writer at a salary of five rupees a month. Jagmohan Ray was requested to spare some space for the printing machine in his house until the company acquired its own premises.

In the end, everyone present requested Gourishankar to start publishing a magazine in Oriya under the auspices of the company at the earliest opportunity.

Puri, July 1865

At midday on 3 July 1865, the steamer carrying the commissioner, T.E. Ravenshaw, reached the Puri coast. He had set out from

Calcutta the day before. Since there was no harbour at Puri, the steamer had to stop some distance from the shore and passengers had to be ferried ashore.

The news had been telegraphed to Cuttack and Bichitranand had come to Puri to receive the commissioner. The police superintendent, Lacey, and the deputy collector, Ramakshoy Chatterjee, were waiting on the sandy beach with a palanquin. When the steamer sailed into view, they went out to it by boat and brought Ravenshaw ashore.

Ravenshaw looked about him with marked distaste. He had not wanted to be posted to Orissa. The last sixteen years of his service had been spent mostly in different parts of Bengal and in Patna. A few days after he went from Patna to Birbhum as judge, he got promoted again and was transferred to Cuttack. Ravenshaw went to Calcutta and protested against his Cuttack posting. His reluctance to go to Cuttack had another reason: the job of judge was more to his taste than any position that involved land revenue administration and now, as commissioner, most of his work would relate to that area.

But the board wanted him to go to Cuttack as early as possible because Shore, who was commissioner in Cuttack, had already left. Ravenshaw was asked to join as officiating commissioner at the office of the board in Calcutta and he was assured that he would be recalled to Bengal within a short time. Mrs Ravenshaw expressed her unwillingness to accompany her husband to Cuttack and went back to England. Ravenshaw set off for Orissa after spending a few days going through records relating to Orissa at the board office.

Ravenshaw knew absolutely nothing about Orissa. He had heard strange things about Oriyas from officers who had served in the province at some point time and were now working at the board. Cockburn, a member of the board, who had himself been commissioner in Cuttack a few years earlier, gave Ravenshaw a great deal of advice on matters relating to the administration of Orissa. After hearing all this, Ravenshaw was convinced that the Oriyas were no good at all.

Old accounts gave credence to this view. A collector in Cuttack had written in a report in 1818 that, of all the races under British rule, Oriyas happened to be the most stupid and ill-mannered. A similar view found a place in Stirling's account of Orissa: 'Abul Fazl was right when he described the Oriyas as an effeminate race, devoid of manliness and vitality.'

Thus, on account of all this, Ravenshaw's head was full of bizarre notions about Orissa when he stepped on its soil. He was preoccupied with the thought of going back to Calcutta. It had been arranged that he would spend the day in Puri and leave for Cuttack the next day. He was to stay at the collector's bungalow. In those days, the collector of Puri shifted his office to Cuttack for four months from July to October for Puri was unbearably hot at that time of the year. Mr Barlow, the collector, had left for Cuttack on the first of July, and his bungalow lay vacant at the time.

In the evening, Ravenshaw went around the town. The roads had become dirty and they stank because of the rains. He expressed his wish to enter the Jagannath temple, but he was informed at the Lion Gate of the temple that he would not be allowed in. And yet a priest came up to him and asked for money. A sudden shower soaked him through and as he walked along the main street of Puri, a leper tried to touch his feet. When he returned to the bungalow he was told that the raja of Puri would call on him. After a while someone who came with him baskets of sweets and fruits was presented to him as the raja. He was a mere boy, aged about eight or ten.

Having spent a day in Puri under such unpleasant circumstances, Ravenshaw reached Cuttack on 5 July, travelling by palanquin. He cursed his fate and cursed Orissa and the stupid, ill-mannered, effeminate Oriyas.

Cuttack, July 1865

When Barlow came to Cuttack to escape the unbearable heat of Puri, he had thought he would spend four months in peace in the circuit house. But when Barlow went to call on Ravenshaw the day the latter arrived in Cuttack, Ravenshaw said, 'I am alone. Come and stay with me.' A reluctant Barlow had to come and reside in the commissioner's bungalow at Lalbagh. For a subordinate, a superior's request is, after all, as good as an order.

Barlow did not want to come to the commissioner's because managing servants scared him. For the sahibs, dealing with servants was as important as ruling the colony. A sahib's bungalow was crowded with an army of servants who included messengers, chaprasis, ostlers, *durwans*, *khansamas*, water-carriers, *beheras*, *hamals* and torch-bearers. Since Barlow's ailing wife lived in England, he had to deal with these himself. His responsibilities included giving the servants money for the purchase of provisions from the bazaar and getting them to render accounts, making them do their allotted chores, and, most important, settling their never ending squabbles. He had thought he would escape this ordeal for at least four months by staying in the circuit house but, at Ravenshaw's bungalow, he had to involve himself in the mess again.

Ravenshaw was a sociable man of gentle disposition and was a solicitous host to Barlow. For the first few days, Ravenshaw did not go to office, spending time sprucing up the bungalow and going through files at home. But he was more interested in readying a tool shed than in smartening up the sitting room or the bedroom. He placed a table in the shed in the back garden and arranged on it tools like knives, screwdrivers, tongs, a hammer and a saw. He also had plans to set up a lathe machine. This was where he spent a lot of time. At the moment, he was busy with a saw, cutting a bookcase to make it smaller.

Barlow noticed that Ravenshaw had no interest at all in his official work. Perhaps he knew he would get transferred shortly and so there was no need for him to find out more about official business relating to Orissa. His attitude made this abundantly clear. A few days after his arrival in Cuttack, Ravenshaw spread out a map of Orissa before Barlow and selected the places he wanted to see before he left the province.

At last it was decided that Ravenshaw would go to Balasore to hold the sessions court there, this being the commissioner's responsibility, for there was no judge for Balasore. There was other business to attend to but Ravenshaw was happy to go there for he liked sessions work more than dealing with revenue matters. On 22 July he left for Balasore on a three week tour.

Barlow passed his days pleasantly enough during this period. His daily schedule was as follows: he got out of bed at five in the morning, spent two hours riding along the bank of the river Katjuri, came back and read the *Englishman* which had been sent from Calcutta. He had breakfast after a bath and at ten o'clock opened the dispatch box sent from Puri and went through the letters and files it carried. He wrote out his orders and rested after lunch at twelve. He then played a game of racquets at four in the premises of Barabati fort and spent the evening in the station club there.

Cuttack was home to several sahibs including the pastor, the civil officer, the PWD engineer and the employees of the Irrigation Company. Sahibs from other stations visited Cuttack because it was the headquarters of the three districts of Orissa. Besides, a regiment of the Madras infantry was also stationed there and six or seven of its officers lived in Cuttack with their families.

For these reasons, Cuttack found great favour with the sahibs. Since some of the sahibs knew little about the place, they were unwilling to leave Calcutta for a posting here but once they had spent a few days in Cuttack, they did not want to leave.

Cuttack offered opportunities for good living as well. It had many open spaces. There was a race track in Chauliaganj, and the raja of Vijaynagar used to send his horses to race there. At the parade ground close to it, a band played in the evenings. At night, the sahibs and their wives and children got together at the station club situated in the fort premises. The other places where the sahibs met for recreation included the Lodge Star of Orissa run by the Freemasons and the club of the Irrigation Company in Jobra. For these reasons, coming to Cuttack felt like one was coming to a city.

Barlow received few important letters from Puri. The Car Festival, which was the event of the greatest significance there, had passed off smoothly. The dowager rani and the underage raja had caused no trouble. The superintendent of police, W.C. Lacey, and the deputy collector, Ramakshoy Chatterjee, were both able officers and Puri was safe in their hands.

Balasore, August 1865

The ghat of the Gadgadia pond, which lay on the outskirts of Motiganj Bazaar of Balasore, was a nice place to spend time with one's friends. Sadar Kanungo Sundar Narayan Ray's house stood on the eastern side of the pond and Fakir Mohan's was a short distance away on its western side. Radhanath and Fakir Mohan often got together here. In the meantime they had found a new friend in Madhusudan Das. He was the same age as Radhanath. Having passed his entrance examination from Cuttack Zilla School, he had joined Balasore Zilla School as teacher. He had rented a house overlooking the Gadgadia pond.

After school hours Fakir Mohan and Madhusudan got together, but Radhanath could not join them every day for fear of his father. He would come and join them only in the evenings when his father was away from home. Fakir Mohan and Madhusudan always made fun of him for this.

Madhusudan would often recount his personal experiences. After he had passed the entrance examination his father wanted him to work as a clerk in the Cuttack collectorate. But Madhusudan had no intention of doing so, for he had made up his mind that he must appear for his F.A. examination. Seristadar Bichitranand was a friend of his father's, and his father had asked the former several times to find Madhusudan a job. But Madhusudan would not work as a clerk, and he left home the moment he was offered a job at the Balasore Zilla School. His plan was to save some money and then go to Calcutta to study for his F.A.

Madhusudan's mind was full of big ideas. At a time when all that Fakir Mohan and Radhanath wanted was to get an increment of twenty rupees by being promoted to the post of second master, Madhusudan said to them, 'Stop thinking so small. Try to figure out how you can earn hundreds of thousands of rupees.'

The topic that frequently came up in their discussions was the relationship between the Oriyas and the Bengalis. Radhanath could not wholeheartedly participate in this discussion for he was himself a Bengali. However, Madhusudan was quite keen to hold forth on the subject. He had good reasons for doing so.

When Madhusudan studied at the Cuttack Zilla School, there were few Oriya students. The majority were Bengalis who found him an unsophisticated country boy, for he dressed like a villager and wore a pigtail. The Bengali boys wore English shirts made of mill-made cloth. They also wore their hair short. Because of his outfit, Madhusudan had had to endure their ridicule. In fact, one day, a Bengali boy had gone so far as to clip off his pigtail with a pair of scissors.

J.P. DAS

Fakir Mohan, too, had reasons to resent the Bengalis. Barabati School, where he was a teacher, was under the control of Bengalis who made life difficult for him in different ways.

The root of the problem, however, lay beyond these personal resentments. The fact was that few Oriyas at the time had received an education in school or college, or knew English. Most of the jobs in schools, cutcherries, courts and offices were, therefore, in the hands of Bengalis, and these Bengalis looked down on Oriyas.

When Fakir Mohan and Madhusudan talked excitedly about the education and progress of the Oriyas, Radhanath kept somewhat aloof; but his eyes lit up whenever the discussion turned to literature. Although his mother tongue was Bengali, he had studied classical Oriya literature and had learnt Urdu from Maulvi Ghulam Rasul and Sanskrit from Sadashiv Nanda. He had memorized the sonnets of Michael Madhusudan Dutt and could recite Sanskrit verses beautifully. He used to tell his friends that Balasore badly needed a library. Luckily for him, a businessman in Sunhat, Damodar Prasad Das, had set up a library in his own house which Radhanath visited regularly.

In August, the new commissioner, Ravenshaw, and his seristadar Bichitranand Das arrived in Balasore. Ravenshaw called a meeting of the zamindars of Balasore to discuss with them the arrangements to be made for an agricultural fair. Madhusudan went there to meet with Bichitranand Das who tried to persuade him to take up the job of a clerk. Bichitranand himself had risen from the positon of a lowly clerk to become a seristadar and the right-hand man of the commissioner. But Madhusudan had not gone there to ask for a clerk's job or to listen to Bichitranand's advice. Nilamadhab Das, a relative of Bichitranand's, was then working as a clerk in the Calcutta High Court. Madhusudan wanted Bichitranand to write Nilamadhab a letter which he could take to Calcutta. Bichitranand, on his part, prevailed upon

Madhusudan to join the registration office in Balasore as clerk. Madhusudan did report for his new job. At the same time, he did not forget to get Bichitranand to write a letter to Nilamadhab, which he kept with him.

Puri, September 1865

The servants were no longer able to control Divyasingh. He was ten and a strong, well-built child, and he easily outdid servants when it came to obscenities. He beat them whenever he felt like it and even had a special cane fitted with a silver handle to do so. The servants were now afraid of him and complaints about Divyasingh breaking someone's head or hand reached Suryamani at regular intervals.

After making several attempts at giving him an education, Suryamani finally gave up on Divyasingh. The system of teaching a prince which prevailed in the palace was a strange one. The teacher had to remain standing while his student sat on a chair. To teach his royal pupil the alphabet the teacher had to say: May His Highness be pleased to say *ka*; may His Highness be pleased to say *kha* and so on. But, instead of the letters of the alphabet, Divyasingh only showered filthy abuse on the teacher. The teacher was also pulled up by the queen for his failure to teach his pupil properly. Under such circumstances, few teachers lasted very long. Finally, after Divyasingh raised a stick to beat one of his teachers, even the love of money failed to tempt anybody to come into the palace and teach His Highness.

Divyasingh was no longer afraid of Suryamani. He had realized that he was the raja, after all, for he had been treated with great respect on the day of the Car Festival and on other festive occasions. Whenever a big sahib visited the temple city he was always invited to meet him. Inside the palace, however, his only friends were the servants. Divyasingh was convinced that to keep them under control he must possess bodily strength. To this end, he developed a keen interest in physical exercise. He had wrestlers from the gymnasium in town brought in and he practised wrestling with them. In Upadhyay, a north Indian servant in the palace, he found his mentor. On Upadhyay's advice a wrestling pit was dug near the palace wall and it was decided that Divyasingh would begin his wrestling practice on an auspicious day.

A few days later, on *Sunia*, which fell on the twelfth day of the bright fortnight in the month of Bhadrav, a new regnal year began. Divyasingh sat through the puja in the morning in his silk robes and after it was over, the royal priest wrote on a palm leaf and announced that the regnal era of Sri Sri Divyasingh Dev began that day. Every Sunia, Divyasingh felt very happy, for on that day he was treated with every mark of respect due to a raja.

In the afternoon, he took off his silk clothes and wearing a loincloth, went to train as a wrestler. In the pit, an expert wrestler from the town gymnasium laid him flat in a minute. Divyasingh groaned as he fell on the hard, dry ground, slapped the wrestler and roundly abused Upadhyay who threw himself on the ground and said, 'Your Highness, the ground has to be softened.'

Divyasingh said, 'Go, you bastard, get some water, and tread on the ground.'

To buy time, Upadhyay said, 'Your Highness, we need rain water for this.'

Divyasingh and Upadhyay looked up at the sky. Small clouds sailed across it. Upadhyay said, 'The rains will come any minute now.'

Divyasingh sat waiting in the hope that the rains would soften the wrestling pit. But it did not rain that day.

The king waited for the rains the next day. But it did not rain that day, either. Not even on the day after that. Nor on the day after.

two

Cuttack, October 1865

Barlow was depressed at the prospect of having to return to Puri in a few days. Moreover, he had not received any letters from his wife for a long time. To add to his problems, the police reports which had reached him during the last few days worried him. They warned about the possible failure of crops since there had been no rain since mid-September. The reports predicted a rise in the price of rice and a shortage of foodgrains in the market.

Around this time in previous years, one could buy thirty seers of rice for one rupee. But this year, one rupee bought only ten seers. In several villages under the Gop police station, no rice was available. The *Panas* and the *Bauries*, who belonged to the lower orders of society, survived on roots and tubers gathered from the forests. One could get twelve seers of *mandia* cereal for a rupee. So, even people from good families had started eating mandia. Many from the villages under the Gop police station migrated to Cuttack in search of work. In Srichandanpur village, even the police inspector could not buy a seer of rice. For fifteen days, no rice was brought to the Lataharan weekly market, which used to be a major centre for trade in rice. Many people in Puri had submitted a petition complaining about the scarcity of rice in the town. In addition to all these reports, there was a letter from Babu Ramakshoy. This in hand, Barlow waited for Ravenshaw.

From Baboo Ramakshoy Chatterjee, Deputy Magistrate of Pooree, to G.B.N. Barlow, Esq., Magistrate of Pooree, (No. 68, dated the 25th October 1865.)

Sir,

I have the honour to state that yesterday I forwarded to you a petition made by many persons complaining about the scarcity of rice in the station. The circumstances described therein are too true to be denied. In many places in the mofussils, the inhabitants, I have been well informed, are not getting rice, and are obliged to live on fruits and roots, and many of the poorer classes are leaving their houses with their wives and children for Cuttack, with the hopes of being employed in the Irrigation Department. Yesterday, I got a chullan of a theft case from Pooree Division; the two prisoners forwarded, on being asked, openly declared that, having fasted for three days with their family they were compelled to steal a neighbour's corn, who having a sufficient quantity, was reluctant to part with a portion of it.

At the station, though there is a large quantity of rice in the ganjes, and though the supply from some parts in the mofussils is daily coming, still the exorbitant rate at which the rice is selling has put the people into greatest inconvenience and trouble. Yesterday the rice was sold by the ganjwallahs at three annas a seer. If there be no rains in the course of three or four days more they will enhance the rate more arbitrarily, and famine will undoubtedly rage in the district. This state of things loudly calls for an interference from the Authorities.

It is to be regretted that we have no stock of rice in the Jail at this time, and I am at a loss how to procure rice for more than (80) eighty prisoners. A certain number of the prisoners had already been ordered to be sent up to Cuttack Jail today. Still we have many, and expect to have many more daily at this time of scarcity.

The muttwallahs and many zemindars, I am informed, have immense quantity of rice in their stores, so much so that they can supply the whole district with rice for two years, but they would not do so unless urged by the authorities.

In bringing these circumstances to your notice, I hope that some measures can be adopted by Government to remedy the crying evils in time.

P.S.: While writing the above, three petitions with two lists containing the names of the muttdhars, & e., who have got rice in their stores, are brought before me by the inhabitants of the station and the police officers. They have represented the grievances in a very pitiable manner. Now, I think it is to be a high critical time, and it requires your interference. Inspector Sadhoo Singh, who is now before me, says that he was in the morning obliged to go to the ganj at Moniram to keep the peace, as the people assembled there only to get some rice.

When Ravenshaw came out, Barlow told him in brief about the scarcity of rice in the Puri district and such matters, but Ravenshaw did not seem at all interested. On the other hand, he talked to Barlow about his tour of Balasore and arrangements for the agricultural fair. When Barlow gave him Ramakshay's letter to read, Ravenshaw said, 'You write out a report, I will forward it to Calcutta.' Since his discussion with Ravenshaw had led nowhere, Barlow sat down to write out a reply to Ramakshay's letter.

That evening Barlow did not accompany Ravenshaw to the club, but decided to meet Reverend John Buckley and speak with him about the problem on hand. Buckley had spent more than twenty years in Orissa, was fluent in Oriya and was secretary of the Orissa Mission. He was of a serious disposition and he listened to Barlow very attentively. In Buckley's circle there were three hundred Christian farmers with whom he regularly kept in touch. From them he had already received news of the crop failure the previous month and he had no doubt that a terrible disaster was around the corner. That very morning Buckley had written a letter mentioning this to the Mission Society in England.

From Buckley's house Barlow went to the club. There he came across W.J. Money, collector of Cuttack, and Captain G.B. Fisher, superintendent of police. Barlow expected to get some information from them about the situation regarding the crops. But both of them were shallow people, and they told Barlow flatly that they would not discuss official matters in the club.

The next day, Barlow talked to others and found out that the situation in Cuttack was no less alarming. Rice sold at eight seers a rupee and so many people gathered to buy rice on 26 October that the rice market had to be closed down. Only one shop had remained open, and people took away the rice by force without paying for it. In shops where rice was being sold under police protection, the guards got the shopkeeper to sell rice only to their men, and others had to go away empty-handed. There was no rice for the soldiers stationed in the Cuttack cantonment, and the lawyers in Cuttack had petitioned the judge complaining about the scarcity of rice. The situation in Cuttack was really alarming.

Puri, October 1865

When Ramakshoy arrived at his office, he found a small crowd assembled outside. In the crowd, he spotted many rice traders as well as Dukhishyam of the Emar Mutt, one of the many abbeys of Puri. They followed him into the office. After he settled his chair, Dukhishyam placed a bunch of keys on the table. Others followed his example and said in chorus, 'We are told you think our godowns are bursting with rice. Please come and see for yourself how things are.'

They did not listen to Ramakshay's protests and insisted that he himself inspect their godowns. Ramakshay first went to the godown of the Emar Mutt. From there he was taken to the godowns of the Sriramdas Mutt and the other mutts. In fact, they had only a small quantity of rice. His point made, Dukhishyam said, 'Although we do not have a lot of rice, we are nevertheless willing to sell it at a fair price. But the sale cannot be carried out without police protection.'

Ramakshoy said, 'Don't worry, I will be here. Start selling the rice.' In his presence, rice was sold at fourteen seers a rupee though the market price the day before was only five seers to a rupee. No one knew how the news of this spread, but in no time a crowd of about a hundred people gathered in front of the godown. It was difficult to manage the crowd and the sale of rice had to be stopped. Ramakshoy sent for Inspector Sadhu Singh and constables. The crowd was brought under control and the sale was resumed. But in the space of only two hours all the rice brought out for that day was sold out and half the people had to go back empty-handed, complaining bitterly.

Back in his office, Ramakshoy chalked out a plan for selling rice in consultation with Sadhu Singh. It was decided that from the next day, all the mutts and rice traders would sell rice under police protection.

While they were working out their plan, Ramakshoy received a letter from Barlow, which said:

My dear Baboo,

Your official letter regarding the price of rice reached me today, and I hasten to reply to it. The matter is very serious, and the same condition of affairs appears at Cuttack also; with the additional complication that the dundeedars have combined, so as to altogether close the moddes' shops, and no rice is to be had at any price whatever from a single shop in the town here. This, in a place where there are troops to be fed, is most inconvenient.

I gather from your letter that we are so far better off at Pooree, that rice is being sold there though at enhanced rates, and it is a great comfort to know that there is sufficient rice stored up to feed the people, if ultimately it can be reached. I wish you to see personally the principal mohunts and holders of rice, and endeavour to induce them to continue offering their rice for sale, even if it be at their own prices, and if you can find out by any approximate guess what quantity or supply of rice there is stored in Pooree, I shall be glad to know it. Let me know regularly the condition of affairs, and how the price fluctuates, as well as prospect, of the opportunity for purchases (at any rates) being continued. Inform Sadhoo Singh that he must manage somehow to keep the peace and to supply you faithfully with reports of the state of affairs and of the public feeling in the matter.

What becomes of the rice coming in from the mofussils? Of course the reply is the dundeedars secure it all for the buniahs by whom they are employed. Ask Sadhoo Singh if a public haat was opened by me, say in the *Barodand*, where any one who chose to sell could come and sell at his own rate, how many maunds per day he would guarantee, should be offered for sale there.

Now, Baboo, look sharp after this matter. Keep your eyes open and head cool, so as to derive a calm judgement as things progress, which be sure to communicate to me regularly and plainly.

P.S.: Write to me demi-officially always about this, and tell me if you see any indication of the buniah and dokandars closing their shops altogether. Try and persuade people to send out into mofussils to buy in their own rice. Promise help from Foujdaree if any one seizes a bonafide stock in transit.

Ramakshoy read out the letter to Sadhu Singh. The plan to set up a weekly rice market on the main Badadanda street of Puri was not a bad idea. But before doing this, two precautions would have to be taken: the Telugu traders who came to purchase rice here must be stopped and arrangements must be made to stop middlemen from buying up rice sent from the mofussils to the town. Sadhu Singh was of the opinion that if these measures were taken, rice would be supplied to the market by the villagers.

However, the price of this rice had to be fixed every day in consultation with the shopkeepers. The government had to play the role of mediator in these transactions in order to make the market function properly. This formed the substance of Ramakshoy's reply to Barlow's letter.

There was still no sign of rain in Puri. In the evening, hot winds blew. Looking up at the blazing sky through the window, Ramakshoy added a postscript to his letter: 'The weather is unbearably hot here. A hot wind blows all the time and a fever epidemic has broken out.'

Ramakshoy was a pious man. He sealed the letter, bowed his head to the Almighty and prayed, 'May Barlow return soon and manage the situation here.'

Balasore, October 1865

The situation in Balasore, another district of the Orissa division, was not all that good either. There was no rain and therefore, no crops, and the supply of rice to the market had stopped. People walked about all day, hoping to buy some rice but they always came back disappointed. In spite of all this, sixty-nine ships from Madras had dropped anchor in the river and were waiting to purchase rice. The year before, the harvest in Balasore had been an unexpectedly good one and Telugu traders had exported vast quantities of rice from there to Calcutta and Madras. So no one in Balasore now had any rice left over. Every year, Balasore exported about two hundred thousand maunds of rice but the previous year about eight hundred thousand maunds had been exported and as a result, the godowns lay empty.

Although rice now sold at sixteen seers a rupee, the Telugu traders were busy buying up whatever rice they could find and were willing to keep buying until a rupee would buy ten seers. But there was no sale of rice. Having bought an enormous amount of rice, they were now waiting for the tide to take their ships to sea. The plan was to sail to Burma and procure rice from there.

The scarcity of rice gave rise to law and order problems in Balasore. Rice was looted from people on the roads. The houses of people who refused to lend rice to the hungry were burnt down. In Aulda, a similar incident took place and a lot of property was damaged.

Groups of people were now seen wandering about all over the place. Some of them were looking for work; others went from village to village to buy rice. The number of beggars had increased vastly.

On 25 October, Padmalochan Mandal met the collector to submit the following petition on behalf of the zamindars of Balasore:

Sir,

We, the undersigned zemindars of the district of Balasore, beg most respectfully to bring to your notice the following circumstances under which we sincerely depend upon you that you would be kind enough to grant us one month's time to pay the khajanah due for the two quarters of the last year on the 8th of November 1865, viz:

1. That for want of rain the main crop of this district has severely suffered from the scorching heat of the sun, and we therefore do not in the least expect any produce this year.

2. That the practice was, the ryots did always receive advance from mahajans to pay the last instalment of rent of the past year, depending upon the crop of the present one; but they say they could not get it, and we have no reason to disbelieve their statement.

3. That the poor ryots blindly disposed of all the produce and could not keep any stock for this year, owing to the over exportation of rice last year.

Under the circumstances above alluded to, the poor ryots are not in a position to pay rent to us, and consequently we are unable to pay it in due time, unless we are favoured with one month's time to get money elsewhere.

Obediently,
Zemidars of Balasore

The collector, H. Muspratt, forwarded this petition to the commissioner with the comment that the zamindars' request deserved consideration. But Ravenshaw responded to the petition by writing that only fifty per cent of the crops had failed, therefore, the zamindars had the resources to pay the revenue. Muspratt wrote again to the commissioner about the crop failure and the scarcity of rice in the district and said in his letter that he was persuading people to sell rice. In his reply, Ravenshaw wrote:

Sir,

I have no doubt there is more rice in your district than you imagine, and further that the crops of the current year will suffice for the year's supply. You must on no account interfere with legitimate trade, either export or import, or hold out any promises or inducements beyond encouraging dealers to sell and buy without restriction at such prices as they may find to be for their interests.

The rise in price, so far as it goes, will have stopped export in very large quantity and should the price rise higher than at present, I have no doubt but that you will find grain being imported in place of exported.

T.E. Ravenshaw

Muspratt chose to keep quiet. The houses of people who had some rice in store were broken into. The superintendent of police, Shuttleworth, was at a loss to decide what to do about these incidents, for, when caught, the culprits readily pleaded guilty and happily went to jail. The Balasore jail was already so crowded it could not accommodate any more prisoners.

In Balasore, Netra Senapati was lying on his bed, resting at midday. But he was restless as news of houses being looted reached him daily and he had reason to feel apprehensive for he had some rice at home. The sound of footsteps outside made him rush to his front door. He opened the door and looked around. But there was no one outside. When he went inside and closed the door he found a piece of paper lying on the floor. It carried the following message scrawled on it in big, clumsily written letters: 'If you will not sell your rice, we will set fire to your house.'

Ganjam, October 1865

Although Ganjam was an inseparable part of Orissa from all points of view, for administrative purposes it had been placed under the jurisdiction of Madras. Ganjam had very close links with Orissa in general and Puri in particular, and rice from Orissa was brought to Ganjam by way of Chilka lake which bordered the Puri and Ganjam districts.

This year, however, rice was not supplied to Ganjam from Orissa and the ships sent to procure rice had not returned yet. Ganjam used to import rice every year. This year, importing rice had become essential because the harvest had not been a good one. Traders from Rambha and Ganjam wrote to the collector, demanding that the government of Bengal withdraw its order banning export of rice from Orissa.

In fact, the government of Bengal had issued no such order. Nevertheless, G. Thornhill, collector of Ganjam, wrote to the commissioner of Cuttack regarding this matter. Ravenshaw promptly replied saying that no order banning rice export from Orissa had been issued, nor had any restrictions been imposed on trade. The rice traders had perhaps ganged up together to raise the price of rice.

On receiving such a reply from Ravenshaw, Thornhill sent the following telegram to the Bengal Chamber of Commerce:

There has been cessation of sales of rice throughout Ganjam District owing to stoppage of supply from Cuttack, and much distress is felt. Price of rice in Berhampore is seven Madras seers per rupee, and other grain in proportion, and procured with much difficulty. Kindly inform merchants that any rice shipped to Gopalpore or Ganjam would find ready sale as above. If plentiful in Arracan and Burmah, kindly communicate there also.

Cuttack, November 1865

Ramakshoy's letter made Barlow want to return to Puri as soon as possible. The situation there was going from bad to worse. With great difficulty, Ramakshoy had made arrangements for the sale of rice in the open market but so many people thronged the shops, it became impossible to manage the sale. In the mutts rice was sold from 6.30 a.m. till 10 a.m. But people arrived the night before and camped in front of the mutt. Selling rice was not possible without police protection and Ramakshoy had to go personally to all the points where rice was being sold. At times, the mutts created problems by refusing to sell rice on Thursday or on a full-moon day or on some such pretext. Ramakshoy wrote to Barlow saying that the latter's presence in the district during an emergency like this was absolutely essential.

Barlow had managed with great difficulty to find an opportunity to discuss the situation in Puri with Ravenshaw a few days earlier. In spite of all that had come to pass, Ravenshaw still believed that plenty of rice had been stored up in the countryside. When Barlow mentioned his plan to set up a haat in the main street of Puri and fix the price of rice, Ravenshaw showed him two letters. One was a copy of his cable to the government of Bengal sent on 21 October. It said:

Owing to bad prospect of rice crop Bazaar opened this morning at eight seers per rupee; since noon shops all closed, and rice not procurable. Station and country perfectly quiet. I have sent for principal grain dealers and will endeavour to induce them to open their shops and sell at fair and remunerative rates.

On 23 October, he had received a reply to this from the lieutenant governor:

From S.C. Barley, Officiating Secretary to the Government of Bengal, to the Officiating Commissioner of the Cuttack Division, (No. 5969, dated the 23rd October 1865.)

Sir,

I am directed to acknowledge the receipt of your telegrams of the 21st and 22nd current, and in reply to state that the lieutenant governor, while approving what you have done in sending for the dealers and endeavouring to induce them to open their shops and sell at fair rates, desires that you will be cautious not on any account to interfere with the natural course of trade, or to coerce the Bazaar dealers in grain to sell at rates lower than those which it may be their interest to offer.

You will be good enough to submit, for the information of the lieutenant governor, a full report on the subject of the present scarcity which prevails at Cuttack.

This was the last word on the matter, for the commissioner was under the authority of the board, and the board, in turn, was subject to the authority of the lieutenant governor or the government of Bengal. Unless a matter was extremely serious or critical, it was never referred to the highest authority, that is, the viceroy or the government of India. The letters convinced Barlow that under no circumstances would the government grant him permission to fix the price of rice or act as a mediator in the transactions. He took leave of Ravenshaw and set off for Puri.

The commissioner, Orissa division, had another designation: superintendent of the Tributary *Mahals*. The princely states of Orissa were subject to the authority of the Mahals and as their superintendent, the commissioner exercised administrative powers over them. It had only been four months since Ravenshaw had arrived in Orissa and he was hoping that he would receive his transfer order any moment. He wanted to tour the princely states before leaving Orissa. This he planned to do in winter for it was the best time for travelling. Consulting the map, he decided that he would first go to Banki, then to Nayagarh and from there to Narasinghapur which lay on the south bank of the river Mahanadi, via Duspalla. He would return to Cuttack after visiting Talcher, Kendujhar, Mayurbhanj and Bamanghati. He sent this proposed tour programme for winter in his letter to the lieutenant governor's secretary.

Barlow wrote to Ravenshaw from Calcutta to say that his tour programme had been approved. However, Barlow added that the lieutenant governor hoped Ravenshaw had made all arrangements for bringing aid to people in the Cuttack division who found themselves faced with a terrible drought.

But the letter did not find Ravenshaw in Cuttack. He had already left for Banki on 20 November, two days after he had sent his tour programme to the lieutenant governor.

Calcutta, November 1865

Although the situation in Orissa gave Ravenshaw, the board of revenue in Calcutta and the government of Bengal no cause for worry, it made people in the know in Calcutta deeply anxious. On receiving the telegram from the collector of Ganjam regarding the scarcity of rice there, the vice-president, Bengal Chamber of Commerce, R. Scott Moncrieff, resolved that he must do something about the matter. He was a highly placed official in a business organization called Gisborne and Company. On 3 November, he submitted, on behalf of his company, a long and detailed proposal to the lieutenant governor.

In the proposal Moncrieff said that importing rice to the famine affected areas had become a matter of extreme urgency. It should now be found out from where rice could be procured, and procured quickly. Burma possessed large stocks of rice. Rice procured from these places could be sent by small vessels to famine hit areas in Orissa and Bengal. However, caution must be exercised while doing so. If word about the government buying supplies of rice spread, the price of rice might shoot up. Messrs. Gisborne and company was a reputed organization, and if they procured rice no one would have any cause for suspicion. Should the government entrust this company with the task of procuring rice, it would be able to ship one thousand tonnes of grain to Calcutta in six weeks' time without charging anything for their labour.

When this letter was forwarded to the board of revenue, the secretary of the board, R.B. Chapman, made the following observation:

> The Board however, have very little doubt that the extent of the calamity which has befallen these provinces is considerably exaggerated in Messrs. Gisborne and Co.'s paper. It will probably not give a very erroneous impression if it be said that in the Divisions of Behar, Bhagulpore, a part of Chota Nagpore and Orissa there will be about a quarter crop; in Central Bengal, including the Burdwan, Nuddea, and Rajshahye Divisions about a half crop, and in the Eastern Districts a full crop. Beyond the western boundary of the Lower Provinces, it is pretty well ascertained that the scarcity does not extend further than the Benares Division.
>
> It is also most important to make it clear at once that the State will not step in and relieve from their responsibilities the wealthy landholders who have been created by the permanent settlement at an enormous sacrifice of revenue expressly as one main object to intervene between Government and the people in season of pressure such as the present.

The Board, therefore, while again acknowledging the laudable motives that prompted Messrs. Gisborne and Co.'s proposal, advise the Government to decline to accept it.

The lieutenant governor, Cecil Beadon, shared the views of the board and informed Moncrieff that he would not be able to accept his proposal. Beadon felt his duty was over when he sent a copy of the letter and other papers to the government of India. In a few days' time the viceroy wrote back to say that the governor general-in-council had approved the reply to Moncrieff's proposal.

At the time, British officials in India were being guided by an invisible counsellor, John Stuart Mill. He had once been an employee of the East India Company and was a leading light of the Utilitarian Society and member of the British parliament. His writings on political economy and philosophy had inspired the intelligentsia. British officials in India, in particular, had been profoundly influenced by his writings. They were all familiar with the following observation made by Mill:

> Direct measures, at the cost of the State, to procure food from a distance are expedient when, from peculiar reasons, the thing is not likely to be done by private speculation. In any other case they are in great error. Private speculators will not, in such cases, venture to compete with the Government, and, though a Government can do more than any one merchant, it cannot do nearly so much as all merchants.

Puri, November 1865

Ramakshoy heaved a sigh of relief when Barlow returned to Puri in the first week of November. Life had been terribly hectic for him during the last few days. He had no time for official business in the court or the cutcherry; all his time had been taken up visiting the shops of rice dealers and maintaining law and order there with the help of the police. Wherever he went, groups of people carrying baskets and sacks and money ran after him in the hope of being able to buy some rice.

As soon as he arrived in Puri, even before entering his bungalow, Barlow sent for Ramakshoy. The situation in Puri was getting worse by the day. So many people gathered in front of the mutts to buy rice these days that only the strong ones could push their way to the front while the weak hung back and came home in the evening after a long wait, bruised and empty-handed.

The petty dundidars made matters even worse. They had spread rumours in the mofussils that anyone bringing rice to Puri would be forced to sell it at twelve seers per rupee. Half of the rice coming to Puri was bought up by them on the way. Lest they should be caught doing this, they got a few poor women to do it for them. To escape being caught, the women carried the rice in baskets with dried cowdung cakes piled on top.

If this was the situation in Puri, the situation in the mofussils was no better. From the mofussils came police reports of the misery endured by the people. Although the zamindar of Krushnaprasad distributed relief, some families in Nabapatna were utterly helpless, and people were dying of starvation. In Banpur, rice sold at seven seers per rupee. Rice was sold in Bhusandpur with the help of the police, but it had run out. People from villages like Bayalisbati and Balrampur used to purchase rice from the weekly markets of Nagpur, but supplies of rice to the markets had stopped. News of the death of two children due to starvation was received from Baulani. In Pipili, rice was sold at eight seers a rupee. Not able to get any rice, people now survived on roots, stems of water lilies, tamarind leaves, etc.

News of the extreme distress that the people suffered came from places on the shore of Chilka, especially in Parikud and Malud. Two persons died near the salt office in Malud. People there were undergoing great hardship since salt-making in the area had been stopped. When the rains failed, people from this area had migrated to other places in search of work. The condition of the women and children left behind was wretched beyond words. Police constables also sent a petition stating that they found it difficult to survive on their present salary. They requested that they be given an extra allowance in view of the high price of rice.

After he returned to Puri, Barlow set to work tirelessly day and night. Touring the town, he inspected arrangements for the smooth sale of whatever rice was available. He informed Ravenshaw that he was absolutely mistaken in believing that there was plenty of rice in the district. There was no rice in the region, and it had to be procured from outside. He added that unless a shipload of rice was sent to Parikud and Malud from Calcutta, people there would die of starvation.

Ravenshaw was an expert at writing letters. A reply from him promptly reached Barlow. It said:

Demi-official letter from T.E. Ravenshaw, Esq., Officiating Commissioner of the Cuttack Division, to G.N. Barlow, Esq., Magistrate of Pooree (dated the 14th November 1865)

My dear Barlow,

I am in receipt of yours of 13th reporting the deplorable state of things in Parikood and Mallood. I only hope your informant may have put a little colour on his story. The accounts I get from all parts are full of grumbling, but I am certain that, with the exception of a few fields on the higher lands which are entirely lost, the crops nowhere fall short of 8 annas, and in many places will be very nearly a full crop, particularly on the lower part of the Delta between the Mahanuddi and Katjooree; a zamindar from that part was with me yesterday and said he had a full crop. Perhaps you may be able to draw supply for Pooree from that direction.

Parikood and Mallood are peculiarly situated, and are, I fancy, entirely depending on the rainfall for a crop, the water on both sides being salt, but the distress there would appear to be exceptional. I have reported the matter to Government. It will be a difficult matter to find funds, or having got funds, to provide food for the people there until the rain comes in; the only chance will be to get them to emigrate for a while to some place where they will be more accessible in case relief is given, or if there be work of which they are capable, but this latter alternative won't help the old or infirm. The Mallood Pergunnah belongs to Jagirdar Jameeloodden, who was committed for trial. Can't you persuade him of the necessity of keeping his ryots on the estate? The Parikood Raja ought to be in a position to do something for his people. You must try and induce the landed proprietors to do their duty, and not to throw themselves and their people on Government, and on all accounts and all occasions put the best colour on affairs. Don't let people get downhearted, with the prospect of even half a crop there ought not to be a famine, reassure every one and try and get the people to help themselves, a somewhat difficult matter you will say in Orissa, but there is nothing like trying. The whole revenue of the country has to a great extent been absorbed in the country and by the people, to say nothing of the large export, which, if it has expended rice, has brought money, and money will buy food, and food will, if in existence, go towards where the want exists. It's hard times for poor folks, but what's to be done? Can your Unnochutter Fund help you? Stop feeding the fukirs in Pooree for a bit, and throw them on the charity of the town, and send the available proceeds in rice to the Parikood and Mallood people, try to get by any means some local subscription, buy a few bags of rice and send them under such superintendence as will ensure its reaching the mouths of the hungry.

Any khas mehal enquiries into loss of crops should be made at once before the grain is cut; it looks like rain here; we are in hopes it may fall. Perhaps with further inquiry you may find the reports from the Chilka not quite so bad as you expect. I only hope it may be so.

Yours faithfully,
T.E. Ravenshaw

This Ravenshaw is a funny fellow, thought Barlow to himself. He lives in a fool's paradise. He put the letter aside and looked out of the window. There were clouds, but no sign of rain. The previous night, not more than two spoonfuls of water had dropped from the skies. In Puri, rice now sold at six and a half seers per rupee.

Mithakua, November 1865

Police Superintendent Lacey had begun his tour ten days ago. His chosen destination was Fatepur, but not because he wanted to shoot birds. He went there to find out about the state of affairs in the area. He was to send a report by assessing the circumstances during his journey.

The crops in Khurda were not too bad and the situation there had improved slightly during the previous week on account of the cloudy weather. But the scene shifted as he approached Bolgarh. In the area lying between Jankia and Tangi, the crops had wilted; at places farmers had tried to save whatever crops they could by irrigating the fields. Lacey set up camp at Jankia. His servant bought rice from the bazaar. Old rice sold at eight seers a rupee, and new at ten seers a rupee.

After setting up camp on the shore of the Chilka lake, Lacey went off to Sunakhala. The crops there had failed completely. Not even one ear of grain was to be seen in the fields, and the cattle browsed on the stubble. The sarbarakar informed Lacey that many men had left the area for Cuttack and Ganjam in the hope of finding work there.

Lacey got off his palanquin and covered the distance between Balugaon and Banpur on horseback. A peasant took him to show him his plot of land by the roadside. It was a large one, measuring ten acres. On all this land not even one ear of paddy was to be seen anywhere. The owner would have to go out and beg. The sarbarakar pressed the peasant to pay his taxes. If the former insisted on being paid, the poor man would have to sell off his livestock and his bullock cart. When Lacey entered the pragana comprising Parikud, Malud and Bajrakot, he got off his horse and toured the villages on foot. He went from the Mangala outpost lying on the shore of the Chilka to Nabapatna and from Krushnaprasad to the fort. In all these places the crop had failed completely. Only in a few villages had the Brahmins managed to save what crops they could. The condition of the people was worse than that of people living anywhere else.

Lacey was told that twenty to thirty people in these villages had already died of starvation. What he came across during his tour convinced him that the number must be increasing by the day. Badachur was a large village, but it now lay more or less deserted. There were only women and children in the houses. Lacey entered a few houses to see for himself how they fared. The head of one family had gone away, abandoning his wife and children to their fate. His unfortunate wife, dressed only in rags, lay huddled inside. She showed Lacey her two daughters. They were all skin and bones; drained of all their strength by hunger, they were unable to get up and move. Other women placed in similar situations narrated to him their tales of woe. Two days ago, three children had died in one family and one child had died in another. A couple had died of starvation in yet another house; in fact, they died because they were forced to eat food that was inedible or even poisonous.

The terrible effects of the famine were evident everywhere in the area. Everyone in the villages—men, women and children—

plodded through mud and water to collect *dohana* roots. This was what they survived on. But stocks of this would run out soon and there would be nothing left for people to eat.

The raja of Parikud was doing a commendable job. The raja had a large stock of rice, and for the last two months he had kept his ryots alive by doling out grain to them. In his farmyard fifteen boys were housed and fed; in another place seventeen orphaned girls had been accommodated. For the destitutes, he had set up a free kitchen.

The tour was a heart-rending experience for Lacey. The terrifying shadow of death hung over the whole region he had passed through, and the sky was rent by the cries of helpless and desperate people. Lacey spent a night at Mithakua writing out a long and detailed report of his tour and returned to Puri along the seashore, carrying in his heart a harrowing tale of grief.

Calcutta, November 1865

On the morning of 25 November, Chapman, secretary of the board of revenue, received a telegram from Barlow. It read as follows:

> Starvation at Parikood, Mallood; deaths increasing. District Superintendent viewed distress. Men deserted and families destitute. Organization of local relief attempting, but difficult from general scarcity. Ask public aid. Grain shipped to Metacooah better than money. Parikood zemindar behaving well.

This telegram was sent to the subordinates along with other papers. Two days later, when they came back to him in a file with notes, Chapman sent the following reply by wire:

> Send more particulars about Mallood. How many persons are known to have died of starvation, and how many families are deserted? What is the population of Mallood and Parikood

together? Are there no wealthy people? What number of people are supposed to be actually starving?

Before answers to the above questions were received, Moncrieff was consulted about sending rice to areas around the Chilka lake. Moncrieff indicated that given carte blanche, he could land 800 tonnes of rice from Akyab on the Orissa coast within twelve days. He added that if he could be informed by morning, or even by four o'clock in the afternoon of 28 November, he would immediately send at least 250 bags of rice by a steamer from Calcutta to Orissa.

However, after everything had been set in motion, A. Grote, a senior member of the board, put a spanner in the works. On 28 November, he wrote on the file that under the present circumstances, people in Mithakua must have migrated elsewhere in search of work and food before help could reach them. Therefore, there would be no point in sending supplies of rice to this place. Besides, shipping rice there and distributing it among people free of cost could land the government in difficulty. Since a member of the board had made such an observation, all the papers were forwarded to the lieutenant governor, Cecil Beadon. He went through them the same day and promptly wrote to Grote:

> I think we may send down 250 bags by steamer to Metacooah to meet the present emergency but before embarking on any larger operation I should like to have the Board's advice. The cost of the 250 bags should be debited to the Relief Committee and they should be responsible for the economical disposal of the rice. You might suggest the employment of the Mallood zemindar, but it is best, I think, to leave all such details to be arranged by the local authorities.

After writing to Grote, Beadon wrote to Chapman, secretary of the board of revenue:

Under the exceptional circumstances shewn to exist in the south of Pooree, I think the Government may properly depart from its rule of non-interference and send rice to Metacooah for sale at cost price to the people, and for gratis distribution to the absolutely helpless and destitute at the discretion of the local Relief Committee. You can therefore send down 250 bags by the steamer.

The very same day, a telegram from the office of the board was sent to Ravenshaw. It said: 'Would it do any good to send cargo of rice to Metacooah, and could you arrange to get it sold at cost price, say 12 seers for the rupee?' Another telegram was sent to Barlow, collector in Puri. It carried the following message: 'Two hundred and fifty bags of rice will be delivered at Metacooah by the steamer which leaves Calcutta on the 1st. Send a careful officer to make arrangements for receiving the rice, and distributing it with the utmost economy. It is to be sold, if possible, at 12 seers for the rupee. The Government expects the Local Relief Fund to pay for it. Distribute gratuitously only to the absolutely helpless.'

Barlow felt very happy when he received the wire. On 29 November he sent a reply to Chapman's telegram, although it served no useful purpose now: 'By inquiring, 96 deaths and 992 persons left the country: deserted families not computed. Population of Mallood, Parikood, and Sathparah estimated 12,000: no wealthy people. Parikood zemindar helps own ryots somewhat, perhaps 8,000 destitutes.'

Duspalla, December 1865

Ravenshaw left Cuttack on 20 November and after touring Dompara, Banki, Khandapara and Nayagarh, he set up camp at Duspalla. A large tent had been put up in a mango orchard for the commissioner's accommodation. People accompanying him were put up in small tents a short distance away. Elephants and horses were kept tethered outside the orchard. The camp swarmed with chaprasis, sepoys, khansamas and bearers. A crowd of people stood there, waiting to meet the sahib. The whole place had the look of a fairground.

Ravenshaw sat on a chair outside his tent, smoking a hookah, and ran his eyes over papers relating to Duspalla which he had brought with him. He had not liked Orissa at all during the first few months of his stay there. Gradually, however, he began to find out more about the province, and the weather in winter was not unpleasant. He had plans to organize an agricultural fair on a big scale but unfortunately everybody insisted that it be postponed in view of the famine. The famine was now the centre of attention. Although the situation in Cuttack was not much better than that in Puri, the collector of Cuttack did not bother himself too much with it. But Barlow sent him piles of letters from Puri. Ravenshaw concluded that Barlow was one of those who got easily flustered by small problems.

This time, when he started his tour, he had decided that he would find out for himself the condition of the crops. Those who came to meet him in Cuttack gave him to understand that there was no need to worry. A zamindar from Puri told him that there had been no crop failure in his area. Brundaban Marwari from Cuttack informed him that plenty of rice was stored in the district.

While being borne in his palanquin, Ravenshaw examined the rice fields on either side of the road, and occasionally got off the palanquin and went into the fields to take a closer look. In many places, the crops had been gathered in and the fields lay empty. His inquiries in Dompara convinced Ravenshaw that only fifty per cent of the crops had been lost. At many places in Banki, rice stalks had withered in the heat before they could put out ears of grain. But, wherever there was some water, seventy-five per cent of the crops had been saved. Khandapara had had a good harvest, but in Nayagarh farmers hoped to get only twenty-five per cent of the harvest.

Ravenshaw came across something new in Nayagarh. People belonging to the lower castes bought salap trees from the Khonds in Khondmal. They chopped and pounded these, and cooked the powder after straining it. Ravenshaw was pleased that people had discovered a new source of food. But when he tried to persuade them to plant salap trees, they said that these trees should be planted by Khonds, and they would only eat its fruit and the flour obtained from its trunk, but never plant it.

All this made Ravenshaw conclude that the situation was far from alarming. This view he conveyed to the board in a letter. He had of course come across quite a few destitutes wandering about in the course of this journey. After finishing his business at Duspalla, he began thinking about the poor people. Something had to be done about them. After much thought, he wrote out the following letter addressed to his three collectors:

Sir,

As present season of scarcity is likely to be and indeed is already severely felt by the poorer classes of the inhabitants of this division, I have the honour to suggest that a charitable subscription be started for distribution of food and assistance to the really starving or needy. The proceeds of this fund are to be under the management of, and in connection with, that admirable establishment we already have, the Unnochutter Fund.

The present call might legitimately be made by appeal to the charity of all classes of the community, and be headed and promoted by all government officials. Should sufficient funds be procured, branch Unnochutter houses of relief might be temporarily established in those parts of the country where the greatest loss of crops and consequent distress prevails. I should be glad to hear that you have called a special Unnochutter Relief Committee Meeting in your district, and to know the results of the arrangements you may make.

You are at liberty to place my name on the subscription list for Rupees 50, with promise of increase should circumstances require it.

T.E. Ravenshaw

Mithakua, December 1865

Barlow left Puri on 3 December 1865 and came to Nijagarh Balabhadrapur and set up camp there the same day. The next day, in the morning, he set off for Satpada. There, the headman told him of the terrible sufferings the people were going through. In the whole area, only two *Kumuti* shops had rice. The shopkeepers had brought rice over from Banpur and were selling it at seven seers a rupee. Although they still had some rice left, people now had no money to buy it.

The news of the magistrate's arrival at Satpada brought people from the neighbouring villages. They were small farmers who owned a little land but after the crops had failed, they had been reduced to begging for their survival. They had come to take the magistrate to their villages. They believed that once the sahib himself saw their condition, a solution to their problems would definitely emerge. Visiting these villages was not part of Barlow's tour programme. But the villagers insisted that he visit them. They went away only after Barlow assured them that he would visit them later.

From eleven to five Barlow toured the Nabapatna, Bhutapatna, Nuagan and Bajamunda villages on foot. The situation everywhere was terribly depressing. He visited all the houses in four villages and found that only two had a small quantity of rice. In one house he saw five children and a cat eating a handful of rice off a leaf. In another, he found a quantity of unhusked paddy. The owner said he had bought this two days earlier. He had left it uneaten for he hoped to use it as seed next year if he survived the famine.

In front of all the houses green leaves and kanika roots were drying in the sun. These were to be boiled; but the children sometimes ate them raw. The condition of starving children, in particular, was extremely painful. They lay listlessly on the floor. Some were in such bad shape that when someone lifted them up for the sahib to have a look at them, they cried in pain, but no sound issued from their mouths.

In one house lay the corpse of a seven-year-old child. He had gone with other children to gather green leaves but could not proceed after going some distance. He came back home, and there he dropped dead.

Many houses in the village now lay empty. The men had left for Cuttack or Chabiskud in search of work. The women, too, had gone off to their relatives. The doors of most of the houses stood open. Some had left dry thorny branches across their doorsteps. There was not even a piece of straw to be found in these houses.

No one in these villages had any money. Nor did these people have anything which they could sell off. Barlow saw only six bell-metal utensils in the fifty households he visited. The livestock had already been sold off, and the domestic animals which had not yet been sold found no customers.

That evening, back in his camp, Barlow's thoughts went back to his wife, for some strange reason. He broke down and wept. Soon he collected himself and wrote in his diary:

My first impression on meeting the people in their villages was surprise at their condition and appearance not being so bad as I expected; but I soon perceived that it was the unexpected patience, and I might almost say, cheerful resignation with which, so different from what European ideas associate with starvation, the people seem to await their fate, saying, 'Yes, we have nothing to eat but weeds, and shall go on, until we die, feeding on this.' This was misleading me, and at the end of the day the conclusion I had come to was that the population, as a mass here, are actually starving, and it is only a matter of time how long the strongest of them can hold out.

After it was learnt that supplies of rice were being shipped to Mithakua, small boats were arranged to unload the rice from the steamer. Word had spread in the locality that the rice would arrive on 5 December and on the morning of that day, people started to gather around the dak bungalow in the hope of getting some food to eat. All of them carried earthen pots, shards or leaves off which to eat. For months they had not set their eyes on even a grain of rice, and cooked rice had been a dream for them. They had not stopped to think who would cook the rice when it arrived. By ten in the morning, nearly a thousand people had assembled near the dak bungalow.

Barlow had decided to come to Mithakua for he had been informed that rice was being shipped there. But before he left Puri, he received a telegram saying that the steamer would not bring the rice to Mithakua but that another ship carrying rice for traders was on its way to Gopalpur. Nevertheless, Barlow did not change his tour programme and proceeded to Mithakua. He informed everyone that rice would not be coming to Mithakua. But the people who had come from far-off places hoping to get some rice to eat did not believe him. They sat there, waiting, until late into the night.

Fatepur, December 1865

Early in the morning, Barlow set out to tour the villages nearby. The situation in Gurubai was not all that bad. Since the waters here were shallow, catching fish was easier and the raja of Parikud was selling rice at sixteen seers a rupee. But after a month, edible kanika roots would no longer be available and once the water dried up, fishing would stop.

Twenty-eight people had been engaged in making salt by the salt *daroga* of the area, who gave them a daily wage of two paise each. But the coolies had grown so weak that they could make only five hundred maunds of salt instead of a thousand, which was the expected output. Besides, their wages were so meagre that picking green leaves seemed a more sensible thing to do than buying any rice with it. Barlow ordered that they be paid four paise, instead of two.

In the village of Chechudi, Pandab Sahu's son had died of starvation the day before. Barlow entered his house and found that his other four children too, were not likely to live for very long. In Alanda three members of a family had died; the others were only waiting for death. The hands and legs of the old woman sitting on the doorstep were thin like sticks, and weakness and hunger had fixed her eyes in a stony stare.

The raja of Parikud called on Barlow and said, 'Now that you are here, our bad days have come to an end.' But he was only trying to reassure himself. He was himself in a bad shape. After paying the *peskish* levy to the zamindar of Malud, he was left with only forty-five hundred rupees. Recently he had spent sixty thousand rupees on a case relating to property rights, and his purse was now empty. But he was doing his utmost to help the people.

The condition of Fatepur was even more distressing. Women with their children assembled in front of Barlow's tent. When Barlow came out of his tent, his eyes fell first on a woman who carried held a baby on her hip and held two children by the hands. It appeared as if the baby were dead. Barlow went near the woman and touched the baby. He found that the baby was moving its limbs and was breathing with difficulty.

Skinny women, who had covered their emaciated bodies with rags, surrounded Barlow, holding out their half-dead babies and cried, 'Babu, give us rice.' Barlow made his way through this milling crowd of women. The forty houses in Fatepur had already witnessed ten starvation deaths. Barlow came across about fifty children, who, it seemed, would not live more than two weeks. There were some among them who made one think they were already drawing their last breath.

The woman whom Barlow had seen first when he came out of his tent, now followed him with her three children as he walked round the village. The baby she was carrying on her hip had died in the meantime, but she absolutely refused to accept the fact that it was dead.

From Fatepur Barlow wrote the following letter to Ramakshoy:

My dear Baboo,

A thought has just struck me which, if we can see it carried out, will be the making of the country just now, and I send you a line to ask you to take the matter up at once and try to get it in hand against my return. I forget if I told you that some time ago a proposition was made by some of the Pooree people to repair the Naraindra tank, and it was said the people would subscribe Rupees 30,000 for this purpose.

If this work could be put in hand at once, (in addition to other works already under suggestion by me to Government), an immense deal would be done towards providing relief for the people. I want you, therefore, to stir in the matter and see what can be done. Nursingha Chander Baboo is one of the people interested, but is away; meanwhile ask the Moonsiff to join you in starting the matter. The Raja of Pooree, Mohunts, & c., and all the principal people should be consulted to see what they say, and inform the Raja that, should this scheme be carried out, it will probably supersede my intention of the Rupees 1,000 subscription to which he agreed, as that does not appear likely to succeed. I want the matter to be got up and to proceed under the management of the Natives themselves. I will give all the help I can on part of Government, and indeed a private subscription myself, but the subscription should be proposed by the Native public, their own Committee appointed, &c., and work set about as soon as possible. Just move in the matter, so as to report progress as soon as I come in. Rughoonath Chowdhry will come down handsomely as he was one of the persons who spoke to me, and he was just written to and asked to come to Pooree to consult about it; if he comes before I get there, take him into your counsel. Nursingha Chander Baboo will probably get a subscription from Denkenhal Raja, and if the public unite in pressing on the Pooree Raja, I hear he had promised to give whatever was considered a fair share. Your plan is, after starting the thing, to retreat as much as possible yourself into the background, looking after it indeed, but making every person who comes into the tadbir a confidant, and so an active partisan in persuading others, so as to give the affair as much the appearance of a public general movement as possible. Radhasham Nurindra of Cuttack should be asked to join, as he is most anxious about the affair. Now try hard and develop the idea.

Barlow

Along with this letter, he sent a message which was to be telegraphed to the board:

Passed six days through Sathparah, Parikood, and Mallood. Previous accounts confirmed. Destitution general and complete. Deaths occurring. Sanction of Rupees 5,000 expenditure from Improvement Fund for construction of substantial tank in Khas Mehal Sathparah. Work will support lives now, and be profitable hereafter. People anxious to begin and recalling deserted relatives; there is no alternative measure if this be rejected. Telegraph reply. I am waiting at Sathparah to begin.

That night Barlow wrote in his diary:

The advanced state to which starvation and misery have progressed upon all could not be seen without an oppression of mixed pain and alarm coming upon one ... there is, I am afraid, the saddest fact to be accepted that the whole population of this place, young and old, must starve and nothing to save them, while it is only a matter of lasting out from day to day until the last perishes.

Puri, December 1865

That day rice did not reach Mithakua. But, through an irony of fate, a ship carrying rice got shipwrecked near the Puri coast.

The French ship, the Philaneme, belonged to the Robert and Sharial Company. It was carrying rice for another company and was on its way to Gopalpur and Madras. No one was around when the ship ran aground; the sailors disembarked and the rice was unloaded. When Ramakshoy first got news of the shipwreck, he thought that the ship sailing to Mithakua had reached Puri by mistake. The sailors could not provide any definite information. Ramakshoy sent a wire to Calcutta: 'The ship, the Philaneme, has dropped anchor off the Puri coast on Monday in the evening. Its cargo consists of rice. The owner is Robert and Sharial, Calcutta.'

About six thousand bags of rice were unloaded from the ship. These were stored on the shore, covered with a tarpaulin sheet. A crowd of people gathered when they saw the rice being unloaded from the ship and wanted to buy it. Although they were repeatedly told that the rice was not for sale, they refused to leave. At last, the police had to be called to guard the rice and disperse the crowd.

Barlow returned to Puri on 18 December. While he was on tour, five thousand rupees had been sanctioned for a pond to be dug in Satpada. Before he got this news, he had spent one hundred rupees on getting an old pond renovated. Nearly five hundred people were engaged in this work, and they showed some signs of life. Through such work, these people earned a little money with which they could buy some rice. Around this time, sanction was obtained to employ people to construct the Khurda–Puri road, and thus many people found work.

There were no instructions yet regarding the shipment of rice lying on the Puri coast. However, news that rice had arrived from outside brought the price of local rice down. But it soon became clear that this rice was not for sale because it did not belong to the government and was not meant for Puri. Besides, a dispute broke out between the owner of the ship and the company which had insured the rice. For this reason, there was no question of this rice being made available to people in Puri. Once this became public knowledge, the price of rice went up again. But the crowd of hungry people who had surrounded the rice bags lying on the shore did not thin out.

Since the rice from the Philaneme was not available, Barlow wrote to the board asking for supplies of rice. Although the board sanctioned funds for the construction of the Cuttack–Ganjam and Cuttack–Puri roads, the government was of the view that there was now no need to send rice to Puri.

Under these circumstances, six thousand bags of rice lay surrounded by the police and hungry destitutes.

Cuttack, February 1866

Ravenshaw returned to Cuttack on 31 January after his tour of the princely states and suddenly found himself buried in work, much of which related to the famine. He had supposed that the solution to the problem lay in setting up relief committees in every district. But the plan did not work. Muspratt wrote to say that the relief committee in Balasore had managed to collect only five hundred and forty-four rupees, which included Ravenshaw's donation of fifty rupees. The relief committee of Cuttack convened a meeting but not many attended it and little work got done. From Puri, Barlow wrote to inform Ravenshaw that he had not organized a meeting of the relief committee for he knew that no good would come out of it.

Barlow suggested that the government restart salt-making operations in the areas near the Chilka lake to give people employment. But, since work on the construction of roads had begun in many places in Cuttack and Puri, Ravenshaw wrote to the board saying that taking up salt-making would no longer be necessary. He wrote to Barlow: 'Don't take up too much work. If people are really starving, they will be prepared to walk ten to twelve miles in search of work. So, there would be no point in starting any work programmes in villages where people are starving. People should go out to find work; work should not find them.'

In the Puri district, famine was soon followed by cholera. The outbreak of cholera was nothing new but this year, people had been forced to eat much inedible food and the situation was likely to be worse. In the Sorada and Nagpur villages under the Gop police station, cholera had claimed 163 lives. It was feared that more lives would be lost if pilgrims started arriving as they did in a normal year. In view of this, Ravenshaw wrote to the government of Bengal suggesting that newspapers there give publicity to the outbreak of cholera in Puri, and that posters warning people about this be put up beside railway lines and roadways. Accordingly, the government of Bengal made the news known everywhere and notices in Bengali and Urdu were put up at all police and railway stations cautioning people against visiting Puri.

In the meantime, Barlow had collected five thousand rupees in subscriptions but providing the labourers with rice was a problem. Many people came to work on the Cuttack–Puri road but no arrangements had been made to give them rice. In the evening, they would go from village to village but no matter how much money they offered, rice was not available anywhere. The labourers therefore had often to go without food.

Nolan, the Public Works Department (PWD) engineer who was superintending the laying of the road, decided after discussing the problem with Barlow that he would advance twenty thousand rupees to the latter. Barlow, on his part, would make arrangements for procuring rice for the labourers. Nolan wrote to the departmental secretary seeking approval for this course of action: 'Not only does our work depend on advancing money for procurement of rice, people's lives depend on this as well.' But Nolan received the following wire in response to his request: 'This department cannot have any concern with providing rice.'

Nolan now expressed his inability to advance money to Barlow. Labourers refused to come to the work site. The scarcity of rice had led to an alarming situation. There was no alternative but to import rice to Puri from outside. Barlow went to Cuttack to explain this to Ravenshaw. After much persuasion, Ravenshaw sent the following telegram to the board: 'Famine relief is at a standstill. Public Works Department refuses to advance money to collectors to purchase rice. Pooree must get rice from elsewhere. May I authorize advance for the purpose for Cuttack, Balasore, or Pooree?'

The next day, when Barlow was sitting in Ravenshaw's office, a reply to this arrived. Ravenshaw handed the piece of paper to Barlow and said, 'From now on don't ask me to do anything about this.' The brief message from the board was as follows: 'The Government declines to import rice into Pooree. If the market favours imports, rice will find its way to Pooree without Government interference which can only do harm. All payments for labour employed to relieve the present distress are to be in cash.'

Puri, February 1866

Barlow found it difficult to concentrate on the relief work, for now he had to shoulder another responsibility. He received the news that the lieutenant governor, the member of the board of revenue, Cockburn, and Colonel Nichols, secretary of the PWD, would first come to Puri and from there travel to Cuttack. The lieutenant governor was coming to inspect the construction of the canal by the Irrigation Company and to hold a durbar in order to meet the rajas and the zamindars of Orissa. This was his first visit to Orissa and everyone wanted to make sure the arrangements left nothing to be desired. These occupied Barlow for a few days and he had to set all other work aside.

Although the lieutenant governor was to spend only a day Puri, arrangements had to be made on a grand scale. A reception committee was formally set up and a number of meetings held to decide matters such as the number of floral gates to be put up at different places in the town to welcome the lieutenant governor. A list of gentlemen in the town who would be invited to meet His Excellency was drawn up. The committee also decided what the lieutenant governor would see in Puri during his stay and at what time. A detailed itinerary was worked out. Schools were instructed on the correct way to welcome the lieutenant governor, should he want to meet students there. Besides, steps were taken to clean up the beach and the roads of Puri. The collector's bungalow was given a fresh coat of paint as the lieutenant governor was to stay there.

But while doing all this, Barlow made sure work relating to the famine was not neglected. To check the spread of cholera, medicines had been sent to all police stations. The renovation of the Narendra tank in Puri and the construction of roads by the Public Works Department went on. Barlow had offered to buy the rice from the stricken vessel at thirteen seers a rupee but the owners of the ship had not agreed to the proposal. Now Barlow was informed by the board in Calcutta that the government would not purchase the rice, and the matter ended there.

The lieutenant governor arrived in Puri on 13 February. Ravenshaw was to meet him there but he did not come as preparations for the durbar in Cuttack kept him totally occupied. So it fell to Barlow to organize the reception for the lieutenant governor in Puri all by himself. Everything went off smoothly when the ship came ashore: fourteen guns saluted the lieutenant governor, and a military band played. A pandit recited a sloka welcoming His Excellency. From the seashore a horse-drawn open coach brought him along the road to the collector's bungalow, passing through flower-decked gates on the way. All along the way large crowds greeted the lieutenant governor. Cecil Beadon was pleased at this spontaneous display of loyalty and respect. However, amid the pomp and pageant of his reception, it escaped Beadon's notice that there were among the crowd a large number of destitutes and they were begging for rice, not singing his praise. The lieutenant governor would also have seen, had he wanted to, the rice bags piled on the beach.

Having rested in the afternoon, the lieutenant governor and his companions had dinner with the English officers in Puri. Then they went to watch the fireworks on the beach. The lieutnant governor had heard about the skills of the firework-makers of Cuttack and it gave him much pleasure to see the evidence with his own eyes. In this way, the programme of the day was satisfactorily concluded.

On the morning of 14 February, the lieutenant governor set out to tour the town after breakfast. He saw the Aruna Pillar near the Lion Gate of the temple; from there, he was carried round the temple on a sedan chair by four carriers and saw as much of the temple as possible from outside. He got off near Radhaballabh Mutt, climbed to its terrace and surveyed the temple from there. Then he took Barlow with him and went to see the collector's cutcherry.

People from villages around Puri had assembled near the cutcherry in the hope of telling the lieutenant governor about their problems. They had carried kanika roots and the stems of water lilies in order to inform His Excellency that they had to live on them after their crops had failed. But the lieutenant governor did not meet them; he went straight into the office and discussed matters of revenue of the district with Barlow. Cockburn chose to sit on the veranda for he was not feeling well. People now surrounded him. Cockburn found the seristadar, Purushottam Pattanayak, standing close by, and called him over. He had know Purushottam when he was commissioner in Cuttack. Purushottam took the roots and stems the people had brought and showed them to Cockburn, and explained to him that the people had to eat them on account of the famine. When Beadon came out, Cockburn showed him the stuff. Barlow took the opportunity to give them a brief account of the measures he had taken to cope with the famine in Puri.

In the afternoon, at the collector's bungalow, the lieutenant governor met some important people in Puri who included the raja of Puri, the zamindar of Kotdesh, the mahant of the Emar Mutt and some others. Satisfied with his visit to Puri, the lieutenant governor set off for Cuttack with his companions the very same evening.

Cuttack, February 1866

The lieutenant governor spent 15 February, the day he arrived in Cuttack, resting. The next day he proceeded to tour the city. As expected, arrangements for his reception were more gorgeous than those made at Puri. Floral gates had been erected at all important points in the city. The intersections were trimmed with leaves and flowers, and arrangements for musical programmes had been made to welcome the lieutenant governor. All small roadside shops had been removed, and for the last two days the sweepers had kept the roads clean and dust free by spraying water on them. Given a facelift, the government offices now sparkled. A festive mood had swept through the whole city which now resembled a fairground. The only thing that spoilt the show was the sight of haggard destitutes, men, women and children, who wandered about, crying, 'Give us a little rice gruel, mother.'

The lieutenant governor inspected the jail after having spent some time at the commissioner's office. When he was about to enter the jail premises, some people came to meet him, ignoring the police who tried to stop them. They were not beggars, just ordinary townsmen. They said in a chorus, 'The government should fix the price of rice.' The lieutenant governor assured them that he would talk about this matter at the durbar.

According to the lieutenant governor's programme, the native gentlemen were to meet him in the afternoon. They included all the rajas, zamindars and other men of rank and substance. Crop failure in Orissa figured prominently in what they told the lieutenant governor. On behalf of the zamindars, Jamaluddin, the jagirdar of Malud, requested that they be exempted from paying land revenue. Zamindar Radheshyam Narendra urged the government to import rice because it was so scarce in the province. To all of this, His Excellency responded that he would deal with all these matters in the lecture he was to deliver at the durbar. Beadon had prepared a lecture before setting out from Calcutta. At night he revised and enlarged it, convinced that the draft speech was not comprehensive and interesting enough.

On 17 February, a Saturday, the durbar was held in Jobra on the premises of the Irrigation Company. Great care had been taken to decorate the building with coloured paper buntings, leaves and flowers. A carpet covered the floor of the durbar hall which now resembled the interior of a palace. On one side of the hall, chairs had been placed on a raised platform; on the other, chairs had been arranged in rows to seat invited guests. Besides rajas and zamindars, government officers too, had been invited. For the invitees, the rajas of Keonjhar and Puri were the centre of attraction, for both were minors. Dressed in gorgeous clothes, they sat in the second row and everyone turned to take a look at them. But the two boys did not seem bothered by the attention they received and seemed to be thoroughly enjoying themselves.

For the city of Cuttack, the durbar was a unique experience. It was swarming with the paiks, sepoys, horses and elephants belonging to the hundred or so rajas and zamindars who were attending the durbar. The area around Jobra was packed with people and mounted police had to keep the crowd under control.

The durbar began with a Brahmin chanting a sloka, wishing the lieutenant governor a long life. This was followed by a welcome song sung by three prostitutes of Cuttack. After this, a welcome address was read out on behalf of the citizens of Cuttack which contained praise for Queen Victoria, the British government and the lieutenant governor. The government was requested in the address by the citizens to exempt them from paying taxes and to fix the price of rice.

The hall resounded with the sound of clapping when the lieutenant governor stood up to speak. Divyasingh, the minor raja of Puri, nudged Dhanurjay of Keonjhar, who was sitting next to him, and said, 'This man looks like a red-faced monkey in our palace.'

The lieutenant governor began his lecture:

My friends,

I gladly welcome the opportunity I have at length of being able to enjoy meeting you here in public durbar, and of assuring you in person of the lively interest which the British Government—the Government of Her Majesty Queen Victoria, of which I have the honour to be the local representative—ever takes in the welfare of all its native subjects, and its anxious desire to secure them in the enjoyment of their just rights, and to promote their prosperity and advancement. I regret that unavoidable circumstances have hitherto prevented me from visiting Cuttack; and that I come among you at a time when you are suffering from the calamitous effects of drought. Such visitations of Providence as these no Government can do much either to prevent or alleviate. The seasons are in God's hands, and no man can control them.

After saying this, the governor stopped for a while and took a long breath, for the next sentence of his speech was rather long.

But if a people enjoy the blessing of good government, if every man is safe in the enjoyment of his own property; if crime is repressed, and the strong are prevented from oppressing or plundering the weak; if justice is promptly and impartially administered, if all vexatious imposts and restrictions upon trade are prohibited, if means of a sound education are afforded to all who desire it; if local improvements, especially in the way of transit by land and water, are encouraged and promoted; above all, if taxation necessary for carrying on the administration of the country is fair and moderate, the rest depends upon the energy, the prudence, and the self-denial of the people themselves, and especially on those who enjoy wealth and social influence, and by whose example the people at large are mainly guided.

Leaving the solution of the problem to kings, zamindars and ordinary people, the lieutenant governor went on to dwell on how the British government was working for the good of its subjects and how the commissioner, the magistrate and the collector were efficiently and devotedly running the administration. Now he came to the specific demands of the people:

> I have been asked, since I came to Cuttack, to attempt to mitigate the prevailing scarcity and dearness of food by compelling the dealers of grain to sell their stores at fixed prices. If I were to do this, I should consider myself no better than a dacoit or thief who plunders his neighbour's property for his own use.

These remarks from the lieutenant governor created a mood of dejection among the natives present in the hall. But the lieutenant governor, busy as he was reading out his lecture, did not notice this. He went on:

> Dealers in grain are often supposed to be public enemies, but in fact they are the best friends the people have; for without them there would be no stores of grain, the harvest would be eaten as soon as reaped, and the first bad season must produce starvation and misery to a degree which is now impossible.

Then he touched upon matters such as irrigation in Orissa, the canal which was being dug to facilitate communication and the settlement of land. Regarding the demand for establishing a government college in Cuttack, he said that the government would set up the college only when there were enough students whose fees could meet a large part of its expenses. Now the lieutenant governor turned to look at that part of the durbar hall where the elegantly dressed kings and zamindars were seated and concluded his speech with this:

> Chiefs of the Gurjat! I am happy to hear from your Superintendent, Mr Ravenshaw, who has recently returned from a tour through your estates, that in most cases you pay attention to the management of your estates and consult the good of the people

who are in a peculiar measure under your care, and who look to you chiefly for that protection, which in other parts of the country they enjoy under the regular operation of British Law administered by British Officers. You enjoy great privileges and immunities, and it behoves you to show that you appreciate them. During the time of the mutinies, you were all loyal in your attachment to the British Government; and some of you (I allude especially to the late Maharaja of Keonjhar) rendered efficient and valuable service to the State on that occasion. This was rewarded at the time, and I am now happy to acknowledge it in person.

The lieutenant governor did not forget to thank the Irrigation Company in whose building the durbar was being held. He said that this was one of the best durbars over which he had presided.

The day after the durbar was a Sunday, and the lieutenant governor decided that he would only rest. That day, all decorations were removed from the roads by evening and the attendants of the kings and zamindars left the city. Cuttack returned to its old state.

On Monday, 19 February, a grand lunch was organized in honour of the lieutenant governor. The last thing he would do, while in Orissa, was to inspect the construction of the canal. Having completed this, Sir Cecil Beadon felt that his visit to Orissa had been a great success. That day, in the evening, he took leave of the officers and boarded a ship at the lighthouse.

three

Puri, March 1866

By the end of February, Puri was in the grip of a terrible epidemic of cholera. It began in Rambha in Ganjam and spread to Puri through Parikud and Malud. Its worst effects were visible in Satyabadi, Pipili, Balianta, Astarang and Kakatpur. In spite of warnings issued by the government, a large number of pilgrims had come to Puri for the *Dola* festival, and they caused the epidemic to spread fiercely.

Things came to such a pass that every morning, ten to fifteen dead bodies could be found on the streets of Puri. And because there were no arrangements to have the corpses removed, they would lie there for days. In the end, Barlow ordered that six sweepers be employed in Puri on a contract basis and they be supplied with four litters. In the beginning, bodies were cremated in the cremation ground but later, when a large number of corpses arrived from the jail, the hospital and Kumbharapara, the sweepers simply dumped the corpses Soon, many corpses lay in the area and the unbearable stench made it almost impossible to approach the area. It was said in town that even dogs and jackals were averse to going near the corpses.

The sweepers had received instructions that if they found someone alive, they should take him to the hospital. But the patients, if they had any strength left at all, refused. In the first place, they were afraid of going to a hospital run by the sahibs. Then, people feared that they would lose their caste if a sweeper touched them. They would rather die by the wayside.

As the days went by, the number of beggars and destitutes swelled. These people had left their villages because they could not get anything there. In the main street, as in the lanes and bylanes of Puri, groups of beggars carrying earthen pots went from house to house pleading, 'Mother, give us a little rice gruel.' Their pathetic cries never ceased and people would shut their doors the moment they heard their voices.

At this time, cases of 'rice dacoity' became more frequent. No one dared to take rice or paddy anywhere because if the destitutes came to know of it, they would snatch it away. If needy neighbours found out that someone in their village had some rice, they would break into his house and take it away. According to law this amounted to dacoity but when caught the culprits said that they had done so because they were starving. They confessed to their crime and happily went to jail. The jail in Puri was soon overflowing.

Barlow was glad that relief work was going on in full swing everywhere. With a grant of ten thousand rupees from the government, he had begun a new project: a road from Khurda to Pipili. Barton, the assistant magistrate in Khurda, was in charge of this. People from far-off places, even from Satpada, had come to work there. The Public Works Department had taken up work on the stretch between Jankia and Barkul on the Cuttack–Madras road. The coolies received a daily wage of two to three annas. Around eight hundred coolies including women and children were engaged in digging a pond at Satpada. Children earned wages of from three to eight paise.

Procuring rice was Barlow's main problem. The supply of rice from the mofussils to Puri had stopped completely. The government provided people with work and paid wages in cash. But what could they buy with the money? At the end of the day, they wandered in search of rice, but in vain. Barlow could not decide if he should approach Ravenshaw once more and talk to him about importing rice.

Since the government refused to buy the rice, the owners of the six thousand bags from rice of the ship Philaneme sent the stock by steamer to Madras. This rice could not be used to feed the hungry but in the whole exercise, the rice trader, the shipowner and the insurance company incurred heavy losses.

Calcutta, April 1866

The *Hindu Patriot*, published from Calcutta, carried a long letter to the editor from Ramakshoy Chatterjee on 5 March:

Sir,

In your issue of the 19th instant, you have extracted from the report of the Cuttack commissioner, stating that famine and cholera are raging to an alarming extent in the district. On the recommendation of the Commissioner of the Division, Government has desired all Commissioners to dissuade the people from proceeding on a pilgrimage to Pooree this year. The above notification of Government was made on the strength of the report of the local authorities for December last. But the present state of things in the district is much worse. The mortality by epidemic cholera due to scarcity of food has become alarming. Starvation, in its literal sense, is to be seen in every part of the district. When such is the state of things seen during the harvest season, it is impossible to imagine what disastrous consequences will follow in a short time. At a meeting held this day at the Magistrate's bungalow for making arrangements with regard to the distribution of Rupees 5,000 which has been already collected from the district among the most distressed people, it has been resolved and carried unanimously that house relief system be at present adopted. The object of this relief system is to support the truly distressed families for the next six months. But as the fund at the disposal of the Committee is very limited, I fear their operation for affording relief will not be on an extensive scale. Owing to this, it has been also resolved that the public be invited to contribute their mite to the Pooree Relief Fund. The European members of the Committee have undertaken to move the European gentlemen at Calcutta, and also to write to the Secretary to the late Cyclone Relief Fund to assist them with funds. I take, therefore, the opportunity of requesting you to stir the matter and induce the native community to co-operate with us in this laudable cause by granting donations. It will not be out of place to mention here that this district, poor as it is, was forward in extending relief to the people of the North-Western Provinces in 1861, and to the people of Lower Bengal who suffered from the late cyclone. Baboo Khetter Mohun Bose, Head Clerk of the Pooree Magistracy, has been appointed to act as Secretary to the Relief Committee, and to receive subscriptions from the charitable public.

Yours obediently,
Ramakhshoy Chatterjee

Apart from publishing this letter, the *Hindu Patriot* severely criticized Cecil Beadon's speech at the durbar in its editorial of that issue

When people were dying of starvation Mr Beadon had waxed eloquent about the blessings of British rule. When people were unable to save their lives, Beadon held forth on the need to protect their property. When they were being swallowed up by an all-devouring famine, he had chosen to dwell on the eradication of crime and on how to speed up the delivery of justice. He talked of food for the mind when people were desperately begging for food for their bellies. When all around him the air rang with the cries of the hungry, he chose to focus on local development. How would the hungry millions benefit if they were told that the government's intentions were just and generous?

G.S. Sykes, a young businessman of Calcutta, had read about the famine earlier, but had not given it much thought. On reading what the *Hindu Patriot* said about the lieutenant governor, he was convinced that the British government had not done its duty by its subjects and he thought that he should do something. He had never been to Orissa but, as the representative of American Baptist missionaries, he was in touch with Christian missionaries in Orissa. He promptly wrote letters to the governor general and to the lieutenant governor, and drafted an appeal, which he personally took to the offices of all the newspapers in Calcutta. It was published in the *Englishman* on 14 April 1866:

ADVERTISEMENT

ORISSA FAMINE FUND

Subscriptions and donations are solicited in aid of the above fund for the relief of the sufferers by the famine now prevailing in the Orissa Districts, and will be received and forwarded byMessrs. SYKES and Co., 1, Vansittart Row, Calcutta

Cuttack, April 1866

Bichitranand and Gourishankar no longer met at their houses, nor did they spend time together in Bichitranand's house in Tulsipur. Instead they got together at the office of the Cuttack Printing Press where the press lay unused in Jagmohan Ray's sitting room in Alamchand Bazaar. After Jagmohan Ray's wife and other members of his family died of cholera, he had taken long leave, left Balasore and was now staying in Cuttack.

Today, their discussion centred on the famine and the situation it had caused. The scarcity of rice presented a most pressing problem. A few had tried at a personal level to sell rice at a fair price but without success. All the rice Brundaban Marwari had was exhausted in only three days. Zamindars like Raghunath Das, Ramnath Raychoudhury and Golakchandra Bose had begun selling rice from their own houses in an attempt to help people but they could not sustain the effort for long. The lieutenant governor's speech at the durbar had given the rice traders the feeling that they could now do as they pleased and so they arbitrarily fixed prices. Rice now sold at five seers and a half per rupee.

Bichitranand wanted the printing company to make arrangements for selling rice but Gourishankar thought the company should confine its activities only to printing. In the meantime, the printing press had made some progress. Two people from the Irrigation Company had been appointed one after the other but they had not proved very useful. However, Bhagirathi Sathia had become an expert at lithography. A sahib called Utin was appointed to operate the printing machine which had been brought from Calcutta, and he was able to get the machine to work in a short space of time. With this machine, texts in English could be printed, but Oriya type had not yet been obtained and it was not possible to print Oriya texts. It was learnt that Oriya type would be available in Calcutta, but as the shareholders of the company had not paid their contributions, the company did not have the funds to buy the types.

There was a difference of opinion regarding the company's getting involved in the rice trade. So it was decided that a separate meeting would be called to deliberate on the matter and that to this meeting would be invited, besides the directors of the company, zamindars, officers and businessmen. The meeting was held on 1 April at the press office. Quite a few people were present on this occasion and the meeting was presided over by Bichitranand Das. After a lot of discussion, some decisions were taken.

A company called the 'Rice Selling Company' would be set up. It would sell rice at the same price throughout the year in the city. It would begin its operations from the first day of Baisakh or 14 April. It will have a capital of 20,000 rupees. At fifteen shops in the city, 4500 maunds of rice would be sold at the rate of ten maunds a day per shop. No one would be allowed to purchase rice worth more than one rupee. In this way, nearly 8000 persons could be supplied with food every day. Rice would be stored in a rented pucca house in either Balu Bazaar or Chaudhury Bazaar, and every Sunday, at least three directors would meet in order to fix the selling price of rice.

The places where the fifteen shops would be opened were chosen. The office-bearers of the company were: Babu Gourishankar Ray, secretary; Babu Dinanath Sarakar, treasurer; and Babu Brundaban Marwari, manager.

The gentlemen present at the meeting promised subscriptions, and it was expected that a sum of 8240 rupees would be collected.

The next day, a notice signed by Bichitranand and Gourishankar was sent out to sixty-eight zamindars and other men of means informing them of the quantity of rice the company expected to purchase from them. In response to this, only zamindar Radhashyam Narendra, Bhagirathi Mahendra, the king of Dhenkanal and zamindar Raghunath Das conveyed their willingness to supply rice, but in small quantities. The others wrote to say that they had no rice to spare.

Attempts were made to procure rice from Ganjam but they came to nothing, for those who had promised to contribute to the company's capital did not pay. A way around this problem could possibly have been found but, on 11 April, Bichitranand went away with Ravenshaw on a tour. Thus the Rice Selling Company died an untimely death.

Balasore, April 1866

Besides cholera and smallpox, dacoity too added to the woes of Balasore. More dacoities were now reported in a week than used to be reported in a whole year. The police spent all their time investigating these cases and catching the dacoits. Fifty more constables were employed in the district to deal with this crisis.

All the cases of dacoity were similar. The starving people in a village would break into the house of a villager who had rice and would take it away by force. That the owner of the house might recognize them did not bother them in the least. When caught, they returned whatever rice was left and pleaded guilty in court. In one instance, the dacoits found some cooked rice in a kitchen. They tied up the owner of the house, ate the rice, and then proceeded to commit the burglary.

The news of the increasing number of dacoity cases in Balasore disturbed the lieutenant governor. He wrote to Ravenshaw asking him to go to Balasore and investigate the matter and send a special report. Ravenshaw reached Balasore on 12 April. On 15 April, the lieutnant governor went off to Darjeeling to escape the heat of Calcutta.

From a discussion with Collector Muspratt, Ravenshaw learnt that between 1 January and 12 April, fifty-three cases of dacoity had been reported in Balasore. Seven hundred and thirty dacoits were involved in these, out of whom 566 had been caught. Eight out of them had died and 106 had been sentenced after trial. The remaining cases were being investigated and tried.

Two days after Ravenshaw's arrival in Balasore, cholera broke out in the jail there. On the civil surgeon's advice, the prisoners were shifted to a temporary camp. That very night, a hundred of them managed to effect their escape. The police chased them and captured a few. In the scuffle one prisoner was hurt in the shooting and another sustained a cut. The leg of the prisoner who had been shot was amputated. On receiving news of this, Ravenshaw decided that in his report to the government, he would recommend whipping as a substitute for sending criminals to jail.

It was in Balasore that Ravenshaw came face to face with the misery of the people for the first time. Here, a free kitchen set up by zamindar Shyamanand Dey and others fed the destitutes. There was such a melee during the distribution of cooked rice that only those who were physically stronger could push their way forward. Women, children and the weak had to return hungry and empty-handed. The spectacle was heart-rending, for the destitutes fought each other bitterly for a handful of rice. One destitute snatched food from another, and women and children, unable to get a share, howled pitifully.

Ravenshaw went to distribute money in one such gathering of destitutes. In spite of police protection the destitutes surrounded him as soon as he got there and snatched at his purse while he was giving away the coins. They even thrust their hands into his pocket and took his money away. Somehow Ravenshaw escaped. On another occasion, seeing a scuffle at a free kitchen, he rushed into the middle of the brawling destitutes to make peace. They threw him to the ground as they fought their way towards the rice pots. Having had such experiences, Ravenshaw realized that the situation in Balasore was much worse than that in Cuttack.

He would have stayed a little longer at Balasore to study the situation and write a report. But news came from Mayurbhanj that people in Bamanghati had driven out the police there and spread anarchy. Ravenshaw, therefore, immediately proceeded to Mayurbhanj. All along the way, he came across harrowing scenes of deprivation caused by the famine. There were destitutes everywhere and their cries for rice filled the air. On his way to Mayurbhanj, Ravenshaw forwarded the following letter from the camp:

My dear Muspratt,

I didn't get in here until 12 today, and arrived nearly too late. The elephant was so done up, he positively came down on his nose and nearly sent me flying. The famine here is, if possible, worse than in Balasore. I am swarmed with poor hungry wretches. I have just got a glorious boiling pot of rice going, and have found a Brahmin to cook it much against his will. The poor wretches shall have a belly full for once.

I forgot to bring your map containing Mohurbhanj and Bamunghattee; it was mounted on a roller, and though it did not give the country in detail, it would answer my purpose, so send it out to me by return of post, as I can't get on without a map. Could you have it taken off the roller and folded up? It would be more convenient to send out; it is just sunset, and no dak in yet. Depute Mr Norin or someone to see that my daks are sent off regularly, and should my telegrams from Government come, they can be brought with the dak.

I saw a poor wretch, said to be insane, who had been found devouring a human body; he was at Kemna outpost; he had better be sent in to the Doctor and examined; or it will get abroad that people are reduced to eating one another.

Yours sincerely,
T.E. Ravenshaw

Calcutta, May 1866

The governor general and the lieutenant governor sent donations to Sykes and Company, and after the appeal was published in the newspapers the company received some money every day. Not satisfied with this, Sykes sent another appeal and receipt books to his friends and acquaintances. His appeal was accompanied by excerpts from two letters from Reverend Buckley in Cuttack and Reverend Miller in Balasore in which they had mentioned the difficulties they were facing in running their orphanages. Buckley wrote: 'Of course our first care is for those immediately dependent on us, but we are not insensible to the cries of those who know not Christ.' Since the price of rice had gone up, more money was needed to run the orphanages but they did not have the necessary resources. Miller said in his letter, 'I cannot bear the thought of transferring all the orphans to the graveyard, yet there they must go unless liberal and timely relief is afforded.'

Moncrieff, too, did not sit idle in Calcutta. On 12 May, he wrote a long letter to the lieutenant governor, who was relaxing at the time in Darjeeling. He wrote: 'People are dying in Orissa while rice is super abundant in Arracan. We, English, have the money here wherewith to transport the rice across, but, under the circumstances of the case, unless Government will come forward and buy the cargo to be distributed through its own officers not a maund of it will find its way from Akyab to Pooree. A telegram from you will secure a cargo of rice at Akyab within ten days from the order leaving Darjeeling. The people have four months of famine yet before them, but prompt action on the part of government will bring them relief within one month.'

Moncrieff also wrote to the governor general, who was then spending the summer months in Simla. The governor general forwarded this letter to the lieutenant governor, who left it to the board of revenue to decide whether rice should be imported into Orissa. On 22 May the board informed the lieutenant governor that there was no need to send rice to Orissa for rice in huge quantities was stocked in the province.

Cuttack, May 1866

Ravenshaw returned to Cuttack on 25 May in the afternoon. Finding a solution to the Mayurbhanj problem had proved easy. The tribals of Bamanghati and the raja were never on the best of terms. The land was being settled and the raja's officials were harassing the tribals. When their tyranny exceeded the limits of endurance, the tribals drove out the raja's police and spread chaos in the region. On reaching the troubled place, Ravenshaw had a talk with the rebel leaders and worked out an amicable solution. It was decided that the oppressive officials would be thrown out and Bamanghati would be placed under the jurisdiction of the deputy commissioner of Singhbhum. The tribals agreed not to create any more trouble if these changes were put into effect.

While Ravenshaw was busy sorting out these problems in Mayurbhanj, he was not allowed to forget the famine. The destitutes milled around his camp and about four hundred destitutes lived on the rice Ravenshaw gave away every day. Not a single moment passed during the day without Ravenshaw's running into a destitute. During his stay in Mayurbhanj, Ravenshaw realized that the situation was really bad. This trip opened his eyes, although he had not been able to attend to relief operations during his month-long absence from Cuttack.

The situation had grown to alarming proportions by the time he returned to Cuttack. Reports from Puri and Balasore conveyed information about the deteriorating situation there. The town of Puri was now teeming with destitutes. Most of these were women and children who had come to the town after the men in their families had died of hunger. In April, there were eighty-five families on the relief list; by May, there was no sign of thirteen of these; it seemed all their members had perished. Large groups of destitutes entered people's homes, looking for food. They surrounded the houses of government officials. Barlow wrote to Ravenshaw that he did not know what the government's responsibilities and duties should be according to the principles of political economy, but he had no doubt about one thing: the time had come to feed the starving and save their lives.

The superintendent of police, Balasore, informed the commissioner that given the rising incidence of crime, he would soon have to accommodate 1500 prisoners in a jail which had space for only 150. Every day a few destitutes dropped dead and removing their corpses kept the sweepers of the municipality busy. Nicolls, the superintending engineer of Balasore, sent a telegram saying that he had no use for the sixty thousand rupees the government had sanctioned for Balasore; what he really needed was rice. Rice was not available even if one offered cash. The labourers therefore were leaving the work site.

W. Cornell, the new collector of Cuttack met Ravenshaw to apprise him of the situation prevailing in his district. While his predecessor had taken his job lightly, Cornell was a competent and committed officer. He was of the view that things were getting out of hand in his district. The coolies of the Irrigation Company looted a shop in Jobra when the shopkeeper refused to sell them rice. The only rice trader in the cantonment bazaar used to sell rice at three and a half seers a rupee. He had stopped selling rice and it was feared that the military police would mutiny when they were not able to purchase rice.

At long last Ravenshaw realized that there was no alternative but to import rice into Orissa. On 28 May he sent the following telegram to Calcutta:

> Rice with utmost difficulty procurable in insufficient quantity at 4 ½ Cuttack seers per rupee. Bazaars again partially closed. Only one day's rations in store for troops, who are reported discontented. Commissariat have refused assistance; crime increasing daily. Public works and relief works stopped for want of food. I recommend immediate importation of rice for use of troops, for jails, and to feed labourers on relief works, and supply food to starving through Relief Committees. Rice can be landed at Balasore River, False Point, or mouth of Dhamra River for Cuttack. I will arrange to do so.

On 29 May the Famine Relief Committee, Cuttack, sent a telegram to Darjeeling requesting the government to send rice worth one lakh rupees from Calcutta by steamer to the lighthouse. The same day the lieutenant governor issued the necessary orders for shipping rice to Orissa.

four

On 4 June, two ships loaded with rice reached the lighthouse. One of these carried 8600 bags and the other, 3000. Since these big ships could not come ashore, the rice was to be unloaded with the help of small boats. But these boats had not been arranged until the ships arrived. As a result, the unloading of the rice was delayed.

When the work of unloading the rice was begun with the help of coolies, it was found that they were too weak to exert themselves. So they had to be first fed properly and rendered fit for work. The cargo of the smaller vessel was unloaded by 13 June but unloading the cargo from the bigger vessel went on till the end of the month.

In the meantime another ship carrying about 4000 maunds of rice for the soldiers had arrived on 12 June.

Now a new problem arose: that of transporting the rice from the lighthouse all the way to Cuttack. The rice could be taken in boats as far as Taladanda from the lighthouse down a canal. From Taladanda the rice was to be transported by means of bullock carts. The boats took seven days to reach Taladanda and the bullock carts took five to reach Cuttack. Since the rains had made the roads difficult to negotiate, it took a long time to bring the rice to Cuttack. While it had taken only thirty hours to ship the rice from Calcutta to the lighthouse, it took fifteen days for the rice to cover the distance from there to Cuttack.

In the fitness of things, Ravenshaw should have stayed in Cuttack and supervised the transport of rice from the lighthouse to Cuttack. But he went off to Puri on 3 June and returned to Cuttack from there on 19 June. When he came to know how difficult it was to bring rice from the lighthouse to Cuttack, he wrote to the board saying that there was no need to ship rice to the lighthouse. But by this time another four ships loaded with 28,630 bags of rice had already left Calcutta for Orissa.

The famine in Orissa had aroused public opinion in Calcutta and the government had now become slightly more concerned. Besides sending rice to Orissa, the government also sent three assistant collectors to oversee relief work. G.M. Currie was posted in Puri and R.F. Rampini to Balasore. T.M. Kirkwood came to Cuttack and reported for duty on 27 June.

Kirkwood buried himself in work as soon as he arrived in Cuttack. At that time six relief centres in Cuttack were distributing rice. Kirkwood took Crouch, the assistant superintendent of police, with him to inspect the relief centre at Taladanda. The nazir of the collectorate was responsible for the sale and distribution of rice here. The place presented a sight which was as gruesome as it was pathetic. There was mud everywhere after the rains and there lay a few dead bodies which had not yet been picked up by the sweepers. Nearly a thousand destitutes clamoured in front of the shed where rice was being doled out, and were trying to push their way to the rice. Those who had managed to get some rice sat and chewed the uncooked grains. Others around them tried to snatch it from their hands. A hungry mother took rice from her wailing child's hand by force and devoured it. Some, who were too weak to get up, lay on the ground screaming, 'Give me rice.'

Kirkwood took steps to improve the arrangements at this relief centre. He decided that cooked rice instead of plain rice would be distributed here. Kirkwood set to work without delay. By the next day, bamboo sheds were erected near the shed where rice was doled out in order to control the movement of people. A Brahmin was employed to do the cooking.

The next day, the Brahmin finished cooking the rice at about four in the afternoon. But when the rice was distributed, new difficulties arose. The people pushed each other in their eager hurry and so the weaker ones fell down and got trampled over. Those who managed to receive some rice had it snatched away from their hands. Soon, bitter squabbles and fights followed. Under such circumstances, Kirkwood had to find a way out. He asked the distribution of rice to be stopped, and taking some of his men with him walked away from the relief centre. The destitutes who were a little stronger than the rest followed him. As a result, only the very weak remained near the relief centre and now they could be fed.

Before leaving Taladanda, Kirkwood placed a local native Christian, Kangali Mohapatra, alias John, in charge of the relief centre, for John had rendered Kirkwood much help.

Calcutta, June 1866

On 16 June, the lieutenant governor returned to Calcutta after two months in Darjeeling. On Monday, 18 June, he called a meeting of the board to discuss matters relating to the famine. He had been urged to invite to this meeting Europeans and native gentlemen, besides officers. But Beadon invited only two non-officials: zamindar Digambar Mitra and Moncrieff of the Bengal Chamber of Commerce. The meeting was held at the board office and various reports on the famine were presented here. Moncrieff felt that even now the members of the board and the lieutenant governor himself had not been able to appreciate the gravity of the situation in Orissa. Beadon insisted that rice should not be sold at less than its market price. The lieutenant governor was not willing to believe that the situation in Orissa was becoming impossible to control.

Moncrieff kept quiet at the meeting. But on 21 June he addressed a stiff letter to the secretary of the board.

My dear Chapman,

There is a very strong feeling indeed outside official circles that famine is steadily increasing, and that Government will not admit the full extent of the danger, and does not even adequately meet the scarcity which it allows.

You must supply Orissa from Rangoon, and instead of sending rice from here down the coast you must send it into the interior. And in the distressed districts it should be made known as widely as possible that rice will be sold at certain depots in quantities not exceeding 5 or 10 maunds to one man at 10 seers the rupee.

The difference between that and cost must be borne by the Famine Fund. When the Lieutenant-Governor talks of selling rice at cost price he simply mocks the starving.

The Board should immediately secure 5 or 6 lakh maunds of rice for delivery within three weeks. I entreat you to get this at once, for I believe that in another month matters will be much worse than at present at our very doors.

Show this to Mr. Grote and to any one else you like. My belief is that if the Government of Bengal does not act as if matters were ten times worse than it admits, the public, Native and European, will speak out very plainly.

For I will certainly get up a meeting at the requisition of the Sheriff, for the discussion of the subject.

Yours sincerely,
R. Scott Moncrieff

Balasore, June 1866

On 9 June, a ship called the Nemesis carrying 25,600 bags of rice reached Balasore. Earlier, businessmen in Balasore used to bring some rice by bullock cart, but after the rains, the roads became so bad that this was no longer possible. The businessmen also tried to get rice from Madras but at this time of the year sailing across the sea in sloop boats proved difficult. So they waited for good weather.

After the arrival of the Nemesis, the price of rice in Balasore went down a little and the situation changed for the better. In the hospital, seven hundred invalids and patients were being given food. A community kitchen had been set up near Dharmasala, where rice was distributed to 5000 destitutes. In addition, 2000 coolies engaged in digging work were given rice as their daily wages.

Managing the destitutes at the community kitchens was a very difficult task in the beginning. They were not sure for how long they would be provided free rice so they stuffed themselves with as much food as they could for fear that they might get nothing the next day. Able-bodied people did not want to go to work; they came to the kitchen for free food and would not leave unless they were thrown out. They sometimes preyed on those weaker than themselves and once, when someone snatched rice from a woman, in the scuffle, her child fell from her lap and died.

It was decided that tickets would be issued to the destitutes in order to prevent anyone except the invalids, the genuinely needy and the women and children from entering the community kitchen. But, it was discovered later that the destitutes sold these tickets. Besides, some people stole these tickets from the destitutes, or forcibly took them away. Around this time, fake tickets also started circulating and investigation revealed that schoolchildren and policemen were involved in this racket. Taking advantage of all this, many able-bodied men appeared at the community kitchens carrying tickets and soon the practice of issuing tickets to the starving had to be abolished.

In Balasore, the disposal of garbage gave rise to a new problem. All the men belonging to the lower scavenger castes were employed to remove corpses. But people belonging to other castes were not willing to have anything to do with clearing the garbage and so the area around the hospital had grown filthy and no one could enter the premises.

Thatched sheds had been constructed to provide shelter to the destitutes but they did not stay there. They wandered all over the town, begging, and ate whatever they could get. They were reluctant to stay away from the community kitchen and at night they slept under a tree or on someone's veranda instead of going to the sheds. They would sell off their clothes and the palm leaf umbrella which they had received from the government and buy opium with the money.

Fakir Mohan and his friends did not spend time at the Gadgadia ghat any longer. A lot of destitutes now lived around the pond, and the ghat had become extremely dirty. Occasionally, Fakir Mohan and Radhanath chanced upon each other in the streets. Meanwhile, Madhusudan had suddenly left Balasore without informing anyone. People whispered that he had made off with the cutcherry funds.

One evening, Radhanath came back from school and threw up in front of his house. He had by now got used to the crowds of destitutes and their pathetic moans but that day he had come across a child eating the flesh off the hand of a dead body. When he said this to Sundar Narayan, he was scolded and advised not to wander about outside. When Radhanath entered his house he found a skinny child sitting in the courtyard. He screamed. Sundar Narayan rushed in and explained that he had picked up the child, whose name was Anand, from the wayside and had brought him home.

Puri, July 1866

The rice imported to Puri reached after a long delay. On 30 June a government steamer loaded with 2549 bags of rice arrived. Another steamer carrying twelve bags of rice reached Puri on 7 July. Because of the monsoon, the rice could not be unloaded on to the small boats which the steamers carried. For that, boats needed to be sent to the steamers from the shore. However, there weren't many such boats in Puri. On 12 July, forty bags of rice fell into the sea and on 16 July, one of the boats sank. Then a storm began blowing and the work of unloading had to be suspended for a few days. On 19 July, one boat broke and another sank. Afraid of such incidents, fishermen now refused to take their boats to sea. Every day, boats either broke down or capsized, and many bags of rice were lost. Barlow brought thirty-one fishermen from the mofussils and fed them well to render them fit for the work of unloading.

By the end of July, even a thousand bags could not be unloaded from the steamers. Out of nineteen boats, fifteen had been lost; three fishermen were killed while three were being treated for injuries sustained. Such a situation would never have arisen if the steamers had been sent earlier. Now, with so much rice lying in steamers anchored off the coast in Puri, people in the town were dying of starvation.

Until June, Kumuti traders used to procure rice from Gopalpur and sell it in Puri. But after the rains came, the sale of rice stopped. A ship carrying 1500 bags of rice dropped anchor off the shore of Puri. The vessel also carried boats and labourers to unload the rice. But the weather turned so bad that a part of the ship was damaged and it sailed back to Gopalpur with its cargo.

Reverend W. Miller had set up a community kitchen with the five hundred rupees he received from the Sykes fund. The kitchen fed about three hundred destitutes. By July, more than a thousand destitutes flocked to it daily. The members of the relief committee were given the responsibility of issuing tickets to destitutes in exchange of which they got rice. But it was discovered that the members took their jobs lightly and issued tickets according to their whims. As a result, some people could collect twenty to thirty seers of rice each. Among the ticket-holders there were also a few priests of the Jagannath temple. In view of this, many tickets had to be cancelled and committee members were asked to be more careful while issuing tickets.

At this time, a large number of orphans wandered the streets of Puri. Their parents had died and there was no one to look after them. Reverend Miller took them under his wing and housed them under a single roof.

Community kitchens were set up in other places in the Puri district too. In the Khurda sub-division, nine community kitchens were set up under the supervision of Barton. In these kitchens cooked rice was provided to the destitutes. The work of the kitchens suffered when the rains came. June and July were particularly bad for Puri. But people predicted that the month of August would bring even greater suffering.

Cuttack, August 1866

All the reports which reached Ravenshaw these days carried bad news. The expectation that the import of rice would improve the situation was thwarted by the rains and the floods, which actually made things worse. From 6 August it drizzled for three days on end and it was not possible to send rice to the mofussil areas. On 9 August the embankment of the river Bhargabi gave way and a number of villages got washed away. Soon afterwards, the embankment of the river Luna gave way. There was floodwater everywhere and rice could not be sent from Cuttack to Khurda, and the relief centre at Khurda faced closure. The relief centre at Tangi had to be closed down and a thousand destitutes again went without food.

By the end of July the rice supplied to Balasore ran out and in August the rice shops had to be shut down for there was no stock left. The community kitchen was run somehow by borrowing 500 bags of rice from the jail. A ship carrying rice had arrived on 21 July but on account of the foul weather it had to drop anchor eight miles from the shore. Since the weather showed no signs of improving long after it had dropped anchor, the ship sailed back. It was as if someone had literally snatched food away from hungry mouths.

During the first twelve days of August, 1013 persons died of starvation. On 8 August, there was a storm and 245 persons died. They were followed by another 151 the next day. These days, the disposal of the dead bodies kept the police occupied all the time. Four carts were used for this purpose and it took three days to remove all the corpses.

The condition of the mofussils went from bad to worse when the rains came and the rivers swelled with floodwater. In Dhamnagar, rice now sold at one seer a rupee. In Bhadrak, no rice was available and the destitutes received cash instead of food.

The rains and the flood had compounded people's misery in Cuttack too. Whereas one thousand destitutes had been provided relief in June, in August, their number swelled to eight thousand. People now dropped dead like flies. In the town of Cuttack, an inspector of police buried two hundred dead bodies in the sands of the annicut in the course of a single day.

On 20 August, assistant magistrate Kirkwood went to inspect the relief centre at Taladanda. Two months earlier, he had ensured that everything was in order here. Now he found that the floodwaters had damaged the godown and the kitchen. Kangali Mohapatra, whom he had appointed as manager, was guilty of not doing his duty properly. The people in charge of the centre were harassing the destitutes in different ways. Kirkwood went through the records and listened to the grievances of the destitutes. He immediately threw Kangali Mohapatra out of the centre and ordered that action be initiated against all the employees.

During the monsoon, Orissa was cut off from the rest of the world, and it was not possible to import rice from outside into the province. It was now like a ship in the middle of the sea, which had run out of provisions. During this time, every bag of rice, whether sold, given away or stolen, saved a human life.

Ironically, the famine brought unexpected profit to the Cuttack Printing Company. It had only English type, therefore, only material in English could be printed here. The company could have printed official forms for the government but they were being printed in Calcutta. However, on account of the famine, many new types of forms needed to be printed and from July, the company received plenty of orders. The press worked day and night in Jagmohan Ray's living room, and, setting office work aside, Gourishankar spent all his time at the press. In addition to overseeing the printing, he was busy annotating Upendra Bhanja's poem 'Prema Sudhanidhi' in collaboration with Banamali Singh. Bichitranand and he had resolved to bring out an Oriya magazine. If Oriya type were not available, they were prepared to print it lithographically with letters carved on a stone slab.

On 4 August, the twenty-second day of the month of Shravan, was published the first issue of a magazine called the *Utkal Dipika*. It had been printed by the lithographic process and it was priced at four annas. On the day of its first publication, the magazine reached every one who mattered in Cuttack. This issue of the magazine focused on the famine and pointed out lapses in the relief operation. It became clear to everyone that this magazine would be the conscience keeper of Orissa.

Gourishankar now spent all his time collecting news for the *Dipika* and writing articles for it. In August he visited the community kitchen and rice shop in Cuttack and reported:

Last Sunday, we went to the community kitchen at Lalbagh and found that the Brahmin cook and the jamadar lorded it over the place. Many destitutes, who had brought tickets with them, returned empty-handed. One of the servants in the kitchen said that they had been asked to be present at three o'clock. But they came late, and there was no rice left. Where would rice for them be brought from? But we saw that two mendicants were given rice from the kitchen at that very moment. An old woman informed us that the servants beat the emaciated famine-stricken destitutes so mercilessly that the blows would kill them even if hunger spared them. It is therefore necessary to appoint a good and able manager. It would not do to rest content by leaving everything to menials.

What a surprise! Is it not possible for the government to sell rice without beating people? When we paid a visit to the rice godown at Chandini Chowk we got the impression that it was a Bazaar where blows were sold, not rice. On 21 July, the sahib was not present at the sale of rice. In spite of their best efforts, the guards failed to control the crowds. Only those destitutes who had a little strength left, or those of them who had their backs covered with a piece of black rag somehow managed to collect some rice. But the rest received a few blows as soon as they reached the door-step of the godown, and the pain in their back dulled the pain in their belly. This place makes one realize that greed is the root of all evil.

In the first week of August, the lieutenant governor went again to Darjeeling. The *Dipika* did not keep quiet and reacted to this by saying:

We learnt from the *Englishman* that the lieutenant governor has again made a trip to Darjeeling in the first week of this month. Health has been mentioned as the reason behind this trip. People are dying here on account of the famine. Rather than tour places hit by the famine and find out ways of mitigating people's suffering, His Excellency has chosen to live in a quiet hill station in order to recover from his illness.

Cuttack, November 1866

The situation improved slightly from September, for more rice had arrived in the meantime and the relief work was managed more efficiently. Nevertheless, many people continued to be in terrible distress. Rice sold at five to six seers a rupee. Also, when people ate after a long period of starvation, they took ill and died. These problems dominated in October too. In November, when harvesting commenced, it seemed the worst was over. Except for the very needy, the invalids, widows and orphaned children, most people returned to their native places and occupations. The destitutes who had migrated to Calcutta were given some rice, clothes and three rupees each and shipped back to Orissa. It appeared as if the black shadow of death and destruction that had hung over Orissa for so long had at last lifted.

The officers who had been working tirelessly day and night now found time to relax. That day, E.J. Barton, assistant collector, Khurda, J.S. Armstrong, assistant collector, Jajpur, and T.M. Kirkwood, the relief magistrate, sat in a dimly lit corner of the Station Club, each holding a glass of brandy. All three were young men who had joined service only recently. India, for them, was an absolutely new experience. But they had had to suddenly deal with a terrible famine. The relief work had occupied them so much that they could not come to the club often. Only occasionally had they met at the bandstand in the evening. That day, the three had got together after a long interval.

Ravenshaw left after spending a little while with them. He had returned after his tour of Kendrapara that same day and he was rather upset. The famine was over but it had left its mark everywhere. On his way back he had counted 238 human skulls in only ten miles. One painful experience, in particular, he found difficult to put out of his mind: a woman holding a baby threw herself at his feet near the sub-division office in Kendrapara; when he bent down to pick her up, he found that she was dead.

After Ravenshaw left, the three young officers spent some time making fun of him. Whenever they got together, they never missed the chance to criticize his style of functioning. Ravenshaw was an excellent human being but his thinking and manner of getting things done were rather peculiar. However, today, the officers did not discuss the commissioner or the famine; they talked about the *Utkal Dipika* and its criticism of British officials. No happening, big or small, ever escaped the *Dipika's* notice. It carried the following piece on Kirkwood's visit to the relief centre at Taladanda in August:

> We came to know that Kangali Mohapatra, the rice daroga of Taladanda, and his chaprassi and dundeedar have been dismissed and that criminal proceedings have been initiated against them. The case is being tried in the court of the assistant magistrate, Kendrapara. We have heard that the said Mohapatra was appointed manager on the recommendation of the missionary sahib, because he is a Christian. But who is to blame if Kangali fails to sympathise with the Kangalis, which literally means destitutes in Oriya!

In another news item, Ferron sahib, engineer, Balasore, was criticized for having beaten a coolie to death. The magistrate, who acquitted the sahib after the trial, also came in for criticism.

The chief target of the *Dipika* was Kirkwood. The 29 September issue of the magazine carried a long article on him. On 25 August, he was in Jajpur *kothi* to inspect the community kitchen there. At 3 a.m. he sent for the lessee of the river ghat, for he wanted to be ferried across the river. When the *ijaradar* failed to carry out the order promptly made excuses and, Kirkwood flew into a rage, landed five or six blows on his head and dragged him over the gravel, pulling him by his hair. Even after all this, the sahib did not calm down. On his orders, his chaprasi gave the ijaradar a good beating with a stick. The ijaradar suffered a great deal of pain and the doctor's certificate revealed that his hand had received a deep wound. The case was referred to the deputy magistrate Mr Taylor, but since the complainant failed to appear on the specified date before the court, it was dismissed.

The above account was accompanied by other instances of Kirkwood's high-handed behaviour: once when he went to inspect a government rice godown, he found the rice daroga, Durlabhnath Ray, absent. Kirkwood went to the daroga's house and beat him up there. Durlabhnath resigned after this. Another rice daroga, Mathura Mohan Sen, also resigned because he was beaten by Kirkwood. Then it was the turn of the sadar overseer, Kahnuram Chakravorty. He received such a severe beating that he could not leave his bed for two days, A Brahmin cook in the Lalbagh community kitchen got a beating from Kirkwood for some delay in cooking rice. A few days later, a constable, Madhu Behera, was beaten up by Kirkwood. He complained to the superintendent of police. The matter reached the collector, and Kirkwood received a letter reprimanding him for such behaviour.

The *Dipika* had given Kirkwood a nickname, 'The Thrashing Phiringee'. It wrote, 'Unless Kirkwood sahib reforms himself and acquires a calmer disposition he can never enjoy the respect of the governed, and he will lose people's affection.' The piece was followed by a doggerel which contained the following description of Kirkwood:

> On Kirkwood there's no check
> For he must his anger wreak
> On whosoever crosses his path;

At the slightest bungling
He goes about pummeling
There's no reason to his wrath.

When English officers were posted to India they used to be given one special piece of advice: 'Do whatever you like to natives, but remember never to hit them yourself. They might die, for they suffer from spleen disorders.' Kirkwood had not bothered to follow this advice.

However, the *Dipika* did not always criticize British officers. When Barlow, collector, Puri, took three years' leave in September and left for Britain, the *Dipika* wrote: 'We pray to God that Mr Barlow will return to India.' When Ravenshaw wrote a report against Mr Cornell, collector, Cuttack, and removed him from office, the *Dipika* stood solidly behind the latter.

The young officers refrained from discussing another item published in the *Dipika*, for it had to do with Barton, who was present among them. A woman from Khurda had demanded maintenance from Barton for she claimed that he was the father of her year-and-a-half-old daughter. People believed her story, for the little girl was of a very fair complexion. However, the case was dismissed for lack of evidence.

The officers pulled Joseph Armstrong's leg because he was a subscriber of the *Utkal Dipika*, and had paid an advance of four rupees and two annas towards six months' subscription and postage to receive the magazine at his Jajpur address. It was decided that Armstong would atone for this by reading the magazine and keeping his colleagues informed of what it published about whom. Before taking leave of his friends Armstrong promised to do so. He also informed them that the *Dipika* was publishing a discussion on the subject: 'Are Oriyas Stupid by Nature?' He said that he would let them know the conclusions that emerged from the discussion.

Calcutta, November 1866

Although the news of the famine in Orissa arrived late in Britain, it caused great anxiety there and stirred much public opinion. People were convinced that the government had not taken any steps to prevent the situation in Orissa from getting out of hand, and this was the reason why so many had suffered and so many lives had been lost. From London, the secretary of state instructed the government of India to appoint an officer to investigate the matter.

On receiving this order, the lieutenant governor entrusted the commissioner of Nadia division, H.L. Dampier with the task. One of the allegations against the officers dealing with the famine situation was that they had not taken the crisis seriously enough. So the decision to put one of these same officers in charge of the investigation was widely criticized. Therefore, the governor general modified the lieutenant governor's earlier order and appointed a Famine Commission. This commission was headed by Justice George Campbell. The other two members of the commission were Dampier and Colonel W.E. Morton of the Royal Engineers.

The commission was asked to investigate the following and submit its report: What were the causes of the famine? Were timely and appropriate measures taken to relieve people's distress? If not, why not? What steps should the government take in order to prevent such calamities from recurring in future, and to deal with the consequences if they did?

As soon as the order relating to the formation of the commission came, everyone from the lieutenant governor down to the assistant magistrate started putting his papers in order.

five

Puri, December 1866

The members of the famine commission reached Puri on board a ship called the Pheroze on 17 December. They were accompanied by the secretary to the commission, P. Dickens. The ship had also brought nine hundred bags of rice.

Justice Campbell was accompanied by Mr Raban, the newly appointed collector of Puri, on a visit to the cutcherry to find out what arrangements had been made to facilitate their work. There was no reporter in Puri at the time who could set down the depositions made by the witnesses. Word was immediately sent to Cuttack to arrange for a reporter. Before the arrival of the commission, a notification had been issued that interested persons might present themselves for getting their depositions recorded, but they were forbidden to publish their depositions before the inquiry was completed. Copies of this notice had been pasted on the door of the collector's cutcherry where people were to depose before the commission.

The commission set to work on the morning of 18 December. Spectators had occupied all chairs and benches except those set apart for the members of the commission and the witnesses. The first witness on the first day was the deputy magistrate and deputy collector, Babu Duryodhan Das. He was in Kendrapara when the famine was at its worst and had been transferred to

Puri three months earlier. The gist of the replies he gave to the questions put to him was as follows:

He had been in government service for thirty-five years. In the past, he had witnessed periods of scarcity in 1829 and 1841. But no famine had occurred at the time. During 1865–66, seventy-five per cent of the crops had failed and by March 1866, people had begun of starvation. The death toll grew heavier during April, May and June, and in July, the outbreak of cholera had made matters worse. Twenty-five per cent of the population of Kendrapara must have perished in the famine. The situation improved somewhat when the winter paddy was harvested. In July, the chaprasis and the constables had reported to him that a hungry man in the town of Kendrapara had eaten human flesh. A Hindu belonging to a low caste had picked up the corpse of a child from the river Gobari and had cooked its flesh. Low-caste people generally ate beef, and, occasionally, flesh in the raw.

Duryodhan Das was followed by Ramakshoy Chatterjee. He presented an account of the famine in Puri and gave a list of people who had died of starvation. According to this list, in all of Puri excluding Khurda, 1,67,356 persons had died out of a total population of 4,01,501. This report had been compiled by the police for the period ending in October.

From the deposition of the next witness, sub-assistant surgeon Uday Charan Dutt, it was learnt that out of about fifteen hundred destitutes being served by the community kitchen, about six died every day. The commission concluded its business for the day after recording the deposition of the doctor.

The commission spent another four days in Puri and recorded the depositions made by twenty-one witnesses. Over all these four days, spectators thronged the cutchery and listened to what the witnesses said. The commission's work continued till evening every day. Among the witnesses, barring the government officials, were zamindar Raghunath Choudhury, Babu Sashibhusan Mukherjee, Marwari Rambagan Ram, Lachua Patra, a Kumuti businessman, Gopi Panda, a temple priest, and the zamindar of Kotdesh, Bhagban Raet Singh.

One of the principal witnesses, relief assistant collector, G.M. Currie said while deposing before the commission that during his visit to a village near the Chilka lake he had found that only two persons out of twenty-eight families were alive. He thought it was likely that about fifty per cent of the total population of Puri had perished during the famine.

On 22 December, after going through records relating to the famine at the cutcherry in Puri, the members of the commission set off for Cuttack, borne in palanquins. For many days afterwards, people in Puri kept discussing the depositions made before the commission.

Cuttack, January 1867

Before beginning the inquiry in Orissa, the commission had tried to assess the extent of crop failure by sending to zamindars and others a questionnaire. But no one replied to this for fear that their answers to the questions might lead to an enhancement of land revenue.

From 24 December the commission set to work in the cutcherry. After consulting the records, they prepared a list of witnesses to be called. On 26 December, the depositions of Siba Prasad Singh, munsif, Kendrapara, Police Superintendent Lacey, Reverend Miller, Henry Crane, engineer, zamindar Rasul Bux, and Cornell, collector, Cuttack were recorded. On 27 December the commission took down the statements of only three witnesses and spent the rest of the day inspecting rice godowns, the community kitchens and the orphanages. That day, it received information that the statements made by the witnesses before the commission might be published by the *Utkal Dipika*. So, the next day, before the commission began its proceedings, the following notice was put up in front of the cutcherry. 'The famine commission welcomes any gentleman who wishes to remain present during the deliberations. But no one will be permitted to take the statements down, nor to publicize these.' The *Dipika* immediately published a protest against this: 'If the commission wants to be impartial in doing its job, it must withdraw this notice and allow its work to be given publicity.'

On the following day, the depositions of officers who had dealt with the famine were recorded. On 5 January, Ravenshaw appeared before the commission. Everyone held him responsible for the famine, for he had decided not to import rice into Orissa, acting on the assumption that there was plenty of rice in the province. Since the commission put a lot of questions to Ravenshaw, the business could not be concluded that day. Ravenshaw appeared again before the commission on 7 January. Some of the important questions put to Ravenshaw during the cross-examination and the answers given by Ravenshaw were as follows:

Question: In your letter No. 255 1/4 to the Collector of Balasore, dated 3rd November 1865, you expressed the opinion that there was more rice in his district than he imagined, and that the crop of the current year would suffice for the year's supply, the Collector having then given a very bad report of the crops in his district: Will you mention on what information you founded your opinion?

Answer: I cannot at the present moment recall to my recollection the precise grounds on which I formed that opinion, nor have I the correspondence before me that would enable me to state precisely on what grounds I founded an opinion that there was more rice in Balasore district, or that the crops would suffice for the year's supply; but speaking generally, I may say that I was aware that the people were in the habit of hoarding grain, and I hoped that they had more than the Collector had been able to ascertain.

The following questions were asked regarding Ravenshaw's two-month-long tour of the princely states in November:

Question: Were you not aware by the end of November and beginning of December that there was very serious alarm in the British districts regarding the failure of the crops? Did it not strike you that it was your first duty to visit the proper British districts of Pooree and Balasore with which you were personally entirely acquainted, before proceeding to remote Tributary Mahals?

Answer: At the time I started on my tour in the Tributary Mahals, I was aware that very great scarcity prevailed in and about the Chilka Lake districts in Pooree. I did not, however, anticipate anything approaching general scarcity or famine throughout the district or province. I could as easily have superintended matters through correspondence from my camp as from headquarters.

Question: Did you at any time before June 1866 visit the Pooree district?

Answer: I did not.

Question: After reaching Cuttack in August did you visit the Balasore district before you were directed by the Government to do so in April 1866?

Answer: I did not, but my intention was to visit Balasore on my return from the Tributary Mahals. My tour was interrupted by the intelligence of the lieutenant governor's intended visit, and also by my wife's unexpected return from England. After the lieutenant governor had left Cuttack, I found that my work had accumulated to such an extent that it was impossible to go out on tour again immediately.

Ravenshaw was asked about the visit of the lieutenant governor and his answer was as follows:

Answer: I believe that the principal object of the lieutenant governor's visit was to see the irrigation works, and that he took the opportunity of holding a durbar to meet the native chiefs. I am not aware that one of the objects of the lieutenant governor's visit was to enquire into the scarcity. There was no official consultation or discussion on the subject during his stay here, that is, there was no gathering of public officers for the purpose.

Question: Are you aware whether the subjects connected with the prevailing scarcity, which had been matter of recent correspondence, and especially the dearth in Pooree district, and the difficulty in carrying on relief works owing to the order prohibiting the purchase of grain, were in any shape topics of representation and discussion during the lieutenant governor's visit?

Answer: I believe that the lieutenant governor spoke to me privately several times on the subject of the scarcity, and I expressed an opinion that there were probably sufficient stocks of grain in the country, and that though it might be dear, it would be procurable for money.

Question: You have mentioned that the rajahs and respectable persons were presented to the lieutenant governor. Had the poor also any opportunity of representing their grievances?

Answer: I should say, certainly. I recollect at the cutcherry the lieutenant governor stopping and speaking to the people who were there, and also to a crowd of people outside the school-house; also on one or two occasions his stopping in the street when petitions were presented. The universal petitions were only to cheapen rice.

Question: Are you aware whether the lieutenant governor was impressed by anything he had heard at Pooree regarding the distress in that district?

Answer: I had no conversation with him on the subject.

Question: Can you at all specify the authorities on which you founded your opinion that there were such large stocks of grain?

Answer: I was in constant communion with zemindars, European and Native officers, the Irrigation Company's officers, and others, and the universal opinion was that the stocks in the country would be sufficient generally for the year.

After this Ravenshaw said that he saw the distress of the people with his own eyes for the first time during his tour of Balasore in the month of April and believed that severe famine existed to any extent.

Question: Did you then think that the time had come for emergent measures on the part of Government to relieve the frightful starvation and distress described by you ?

Answer: I certainly did so.

Question: What emergent measures did you take to secure the aid of Government?

Answer: I described what I had seen in a demi-official letter to the lieutenant governor, but I do not recollect any other special measures of relief to have been either proposed or adopted.

As for his visit to Mayurbhanj again towards the end of April for more than a month, Ravenshaw said that such a visit was necessary.

Question: Did you not think the famine in the British districts at least as urgent?

Answer: Quite as urgent; but I had already turned my attention to the famine and done all that I considered necessary at that time.

Whenever the meetings of the Cuttack Relief Committee had been called, only one native gentleman used to be invited. All the other members of the committee were of European origin. The commission wanted to find out why the cooperation of more natives had not been sought. To this, Ravenshaw responded by saying that, in his opinion, people of the province were extremely apathetic and indolent.

Ravenshaw's statement before the famine commission led to lively discussions in Cuttack and people were all praise for the forthright questions put by the commission. Gourishankar was unhappy at not being able to print such important and exciting news in the *Dipika*. However, he and Bichitranand discussed the matter every day in the evening. The day Ravenshaw's deposition came to an end, Bichitranand said, 'This sahib insists even now that plenty of foodgrains were in store in Orissa.' Gourishankar knew Bichitrananda had a soft spot for Ravenshaw. So, without responding directly to this, he merely said, 'How does someone who has no grain, benefit if his land is full of it? All of us believe that there is nectar on the moon, but can this belief make us immortal?'

In point of fact, Orissa now had no shortage of rice. In addition to the yearly harvest, by the end of December, four lakh maunds of rice had been imported into the province.

Calcutta, March 1867

The members of the commission stayed in Cuttack recording depositions of witnesses until 16 January. Then they sailed to Balasore from the lighthouse. In Balasore they spent five days recording statements from official as well as non-official witnesses. Travelling through Jaleswar and Medinapur they finally reached Calcutta. There they recorded the statements of members of the board of revenue, the inspector general of police and the secretary, PWD. Some people like Moncrieff, Sykes and zamindar Digambar Mitra who were involved with the relief work also appeared before the commission.

The lieutenant governor had submitted a long written account of his actions during the famine. But the commission was not satisfied with this for it had been alleged that, like Ravenshaw, the lieutnant governor, too, was responsible for help not reaching Orissa on time. So he was called to appear before the commission and make an verbal deposition. This was somewhat ironic since one of the members, Dampier, was till recently a subordinate of Beadon's. However on 5 March the Hon'ble Sir Cecil Beadon appeared before the commission. Some of the important questions asked and the answers given were as follows:

Question: We believe Your Honour is aware that towards the end of November Mr Ravenshaw started on a tour to the Tributary Mahals. Does Your Honour consider that, in the face of the warning conveyed in your Secretary's letter No. 6908 dated the 1st December 1865, Mr Ravenshaw was warranted in leaving the Regulation Districts and going into a remote part of the country, where his presence did not seem to be so urgently required?

Answer: The inspection of the Hill tracts has always been considered a very important part of the Commissioner's duties in his capacity of Superintendent of Tributary Estates. In his letter dated the 14th December the Commissioner wrote that he anticipated no necessity for special measures in connection with the scarcity, and on this assurance from him, I approved of his proceeding then and must approve of it now. Assuming that the circumstances in the Regulation Districts were as he then represented them, I think he was quite justified in going into the Tributary Estates.

After this, Beadon faced questions relating to the credibility of Ravenshaw's report that Orissa had plenty of rice. The members wanted to find out from him why he had believed Ravenshaw when everyone else in Orissa had talked about the scarcity of rice.

Question: We find that in the months of January and February a very considerable correspondence was carried on regarding the difficulty of obtaining grain in Pooree, and more especially with reference to the public works which were then ordered by Government with a view to relieving the existing distress. We find that both the Collector of Pooree and the Officers of the Public Works Department represented in very strong terms that rice was not to be obtained in the market; that although there was a nominal price, rice was in fact not to be got in any quantities, and that to render the works practically operative, it was absolutely necessary that grain should be imported and stored in some shape. The Commissioner seems also, on two previous occasions in a somewhat undefined manner, to have proposed the importation and storing of grain, and, on his return from his tour, the information which reached him was such as to induce him to send to the Board of Revenue a very emergent telegram in these words: 'Famine relief is at a standstill. Public Works Department refuses to advance money to Collector to purchase rice. Pooree must get rice from elsewhere.' To that telegram the Board, on 1st February, returned a very decided answer in the words, 'The Government declines to import rice into Pooree.' The consequence of which was that the Commissioner, considering that the Board of Revenue and the Government had finally and conclusively decided against the importation of rice and payment of labour in grain, issued a series of orders to the Collectors in that sense. The Secretary and senior member of the Board of Revenue have informed us that the words 'the Government declines to import rice into Pooree' were used on a general knowledge that it was the established policy of Government not to import rice, and in fact, the senior member said the matter had already been reported to Government, which declined to import rice. It has also been stated that the personal communication between the Board of Revenue and Your Honour was at that time intimate, the senior Member especially being in frequent communication with the Government. Does Your Honour remember that the general subject of the difficulty of procuring rice in Pooree and the consequent stoppage of relief works and the question of importation was at that time brought to Your Honour's attention?

Answer: The only ground that the Board could have for saying that the Government declined to import rice into Pooree was the answer given to those letters which Messrs. Gisborne and Co. wrote in the month of November. Certainly, I had several interviews with Mr Grote at that time, and I have no doubt that I must have repeated, in my interviews with him, that the Government had determined not to import rice by sea into Pooree. When it was reported by the Officers of the Public Works Department that they had a difficulty in getting labourers because they could not obtain food with the money themselves, and when they proposed to purchase rice and pay the labourers in grain, the answer I authorized was that the Public Works Department had nothing to do with the procuring of rice, but that the supply of rice to the labourers must be managed through the Civil Officers, and the instruction I desired Colonel Nicolls to give to the superintending engineer was that he should arrange for the feeding of the labourers in communication with the Commissioner of the division. The system I supposed to prevail was that wherever public works were going on the Public Works Department were paying the labourers in money, and the labourers would be able to supply themselves from the shops established by the Civil Officers. The orders that were actually issued by the Board, directing that labour employed by the Local Civil Officers should be paid in money and not in grain, so far from being in accordance with my wishes, were opposed to them; my wish was that the labourers should get their grain from the Civil Officers. The Board's orders were founded on an entire misapprehension of the orders I issued in the Public Works Department. I don't remember to have seen the letter which was issued; but if I did, the point must have escaped my attention; if I had observed it, I should have undoubtedly set the Board right.

Question: Is it Your Honour's impression that at that time the fact that the Civil Officers were unable to make arrangements for the supply of grain for the labourers employed in public works was not brought to your attention?

Answer: I was under the full impression that such arrangements had been made.

The lieutenant governor was then asked questions about his Orissa visit.

Question: Did Your Honour arrive at Pooree on one day, and leave the next?

Answer: Yes, we arrived in the morning of one day and left in the evening of the next.

Question: Did Mr Barlow, the Collector of Pooree, have full opportunity of reporting all that he knew or feared?

Answer: The fullest opportunity. Besides being in constant conversation with him, he had a special separate interview with me for the purpose of talking over all matters of interest in the district. I was a guest in his house.

Question: Did Mr Barlow then take a very gloomy view of the state of his district?

Answer: No, certainly not.

Question: Did he not report that there was considerable mortality from want?

Answer: There was a report of such a state of things previous to my arrival; but in every instance in which sickness and distress and mortality were alluded to, Mr Barlow told me that by late accounts there was a decided improvement.

About some people having shown him roots they were eating while he was in Puri:

Question: Some of the witnesses have informed us that people suffering from want produced the roots and jungle produce on which they had been living, and that Mr Cockburn took those things and showed them to Your Honour. Will Your Honour tell us the circumstances?

Answer: I heard that story the other day. The only thing I can recollect was this. We were walking along the road, and there were people with roots in baskets sitting near the cutcherry. They said something in Oriya which I did not understand. I asked Mr Cockburn what the roots were, and he said that those were the roots the people live on, and he brought the roots to me. But that was not mentioned as symptomatic of distress, but rather as specimens of roots which form the ordinary food of the people at that season of the year.

Question: Some of the native officials have told us that they were aware that considerable mortality was going on and was likely to increase, and that they had interviews with your Honour and said so. Will Your Honour tell us if such was the case?

Answer: I saw several of the natives; in fact all who wished for an interview I saw and talked to; and what they said to me about the famine was very much the same as what Mr. Barlow had said to me. No doubt they said there had been a failure of crops and that people were dying; but as far as I remember, they all seemed satisfied with what was done, and all I was asked to do was to fix a *nerrick* and prevent exportation.

Question: Was it brought to Your Honour's knowledge the cargo of the ship Philaneme was then on the Strand in Pooree, and that the agents would not or could not sell?

Answer: Yes, I heard of it.

Question: What was the special object of Your Honour's visit to Orissa?

Answer: As far as it had any speciality in it, it was with reference to the famine. I had not had an opportunity of visiting Cuttack before, and took the opportunity of going down to see the Officers and people there, and particularly also to see the irrigation works going on there.

Questions then turned to the absolute trust put on Ravenshaw's reports, and the Comission wanted to know why the lieutenant governor believed Ravenshaw rather than everyone else who were reporting the scarcity of grains.

Question: Did Mr Ravenshaw bring to Your Honour's notice that some of the officers in his division held the opinion that there was no sufficient stock of grain in their districts, but that he, for such and such reasons, did not agree with them?

Answer: No, he did not.

Question: Up to that time, had your Honour reason to think that Mr. Ravenshaw's conduct was reliable and prudent, or that he hazarded somewhat rash opinions, he not being fully cognizant of the state of his districts, in as much as he had not visited them himself?

Answer: Mr Ravenshaw is an officer with intelligence. It never occured to me to question his opinions, because I had no ground to raise any objection to them.

Question: Did Mr Ravenshaw seem to be in some considerable degree credulous as regards the people amongst whom he was more immediately thrown?

Answer: No, not in the least.

About the lieutenant governor leaving Calcutta and going to Darjeeling:

Question: Before Your Honour left Calcutta for Darjeeling, was it by anyone, as far as Your Honour remembers, brought to Your Honour's notice that there was a famine of a very severe character in Balasore?

Answer: I had not any information on the subject before I left Calcutta beyond what is contained in the papers before the Commission.

It took a whole day to record the lieutenant governor's statement. Five more witnesses were cross-examined before the commission brought the inquiry to an end. In all, 130 witnesses had appeared before the commission. Only two key witnesses had not been able to depose before them. One was Cockburn who had taken ill during the lieutenant governor's visit to Orissa and expired soon afterwards. The other was Barlow, collector, Puri. He was at the time in Britain on furlough.

Cuttack, April 1867

The famine commission submitted its report on 6 April. In it the commission accused the officers of dereliction of duty. Some of the remarks which the government of India made on the report before forwarding the report to England were: Ravenshaw was unfit to cope with the extraordinary situation in his role as commissioner; the board of revenue was guilty of having failed to manage the crisis; the manner in which Sir Cecil Beadon had dealt with the calamity was far from satisfactory.

Copies of the report and the remarks made by the government of India were given to all the officers concerned. These made Ravenshaw deeply unhappy. He had grown to like Orissa over the last year and a half and he no longer wanted to get transferred elsewhere. His wife, too, had grown very fond of Cuttack. His failure at dealing with the famine oppressed him and he now wanted to do something for the betterment of the province. The remark on his unfitness for the position of commissioner hurt him less than the one that had suggested that he harboured anti-Oriya feelings.

Although the national character of Oriyas did not lie within the scope of the commission's inquiry, the witnesses had been asked to express their opinions on this subject. There was a special reason for doing so. Some were of the view that the Oriya character was responsible to a large extent for the wretched misery of the people during the famine. To substantiate this view, it was claimed that people chose to die of starvation at home rather than go out even when opportunities for work were provided to them. However, the commission observed that this was not the case. Those who were used to physical labour did come out to work if it was available near their village. It could be that some were unwilling to venture to far-off places in search of work, or, people unaccustomed to physical labour did not do any work, even when it was available near their villages. The commission added that, even in England, people not accustomed to physical labour would not send their wife and children to work on the construction of a road in some far-off place unless driven by dire necessity.

In the course of his deposition before the commission, Ravenshaw had let it slip that Oriyas were extremely apathetic and indolent and that they did not do all they might have done for themselves. But seeing this remark in cold print, he felt deeply embarrassed. In the hope of defending his disparaging statement on Oriyas, he went through the depositions of other witnesses and prepared a list of the things said by them about the Oriya character.

Babu Shiba Prasad Singh thought that Oriyas clung so tenaciously to caste and respectability that they would not come to the centres for public charity until they were in the last stages of debility, so far gone that they could not recover. Reverend W. Miller, the padre of Cuttack, felt that Oriyas were tolerably industrious cultivators, but rather improvident. In Cuttack collector W. Cornell's opinion, Oriya ryots were poorer than those of the eastern districts of Bengal and more superstitious, also more idle. But T.H.H. Shortt, sub-divisional officer, Bhadrak, was of the view that Oriyas were improvident and lazy. Babu Rangalal

Banerjee, deputy collector, Cuttack, claimed that Oriya ryots were more industrious than the Bengalis. To H. Muspratt, collector, Balasore, Oriyas were much inferior to other natives of India. R.M. Rampani, relief assistance collector, Balasore, had a very low opinion of the character of Oriyas generally. In A. Miller's view, the Oriyas were a bad race of people, very deceptive and indolent. This opinion was echoed by Revered J. Phillips, who said that Oriyas were a perverse and deceptive people and difficult to deal with. Suprintending Engineer H. Leonard too saw Oriyas in an equally unfavourable light. He thought that Oriyas were less able to help themselves than any people he had seen in other parts of the country. He had seen people begging for relief actually on works in progress and who, when work was offered to them, refused it, because they said they had never done that kind of work. He had also seen people dying close to the relief stations because they would not eat the food offered to them as being against their caste. However, zamindar Babu Digamber Mitra expressed the view that Oriyas were more tenacious than the Bengalis and they were likewise more indolent. Rahmatullah Khan's view of Oriyas was uncomplimentary. He believed that Oriyas were inferior to the other people of this country. Firstly they were poor which was the chief of their defects; they had no industry except agriculture. They were good agriculturists so far as their knowledge went. But they were not more fraudulent than Bengalis. To Padre O.R. Bachelor, Bengalis were more proficient at dishonesty and Oriyas obstinately adhered to their own ways. A more balanced view of Oriya character came from A. Bond, who thought that Oriyas were worse than the Bengalis. They were equally lazy but not so sharp.

After preparing the list Ravenshaw cheered up for he had found that others held opinions on Oriyas which were far more contemptuous than his. The last word on the subject had been written by the commission: 'The Oriyas are not as clever or hard-working as the Bengalis. Since they are not educated, they happen to be more stupid. However, they are quite hard-working, considering their limitations. They are not entirely without intelligence. In some respects they are more trustworthy. The bearer who serves sahibs in their homes is a fine specimen of the Oriya race.'

Ravenshaw decided that he would write to Englishmen in Cuttack and ask them to state that he harboured no ill feelings towards Oriyas. He had a talk with a couple of Englishmen about this, and in no time the news reached all sahibs in Cuttack. They were all fond of Ravenshaw but at the same time, they made fun of him for his love of ease, his simplicity, his openness and plain dealing. Now the sahibs remarked to each other that the finest specimen of the Oriya race was none other than Ravenshaw himself!

Calcutta, September 1867

When he forwarded the report of the famine commission to England on 22 April, the governor general, Lord Lawrence, made the following remark about Cecil Beadon: 'The highest officer of the government of Bengal was unable to appreciate the gravity of the situation until the very end. As a result, he ignored all the warnings, although these were absolutely clear, and he frittered away valuable opportunities for investigation and action.'

Lord Lawrence deeply regretted the fact that he himself had not instructed Beadon to intervene more actively. Although he had felt the need for doing so, the members of his council thought that the course of action which Beadon was following then was the right one. Nothing was more painful or regrettable than the famine in Orissa during Lawrence's entire career.

As soon as Beadon received a copy of the commission's report, he sent off a long letter to the governor general defending his actions. But when, in spite of this, the governor general made such a remark, Beadon wrote another long letter protesting it. In this he said that the governor general had made his remarks in a hurry since he had to forward the report to England before leaving for Simla. Lord Lawrence had observed that Beadon should have instituted a special inquiry after a crowd of destitutes had kept him encircled during his visit to Puri. In his reply, Beadon said that the crowd of destitutes the governor general had mentioned existed only in the governor general's imagination. He further alleged that the members of the famine commission regarded the officers as criminals and asked such questions as would lead to answers which suited them.

Beadon sent off his rejoinder on 30 April. A few days later, he left India for good as his tenure had come to an end. On 25 July, the secretary of state, Sir Stafford Northcote, took the final decision in this matter and pronounced the lieutnant governor, the board and the commissioner guilty.

On 2 August, the Orissa famine came up for discussion in the House of Commons. The aim of the resolution on the commission's report was to place the blame on Beadon and to acquit the government of India and the governor general. An amendment to this was moved, for the members of the House wanted to hold the governor general and the government of India equally responsible. A heated debate followed. Since the members of the House refused to budge, Northcote conceded defeat. He made the following statement in the House of Commons: 'The catastrophe must always remain a monument to our failure, a humiliation to the people of the country, to the Government of this country, and to those of our Indian officials of whom we have been perhaps a little too proud.'

After the admission of failure, the members withdrew the motion for amendment. However, the matter did not end there. Having been blamed for their role during the famine, the members of the board sent a long explanation consisting of 211 paragraphs in an attempt to exonerate themselves. Needless to say, the government of India rejected the board's petition on 4 September.

Cuttack, December 1867

After the report of the famine commission became public, the government went into overdrive, importing rice into the province even when there was no need for it. Nearly 11 lakh maunds of rice arrived in Orissa and by the end of the year, only five lakh maunds had been consumed. The harvest in 1867 was good and rice sold at fifty seers a rupee. Although imported rice was available at a low price, people did not buy it, and this rice lay unused.

Everyone now seemed to take notice of Orissa, and roads, education and commerce in the province began to receive the government's attention. On the government's taking up different schemes to bring about improvement in every sphere of life in the province, the *Dipika* wrote that the government was trying to atone for its long neglect of the province.

Since the community kitchens were no longer needed, it was decided that they would be gradually closed down from September. By the end of the year, there were only eight hundred destitutes left in these kitchens. Apart from the food being doled out from the community kitchens, rice was also distributed free in the villages. In August, nearly sixty thousand people received free rice; towards the end of the year, however, only two thousand people were given rice free.

Even though one-third of the total population of Orissa had perished in the famine, all marks left by the famine seemed to have vanished. Only occasionally did one come across beggars and destitutes wandering in some places. They were the only reminders that Orissa had just emerged from the vicious grip of a terrible famine. Otherwise, life in the villages had returned to normal. However, the famine had left two problems in its wake: the destitutes who had taken food at community kitchens had problems being reabsorbed into the fold of their caste and the future of the orphaned children.

At the end of the year, there were fifteen hundred orphans to be rehabilitated. Now the government decided that whichever organization would look after these children would receive sixteen rupees per child per month until the child reached the age of sixteen. Allegations about converting these children to Christianity by raising them at government expense were made but no one except the missionaries came forward to claim the children. Two hundred girls who had been purchased by prostitutes in Cuttack during the famine were now being trained for a career in prostitution.

In September, Bichitranand Das called a meeting at the office of the Cuttack Printing Company to discuss the problem of bringing the destitutes who had lost their caste back into the fold of the community. No one accepted water from them and they were ostracised in the villages. This gave rise to many problems and the destitutes led a miserable life.

The company was doing well and it had bought land near Palki Khana, which lay on the southern bank of the pond beside the law court. The *Dipika* came out regularly and had become well known throughout Orissa. The previous year, the company had got an almanac and an annotated edition of Upendra Bhanja's 'Prema Sudhanidhi' lithographed. In August, Oriya type was brought from Calcutta with Ishwar Chandra Vidyasagar's help and the press no longer lithographed the *Dipika*; it was now set in Oriya type.

Other than the gentlemen from Cuttack, mofussil zamindars and pandits from Cuttack, Puri and Bengal attended the meeting convened by Bichitranand. At the meeting, many different views were expressed by the pandits. Pandits from Cuttack and Bengal opined that the destitutes could be received back into their castes. However, while the pandits from Bengal were silent on the need for expiation, their colleagues from Cuttack insisted on the need for this. The pandits from Puri, on their part, said nothing about the destitutes and observed that those who had gone to jail could never be taken back into their castes. In substantiation of the position, a sloka from *Parasar Samhita* was cited which said that, at a time when one's country is in danger, or during exile, illness, or famine, one can save one's life by abandoning one's religion. Later, when one recovers, one can return to one's religion and occupation.

After the meeting ended, Bichitranand compiled the observations of the pandits on how the destitutes could be received back into their castes, and brought them out in the form of a booklet which was printed by the Cuttack Printing Company. Copies of this were sent to rajas and zamindars with the request that they should distribute them in the markets.

SIX

Keonjhar, January 1868

Ravenshaw was only just beginning to recover from the exertions of the famine when the problems arising in the feudatory state of Keonjhar entangled him. The relationship between this kingdom and the British had been excellent. During the Sepoy Mutiny, the raja of Keonjhar, Gadadhar Bhanj, had extended help to the British, and for this he had received praise from the lieutenant governor at the durbar held in 1866. When Gadadhar passed away in 1861, he was survived not only by his queen, Bishnupriya, but also by a concubine. Bishnupriya had no children while the concubine had two sons: Dhanurjay and Chandrasekhar. After Gadadhar's death, Dhanurjay ascended the throne with Bishnupriya's consent. Since he was a minor, he pursued his studies under the supervision of the commissioner. It was he who had attended the durbar addressed by Beadon.

Now the raja of Mayurbhanj claimed that his grandson Brundaban should inherit the throne of Keonjhar, for Gadadhar, before he died, had adopted Brundaban as his heir. Although this was not the truth, Bishnupriya supported the claim for she no longer thought of Dhanurjay's mother as her husband's concubine—she was no more than a mere maidservant. The matter was taken to the commissioner, then to the high court; and now it lay before the Privy Council. In 1867, on the day of Sunia,

Dhanurjay came of age. The queen had petitioned earlier that the coronation be postponed until the privy council pronounced a verdict on the lawsuit, or, if Dhanurjay was enthroned, he should be made to sign a bond.

The western part of Keonjhar was largely inhabited by the Bhuyan and the Juang tribes. The Bhuyans were in the majority and they claimed that it was they who should decide who would sit on Keonjhar's throne. On Sunia, about eight hundred members of the Bhuyan tribe and their chief came to Cuttack from Keonjhar and declared their support for Dhanurjay. Ravenshaw conferred on him the right to rule Keonjhar.

However, Queen Bishnupriya, who was in Keonjhar, did not accept this arrangement and she kept intriguing against Dhanurjay with the help of some tribals. One Bhuyan chieftain, Ratna Nayak, was on the side of Brundaban and the queen. The queen threatened that if Dhanurjay were placed on the throne she would leave Keonjhar. This gave rise to the fear that it would result in a tribal uprising.

The chief problem that confronted Ravenshaw was he had to take Dhanurjay from Cuttack and install him as the raja of Keonjhar. After much deliberation, it was decided that Dhanurjay, accompanied by one official and the tribals, would first go to Anandpur and spend a few days there. It was expected that during this time the queen would begin to relent. Ravenshaw himself would then go to Anandpur and accompany Dhanurjay to Keonjhar. In accordance with this plan, Dhanurjay left Cuttack and Ravenshaw sent a letter addressed to the queen, through an official accompanying him, which said that Dhanurjay wanted the queen to stay on in Keonjhar. However, should she wish to live elsewhere, her wish would be honoured. In the letter the queen was requested to explain this to the tribal chieftains.

Ravenshaw went to Anandpur in November and found that the people of the area had accepted Dhanurjay's authority and everything seemed to be in order. However, he was informed that the tribals living in the jungle remained loyal to the queen. The news did not worry Ravenshaw, and taking Dhanurjay with him, he proceeded to Keonjhar.

The journey proved difficult. People living in villages by the road were scared of the Bhuyans and dared not supply provisions to Ravenshaw's party. The village chiefs were nowhere to be seen, for they had either escaped into the jungle or had gone to Calcutta to complain to the lieutenant governor. On reaching Keonjhar on 5 November, Ravenshaw found that people had abandoned the town which now lay empty. The queen, too, was getting ready to leave the palace. At Ravenshaw's request, she did not leave Keonjhar but moved into a house near the palace. From her subjects' point of view this was as good as abdication.

Ravenshaw spent a few days in Keonjhar and met the Bhuyan and the Juang chieftains there. It proved extremely difficult to bring them round through discussion. The Juangs agreed to accept Dhanurjay as their king but they said that they would take a final decision after discussing the matter with the Bhuyans. The queen was adamant that she would never accept Dhanurjay as king.

In spite of all this, the coronation ceremony was performed inside the palace. Ravenshaw supervised all the necessary arrangements. As the puja was in progress, the queen and her maidservants suddenly appeared and hurled abuse at Ravenshaw and Dhanurjay. Ravenshaw ordered that the ceremony should proceed. For the subjects, however, the coronation was incomplete. Established custom said that a Bhuyan chief should ceremonially place the king on the throne. A few Juangs attended the ceremony but not a single Bhuyan was around.

Ravenshaw had only twenty sepoys with him. Anticipating further trouble, he had another twenty brought over, left them to guard Dhanurjay and went off to tour the hilly areas. On his tour he met Colonel Dalton, who was commissioner, Chotanagpur.

The tribals deferred to Dalton and he persuaded the chieftains accompanying him to extend their support to Dhanurjay. When Ravenshaw came back to Keonjhar at the end of his tour, he found that except the Bhuyans, no one now challenged Dhanurjay's authority. However, Ratna Nayak, who had pledged his support to the queen, did not recognize the coronation and under his influence, the Bhuyans, too, refused to accept Dhanurjay as their king.

In January, Queen Bishnupriya suddenly left Keonjhar and went to live in a village called Basantpur seven miles from Keonjhar. This gave rise to a new problem and as a result, Ravenshaw, who wanted to go back to Cuttack, got stuck in Keonjhar.

Cuttack, March 1868

The famine commission was instructed that when it submitted its report, it should also send a list of those people—official and non-official—who had exerted themselves to provide relief to the destitutes during the famine.

The commission in its report made mention of the following people who had helped in a non-official capacity: the raja of Parikud, Sykes, Moncrieff, and some officers of the Irrigation Company. Only seven government officers from Orissa figured in the list: Barlow, collector, Puri; Muspratt, collector, Balasore; Shortt, assistant magistrate, Bhadrak; Jackson, civil surgeon, Balasore; Harris, assistant surveyor, Dhamra; Barton, assistant magistrate, Khurda; and Kirkwood, relief manager, Cuttack.

During the famine, Kirkwood had thrown himself whole-heartedly into relief work. He remained busy even after the pressure of relief work eased off. He had not found Orissa pleasant initially but he soon began to enjoy his stay in Cuttack. After the relief operations came to an end, Ravenshaw appointed him acting joint magistrate whose job was to try cases. Kirkwood soon made a name for himself as a strict, impartial and principled judge.

However, Kirkwood remained absolutely unchanged in one respect, his foul temper, and he continued to be the thrashing phiringee. Soon, criminal cases were filed by people who had received a beating from him. However, most of these cases were dismissed either through the interventions of fellow British officers or because the complainants failed to pursue the cases. In 1867, Kirkwood was fined five rupees by the court for beating up someone.

These days, Kirkwood had turned his attention to the dress worn by the native clerks which made him fly into a rage. Although there existed no formal dress code at the time for clerks, they attended office in pyjamas, choga chapkan and turbans. Once in the office, they took off their turbans and only wore them in the presence of the sahibs. In time, clerks who did not have to present themselves to sahibs at all stopped wearing turbans altogether. Some even attended office in dhotis. When these deviations from the unwritten dress code came to Kirkwood's notice, he ordered that all the clerks should come to office properly dressed.

There was also a rule regarding shoes. One had to take them off when one went to meet a sahib on some business. Those clerks who came to office wearing shoes took them off and left them near their seats when the sahib called them, or, alternatively, they left their shoes outside the sahib's chamber before entering. This rule applied to rulers of feudatory states as well. Even at a durbar, the rajas had to leave their shoes outside. This rule had led to situations where white servants of rajas and maharajas could enter with their shoes on while their masters entered barefoot. Kirkwood strictly enforced the rule relating to shoes. He had once beaten up a clerk who had dared cross the threshold of his chamber with his shoes on. He had also thrown out a muktar for the same offence.

To Kirkwood's misfortune, in March 1868, the governor general, Lord Lawrence, issued an order permitting all natives to appear before government officers wearing shoes made according to European fashion. However, the older rule would remain in force if the native chose to wear shoes made according to Indian fashion. British officers gathered at the Station Club and severely criticized the governor general's proclamation, for they felt that this would make the natives overconfident. As expected, clerks who were not happy with Kirkwood now entered his court, their brand new English shoes squeaking. These days, Kirkwood, before looking at a native's face, looked down at his feet to find out which shoes he was wearing. The natives understood the situation well, and all had bought English shoes.

Kirkwood may gnash his teeth but there was absolutely nothing he could do. One day, the clerk whom Kirkwood had beaten because he had once appeared before him in shoes, jauntily walked into his chamber fully dressed, and deliberately scuffed his shoes on the floor to provoke the sahib. Kirkwood threw him out and tried to come up with an idea to address the problem. In the end, he issued an order saying that only wearing English shoes would not do, the clerks must put on socks as well. Copies of this order were put up everywhere in the cutchery.

In the past, the clerks used to put on old-fashioned shoes which could be easily taken off. But, since English shoes had laces, taking them off was not easy. The clerks habitually took off their shoes before sitting down to work in office. Now, when socks became compulsory, some of them reverted to old-fashioned shoes. It seemed more convenient to take one's shoes off if one had to appear before the sahib; having to sit in the heat of the office wearing socks was too uncomfortable.

When Kirkwood's order was issued, his old adversary, Gourishankar did not keep quiet. He protested against the order in the *Dipika* for it violated the governor general's order.

Khandapara, August 1868

The astrologers had predicted that a solar eclipse would occur on 18 August, a Tuesday. A total eclipse was expected to be seen in Madras, during which the sun would become invisible for a full six minutes. Since this was an unprecedented event, many European astronomers had come to Madras to watch it.

The Hindus were afraid of the calamities that the eclipse could cause. The eclipse was a significant event for Orissa for another reason. On the exact time of the day at which the solar eclipse would take place depended which almanac—Bengali or Oriya—people in Orissa would use in future.

Before the first Oriya almanac was printed by the Cuttack Printing Company in 1866, Oriyas used to consult the Bengali almanac. However, the *Utkal Panjika* brought out by the company was written in verse and was therefore accessible only to professional astrologers. With the aim of making an accurate yet accessible almanac in Oriya available to people, Gourishankar and Bichitranand contacted Samant Chandrasekhar Singha Harichandan Mohapatra who lived in Khandapara.

Samant Chandrasekhar, popularly known as Pathani Samant, was only thirty-three but had become famous throughout Orissa as a great astrologer. He was a member of the royal family of Khandapara. The king of Khandapara, Natabar, was his nephew. People from different parts of Orissa came to Khandapara to show him horoscopes and to have horoscopes cast by him.

The Cuttack Printing Company published the Oriya almanac on Chandrasekhar's advice. This almanac varied from the Bengali one. Through the *Dipika*, Gourishankar advised people that the Oriya almanac was not a translation of the Bengali one. The almanac and conventions of Bengal should not be followed in Orissa and Oriyas should therefore be guided only by the Oriya almanac. An excerpt from a text called the *Srinivas Dipika* was quoted in support of this.

The almanac published by the Cuttack Printing Company predicted that the eclipse would begin at 8.29 a.m. and last till 11.46 a.m. This prediction was based on Chandrasekhar's calculations. According to the astrologers of Cuttack, and also the Bengali almanac, the eclipse was to begin at 10 a.m. It now remained to be seen which of the two predictions would come true.

Gourishankar waited for the eclipse, an English watch in hand. He had to take a major decision. The almanac published by the printing company was based largely on calculations made by the astrologers of Cuttack. In places Gourishankar had relied on Chandrasekhar's calculations. Today, the time of occurrence of the eclipse would help him decide whether he would base the almanac on Chandrasekhar's calculations or on the Cuttack astrologers'.

Exactly at this time, Chandrasekhar himself was seated in a field near the fort of Khandapara. A saucer containing water mixed with turmeric lay before him. He held a sheaf of palm leaves and he was absorbed in turning these over. A watch had been kept on a wooden box beside him. A crowd of children had surrounded Chandrasekhar and were making a lot of noise. A short distance away, a few adults of the village enjoyed the sight and made fun of Chandrasekhar. For them, Chandrasekhar was an object of ridicule for they found it difficult to see why a member of the royal family should choose to be a humble astrologer. Since Chandrasekhar was not very good looking, there had been a lot of trouble at the time of his marriage. Even years later, memory of this incident had not ceased to amuse people.

The sky had become slightly cloudy in the morning and there was a chance that the eclipse would not be visible. However, the sky soon cleared. Gourishankar calculated that the eclipse began at 8.47 a.m. and came to an end at 11.32 a.m. This was very close to Chandrasekhar's calculation. Gourishankar was happy and went to share the good news with Bichitranand. Chandrasekhar, too, picked up his instruments and started for home. The actual time of the eclipse according to the watch differed slightly from the time he had predicted. Convinced that the watch must be wrong, he adjusted it. Now the eclipse took place exactly in accordance with his calculations. Chandrasekhar started thinking about his treatise on astrology, *Siddhanta Darpan*. He had begun writing it about ten years ago. In fact, the writing of the book could be said to have started when he began studying astrology at the age of fourteen. But the treatise could not reach completion for not only did he have to do a lot of calculations but he also had to observe the movement of the stars and the planets for years. The success of his prediction today convinced Chandrasekhar that he must finish the treatise within a year.

Keonjhar, August 1868

When Ravenshaw realized that it would be impossible for him to leave Keonjhar, and that he would be sitting idle there, he sent for his wife. He had expected to spend a few days in peace and comfort with her but this was not to be. He received information that the Bhuyans, armed with bows, axes and spears, were beginning to assemble in Basantpur where Queen Bishnupriya now lived. After consulting the queen, the Bhuyans had decided to rise in rebellion against the government.

Leaving his wife behind in Keonjhar, Ravenshaw set off for Basantpur with a police force. The police carried guns and it did not take much time to scare the Bhuyans and take them prisoner. Ravenshaw gathered from them that they regarded Bishnupriya as their mother and, since they had given her their word of honour, they were rebelling against the government. If the queen were to release them from their pledge, they would not create any trouble. Ravenshaw had the Bhuyans tied up and brought them to the queen, and told her that if she looked upon them as her children she should release them from the pledge or else they would remain in bondage. The queen did not say anything that day, merely that she would think the matter over. The next day, Ravenshaw took the Bhuyan prisoners to her again. Since the tribals were getting restless, the queen told them that they were free to break the pledge they had made to her earlier. This made the Bhuyans happy and Ravenshaw freed them. They agreed to accept Dhanurjay as their king and to persuade other Bhuyans in the jungle to do so. But Ratna Nayak escaped into the jungle, refusing to accept this arrangement. The police mounted a search for him. The Bhuyans cooperated with them for they had undergone much suffering on account of Ratna. However, Ratna eluded them.

Queen Bishnupriya returned to Keonjhar at the request of the Bhuyans. She also agreed to the proposal that Dhanurjay's coronation be held properly, according to the prescribed customs, once more. The date fixed for the ceremony was 13 February and arrangements were made for a puja in the palace on that day. Early in the morning, the Bhuyans and the Juangs assembled near the palace. One of the Bhuyans impersonated a horse, 'riding' which, Dhanurjay arrived at the place where the puja was being performed. There were a few special guests at the puja: Ravenshaw, his wife, Colonel Dalton, who was the commissioner, Chotanagpur, and his wife, Hess, collector, Singbhum, and his officers. The day after the coronation, the queen gave Dhanurjay a headdress which was a token of her acceptance of his claim to the throne.

Four days after the coronation, a few more rites were performed. The new raja sat on a raised seat outside the palace. Groups of people wearing garlands came to him, beating drums. The chief of each group kissed the raja's feet, and placed them on his head. Then he presented the king a basket containing rice, pumpkins and bananas, and saluted him. After the Bhuyan and the Juang chiefs offered the raja their respects in this manner, they each received a headdress and a goat from him. It was evening by the time all this was over. A feast was held at night.

Ravenshaw was glad that the problem of succession in Keonjhar was satisfactorily resolved. The queen had promised him that she would spend three months in Keonjhar and then leave for Puri after Dhanurjay was secure. It was decided that she would receive a monthly pension of six hundred rupees. Twenty constables stayed back in Keonjhar and the rest of the police force was sent back to the respective stations. Ravenshaw returned to Cuttack with his wife, convinced that he had sorted out a very complicated matter.

However, peace in Keonjhar was short lived. That year the rains arrived late and many old men in Bhuyan villages died. It was rumoured that the crops had failed and people had died because they had failed to put a deserving person on the throne. In April, Ratna Nayak came out of his jungle hideout and called a meeting which was attended by the Bhuyans, the Juangs and the Kohls. In the meeting it was decided that they would drive Dhanurjay out and place Brundaban on the throne.

When news of this reached Keonjhar, Dhanurjay sent some of his trusted men to Ratna Nayak. But they were taken prisoner by the Bhuyan rebels. On 28 April, around twenty thousand rebels seized the fort of Keonjhar and started looting the shops and the market. They snatched guns from the police and damaged the cannon inside the fort. They killed a Brahmin in the bazaar and took the dewan and a hundred persons captive. They kept the fort encircled, and Dhanurjay lived like a prisoner inside the palace. The rebels declared that they would obey the queen, not Dhanurjay. The queen again supported Brundaban.

On receiving news of this, Hess, the collector of Singbhum, led an armed force to Keonjhar and reached there on 7 May. He found that the Bhuyans, armed with bows, axes and swords, had surrounded Dhanurjay on all sides. Hess disarmed the rebels, drove them out of the palace and set Dhanurjay free. But the rebels did not release the dewan and the others whom they held captive in the forest. Administration in Keonjhar had come to a standstill. Faced with this situation, Hess asked for reinforcements. Dalton and Ravenshaw made arrangements for sending troops from Chotanagpur and Cuttack.

On 19 May, Ravenshaw issued an order from Cuttack to the effect that the government had decided to place Dhanurjay on the throne of Keonjhar. Two days later, Brundaban was detained in Balasore on the strength of another order. The raja of Mayurbhanj was scared by these developments and said that he would no longer extend support either to Queen Bishnupriya or to Brundaban in their bid for the throne of Keonjhar. And yet, in spite of this, the rebels did not change their attitude but attacked the police. The situation was brought under control only after Dalton arrived in Keonjhar towards the end of June. His troops rescued the people held captive by the rebels in the forest. They found out then that the rebels had killed the dewan.

Ravenshaw planned another trip to Keonjhar since affairs there were growing more and more complicated. He reached Keonjhar on 7 July and initiated attempts to capture the rebels. About 2200 sepoys and thirteen officers combed the jungle but even so, the operation took a lot of time. Ratna Nayak escaped again and a reward was announced for his capture. The Bhuyan chiefs began surrendering, one after another. At last, on 15 August, Ratna Nayak was caught and the rebels were sent off to Cuttack to stand trial. The rebellion in Keonjhar thus came to an end. However, in order to maintain order, Ravenshaw had to stay back in Keonjhar for some more time.

Puri, Konark, December 1868

One winter evening, a party consisting of about forty men, four palanquins, five bullock carts and two elephants reached Daria Mahavir on the Puri coast. Such entourages usually accompanied rajas who visited Puri during festivals. But this was not the festive season and the fat gentleman who emerged from the palanquin was no royal personage. He was Babu Rajendralal Mitra, director of the Wards' Institute which functioned under the aegis of the board in Calcutta for the education of underage rajas.

At the instance of the Royal Society of Britain, the government of India had set aside a sum of money which was to be used for preparing plaster-of-Paris replicas of ancient sculptures. It had been decided that some people would be trained at the art school in Calcutta to make plaster casts of sculptures. They would be sent to Orissa where they would select beautiful carved figures in the temples and prepare their replicas. Rajendralal Mitra was to help them select the figures and to carry out an archaeological survey of Orissa. He was to take leave from the Wards Institute, and he would not claim any remuneration for this work.

Two months earlier, the *Dipika* had informed its readers of the proposed visit of Babu Rajendralal, and had requested them to extend to him all possible help and cooperation. However, when Rajendralal's party disembarked at the lighthouse and proceeded to Puri by way of Cuttack and Bhubaneswar, word got round that he was a *lakhraj* deputy collector, or an endowment officer, and that he had come to Orissa to confiscate lakhraj land or to dismiss the priests of some mutts. Because of this, the local people were unwilling to render him any help.

Babu Rajendralal put up a tent in Puri and set to work the day after his arrival. His chief associate was Radhika Prasad Mukherjee, who was assistant engineer, Puri. The craftsmen began grinding the gypsum brought from London into powder from which plaster-of-Paris casts of stone figures would be made. Carrying a notebook, Rajendralal, accompanied by Radhika Prasad, began a survey of the Puri temple.

The moment Rajendralal stepped into the temple, he fell into the clutches of a priest called Kashi Singhari. He had to forget all about the measurements, for Kashi dragged him away and made him bow before all the statues of gods and goddesses inside the temple and put sums of money at their feet. Rajendralal, a fat man, was soon exhausted because of the heat, and sat down. Kashi said to him, 'Tell me, sir, can you hear the sea from here?' Rajendralal tried to listen for the sound of the sea. But, although the sea lay close to the temple, even the faintest sound of its waves was not audible. Kashi now explained, 'In the past, the sea used to roar so loudly that the goddess Subhadra shrivelled up with fear and her hands and feet shrank into her body. So the Lord said to the sea, "Roar as loudly as you like, but only outside the temple. Your voice should never carry into the temple." He got Hanuman to make sure the sound of the sea never crossed the boundary wall of the temple. From that day, inside the temple, one can never hear the sound of the sea.'

Rajendralal rose to his feet, went outside the Lion Gate and stood beside the Aruna Pillar. From here, he could distinctly hear the sound of the waves crashing. But, once inside, he could hear nothing. Kashi now said, 'Come with me. You will see another miracle. You may be a very learned man but you are a sinner, after all. Even if you stand before Lord Jagannath, you will never be able to catch a glimpse of Him.' In fact, when Rajendralal went up to the sanctum sanctorum of Lord Jagannath, he could see nothing at all. Scared, he prayed to the Lord for a time, and when he opened his eyes, three deities rose before him in all their splendour. This was truly miraculous! This drama was repeated every day while the survey and the measuring went on.

On the day he was to leave Puri, Rajendralal went to the temple one last time. Kashi stood waiting for him, as usual. Rajendralal instructed him, 'Today, you will lead me into the temple.' Rajendralal closed his eyes tight as he approached the deities. He opened his eyes there and he now had no difficulty seeing them. On previous occasions he had come from light into the dark, so for a time, he was unable to see anything. But he did not face this difficulty today because he had entered with his eyes closed. Releasing his hand from the panda's he came out and told Radhika Prasad about the happy discovery. Radhika Prasad laughed and said, 'You should have talked to me about this earlier. You don't know what cheats these pandas are.'

Rajendralal left for Konark the next day, his work in Puri at an end. The area around the temple there was densely forested and the members of his party dared not go near the temple for fear of snakes. Rajendralal looked at the sculptures from a safe distance and made entries in his notebook. The carved figure of a sleeping lion lying on the southern side of the temple struck him as a thing of surpassing beauty. He wanted to take its measurements and asked a cowherd boy to climb the figure and measure it. He tempted him with an offer of two rupees. But the boy refused to oblige him and ran away. Rajendralal made a rough guess and wrote in his notebook that the figure was about fourteen feet high.

Rajendralal sat under a tree to escape the heat of the day and took out his papers. He located the picture of Konark in Ferguson's book, *Hindostan*, and compared the temple with it. In the picture, parts of the main temple were visible behind the Jagmohan; however, of the main temple nothing remained. Rajendralal was too scared to venture into the jungle to have a closer look at the ruins.

From among the papers, Rajendralal took out a file marked 'Navagraha'. Since the Navagraha slab lay neglected on the ground, the Asiatic Society had been urging the government to get it shifted to the Calcutta museum. The government had granted three thousand rupees for this purpose and the PWD had been entrusted with the task. After much careful thought, engineer Nicolls had decided that the slab would be conveyed to the seashore on rollers revolving on planks along iron rails. From there, it was to have been transported to Calcutta by steamer. According to this plan, a conveyance was constructed and metal tracks were laid out from where the Navagraha slab lay. But soon the money allocated for the job had run out and the project was abandoned.

Rajendralal took measurements of the track: it was about two hundred yards long. The seashore lay another mile away. The fact that the Navagraha slab could not be shifted to the Calcutta Museum filled Rajendralal with regret. Now he turned his attention to the figures on the slab. Stirling, who had written a history of Orissa, had described Venus as a plump, well-endowed young woman. This, Rajendralal found very amusing. In the west, Venus was a beautiful goddess, but here she was Shukra, a wise man.

Rajendralal approached the temple timidly. Although few people went there these days for fear of the wild beasts and snakes, the stones of the temple had been disfigured by names carved on them by visitors. Moving closer, Rajendralal found that all the names belonged to sahibs. Among them, he looked for Stirling's name, but was disappointed when he did not find it.

After his work in Konark was finished, Rajendralal returned to Cuttack. A meeting was held at the Cuttack Debating Club to felicitate him. In his address, Rajendralal said that a genuine well-wisher of Orissa would do his utmost to replace the Oriya language with Bengali in the province. Orissa would never prosper if the Oriya language was not abolished.

Bamanda, June 1869

The question of who would succeed Brajasundar Dev as the king of Bamanda exercised people from time to time. Brajasundar had only one son but since he was born of a maidservant, there was no question of his ascending the throne. Brajasundar had, therefore, decided that his third brother Harihar's son, Basudev, would inherit the throne. This seemed a sensible decision for Basudev was the eldest among all the children in the royal family. Since there was a possibility of someone challenging this decision in future, Brajasundar had sent all papers relating to the choice of Basudev as his heir to the British political agent who was resident at Sambalpur. All this had happened in 1855. Basudev was only five years old at the time.

After this, the title of 'Tikayat' was conferred on Basudev and arrangements were made to give him a proper education. He was taught grammar by Pandit Anand Brahma. Pandit Purusottam Tarkalankar taught him poetry, drama and rhetoric. From Pandit Bhubaneswar Badapanda he received lessons in logic and on the Upanishads. When Basudev grew a little older, Brajasundar sat him down and taught him to manage the affairs of the kingdom. The thought that the kingdom of Bamanda would pass into capable hands after his death gave Brajasundar much pleasure. However, Brajasundar could never have dreamt that his end would come so soon.

The waterfall at Pradhanpat was the nicest spot in Bamanda. Brajasundar went there now and then to rest from his duties. That year, when he arrived at his rest-house, someone came in with the news that there was a cobra on the banyan tree nearby. Brajasundar prided himself on his courage. He claimed that he would be the one to catch the snake.

Some of his attendants, armed with sticks, surrounded the tree. Presently, the snake appeared on one of the topmost branches.

Brajasundar wound his clothes tightly round his waist and climbed the tree. Scared by all this bustle, the snake slithered into a hollow in the tree trunk but Brajasundar caught it by its tail and tried to pull it out. The cobra tried desperately to slip deeper into the hollow, but Brajasundar pulled it out. Holding the snake's head with one hand and its tail with the other, he proudly displayed it to the people assembled below. They cheered him but there was a problem: how was Brajasundar to climb down? An attendant promptly brought a ladder. Snake in hand, Brajasundar climbed down with great difficulty and was heartily applauded.

The snake had been caught at last but the question was what was to be done with it. And even though everyone pleaded with Brajasundar to throw down the snake so that they could beat it to death, the king did not agree. He had gone through much trouble trying to catch the snake and he was not willing to let go of it easily. He called for an empty pitcher.

When the pitcher arrived, Brajasundar tried to push the snake into it. The snake tried to wriggle out and people fell back, frightened. After a great deal of effort, Brajasundar did succeed in forcing the snake into the pitcher but in the process, the snake bit him. Minutes later, Brajasundar fell unconscious. His attendants laid him down beside a well and poured water on him. Someone rushed to a village nearby to fetch a *gunia*. Word was also sent to the capital.

The gunia's incantations and the water poured on his head failed to bring about any improvement in Brajasundar's condition. So he was carried in a palanquin to Deogarh. Here his condition went from bad to worse. The English doctor in Sambalpur was sent for. Realizing that his last hour had come, Brajasundar called all the members of his family and informed them that Basudev would inherit the throne after his death. He then sat Basudev beside him and said, 'Never forget that the blood of satis flows through your veins.' These were Brajasundar's last words.

The 'satis' mentioned by him referred to two women in the royal family who had immolated themselves on their husband's funeral pyre. Six generations ago, Prataprudra had been raja of Bamanda. The British had occupied Orissa during his reign but Bamanda was then under Chhatisgarh, not Orissa. After Prataprudra's death his queen, Chandrakumari, wished to commit sati. Arrangements were made on the bank of a river which flows past Deogarh, and the queen, her husband's dead body in her lap, was consumed by the flames of a pyre made of sandalwood logs. The spot near the river where this happened came to be known as *satighat*.

Prataprudra was succeeded by his son, Sarbeswar. Unfortunately, a few days after ascending the throne, he was killed by an assassin from Rairakhol. The memory of Chandrakumari's self-sacrifice was still fresh in people's minds. So Sarbeswar's wife came under tremendous pressure to follow her mother-in-law's example. She reluctantly gave in, and burnt herself to death on the funeral pyre of her husband. The spot where she committed sati came to be called *satikunda*.

Thus, only nineteen and weighed down by the burden of the blood of two satis, Basudev ascended the throne of Bamanda.

Balasore, July 1869

The library at Damodar Prasad Das's house in Sunhat was the centre of cultural life in Balasore. Fakir Mohan and Radhanath visited it regularly and Damodar Prasad constantly encouraged them to read and write. One day, Damodar Prasad went through a few Bengali poems composed by Radhanath, felt very pleased and said that if Radhanath were to write fifty poems, he would get a collection printed at his own expense. A few days later, Radhanath brought him fifty-one poems. In 1868, Damodar Prasad published these poems in a book titled *Kabitabali*.

They now discussed the possibility of setting up a press where books in Oriya could be printed. In the meantime, Fakir Mohan, at Ishwar Chandra Vidyasagar's urging, had translated the former's book *Jibanacharita* from Bengali into Oriya and got it printed in Calcutta. This book was being taught in the schools of Orissa. Fakir Mohan had also written textbooks of mathematics and grammar. He was now trying to set up a press in Balasore. It was decided that a company would be set up along the lines of the Cuttack Printing Company with Damodar Prasad, Radhanath and others as its shareholders. However, it was also decided that Radhanath's name would not figure in any document whatsoever for his father, Sundar Narayan, strongly disapproved of his taking part in any meeting and of his socializing with anyone.

The P.M. Senapati and Co. Utkal Press was established in Balasore in spite of many difficulties. From July 1868, through Fakir Mohan's efforts, two magazines called *Bodhadayini* and *Balasore Sambad Bahika* began to be published. This was a remarkable and exciting event for Balasore.

The crime rate had grown higher in the city. While it had been expected that with the end of the famine, crime would go down but that did not happen. The stretch of road between Midnapore and Bhadrak was infested with dacoits. These dacoits hid themselves in the jungles of Balasore and Mayurbhanj and some of them operated in large gangs. Notorious among these gangs were the ones led by Nalu Mirdha, Baidi Sethi and Gadei Kandara. The dacoits would not normally dare attack a sahib. However, once the palanquin of Rampini, assistant collector, was looted on the road between Basta and Haladipada; the dacoits were under the impression that the palanquin bore Jogeya, a businessman from Balasore. On another occasion, dacoits attacked the palanquin carrying Ravenshaw's wife while she was travelling from Balasore to Cuttack.

Many social changes were gradually taking place in Balasore. Since a large number of Bengalis were resident in this district, Oriyas came increasingly under their influence. The Bengalis wore their hair short and wore shirts like the sahibs. The Oriyas followed their example by wearing their hair short, entering their houses with shoes on, and by wearing shirts. The other important habit they picked up from the Bengalis was alcohol. At the time, many Bengali officials and gentlemen drank, and they looked down on people who did not. Kishori Mohan Das, the zamindar and moneylender of Sunhat, owned a garden which lay at one end of the Motiganj Bazaar. Parties were held here every Saturday night, where people enjoyed card games, games of chess, wine, opium, charas and the dance of nautch girls. Fakir Mohan soon became a regular at these parties.

Brahmoism had reached Balasore through the Bengalis. Ishan Chandra Basu had come here as the first missionary of the Adi Brahmo Samaj. Prayer meetings were regularly held in Prasanna Kumar Chatterjee's residence near the temple of Jhadeswar Mahadev. Prasanna worked as a clerk in the salt department. After prayer, the followers of Brahmo faith helped themselves to drinks. Among the Brahmos in those days, drinking was an inseparable part of worship. Later, the prayer room of the Adi Brahmo Samaj was shifted to the pukka house of the raja of Mayurbhanjs which lay on the outskirts of Motiganj Bazaar. Fakir Mohan embraced the Brahmo faith around this time.

In 1869, when Radhanath was transferred to the school in Puri as second teacher, Fakir Mohan was left alone. He was not on the best of terms with Reverend Miller, who was secretary, Mission School. His salary was not attractive, either. So he persuaded the acting collector, Mr Percy, to get him the job of *munshi* at the collectorate. But he did not like this job, for it left him little or no time for reading and writing. When Reverend E.B. Hallam replaced Reverend Miller as secretary, Fakir Mohan returned as headmaster to his old place of work. When the students of the school did very well in their examinations that year, Hallam raised Fakir Mohan's salary to twenty-five rupees.

In April, John Beames, who was collector, Champaran, joined as grade one collector of Balasore at a salary of 1916 rupees a month. While in Champaran, he had made a name for himself for having written a treatise on Indian philology. He had started writing a book on a comparative grammar of Indian languages. Since work in the office at Balasore was not very strenuous, Beames concentrated on writing this book. Hallam was at this time engaged in writing a grammar of Oriya, which was aimed at making it easy for sahibs to learn the language. Hallam had a good command over written as well as spoken Oriya. While writing his book, he occasionally took Fakir Mohan's help. When Beames came to Balasore, Hallam took his help. Beames was looking for a pandit who knew Sanskrit, Bengali and Oriya for help in writing his book on comparative grammar. One day, Hallam asked Fakir Mohan to accompany him on a visit to Beames. Beames asked Fakir Mohan a few questions on *taddhita pratyaya* and prepositions in Sanskrit, and was very pleased when the latter gave him correct answers. After this, Fakir Mohan visited Beames frequently and discussed with him matters relating to language and literature. If Fakir Mohan could not come and see him for some days, Beames would complain.

Cuttack, August 1869

Rajendralal Mitra, having delivered his lecture in Cuttack, went off to Calcutta. But his lecture created feelings of antagonism between the Bengalis and the Oriyas. At the time the lecture was delivered, Gourishankar was busy shifting the press of his printing company to its own pukka building. He had praised

Rajendralal's lecture in the *Dipika*. On 18 January the office of the printing company was moved to a house in Dargha Bazaar which stood opposite the jail and this became the *Dipika's* new address. Now many people explained to Gourishankar the dangerous implications of Rajendralal's lecture. So Gourishankar wrote a long essay titled, 'Obstacles to the Growth of the Oriya Language' and published it in the March issue of the *Dipika*. In his view, the Oriya language failed to grow because it was subject to the authority of three masters: the governments of Bengal, the Central Provinces and Madras.

In July, in a long article in the newly published magazine the *Cuttack Star*, Babu Umacharan Haldar expressed the view that Oriya books and magazines should use the Bengali alphabet, for this would make it easy for everyone—the Bengalis, the Oriyas and the sahibs—to learn Oriya. The Cuttack Debating Club promptly held a meeting and supported this view. A few days later, the Utkolollasini Sabha opposed it. On the other hand, the magazine, *Utkal Hiteishini*, supported Haldar's view. Gourishankar wrote a song in the *Dipika* attacking this view:

The fellow opened the pot of cleverness
And took out from it the rule:
Write Oriya in Bengali script.
They are now dancing in joy,
But, I think I will give them
A pair of glasses
So that the myopic fellows
Can find their way!

The real problem arose when Gourishankar printed a letter relating to Rajakrishna Mukhopadhyay who had given a lecture at the Cuttack Debating Club supporting Haldar's view. Published in the letters to the editor column, it said: 'The esteemed Baboo is full of erudition, and has obtained an M.A. degree. It is our good fortune that he has turned his back on his homeland, Bengal, and has descended on our province, determined to bring it prosperity. There is no doubt that such a person would bring Orissa glory. However, a few letters of the Oriya alphabet would have conferred on him uniqueness as a human being. Being extremely clever, the Baboo had dropped the letter "sha" from his degree.' (In Oriya, 'mesha' means 'a sheep'.)

Rajakrishna Mukhopadhyay, who was only twenty-three at the time, was a lawyer and the legal adviser of the High School. When the *Dipika* described him as mesha, or sheep, he immediately wrote the following letter to Gourishankar:

Sir,

The 30th issue of your magazine *Utkal Dipika* (Vol. 4) carries a letter signed off by Sri Ranga Panchanan on 24 July 1869. Since this contains a few remarks libelling me, it is liable to prosecution under article 501 of the penal code. I therefore request you to send me the real name and the address of the letter-writer, so that I could file a case against him in the Sessions Court and another case in the Civil Court demanding compensation. If you do not oblige me, I shall be compelled to take everyone concerned with your magazine to court.

Your obedient servant,
Rajakrishna Mukhopadhyay, M.A. B.L.

In reply to this, Gourishankar wrote:

I placed your letter before the Board of Directors. They have directed me to inform you that the letter contains no libellous material. They therefore express their unwillingness to disclose the name and address of the writer of the letter.

Your most obedient servant,   28 July 1869
Gourishankar Ray

On 2 August, Rajakrishna filed a criminal case in the court of the joint magistrate, Mr Kirkwood. Kirkwood was looking for an opportunity to teach Gourishankar a lesson. So, without going into the details of Rajakrishna's complaint, and believing that the letter was libellous, he promptly sent a summons to Gourishankar. The case was to come up for hearing on 4 August.

On the day of the trial, people flocked into the cutcherry for it was not only a case of libel, it was an open battle between the Oriyas and the Bengalis. They were also eager to see what Kirkwood, the native basher, was going to do to Gourishankar. As for Gourishankar, it must be said he was a little apprehensive. He had, therefore, got one of the best lawyers in Cuttack, Rammohan Mallick, to defend him.

After taking the oath, the plaintiff, Rajakrishna, stated his allegation. He complained that the letter published in the *Dipika* had described him as stupid as a sheep and had suggested that he had obtained his M.A. degree through foul means. This, he said, had disgraced him. He then proceeded to give a list of the degrees he had received from various institutions. This was followed by arguments of the defence lawyer, Rammohan. Kirkwood put to him a number of questions seeking detailed information on the content of the letter at issue. For Kirkwood, to find out how, by adding the letters 'sha' to M.A., the degree could be made to stand for a sheep was a time-consuming and bothersome task but in the end, it proved quite amusing. Having listened to all the arguments for and against, Kirkwood got down to writing out the verdict. Gourishankar felt certain that he would be made to pay a fine. He now thought of ways in which he could appeal against such a verdict.

That same afternoon, after asking the excited crowd in the courtroom to quiet down, Kirkwood read out the following verdict:

When a speech advocating the replacement of Oriya letters and numerals by the Bengali alphabet was made at the Debating

Club in Cuttack, the complainant openly supported the proposal. The letter-writer considered the proposal ridiculous, opposed it, and expressed the view that in supporting such a move the complainant had given evidence of his utter stupidity. The above-mentioned speech undoubtedly concerned a matter involving the general public, and decision on the matter would affect the people of Orissa. The writer of the letter has done nothing more than merely finding fault with the defendant's position on this matter.

Further, the plaintiff claims that he has been disgraced by being described as someone who has 'turned his back on his homeland'. He has also been accused of having adopted unfair means for obtaining his M.A. degree. In our view, considering the circumstances in which the letter was written, no offence was meant when it was said that the complainant had turned his back on his homeland. None of the words used in the letter can be made to imply that the complainant has secured his degree through foul means. The letter-writer has made mention of the plaintiff's degree only in order to play with the letters M and A and to highlight the fact that the latter has revealed his foolishness.

The court feels that, according to section 501, calling the plaintiff a sheep (mesha) does not constitute libel. This falls within the scope of the third exception of section 499. Hence the case stands dismissed, and the defendant, Gourishankar Ray, is acquitted under section 250 of the Criminal Procedure Code.

Puri, February 1870

Like John Beames, William Wilson Hunter, too, was a learned civilian. By 1868 he had already become quite well-known for his books, *A Comparative Dictionary of the Non-Aryan Languages of India and High Asia*, and *Annals of Rural Bengal*. However, Hunter was not on the best of terms with other government officials in Bengal. He believed that this was because they were jealous of him. He also credited himself with having invented a useful system of writing Indian names and place names in the Roman script.

Hunter had been entrusted with the task of writing a gazetteer by the government, and he had sent out letters seeking necessary information. Since it would be some time before he would receive replies to these letters, he decided that he should go to Orissa and write a book on the province which would form the second volume of his *Annals of Rural Bengal*. With this in mind, Hunter left Calcutta on 25 January. But his ship's engine failed, leaving the ship stuck in the Hooghly harbour for a time. It reached Batighar on 28 January and put in at Gopalpur on 29 January. There a palanquin was waiting for him. On 1 February he came to the Chilka by way of Ganjam. Then he sailed to Parikud in a government boat.

Hunter spent some time with the raja of Parikud, Chandrasekhar Mansingh. The raja talked to him about the days of the famine. Out of the total population of 11,178, as many as 5375 had died and 1250 had abandoned their homes. The raja had become a pauper for he could not collect land revenue during the famine and also because he had fed the destitutes. However, a year ago, the government had extended financial assistance to him and had conferred on him the title, Companion of the Order of the Star of India. The people of Orissa were proud of this because at that time, even the lieutenant governor had not been honoured with such a title.

That day Hunter set off at 8 p.m. from Rambha and reached the Puri coast at 7 a.m. on 2 February. A palanquin was waiting for him there, too. Hunter stayed at the staging bungalow in Puri. The next two days he spent looking up cutchery records and taking notes. After this he proceeded to Konark. He started his journey at one o'clock in the night and reached Konark at six in the morning. The temple there was an unforgettable experience.

But a few incidents during his stay in Puri after his trip to Konark left him deeply disturbed. One of these related to what he had seen at Swargdwar.

One evening, during Hunter's stay in Puri, the dead body of an old woman was brought to the cremation ground at Swargdwar. This woman had set out on a pilgrimage some four months earlier. Three out of the twenty-five persons who had come with her had died. The corpse was bathed in the sea and placed on the funeral pyre but the Brahmins would not allow it to be cremated. The pilgrims who were with the dead woman had already given two hundred and fifty rupees to them but the Brahmins demanded more. The pilgrims had no money left. Only after one of them signed a hand-note for eighty rupees, was the corpse of the old woman cremated.

Hunter was deeply affected by another experience during his visit to the Puri jail. The jail had been maintained with great care by its superintendent, the civil surgeon Dr Stewart. There was a good vegetable garden in the jail premises and the inmates were well looked after. Among them the Bhuyans, who had been brought there from Keonjhar, were noticeable. In November, Ravenshaw had tried the Bhuyan rebels who had been captured in August and sent to Cuttack. Ratna Nayak, along with seven others, had been sentenced to death, and twenty-seven had been sentenced to deportation. The rest, about one hundred and fifty Bhuyans, had been given jail sentences. Out of these, forty-eight were kept in the Puri jail. A few months after being jailed, eleven of them died. Two were almost half dead when Hunter went to visit the jail. To have been taken out of their beloved forests and made to live by the sea was a terribly unsettling and painful experience. It seemed as if a deep longing for their beloved hills and forests had worn them out and killed them. When so many of the Bhuyan prisoners died, the lieutenant governor ordered an inquiry. The inquiry revealed that the cause of their death was a change of climate.

Hunter regularly wrote to his wife. The day after he paid a visit to the jail, on 9 February, he wrote:

> Yesterday I inspected the District Jail, a clean, tidy, healthy and hard-working establishment with capital vegetable gardens. Among the prisoners were thirty-seven hill-men, the relics of forty-eight sent here in December 1868. Eleven dead already and two more sinking. My blood boils to think of the way we bully these poor tribesmen. Their only offence was obeying their chief's behests ... This morning I have been hard at work making extracts from the old records, but snatched an hour to refresh myself by reading the *Winter's Tale*, that most romantic of Shakespeare's comedies.

When Hunter was in Puri, Divyasingh, dressed in all his royal finery, went to call on him. He was now a strong and healthy fifteen-year-old. The procession of elephants, horses and drummers who accompanied him impressed Hunter, and the muktar who attended to him praised the raja's knowledge and intelligence. However, Hunter was saddened by the knowledge of the hardships faced by the royal family.

After eight days in Puri, Hunter started for Cuttack, and the collector agreed to accompany him. The arrangements for the journey were slightly delayed because Hunter insisted on using dak palanquins for his travel. Ordinary palanquins were borne by four bearers; these were followed by twelve others, who 'rested' as they ran alongside and took turns to carry the palanquin. As for the dak palanquins, groups of four bearers were stationed at different points on the road, and the palanquin was carried according to a relay system. The palanquin bearers moved at about four to five miles an hour and could cover a distance of twenty-five miles at a stretch. Hunter always preferred this mode of travel. However, there were two drawbacks to this arrangement. One, the collector had to inform the postal department well in advance. Secondly, the schedule of the journey would get upset if a party of bearers failed to turn up. Sometimes, when the bearers belonged to different castes, the problems of caste pollution too, arose. In any event, Hunter had a pleasant journey and went back to Cuttack having stopped over in Khandgiri and Bhubaneswar. The collector returned to his station.

Once in Cuttack, Hunter felt that he had returned to the fold of civilized life. He met many sahibs at the Station Club and he found much material for his book. Dinner at Ravenshaw's house, too, was a very pleasant experience for Mrs. Ravenshaw was an accomplished housewife. However, if Hunter had expected to hold a learned discussion with Ravenshaw, he was utterly disappointed, for the latter was no intellectual. During the time Hunter spent with him, Ravenshaw explained to him the working of the ice-making machine which he had bought for two hundred and fifty rupees in Calcutta. The ammonia-filled cylinder in the machine had to be heated and then dipped into water. The machine produced four pounds of ice in five hours. For Indians, the fact that something cold could be produced from something hot seemed magical. However, the machine was temperamental, and Ravenshaw never allowed his servants to touch it, always preferring to use it himself.

Hunter was very happy with all that he had managed to achieve. That night he wrote to his wife: 'My work is getting on famously. I will write a really great book; at least I have all the material for one. I feel every day that it is the first grand chance I have had in life; and I hope to prove equal to it.'

Balasore, March 1870

After coming to Balasore, Beames immersed himself in work related to office and writing. But his wife, Ellen, felt deeply unhappy all the time. She had left her three sons with a retired doctor in England, as it was not possible to send them to school in India. The eldest was eight years old and the youngest, Robert, was only five.

However Ellen did bring with her her one-year-old daughter, and she was pregnant too. Beames's second daughter was born soon after his arrival in Balasore. The family spent the Christmas holidays in Cuttack, and this was the only good time they had had since they came to Orissa. She went out on a ride with her husband every morning but after that she had to be by herself all day. All she did was wait for letters from her children in England, but they too arrived only once a fortnight. It was a matter of great excitement to have a sahib from outside visit Balasore, and the prospect of Hunter's visit greatly pleased Beames and his wife.

The reason why Beames was so happy was that Hunter had earned considerable fame as a scholar, and he, like Beames, was a philologist. In response to a letter which Hunter wrote him, Beames replied.

Dear William,

I have just received the very interesting series of questions relating to the history and geography of the Province destined to supply materials for your Gazetteer. For myself I can safely promise that they shall be answered as accurately and intelligently as possible. Unfortunately, Balasore is a very uninteresting district, but I will endeavour to give you some information about the little known tributary Mahals of Nilgiri and Mohurbhanj, properly Mayurbhanj, or 'Peacock Country'. I only wish I were still in Purnia. I was four years Collector there, and made many notes upon it.

My object in writing, however, is to notice a point which has probably occurred to you earlier. Personally I may venture to call myself a brother of the craft, as my tolerably numerous contributions to the R.A.S. of London and its Calcutta offspring testify. But how many Collectors in Bengal do you think will care a sixpence for your Gazetteer? How many of them will be bored by the whole thing and hand it over to Baboo Ghose or Bose to expatiate upon? How many will have time for it, or the taste and learning which fit them to be your collaborators? Now I would venture to suggest that, instead of leaving the important task to Magistrate-Collectors, you should apply to Government to make it over to a European assistant specially selected for each district. They would be your subordinates for this work; and many of them have knowledge and the necessary love of the subject. I speak disinterestedly, for, as regards Balasore, I mean to answer your questions myself. It will be an amusement for me in the camping season, for I don't shoot and am more interested in human beings than in tigers. There is no part of India of which we know less than our oldest possessions: Bengal, Bihar and Orissa. I tremble to think of the avalanche of fact and fiction which will be showered on your devoted head if the Gazetteer be left to District Magistrates—in other words, to the Ghose and Bose party.

Yours faithfully,   Balasore
John Beames   12 November 1869

Hunter arrived in Balasore in March. Beames had hoped that during Hunter's stay there he would engage the latter in scholarly discussions. But somehow, when they first met, they failed to hit it off. Beames, with his beard and gold-framed glasses, looked the part of a scholar. Hunter was a hatchet-faced, thin, small man, and one of his hands was deformed. Also, his left eye blinked all the time. On seeing that Beames was unable to take his eyes off his face, Hunter promptly said that a pet goat had gored his eyes when he was a child, and that he had had a fall from a horse and broken his left arm.

Hunter assumed an air of omniscience whenever he took part in a discussion. Beames's first difference with him arose over the meaning of the word 'Utkal'. Having consulted the pandits at Puri, Hunter had decided that it meant a land of artistic excellence. Beames, however, was of the view that Utkal referred to the area beyond the Gangetic valley. This meaning of the word had the support of pandits in Balasore. Hunter devoted himself entirely to the writing of his book and spent all his time collecting material and his endless queries exhausted Beames.

In Balasore, Hunter stayed with Beames, and Ellen would join them at dinner. Beames and his wife loved simple food whereas Hunter wanted to drink champagne every night and he enjoyed good food. So, having Hunter for a guest gave Beames little pleasure. When at last Hunter left Balasore, Beames heaved a great sigh of relief.

The day after Hunter left, Fakir Mohan came to see Beames. It gave Fakir Mohan great pleasure to meet Beames's daughter Margaret, for the two-year-old spoke fluent Oriya. Today, Beames spoke to Fakir Mohan about his book. When Fakir Mohan asked him about something, Beames said, 'Babu, please don't ask me any questions for at least a month. Answering Hunter's numerous queries has left me thoroughly exhausted.'

Puri, March 1870

Radhanath Ray had come to the Puri Zilla School about a year earlier as a second teacher. Madhu Rao should have left school by now, but because he fell ill during his last year at school he could not sit for the examination and had to spend another year at school. This proved to be a blessing in disguise for him, for he got an opportunity to be Radhanath's student and his companion. Radhanath helped Madhu with his studies and since the latter was weak in mathematics, Radhanath went to his house every day and gave him lessons.

Another thing drew the teacher and the pupil closer to each other: their love for literature. By this time Radhanath's book of poems in Bengali had been published and Madhu had read them a number of times. In the evening, the two of them sat on the seashore and discussed Michael Madhusudan Dutt's poetry. Copies of the *Dipika* reached Puri every Sunday and the news published in this was also a topic for discussion. Sometimes, the two of them went to meet Pandit Harihar Das.

Pandit Harihar Das was now busily occupied with work relating to his Sanskrit school. The school was supported by the interest on 5500 rupees which the maharaja of Balarampur in Ayodhya had deposited with the government, and by his annual grant of 1300 rupees for scholarships for poor students. A school for Brahmins did not exist in Puri. Although the Puri Zilla School had been in existence for several years now, the Brahmins did not send their children there for fear of losing caste, and Harihar Das's school was the first institution in Puri where Brahmin children could receive instruction. However, only children from poor Brahmin families came to this school for here, they received a scholarship of three rupees per month. This amount was enough for students to get by. Other Brahmins did not send their children for they thought that they would lose caste. Pandit Harihar was of the view that students should learn English as well as Sanskrit. To this end, arrangements had been made to teach them English at night.

The school did not have a building of its own; it was run on the veranda of the government school. Some people who were jealous of Harihar made attempts to get his school shifted from there, but the collector did not let them have their way. Not only did the collector give Harihar permission to use the veranda of the government school, he also set up a fund for constructing a building for Harihar's Sanskrit school. To this fund he himself contributed a sum of fifty rupees. His example led the superintendent of police, the joint magistrate and even Mahant Hayagrib Das to contribute to the fund.

After passing the entrance examination, Madhu went to Cuttack to study for his F.A. examinations. Radhanath was very sad that Madhu had to leave. However, it was decided that Madhu would pay Radhanath a visit at least once every month. A separate college in Cuttack had not been established at the time. However, two F.A. classes had been added to the government high school there. Madhu enrolled himself and made friends with a fellow student, Pyari Mohan Acharya. The two soon became good friends and whenever Madhu went to Puri, his friend accompanied him.

There were then only two teachers for the F.A. classes: Rajkishore Bandopadhyay, who taught English, and Harnath Bhattacharya, who taught philosophy. Madhu and Pyari Mohan were both very deeply influenced by the latter. Although Harnath had not formally joined the Brahmo order, he regularly attended the morning and evening services at the Brahmo temple every Sunday. Under his influence, Madhu and Pyari Mohan too, were drawn to the Brahmo religion.

When Boxwell, who was the joint magistrate of Puri, decided to take leave and go to England in February, Pandit Harihar resolved to go with him. Boxwell was close to Harihar, and Harihar wanted to see for himself a country that he had read about only in English books. But the matter was quite complicated. One risked excommunication if one crossed the sea and went abroad, and Harihar's decision to go to England gave rise to all manner of controversies.

The news unsettled Madhu, too. Although he had been influenced by Brahmoism to a small extent, in his beliefs and habits of thought, he remained an orthodox Hindu. During his last visit to Puri, Balaramji, who had in the meantime become Madhu's father-in-law, was always critical of Harihar. While all these kept agitating his mind, one night Madhu had a dream.

Pandit Harihar ran desperately along the main street of Puri, carrying a few flaming logs of wood. He flung the logs at anyone who came his way. Finally, Pandit Harihar threw himself into the Narendra tank and found eternal rest and peace there.

The dream haunted Madhu for days. He decided that he would discuss it with Radhanath when he met him in Puri next.

The lighthouse, February 1872

When news reached Orissa that the honourable governor general would visit Cuttack, no one could bring himself to believe it because till date no governor general had come to Orissa. However, when this information was officially released by Commissioner Ravenshaw, several meetings were held to decide how to welcome the governor general. In Cuttack, the leadership in this matter was taken by the Utkalollasini Sabha. This organization set about collecting subscriptions for meeting the expenses to organize a fitting reception for the visiting dignitary. In January, five hundred rupees were pledged. The plan of the reception was as follows: The governor general would travel from Puri to Cuttack in a horse-drawn coach and stay in the commissioner's bungalow in Lalbagh. Awnings would be put up from the bank of the river Katjuri to the commissioner's bungalow, floral gates would be erected, and water-filled pitchers placed on either side of the road.

A few days later, news arrived that the governor general would visit the Andaman Islands before coming to Orissa, and that he would sail from there to the lighthouse, not to Puri. The Utkalollasini Sabha held another meeting and took the following decisions: the area lying between the commissioner's bungalow in Lalbagh and the marquee of the durbar would be illuminated; there would be fireworks on the sands of the bed of the river Mahanadi. For illumination, only lamps with mica shades and using fat as fuel would be used. Crackers of the best possible quality were to be procured. In two places in town, floral gates would be erected and awnings put up, and musicians playing the shehnai would welcome His Excellency. Arrangements for all these were made, and a sum of 1250 rupees was collected. A letter which listed the following details of the governor general's programme arrived:

14 February: The Governor General will disembark at the Lighthouse, travel by steamer up to Kendupatna and stay the night there.

15 February: His Excellency will inspect the canals in Kendupatna for two hours and sail into river Birupa. He will sail down the High Level Canal for some distance and then sail back. At 4.30 p.m., His Excellency will arrive at Jobra, where he will be given a gun salute. His Excellency will be driven over bridge number one of the Taladanda canal to the Commissioner's bungalow in Lalbag past the Commissioner's cutcherry in Mangalabag, the jail at Buxi Bazaar, the Judge's office in Balu Bazaar. The Governor General and his retinue will stay in the bungalow at Lalbag. The lieutenant governor and his retinue will be put up in the Circuit House which is in the upper story of the two-storeyed office of the Commissioner in Mangalabag.

February 16: In the morning His Excellency will go to Naraj on horse-back, and return at 11 a.m. after seeing the sights in a boat. During midday, he will visit some government institutions. A durbar will be held on the same day at 4 p.m. All the covenanted civil and military officials will remain present here. The Commissioner will ceremonially introduce the Rajas of the garjats to the Governor General. The Rajas and zemindars from the mogulbandi areas will be introduced to His Excellency by the Collector.

February 17: In the morning, the Governor General will proceed to Bhubaneswar. He will cross river Katjuri to Purighat, and from there travel to Tankapani in a horse-drawn coach. A marquee will be put up midway between Bhubaneswar and Khandagiri. His Excellency will have lunch here. His Excellency will return to

Cuttack the same day after visiting the caves at Khandagiri. February 18: The Governor General will begin his return journey in the morning and reach the Lighthouse around one in the afternoon. From there he will sail to Calcutta.

The things the governor general would need during his stay in Orissa were brought over from Calcutta. A ship, which arrived on 28 January, carried equipment for pitching tents, three cannons, flags, flagposts etc. Ten horses were shipped to Cuttack on 2 February.

In order to make postal communication faster during the governor general's stay in Orissa, special arrangements were made along the embankment from Marshaghai to Cuttack from 1 February. Two more dak boats were engaged to carry mail from Marshaghai to the lighthouse. Three steamers sailed from Calcutta to the lighthouse and were kept in readiness there for journeys down the river and in the sea.

A list of people to be invited to the durbar was drawn up. It was decided that the rajas of bigger garjats would have to pay 200 rupees each and the lesser rajas 100 rupees as *bheti*, in return for which they would receive gifts of *khilat* or *shiropa*. The zamindars would not have to pay bheti, nor would they be given anything.

From 8 February the rajas from the garjats began arriving in Cuttack. By the 10th, the rajas of Pallahara, Talcher, Athamallik, Khandapara, Badamba, Dhenkanal, Narasinghpur, Madhupur had arrived. They had all brought with them their retinue consisting of paiks, drummers, horses and elephants. The size of the retinue was an indication of the prestige of the rajas, and Cuttack was soon packed with their men. The rajas' attendants wore colourful dresses—some even wore tiger and deer skins and looked bizarre. The whole of Cuttack city now looked like a huge fairground. Never before in the past had the city witnessed such a massive gathering of people.

The managing committee of the Utkalollasini Sabha convened a meeting to modify its earlier programme because the durbar was to come to an end before nightfall. The following decisions were taken: Floral gates would be put up at Mangalabag, Goukhana, Chaudhury Bazaar and in front of the cutcherry of the commissioner. Flagpoles would be set up in these places and *noubat* music would be played.

The fireworks would be let off on the sands of the bed of the river Katjuri. The road leading from Jobra to the bungalow at Lalbagh would be illuminated with lamps with mica shades. If the governor general reached Cuttack by nightfall, a procession with lamps would be organized.

Illumination would be put up on the cutcherry and at Lalbagh with the help of electric devices. The following budget estimate was prepared: Electric lights from Calcutta (two), 500 rupees; floral gates and glass-shaded lamps, 400 rupees; fireworks, 400 rupees.

The festival of Basant Panchami fell on 13 February. Lest all the flowers be used up for the worship of the goddess Saraswati, steps were taken to collect and store flowers needed for the floral arches to be erected in honour of the viceroy. Work on the construction of the arches began early in the morning. Gates were put up and were trimmed with flags. Long stakes were driven into the ground and tied with crackers for the fireworks. The police had the streets and lanes of Cuttack cleaned up, and removed the makeshift shops from the sides of the roads. Shopkeepers and residents of the town placed trunks of banana trees in front of their shops and houses as an auspicious sign and hung garlands. They also made arrangements for lighting lamps at night. Tents were pitched near the venue of the durbar and near the Jobra ghat to accommodate the officers. Distinguished people in the city busied themselves with composing letters of felicitation and getting them printed; pandits and poets occupied themselves with writing poems and slokas welcoming the visiting dignitary.

That evening, a meeting of rajas and maharajas was convened at the two-storeyed building of the Cuttack Printing Company under the aegis of Raja Divyasingh Dev. To mark the occasion, the building had been specially decorated with banana trunks, mango leaves and floral arches. By the time dusk fell, Dargha Bazaar was packed with elephants, horses, palanquins, drummers and sepoys.

Ravenshaw waited with his officers at the lighthouse pier to receive the viceroy. The exact time at which the viceroy's ship, which had sailed from the Andamans, would reach the Orissa coast on 14 February was not known. Since large vessels could not sail up to the shore, it had been arranged that as soon as the ship came into view, Ravenshaw would sail towards it on a steamer and welcome him. Ravenshaw, wearing a blue brocaded dress and a hat, waited. When the ship sailed into view, he set out in the steamer. Now someone noticed something odd about the approaching ship, and handed the binoculars to Ravenshaw. Peering through them, Ravenshaw saw that the flag on the ship, the Nemesis, was flying at half mast. After an hour or so, news arrived that the governor general had been assassinated in the Andamans.

The governor general, Lord Mayo, had arrived at Hope Town in the Andamans on the morning of 8 February. There he spent all day inspecting the jail and other places. At five, he went to Mount Harriet. By the time he descended the hill and came to the Hope Town jetty, it was 7 p.m. and quite dark. Torch-bearers stood waiting to light his way to the ship. Just as Mayo was climbing down the steps, a convict named Sher Ali leapt out of the bushes and fatally stabbed him with a knife. He was dead by the time he was carried into the ship. Mayo's dead body was sent to Calcutta by ship. Another ship was dispatched to Madras to inform the governor of the incident. The Nemesis sailed to the lighthouse. Another ship set sail for Sagar Island, from where a wire was sent to Calcutta.

The lieutenant governor, Campbell, was on his way to the lighthouse. When he received the news, he went back to Calcutta. News of the assassination of the viceroy had been cabled to Cuttack. Collector Macpherson went to the office of the jail and informed everyone of this. When the news reached the Cuttack Printing Company, the meeting of the rajas being held there was called off. But travelling to the lighthouse took time, and since there were no facilities for sending telegrams there, Ravenshaw could not be informed.

On 14 February, in the morning, the collector issued the following for the information of all concerned:

> Queen Victoria's representative was critically wounded by a convict in the Andamans on the 8th of this month. He succumbed to his wounds. Everyone is hereby directed to wear tokens of mourning. Until the arrival of Lord Napier, Hon'ble John Strachey Sahib has been appointed acting Governor General.

By another official order, the cutcherry and other offices remained closed for two days.

Balasore, December 1872

Beames had already spent three years and a half in Balasore. Three children were born to him during his stay there and his seventh child, a daughter, had been delivered only two months earlier. These days, however, Ellen frequently went down with attacks of malaria and other ailments, and rarely stirred out of her house. As for Beames, he remained busy as ever. The first volume of his book on comparative grammar had been published and had received much acclaim in England and Germany. It had also been prescribed as a textbook in a few universities.

Beames had grown to like Orissa and his bonds with the province had become a little more intimate. He had got to know Fakir Mohan when he was writing his book on grammar. An essay he had written on Dinakrishna's *Rasakallol* was published in the *Indian Antiquary*. He read the *Dipika* regularly and when he went to Cuttack to meet Ravenshaw, he met Bichitranand Das. Although he did not know Gourishankar on a personal level, he kept himself informed about the latter. After working for twelve years as an excise writer in the office of the collector, Cuttack, Gourishankar now worked as a translator in court. A magazine called *Bodhadayini O Balasore Sambad Bahika* had been published from Balasore a few years ago but it had folded after the publication of a few issues. With Beames's enthusiastic support, it now reappeared with the name *Balasore Sambad Bahika* and this was printed in the Utkal Press. Some space in the magazine was set apart for official matters. Beames explained the need for this:

NOTICE

With the kind approval of the Lieutenant Governor, Bengal, a magazine called *Balasore Sambad Bahika*, which carries official as well as non-official news, has been founded. We therefore inform the general public that they should treat everything published in the official part of the magazine as conveying the intentions and orders of the Government.

If any of the rules in existence is abolished, reasons for such a step will be given in that part of the magazine which publishes official matters. Any rule replacing an earlier one will be stated and the utility of this new rule will also be explained. The necessity for introducing new rules will be made clear.

Whenever the Government lays down a new law, whatever its outcome, it is always intended to promote the well-being of the subjects and to protect them from harm. The rules framed by the Government also contribute to their well-being. However, the Government is not omniscient. It is run by human beings, after all. The Government feels helpless if the subjects choose not to respond to its measures. It should also be added that it is not easy for the general public to examine laws thoroughly and grasp the intentions they embody. The subjects entertain wrong-headed ideas regarding laws brought into force by the Government. These ideas are the results of ignorance of the Government's intentions. It is hoped that the subjects will gradually shed their prejudices. If the real purposes of the rules are carefully set out, the subjects will doubtless realise how benevolent the government is. In fact, this magazine will function as a messenger between the officers and the general public.

Since I first arrived in the provinces, I have met people belonging to different stations in life, high and low, and have acquainted myself with many important issues. But, I am sure, there are still many of which I have no knowledge as yet. Although I am conversant with the Oriya language, I have not been able to use it proficiently. My inability to pronounce the words clearly has proved the chief obstacle. No matter how well Europeans might learn the language of this province, the natives find it difficult to make sense of their speech on account of their flawed pronunciation. Again, facilities for explaining laws in simple prose are lacking in this province. I, therefore, will publish my comments in the magazine in Oriya on a regular basis.

If anyone has any doubts regarding laws or rules, they should publish them in this or some other magazine. I will address them on the pages of this magazine.

John Beames   20 June 1872
Collector
Balasore District

During his tenure, Beames made friends with another person, Radhanath Ray. Beames knew his father, Sundar Narayan, who had served under him. After spending three years in Puri, Radhanath had been transferred to the Bankura Zilla School, where he worked for only a few months. He returned to Orissa in July and in October he joined as deputy inspector of schools, Balasore.

While in Puri, Radhanath had got married to Parasmani, the daughter of Chandramohan Aditya, a resident of Remuna. He received recognition as a poet when the first volume of his book of poems in Bangla, *Kabitabali*, had come out four years earlier. After Radhanath came back to Balasore, his old friend, zamindar Baikunthanath Dey published the second volume of *Kabitabali*. However, the remarks Dey made in the book's advertisement put Radhanath off. Dey said: 'The poet is a close friend of mine. For a native of Orissa, writing books in Bangla is a ridiculous undertaking and to present such a book to the wider reading public is no less ridiculous an effort. However, one tends to be partial to one's friend's writings, even if they are no good. I hope that the gentle readers from Bengal would read this book in order to encourage its author, reminding themselves that the book has been written by an Oriya.'

Although Baikunthanath treated Radhanath as a friend, the latter knew that deep inside, Baikunthanath nursed a grudge against him. When they were classmates at school, Radhanath had received a double promotion and had become a teacher at the same school. This had made Baikunthanath his student. Deeply embarrassed by such a development, Baikunthanath gave up his studies. However, Radhanath was convinced that his poems were not without worth and they needed no apology. He was also proud of the fact that while Fakir Mohan and others were busy writing textbooks and translating Bengali literature into Oriya, he alone had produced original works.

Soon after Radhanath's return to Balasore, Fakir Mohan went to Nilgiri as its dewan in September. Ravenshaw had given this job to Fakir Mohan on Beames's recommendation. Nilgiri was only eleven miles from Balasore but the four-mile-long road separating Nilgiri from Shergarh was so bad one could not travel along it even by palanquin or on horseback. After taking over as dewan, the first task Fakir Mohan set himself was getting this road repaired. After this task was accomplished, Fakir Mohan visited Balasore every Saturday, and he and Radhanath met each other at Gadgadia ghat as before.

During one such visit to Balasore, Beames said to Fakir Mohan, 'Gourishankar always criticizes me.' In support of this statement, he showed Fakir Mohan a news item published in the *Dipika* which he had underlined in red ink: 'If Beames sahib takes the trouble to find out about the character of his subordinates working at the district headquarters, he will discover how, unknown to him, they oppress the subjects. But who can alert the sahib to all this?'

Fakir Mohan tried to convince Beames that Gourishankar bore no one any ill will, and that, being an outspoken person, he praised goodness wherever he found it and attacked evil wherever he came across it. Beames handed him a sheaf of old issues of the *Dipika* and demanded, 'Babu, show me where anything good about me has been published.'

Fakir Mohan found himself in a tight spot. But he did not admit defeat, and, sitting cross-legged on the floor, he meticulously went through every issue of the *Dipika*. At last, he got up and triumphantly drew Beames's attention to the following report: 'We are glad to report that Collector Mr. Beames is touring villages, and granting assistance ranging from four annas to four rupees, depending on the circumstances, to poor people whose houses have been damaged by the cyclone.'

A smile flitted across Beames's face; he put a red mark on the news item and set aside the issue of the *Dipika* carrying it. However, Fakir Mohan thought it better not to tell Beames that people called him Bhima sahib. Whether this name referred to his ability or his rashness, Fakir Mohan himself was not sure.

Puri, May 1873

These days Ravenshaw took part in all meetings held in Cuttack, especially programmes organized by schools. However, his attempt at combining the Cuttack Society, the Utkalollasini Sabha and the Cuttack Debating Society into a single institution had come to nothing. To his dismay, another institution had come into existence in Cuttack: Pyari Mohan Acharya's, 'The Cuttack Young Men's Literary Association'. From time to time, Ravenshaw went and inspected schools. He studied the *Lilabati Sutra* in Oriya and occasionally asked students to answer tricky questions in arithmetic. He also gave a hundred rupees to the Cuttack High School every year for giving away prizes to students.

When Ravenshaw received an invitation from the Puri Zilla School to grace the occasion of the prize-giving ceremony there, he gave his consent to attend it, but he ordered that a single prize-giving ceremony be held for all schools in Puri. The date he fixed for this function was 25 May. Why he chose this date became clear later.

Ravenshaw also selected a topic for an essay competition for students: Superstition and Blind Belief. While suggesting such a topic, what he had in mind had nothing to do with idol-worship among Hindus or the opposition of missionaries to the worship of idols. A strange incident which was the talk of the town at the time had prompted him to choose the topic. He had also asked Bichitranand Das to find out more about the incident and tell him all about it.

Word had suddenly spread that the goddess Sarala at Jhankad had expressed her desire that people should send offerings in earthen pots to the goddess Bimalakshi in Puri. Once the rumour reached the people, they put rice, mangoes, vegetables and money in earthen pots and left them by the wayside. People travelling along the road would pick up these pots and carry them some distance and leave them by the road leading to Puri. Through this method of relay, these pots were conveyed towards Puri. No one dared steal anything from them for it was rumoured that, if anyone took anything from the pots or failed to carry them some distance towards Puri, he would be killed by *yoginis*.

Bichitranand took Gourishankar with him and tried to find out more about this extraordinary affair. They came across a number of pots lying under trees on the banks of the river Katjuri. Some people picked a few of these pots and carried them towards Puri. A calf broke one of the pots open and ate the rice and the mangoes it contained. Two days later, they revisited the spot to find out what had happened. They expected that all the pots would have been conveyed to Puri in the meantime. But when they arrived, they saw only broken pots lying there. On inquiry, they learnt that a few drunken fellows had smashed the pots and taken the money, beggars had taken away the rice and the mangoes, and whatever was left had been eaten up by cows. The news made Ravenshaw happy and he said, 'Publish this in the *Dipika*. Superstitious people have been taught a lesson.'

On 25 May, the prize-giving ceremony was held in the building of the Puri Zilla School. Commissioner Ravenshaw was the chief guest. At the meeting were present, besides Collector Armstrong and the deputy inspector of schools, zamindars, mahants and other distinguished people of Puri. One whose absence was noticed by all was the raja of Puri, Divyasingh Dev. His sending forty rupees through his muktar was considered even more deplorable than his absence from the function.

The function began on time. In addition to the money granted by the government for prize distribution, money raised through subscriptions from gentlemen of the town was distributed among the students. This was followed by recitation and acting by the students. Boys of the English School staged the murder scene from Shakespeare's *Julius Caesar*. Children from the Sanskrit School recited lines from the Sanskrit *Aja Bilapa*. Excerpts from Upendra Bhanja's poem 'Baidehisa Bilasa' were sung by students from the Oriya School. Prizes were given away to the participants.

At the commissioner's request, first, Deputy Collector Nandakishore Das, then the deputy inspector of schools, addressed the gathering. In his speech, the latter criticized the raja of Puri saying that his remaining absent from the function and sending money through his muktar was a pity; people would have appreciated it if the raja had come in person and given twenty rupees instead of forty, or even if he had given nothing at all. He regretted that the raja displayed no interest in matters relating to the welfare of the people. In his speech, Ravenshaw urged the students to get rid of superstitions and blind beliefs; he encouraged them to pursue higher studies and become judges and magistrates. About the raja he expressed the view that, rather than surround himself with good people, he had preferred the company of men of low birth and low morals, and sycophants. Ravenshaw added that no one became a maharaja simply by calling himself great, and by remaining shut up in his own palace. Earlier, the raja was a minor; now he was aged eighteen. And yet, it was a great pity that he allowed himself to be misled by sycophants.

Ravenshaw ended his speech by informing everyone present that 25 May was the birthday of Queen Victoria. He loudly said, 'Long live Queen Victoria', and everyone supported him by shouting 'Hip hip hurray'. It was dark by the time the meeting came to an end. On their way home, people did not discuss Queen Victoria's birthday, nor did the distribution of prizes interest them. They dwelt on how, misguided by his cronies and hangers-on, Divyasingh had gone completely astray.

Divyasingh, for his part, lay fast asleep, high on opium, by his newly-wed queen. He had married Niladri, the daughter of the raja of Rajpur. The wedding was celebrated with great pomp and ceremony, and for people in Puri, it had been a memorable event. The fireworks, the illumination, the orchestra, the sound of the conch shell, the feeding of the Vaishnavas, the dance of nautch girls, and above all, the sight of the collector enjoying the spectacle seated on an elephant—all these were still fresh in Divyasingh's memory.

seven

Puri, July 1873

In May, J.S. Armstrong took up post as collector, Puri. He had come to Orissa about ten years earlier. During the famine he had done a commendable job in Jajpur. He also spoke fluent Oriya. Although people looked upon him as an eccentric, he enjoyed the reputation of being a good officer. He went deep into the matter in hand, and closely analysed it before taking a decision. As soon as he took over as collector, it fell to him to manage the Car Festival.

Another problem had to be sorted out before the festival. This had to do with the temple drain. The drain into which the rice water from the temple kitchen emptied was in a bad condition, and created health hazards. A year ago, the raja had been fined one rupee for violating sanitation rules. In spite of this, nothing had been done to get the drain repaired. So Geddes, Armstrong's predecessor, had served a notice on the raja. This notice stated that, although the health officer had got a trough constructed outside the temple to receive the rice water, dirty rice water did not pour into it, since the drain inside the temple had not been repaired. The raja was given eighteen days to repair the drain, and he was directed to submit a daily report to the collector on the work done.

Since no steps were taken by the raja, in spite all this, a case was filed against him for having violated sanitation rules. Scared, the raja now hurried through some repairs and reported that since cooking was being done in the temple kitchen every day, it was not possible to get the drain repaired. He assured that he would finish the repairs during the Car Festival, when the kitchen would remain closed. Armstrong made a note that he would look into this matter after the Car Festival.

In order to make sure that everything during the Festival went off without a hitch, Armstrong called Seristadar Ramprasad Singh and made a list of the rituals to be performed at the time of the festival. He also took care to write down the rituals in the order according to which they were to be observed. He called a meeting of the officers, and prepared a list of things that needed special attention. These were: arranging ghats for the pilgrims, facilities for their accommodation, cleanliness of the town, supply of food on time, sanitation, medicine, and facilities for getting a darshan of the Lord. It was also decided which officer would take what responsibility. The raja was directed to make sure that such arrangements were made before the Snana Festival as that would make it possible to bring the idols to the bathing platform by nine the next day. Deputy collectors Kedarnath Dutt and Nandakishore Das were entrusted with the task of inspecting the arrangements made inside the temple premises and reporting to the collector.

On the day of the festival, Armstrong arrived on horseback at the Lion Gate at 9 a.m. sharp. He found that, in spite of so much care having been taken, the temple doors had remained closed, and thousands upon thousands of pilgrims waited outside for darshan. Armstrong rode around the temple and discovered that the other three entrances were closed, too. Directing the police to control the crowd, he went straight to the cutchery, initiated a case against the raja and sent him a summons.

The police went to the palace carrying the summons and caught the raja's muktar and brought him to the court. The raja was fined ten rupees for having mismanaged arrangements for the Car Festival. Armstrong further ordered that for every lapse from the next day in the worship of the deities and in the management of the festival, a fine of one hundred rupees a day would be levied on the raja.

On the day of the Snana Festival, the deities were conveyed to the bathing platform at 11 a.m.; worship was offered to them at 5 p.m., and the temple doors were thrown open. However, from the next day onwards, everything was done on time as per the schedule. On the day of the rejuvenation (*naba yauban*) of the deities, the temple doors were thrown open at 1 a.m. under the supervision of the officers, and by nine in the morning, around a hundred thousand pilgrims had a comfortable darshan of the deities. On the day of the Car Festival, the deities were mounted in their respective cars sharp at 6 p.m. Armstrong personally oversaw all the arrangements. The officials made sure that the cars left for Gundicha without delay. Three days later, at 2 a.m., the deities entered Gundicha temple.

In this way, the Car Festival was organized in a very disciplined manner. Although more than a hundred thousand pilgrims had assembled in Puri, only two police cases were recorded. The brother of the Kanungo of Khurda was sentenced to two months' imprisonment for fondling the breast of a woman. A thief was caught while snatching the earring of a female pilgrim from western India, and was sentenced to a month's imprisonment. The same discipline and efficiency marked the Bahuda Festival, which took place a few days later. For the first time in history, the deities completed their journey in twelve days and returned to their jewelled thrones inside the temple.

Everyone now lavished praise on Armstrong for they had never before seen such a well-managed Car Festival. Some said that the Car Festival had passed off smoothly because the *Malika* had predicted that *satya*, truth, would come to prevail in the 17th regnal year of the raja of the Puri. Others expressed different views regarding the dawning of Satya Yug, the era of truth. The subjects attributed it to the prevention of the excesses of the zamindars; the marwari traders thought such an era had arrived because income tax had been abolished. But a more sophisticated theory was advanced by a pandit in Puri: the mango is called satya fruit or the fruit of truth. Since there was a bumper crop of mangoes that year, one could very well say that truth had finally prevailed!

Balasore, October 1873

In July, Sundar Narayan died of cholera. The death not only left Radhanath deeply distressed, it also put him into a peculiar state of mind. As a child, extremely annoyed with his father, he had often wanted him to die. Now, it seemed to Radhanath as if he were in some way responsible for his father's death. The feeling of relief he experienced after the harsh regime of discipline imposed on him by his father came to an end also made him ashamed of himself.

All his friends came to condole his father's death. Fakir Mohan came from Nilgiri and delivered to him a sermon on the transience of life. Prince Baikunthanath and his father Shyamanand visited him now and then and inquired about how his family was doing. The collector's chaprasi gave him a letter of condolence from Beames. It said:

My dear Radhanath,

I am indeed deeply grieved at hearing the sad news of your father's death. He was an excellent official, very intelligent and active and always rendered me great assistance. I lost my own father many years ago but I have not yet ceased to grieve for him, and I can therefore deeply sympathize with you.

Come and see me as soon as you are able to appear in public. Although I cannot make any promise now about your uncles I need not assure you that I will do all in my power to assist you and your family at this deplorable juncture.

Your sincere friend,   31 July 1873
John Beames

After Sundar Narayan's death the burden of looking after the whole family came to rest on Radhanath's shoulders. He approached Beames for help, and Beames gave government jobs to his uncles, Balaram and Ramanath.

A few days later, when Fakir Mohan came to see him, Radhanath and he sat chatting at Gadgadia ghat late into the night. It was after returning home from there that Radhanath realized that he had been truly released from the stranglehold of Sundar Narayan's disciplining authority. While his father was alive, it would have been impossible for Radhanath to return home so late. On reaching home, Radhanath experienced difficulty in breathing. This was nothing new, for he suffered from asthma; but today he felt as if he were being punished for having disobeyed his father. His father had advised him to take opium for relief but he had given strict orders as to exactly how much opium he was to take. Today, since the pain had not subsided, or maybe because he purposely wanted to defy his dead father, Radhanath had helped himself to a second ball of opium. The pain eased and the intoxication induced by opium brought him a wonderful experience of bliss. But presently, Sundar Narayan appeared before him. Sundar Narayan said nothing but the look in his eyes, and the way in which he shook his head, indicated disapproval of Radhanath's conduct.

Radhanath now immersed himself in his work. As deputy inspector of schools, he had to visit all the schools in the district; he also had to work for the District Education Society. Around this time, Madhu Rao wrote to him repeatedly, asking him to find him a good job.

While reading for their F.A., both Madhu and Pyari Mohan had come under the influence of Professor Haranath Bhattacharya, had embraced Brahmoism and had discarded their sacred threads. This had strained Madhu's relations with his father. Bhagirathi Rao was an orthodox Hindu; he offered worship to god after watering five plants every morning, and would not touch even water before taking nirmalya. When Bhagirathi learnt of Madhu's desire to convert, he had written to him, and in the end had even gone to Cuttack to dissuade his son from taking such a step. But Madhu stuck to his decision.

Pyari Mohan's expulsion from school was another distressing experience for Madhu. Pyari Mohan had been thrown out of school for having written a piece attacking the British in a handwritten magazine which he himself published. But this had not upset Pyari Mohan in the least, and he now spent all his time trying to bring out a magazine. Pyari Mohan 's enthusiasm always inspired Madhu.

After passing the F.A. exams, Madhu, now aged eighteen, had to look for a job because he could not afford to study for his B.A. in Calcutta. He finally managed to get a job as the headmaster of the Middle English School at Jajpur. However, he was not happy with it because most of his students were older than he and were not at all willing to obey a young diminutive boy like him.

At this time, John Beames was president of the District Education Society in Balasore. Through his good offices, Radhanath found Madhu the position of a second teacher at the Balasore Zilla School. On receiving the appointment letter, Madhu travelled to Balasore, accompanied by his wife, his stepmother's sister, his younger brother Jagannath and his wife. They all first stayed with Radhanath. The next day, when Madhu went to school to report for duty, he was informed that he could not join. From Calcutta, Inspector Hopkins had written to say that Beames did not have the authority to appoint Madhu.

Luckily for Madhu, in August, Comissioner Ravenshaw went on three months' leave and in his place Beames was temporarily appointed commissioner. After taking up his post in Cuttack, Beames used his powers to rescind Hopkins's order and wired Radhanath: 'Madhu stays where he is.'

In this way, Madhu joined the Balasore Zilla School and the foundations of a deep and intimate friendship between Madhu and Radhanath were laid.

Dompara, December 1873

Dompara was one of the seventeen feudatory states which the commissioner of Cuttack had to administer in addition to the three districts. When the raja of Dompara, Purusottam Mansingh Bhramarbar Ray died issueless, his cousin's son Raghunath was declared his heir. As Raghunath was a minor, he and his younger brother were sent to the Wards Institute in Calcutta for their education. However, studying at the Institute brought about no improvement in Raghunath's nature and when he came back after finishing school he remained as worthless as ever.

While Raghunath was pursuing his studies in Calcutta, Dompara had been placed under the Court of Wards, and its affairs were managed by the dewan, Nidhi Pattanayak. He neglected the collection of land revenue and the subjects used a lot of land without paying any taxes. To keep them in good humour, Nidhi Pattanayak had given them title deeds and in the process had got a lot of land registered in the name of his kith and kin. When Raghunath returned from Calcutta and ascended the throne, Nidhi Pattanayak's powers got severely curtailed. The raja also decided to get the land surveyed and to levy new taxes.

This went against the interests of Nidhi Pattanayak and the subjects, because this would mean more taxes and would also expose the dewan's illegal deeds. So the subjects rose in rebellion against the proposed survey and the dewan, Nidhi Pattanayak, provided the rebels leadership.

The durbar of the rebels issued a diktat that no one would pay taxes to the raja; no one would go to his palace; no one would take up employment under him, and the washermen and the barbers would not provide any services to him. The rebels looted the houses of peace loving subjects who did not join the uprising and mercilessly beat them up. In fear, palace servants left the palace. The laundry of the palace residents had to be sent to Cuttack for washing. Fearing for his life, Raja Raghunath fled to Cuttack.

When Ravenshaw came back in November, Beames reverted to the position of collector. However, he did not go back to Balasore, for he was posted as collector in Cuttack. Around this time, many ryots came to Cuttack and expressed their grievances to him and pleaded that he intervene in the matter. Raja Raghunath also called upon Beames and requested him to save him from the dewan. Although the raja could have dismissed the dewan with just a stroke of his pen, such a step was beyond him for he was paralysed by his fear of Nidhi Pattanayak.

As collector, Beames decided to go first on a vist to Dompara. There he set up camp in a grove by the river. The dewan and his clerks came to meet him, bringing the official records with them. The raja, looking emaciated and pitiable, clad in a moth-eaten royal robe, and followed by a retinue of paiks and drummers in rags, also arrived in a battered palanquin. For days on end, Beames carried on discussions with both the parties.

The situation was complicated by the fact that the raja was stupid and the dewan an extremely cunning man. The problem could have been quickly sorted out if the dewan had been dismissed and someone from Cuttack had been appointed in his place. But all the records were in Dewan Nidhi Pattanayak's possession, and he was the only person who knew everything about the administration of Dompara. Besides, because he had got a lot of land registered in the names of his relatives and others, he enjoyed the support of a large number of subjects. Under the circumstances, getting rid of Nidhi Pattanayak was no easy matter.

In the end, Beames called the subjects and in their presence, rescinded all the orders issued by the dewan. The land which had illegally passed into the hands of the subjects was taken back from them. Some simple rules for governing the kingdom were framed and these were made known to everyone. Nidhi Pattanayak gave a written undertaking to the effect that he would abide by these rules. Beames warned him that if he failed to do so, he would be thrown in jail.

This done, Beames paid a visit to the raja before leaving Dompara. What passed for his palace was but a huge ruined house. Parts of it had collapsed; bricks had fallen from many of the walls; the door of the main entrance had broken down and hung limply. The area surrounding the palace was overgrown with wild bushes. In the garden near the palace, now full of thorn bushes and creepers, the raja paced restlessly, like a mad man. In a fit of pique, he would not talk to Beames for Beames had not driven out the wicked dewan. As Beames walked up and down the narrow garden path by the raja's side, he tried hard to paufy him. But the raja remained adamant. Whatever Beames said, Raghunath's response was the same: throw the dewan out. When at last Beames took leave, the raja was busy mumbling to himself.

After spending a week in Dompara, and establishing a tenuous peace between the raja and his subjects, Beames returned to Cuttack on 11 December.

Puri, February 1874

Harihar had finished all preparations for visiting England with Boxwell. He had even got a suit made in Calcutta and bought a new pair of shoes. But, in the end, the planned trip had to be abandoned, because he had to raise funds for the Sanskrit School. In the middle of 1872, Harihar set out for important places in India to meet the rajas and get donations from them.

For a year there was no news of Harihar. Suddenly, in June 1873, the *Amrita Bazaar Patrika* in Calcutta carried a small news item about him. People in Orissa were pleased when they read its Oriya translation in the 1 July issue of the *Utkal Putra*, a magazine which had been recently started by Pyari Mohan Acharya. The item said: 'Pandit Harihar Das is an accomplished Sanskrit scholar. But what is amazing about him is that, although he knows little English, he has a very good command over Greek, and can translate Homer's poems into simple Sanskrit.'

Nothing was heard of him after this. A few days later, Sanskrit books worth seven hundred rupees sent by him reached the school. Then one day in December, he landed at a friend's house in Cuttack, ill and penniless, and fell down unconscious. People in Cuttack started collecting donations for his treatment. Gourishankar took the lead in this matter and the *Dipika* published appeals to the general public for donations. Pyari Mohan wrote that, after Michael Madhusudan's death, the people of Cuttack had raised two hundred rupees and had sent it to his children; he urged the people of Cuttack to donate for Harihar with the same generosity.

Kabiraj Fakir Tripathy in Cuttack diagnosed that Harihar was ill with hysteria and prescribed *brihat chhaga ghrita* as a remedy. A hundred rupees were needed for preparing this medicine but from Cuttack, a sum of only fourteen rupees could be collected. Since Harihar's condition did not show any improvement, his relatives shifted him to Puri.

Harihar was taken to his house in Khundheibent lane where he underwent treatment. Here he lost his power of speech completely and showed all the symptoms associated with hysteria. It was rumoured that the pandits of Puri had laid a curse on Harihar for his atheism, and his ailment was a result of this. Around February, Harihar's condition deteriorated further. His madness became so uncontrollable that his relatives sometimes had to keep him tied up.

One day, Harihar's relatives went about their business, shutting him up in a room and locking its door from the outside. Harihar brought out the dress he had got made for his trip to England and put on the suit and the shoes. He wore the hat and paced the room. Suddenly, his dress brushed against the lamp burning inside the room and caught fire. Harihar recovered his power of speech and let out a heart-rending cry. When the door was opened, it was found that his whole body and the dress had caught fire. Bits of his dress, which clung to his body, had to be cut out, and he was laid on a bed made of banana leaves. He lay for four days in this state.

Harihar was able to talk a little and to recognize faces. At his request, all his books were brought over and placed around him. His face lit up when someone held a book or his papers before his eyes. These papers included a letter from Beames to Harihar and a photograph of Beames's mother on which Beames had written in Sanskrit: *mama matri chitra pratima*, a photograph of my mother.

Harihar breathed his last on 9 February, aged only thirty-two. A few moments before he died, he recited a sloka: 'I never worshipped god properly to secure release from the coils of earthly life; I also did not earn the merit which opens the doors to heaven; a woman's pointed breasts and heavy thighs I have never embraced even in my dreams; I was born only to devastate the forest of my mother's youth like an axe.'

This was how, in his last words, Harihar remembered, imagined and summed up his life.

Madhu Rao received news of Harihar's death in Balasore a few days later. He was reminded of the dream he had seen long ago and a nameless dread made him shudder.

Puri, August 1875

After the incident relating to the temple drain, Collector Armstrong wrote Ravenshaw a letter regarding a particularly bothersome problem. At the time, the overseer in Puri happened to be Muslim and so it was impossible for him to get inside the temple and inspect anything. Armstrong had to send a senior official like the deputy collector into the temple compound to find out if the drain had been repaired properly. Armstrong wrote to Ravenshaw requesting him to appoint a Hindu overseer in Puri.

Ravenshaw did nothing about the matter. But during the Car Festival that year an incident took place which compelled everyone to give this matter serious thought. The door of the temple was opened while the deities were at Gundicha temple, and it was found that a huge slab of stone had fallen from the ceiling and was lying in front of the jewelled throne in the sanctum sanctorum. Fortunately, on account of the Car Festival, the temple was empty; at any other time many lives would have been lost. There was now the possibility that many more stone slabs might fall and the crown of the temple might crumble.

Everyone promptly set to work. From Cuttack came assistant engineer Babu Purna Chandra Sarkar to investigate the matter. He went inside the temple and found that four stone slabs of the ceiling lay broken on the ground. These had dropped from a height of about forty feet. The temple must have been slightly damaged when lightning had struck it two years ago. Plants grew in the gaps between the stone slabs and the iron beams supporting the roof had grown weaker. All these factors together were responsible for the unfortunate incident.

Climbing on to the ceiling of the temple was not easy because the flight of stone steps which led there was forty feet above the ground. So a scaffolding had to be constructed in order to enable people to get there. The place was so dark the workers had to carry torches. No one had set foot in this part of the temple ever before. On the steps, and below the ceiling, lay heaped centuries-old lamp soot and bat droppings. Cartloads of rubbish were collected and thrown down.

Babu Purna Chandra Sarkar submitted a report on how the temple could be repaired, and recommended that the deities be removed from their sanctum until the repair work was over, and that no one be allowed inside the premises of the temple during this period. In the course of his investigation, he inspected other temples, buildings and monuments inside the main temple, and reported that *Koili Baikuntha* was in a precarious and dangerous state.

This report was forwarded to the executive engineer, Bond sahib. Since it was not possible for him to enter the temple, he consulted the assistant engineer and then predicted that the Puri temple would meet the same fate which had overtaken the temple at Konark.

While the sahibs kept worrying about the repair and conservation of the temple, the minds of the pandits of Puri were exercised by other problems. The issue at stake for them was: would it be proper to undertake a renovation of the temple, and where would the deities be installed during the renovation work? To find answers to these questions a meeting was organized inside the temple. Two opposite views emerged: the raja of Puri, Mahant Narayan Das and Pandit Gopinath Mishra were of the view that the deities could be shifted to the Jagamohan hall near the sanctum sanctorum. Pandit Markandeya Mohapatra, some other mahants, and the temple servitors opined that the deities should continue to remain seated on their thrones while the renovation work went on; all that was needed was a protective roof which would keep the deities safe during the repairs. In advancing this proposal, the servitors were actuated by selfish motives, for they were apprehensive that if the deities were moved, pilgrims might stop coming to Puri. This would deprive the servitors of their income. They argued that prasad could not be offered to the deities in any place other than on the jewelled throne. To counter this, Mahant Narayan Das cited a precedent from the temple chronicle, *Madala Panji*. In the past, when the temple was being repaired, the deities had been placed under a tree; when prasad was not offered to the deities there by the servitors, the deities had made a dumb person recite a sloka and then made him mute once more and this miracle had made the servitors change their views at the time.

In spite of a lot of discussion the temple servitors kept insisting that the deities must not be removed from their thrones. The raja of Puri opposed them. When the servitors vehemently argued with him, the raja said that unless they obtained permission from the government, they would not be allowed to keep the deities on the throne. The servitors petitioned Collector Armstrong and spread the word that Mahant Narayan Das was a traitor to the religion. The raja of Puri, too, sent a petition to the collector through his muktar.

After going through both the petitions, Armstrong issued an order to the effect that the raja's power in the temple was absolute. The servitors must abide by whatever decisions the raja would take regarding renovation of the temple and the shifting of the deities. They would lose their jobs if they disobeyed the raja.

Now the deities, on returning from Gundicha temple, were placed in the Jagamohan hall. The servitors did not turn up for a couple of days. But they came and performed their duties when they found that their work had been given to others, and realized that they might lose their jobs.

However, this arrangement gave rise to another problem. The prasad which was now offered to the deities at their new residence was accepted by no one except beggars and the raja's servants. A pamphlet written by Pandit Tarakant Vidyasagar of Puri assuring everyone that the prasad was, indeed, holy according to the scriptures, was circulated. But Oriya pandits opposed this view since it was expressed by a Bengali pandit. The few Brahmins who had taken this prasad were ostracised by the pandits of the sixteen orthodox *sasan* villages.

When the raja of Puri was urged to finish the repairs quickly, he complained about lack of funds and demanded that he be given financial assistance from Koili Baikuntha and the Lodging House Fund.

The news of the temple collapsing distressed people all over Orissa. In villages pujas and recitation of Puranas were held. Taking advantage of this mood, many cheats and charlatans started collecting money and ghee from people saying that they would perform a yajna for Lord Jagannath. The repair work of the temple began in the midst of all this controversy and confusion.

Nilgiri, September 1875

After he came to Nilgiri, Fakir Mohan's first few days were spent happily. He was on very good terms with the raja. He was able to come to Balasore once every week, where, apart from seeing to his personal affairs, he could discuss literature with Radhanath and look after the P.M. Senapati and Co. Press. But his happiness was short-lived. He soon fell out with the raja because the raja wanted to make the son of a concubine his heir, and Fakir Mohan supported the claim of the raja's brother's son to the throne.

Two years after Fakir Mohan took over as dewan, he was faced with a serious problem: an uprising by the stone-cutters of Nilgiri. The stone-cutters made plates, tumblers and bowls from granite extracted from two quarries in the Bishnupur hill. There was a demand for these products in Calcutta markets and the stone-cutters made good money by selling their wares to businessmen from Kharagpur. They cut granite with chisels and the raja had levied on them a tax of six and a half rupees per chisel. A tax-collector, *mahaldar*, was responsible for collecting taxes from the stone-cutters. The job of tax collector was auctioned every year and it went to the highest bidder.

During Fakir Mohan's first year as dewan, a man called Kahnei Mishra had bid for the job, offering four thousand rupees. The previous year, the job had gone to someone who had offered two thousand and five hundred rupees. When Mishra was asked how he would pay so much money without increasing taxes on the stone-cutters, he said that there were many who quarried granite without paying any taxes; he would levy taxes on them. The job went to Kahnei Mishra for his bid was the highest.

Kahnei Mishra was right. In the past, one cutter would pay the tax and collect a permit. On the strength of this permit, his brothers and sons went and extracted granite. Going strictly according to the rules, all of them should have paid taxes but tax collectors did not take a hard line in this matter. But once Kahnei Mishra was appointed tax collector, he allowed only the *patta*-holders into the quarry and turned others out. When they were suddenly deprived of a privilege they had been enjoying for generations, the stone-cutters felt deeply aggrieved. They united and stopped cutting stone.

When Kahnei Mishra forced the stonecutters to pay taxes and ill treated them, they petitioned the raja against him. Had

Fakir Mohan dismissed Kahnei Mishra after this, the problem would never have arisen. But he took no such step. He was of the view that removing Kahnei Mishra would mean non-collection of taxes and loss of prestige for the administration. With this in mind, he rejected the stone-cutters' petition.

The stone-cutters assembled before the cutcherry and raised the banner of rebellion. They enjoyed clandestine support from Brahmins in the kingdom and a few palace officials. They were extremely angry with Fakir Mohan because he had refused to dismiss Kahnei Mishra. When the situation get out of hand, the superintendent of police, Balasore, went there to control it. The assistant superintendent of the garjats, Harekrushna Das, too, came to Nilgiri.

The stonecutters raised subscriptions from among themselves and sent twenty of their men to Ravenshaw, who was superintendent of the garjats, to appeal to him. Ravenshaw listened to their grievances, and set out for Nilgiri, because the presence of Harekrushna Das there had not improved matters.

Ravenshaw's investigations revealed that the increase in taxes was the chief cause of the uprising. Since Kahnei Mishra had oppressed the stone-cutters, Ravenshaw dismissed him. This meant the loss of a year's taxes, but the stone-cutters were very happy. Some stone-cutters however, also received punishment for having organized the uprising. In the end, Ravenshaw held Fakir Mohan responsible for the situation and took him to task.

After Ravenshaw left Nilgiri, the raja's attitude towards Fakir Mohan changed. He blamed Fakir Mohan for the loss of a whole year's revenue. Under the circumstances, continuing as dewan in Nilgiri was no longer possible for Fakir Mohan. So, in the end, as any self-respecting man would have done in his place, he tendered his resignation and returned to Balasore after two years and a half, penniless, jobless and humiliated.

Cuttack, August 1876

Suddenly one day, a rumour sprang up, out of nowhere, that a disease called *surukumari* was spreading from Madras by way of Ganjam towards Cuttack. When the disease struck, the person would first feel a pain in his toe, which would then ascend to his waist; the patient would turn black and die shortly afterwards. The disease struck Berhampur in July and it was rumoured that the government was distributing medicine in marketplaces and highways with the help of police constables. On 15 July, details about the remedy were published in the *Utkal Dipika* in its letters to the editor column.

> Get a black goat (it should be completely black and have no other colour on its coat) and feed it all kinds of leaves and twigs. Don't let it drink water or chew its cud before killing it. Cut its belly open and tear out its intestines and take out the food in it with your own hands. Make sure flies do not sit on the food while you pull it out. Dry it and grind it. The stuff should be ground with a stone pestle, and stored in small packets. As soon as the symptoms show, take one packet of this medicine mixed with a small quantity of water. This will cure you.
>
> If one takes ten drops of *navasagar* solution mixed with three ounces of water, one will also get cured.
>
> It may be mentioned here that if the disease spreads up to the waist, this medicine will have no effect. The patient will die in three hours after the onset of the illness.

People promptly set about preparing the medicine. Surukumari turned out to be less a disease than a terrible calamity for goats. Hundreds of goats were butchered, and medicine prepared and sold, and everyone stored it against an emergency. Even vegetarian Vaishnavas kept this medicine although it had been made with stuff pulled out of goats' entrails. The price of goats increased four- to five-fold.

News of the disease reaching Puri and Khurda arrived in August. A few days later, word spread that the disease had struck Cuttack. Surukumari now formed the only topic of discussion there. It was said that a few employees of the court had suffered from this disease and that one person had died of it.

A new cure for surukumari also became widely popular: branding the toe with a hot iron. Now, people started getting their toes branded. The British doctors did their best to convince people that no such disease existed, but people paid no attention to them and went on procuring the medicine. Once people got so panic-stricken that long queues waited until 3 a.m. at the place where the medicine was being sold.

Cuttack was a veritable factory of rumours. From time to time, fantastic rumours would get manufactured here. After the incident of people sending earthen pots to the temple of the goddess Bimalakshi, a rumour spread that the monkey-god Hanuman would pay a nocturnal visit to the town. He would enter a house if its forecourt had not been decorated with chita designs, and destroy all its residents. When they heard this, residents of Cuttack got the space in front of their houses decorated with chita. However, shortly afterwards, the goddess Cuttack Chandi said through a *kalisi* that Lord Hanuman would kill the residents of a house if he found its forecourt decorated with chita. On hearing this, everyone set about erasing the chita from the forecourts of the houses.

On another occasion, someone advised people in Cuttack to remove husking paddles from their houses or else, at night, they would hear the sound of someone pounding rice. If one made the mistake of asking, 'Who is there?' he would instantly go down with an attack of cholera and die. Scared, people put their husking paddles out at night.

Surukumari caused great terror among the natives and much amusement among the British in Cuttack for about a month. When it finally left Cuttack and moved in the direction of Balasore, human beings as well as goats heaved a deep sigh of relief.

Balasore, September 1876

Everyone in the office of the deputy inspector of schools in Balasore was busy at work. However, the chair of the deputy inspector lay empty. This was so because Radhanath hated sitting on a chair and preferred to sit on the floor. At the moment, he was seated in an adjacent room on a mat, adopting *virasan*, his favourite posture. He had taken off his shirt on account of the heat. His snuff box and opium pouch lay beside him. While taking a pinch from these from time to time he pondered over what the past year had been like.

It had been a very good year, on the whole. Six years after marriage, his wife Parasmani had given birth to their first child. For the last two years, Radhanath had been writing down the name of Lord Madhusudan a thousand times every morning before beginning the day's work. Besides, Madhu Rao, who had been transferred to Cuttack High School in February, was Radhanath's daily companion. For both these reasons Radhanath had decided to call his newborn son Madhusudan. However, Radhanath's cousin, Chandranath Ray, chose the name Sashibhusan for the newborn. This was the name by which the child came to be known later; but for Radhanath it was Madhu, the name by which he always called his son.

The presence of Madhu Rao in Balasore created opportunities for literary discussions. Radhanath and Madhu Rao together wrote a textbook *Pratham Siksha* (First Lessons), and published nine thousand copies in the name of Baikunthanath Dey. The book sold out in three months and Radhanath earned a fair amount of money from this venture. However, what brought Radhanath special pleasure was a collection of poems titled

Kabitabali. This had been written together with Madhu Rao and had been published by Baikunthanath Dey and had been dedicated to John Beames. Whatever people might say of this book, Radhanath had no doubt at all that these poems were the first modern poems in Oriya.

While Radhanath was thus immersed in pleasant thoughts, a few gentlemen came to meet him with a strange request. They wanted him to close all schools in Balasore as the disease surukumari had struck the town.

As far as rumours were concerned, Balasore did not lag behind Cuttack. For some years now, in obedience to a certain goddess, old winnowing fans, brooms, bamboo baskets, fish baskets, had been arriving in Dighirahania from Mayurbhanj. These were meant for the goddess Bimalakshi and kept in her temple. In another incident, a man from Pachudia village came running breathlessly to Makalpursahi village and collected seven handfuls of rice from seven families. He told the villagers that a bull was approaching from the south; a banyan tree grew on its back on which was seated Lord Hanuman. He said that everyone in the village should collect seven handfuls of rice from houses in another village, houses from which no one should have have received alms before them. They should offer this rice to the bull when it arrived in front of their houses. If they failed to do so, all the members of their family would perish. On being informed of this, people now ran from one village to the other to collect alms.

However, these were nothing compared to the danger posed by surukumari which struck Balasore. Its first prey was a Muslim woman. She suddenly collapsed, crying, 'Oh my leg is gone, my leg is gone'. Fortunately for her, a local *vaidya* happened to be around at this time. He heated a sickle and branded the woman's toe twice, and she recovered instantly. After this incident, the disease spread rapidly all over the town, and people panicked.

People from the villages stopped coming to the town. Wherever one went—the road, the market-place, the bathing ghat—one found the same thing worrying everyone: surukumari.

Baikunthanath Dey, Madan Mohan Das, Harekrushna Das and others made arrangements for preparing the medicine from slaughtered goats and for getting it distributed. But they could not meet with the swelling demand and now the medicine was being prepared in almost every lane. A goat which normally sold at eight or ten annas now fetched one rupee, even one rupee and a half. Herds of black goats were driven from the mofussils for sale in Balasore.

The *Balasore Sambad Bahika* carried a long piece on the symptoms of the disease and its treatment:

The pain spreads from the toes of both legs and rises upward like the effect of poison. It takes three hours to reach the waist. If the patient receives treatment within two hours he survives. But if the pain ascends to the waist he will certainly die.

Treatment

1. The moment the toe burns with pain, tie it with a piece of string or cloth (cloth is preferable, for it is softer than string, and will cause less pain). Heat a sickle and brand the toe. If the pain does not subside, get all the ten toes branded.
2. Rub the body thoroughly from the feet up to the waist with the juice of the ghrutakumari plant and lemon.
3. Make the patient inhale ammonia. Alternatively, mix ten drops of the same with a little water and give it to the patient to drink.
4. Pour ammonia and dry quicklime in equal measures into a bottle and pour a little water into it and shake the contents. Soon the quicklime will settle at the bottom of the bottle leaving a layer of clear water above it. Drain this water into another bottle. Ten drops of this mixed with plain water should be administered to the patient.

J.P. DAS

5. Get a black she-goat (be sure it is not pregnant) and make it browse on leaves and grass the whole day. Make sure it does not stay in one place, drink water, lie down, or chew cud. Get it slaughtered in the afternoon. Remove the undigested food material from its belly and leave it to dry. Make sure flies do not settle on the stuff while it is being dried. Then grind it, divide it into small quantities and store it in small packets. As soon as the symptoms show, mix the contents of one packet with plain water and administer it to the patient. Give another dose after half an hour. The patient will certainly get well after taking three packets.

Readers, you should never take this disease lightly. As soon as you contract this, adopt one of the five modes of treatment mentioned above according to your convenience.

Since the Bengalis did not believe in the existence of the disease, the *Sambad Bahika* wrote: 'If only one Bengali ways afflicted with surukumari and died, they would recognize the existence of the disease.' On this issue, Radhanath took the side of the Bengalis and, for this reason, he rejected the application seeking closure of the schools.

Fortunately for Balasore, in a few days surukumari left for Calcutta.

Puri, September 1876

By May, the repair work of the Puri temple was finished, and the deities were reinstalled on their thrones. The Brahmins from the sixteen sasans now accepted the prasad offered to the deities. Those Brahmins who had been excommunicated for having taken prasad offered to the deities during their residence away from their thrones were accepted back into their caste after performing suitable rites of expiation and chanting the Gayatri mantra. While this problem was somehow resolved, another arose because of the actions of the raja of Puri.

The rajas of garjats in Orissa paid their respects to the raja of Puri whenever they visited the town. This had convinced Divyasingh that he was above them all, and that the superiority of the raja of Puri should be recognized everywhere. When the lieutenant governor had held the durbar in Cuttack in 1874, the raja of Puri had refused to attend it for he had not been accorded the first place among the rajas of Orissa by the government. When the Prince of Wales held a durbar in Calcutta in 1876, the same story was repeated. Now Pandit Tarakant Vidyasagar was the raja's chief adviser. He had been the *sadar amin* of Cuttack and had gone back to Calcutta after his retirement. He had returned to Puri with a view to spending the last part of his life there, and became a courtier of the raja.

The raja of Puri took Tarakant with him to the durbar in Calcutta. Word spread that the raja was going to present a sword worth a hundred thousand rupees and a betel box worth twenty-five thousand rupees to the prince. However, this had no basis in fact. On Tarakant's advice, the raja, on reaching Calcutta, went to his residence in a palanquin while a band played. This made him cut a ridiculous figure in the eyes of the people of Calcutta. In the hierarchical order of rajas attending the durbar, the raja of Puri had been assigned the thirty-first place. Taking offence at this, the raja refused to take part in the durbar and came back to Orissa, where he was criticized for this behavior. People blamed Tarakant for giving him the wrong advice. But the raja chose to reward the sycophantic Tarakant with the post of dewan.

The affairs of the temple got into an even deeper mess under the raja's supervision. Although the job of temple servitors was held on a hereditary basis, the raja sometimes appointed outsiders if they gave him a bribe. This always led to a conflict between the hereditary servitors and the illegally appointed ones. In a court case relating to this issue, the judge pronounced the verdict that,

J.P. DAS

although the raja of Puri enjoyed unrestricted powers of appointing temple servitors, he was bound by existing conventions to give the job to the eldest son of a servitor family. In spite of this verdict, the raja of Puri did not recognize the hereditary principle of appointing servitors and went on issuing appointment orders favouring outsiders. One such appointment had created much trouble a year earlier.

The illicit relationship of a servitor called Bhobani Kar with his stepmother was common knowledge in Puri. For this, he had been ostracised by his fellow servitors. Later, he was sentenced to two years' rigorous imprisonment for molesting a widow inside the temple premises. After Bhobani had served out the sentence, the raja made him a temple servitor. The other servitors objected to this appointment, but the raja paid them no heed.

The servitors decided to prevent Bhobani Kar from doing his job. Getting wind of this plan, the raja sent his hand-picked bodyguards, Paban Santra and Padma Charan Pattanayak, to the temple. The two musclemen went there accompanied by a hundred and fifty wrestlers. They entered the temple, beat up the hereditary servitors, and saw to it that Bhobani Kar was able to do his job unhindered.

When such instances of abuse of power became quite frequent, the servitors and the Hindus of Puri sent a petition to Ravenshaw in August. It drew Ravenshaw's attention to the following:

> In the past, everyone was allowed to go inside the temple and to watch different temple rituals such as the *prabhat mangal arati* and the *sandhya dhupa*. But the Raja has decreed that everyone now has to pay four annas for this privilege. Out of this amount, two will go to his employees, and the rest will go to the temple fund.
>
> Although the job of temple servitors is a hereditary one, the Raja has given appointment to outsiders through royal decrees in return for bribes amounting hundreds of rupees. This has

resulted in a lot of tension, and disruption of temple rituals. The henchmen of the Raja are manhandling hereditary servitors. He sends one hundred and fifty wrestlers from local gymnasiums into the temple every day to terrorize them.

The Raja has also reduced the amount of *khei* or share of offering, to which the servitors were entitled, by half. This has affected them badly. The offerings made to the deities are now prepared with ingredients of inferior quality. Instead of ghee made from cow's milk, that made from the milk of goats, sheep and buffaloes is being used. This spreads diseases.

No accounts are maintained of the money which the pilgrims give while making offerings to the deities, and the gifts of *pindika* money they leave before the thrones of the deities, and the Raja misappropriates these. The rich have bribed the Raja heavily to get permission to carry torches into the temple and to perform the *chamar* service to the deities.

The Raja has been reduced to a puppet in the hands of his wicked, low-born, stupid and rakish servants, who use him as an instrument of tyranny. The administration has collapsed completely and reached rock bottom.

In view of all this, the servitors urged the government to consider if it should leave the management in the raja's hands or make alternative arrangements.

Commissioner Ravenshaw was aware of the mismanagement of the affairs of the temple. He also knew how devious the servitors were. He, therefore, did not wish to curtail the powers of the raja. In response to the petition, he issued an order to the effect that the government would fully support the raja in his attempt to discipline the servitors.

Dompara, December 1876

After Beames left Dompara in December 1873, the relations between the raja and his subjects remained normal for a few days only. The moment the question of revenue collection came up, the subjects rose against him once more at Nidhi Pattanayak's instigation. Pattanayak went to Cuttack and convinced the sahibs that the raja had gone mad and was tyrannizing his subjects and that this had led to the uprising.

In fact, Raja Raghunath did behave like a mad man. He did not trust his mother, his brother, the servants, even his wife, for he believed that they all wanted to kill him. For fear that someone might poison his food, he lived for years on puffed rice and milk. He did not mix with anyone, lived all by himself, and never met anyone unless he had to. He would sit alone in an isolated room, talk to himself and go on writing in the air with his index finger.

After the uprising broke out, Raghunath left Dompara and spent time in Cuttack and Calcutta. To meet his expenses there, he borrowed money from moneylenders in Cuttack, signing registered deeds. Since he did not send any money to the palace, his mother and other members of his family starved, and, in the end, they sent a petition to the magistrate demanding that maintenance expenses be paid to them.

All this led Beames to believe that the raja had indeed lost his mind. Whenever he sent for the raja, the latter would not come, for Raghunath feared that the sahib wanted to throw him into jail. Had Beames visited Dompara again, the problem might have been sorted out but, under the pressure of work, he was unable to find time.

At this time, Fakir Mohan was staying in Cuttack. After leaving Nilgiri, he had spent a long while in Balasore without being able to find another job. At last he decided to go to Cuttack in the hope that his well-wisher and saviour Beames might come to his rescue. He came and stayed at the house rented by his son-in-law Raghunath Choudhury who was then studying for his F.A.degree. Although he had managed to meet Beames a number of times, Beames had not been able to find any job for him. Having nothing to do, Fakir Mohan spent his mornings horse-riding and spent the evenings at Kalipad Bandopadhyay's house, drinking and playing cards.

Finally, Beames offered Fakir Mohan the job of auditor for zamindaris under the Court of Wards. The monthly salary was seventy rupees. Fakir Mohan told Beames that he would gladly accept the job. However, on consulting his friends, he realized that it would be difficult for him to support himself on this salary. In the Cuttack district there were several zamindaris under the Court of Wards and his job was to visit these and inspect their accounts. For this job, therefore, he would need at least eight palanquin-bearers and one cook—all of which would cost him a packet. When Fakir Mohan presented his problem to Beames, he wrote to the board recommending that the salary be raised to ninety-five rupees.

When no reply from the board arrived, Fakir Mohan again called on Beames. Beames was a little annoyed and said, 'Of course, how long can you keep waiting for a reply from the board?' Fakir Mohan said, 'Huzur, I find sitting idle painful.' To this Beames responded by saying, 'You are right. An idle mind is the devil's workshop'. Then, he thought for a while and said, 'I want to appoint you dewan in Dompara. Would you like to go there?' What a question! Fakir Mohan lost no time in replying. 'Huzur, I'll go wherever you send me.' It was decided that Fakir Mohan would receive three months' salary by way of advance and go to Dompara as dewan.

Before leaving Cuttack for Dompara, Fakir Mohan went to call upon Raja Raghunath Mansingh at his residence in Chandni Chowk. The raja suspected that Beames had sent Fakir Mohan as his spy. He refused to talk to Fakir Mohan and gave no reply to his questions. When, at last, Fakir Mohan said that he was going to Dompara the next day, he said, 'All right. Go there and increase the taxes by four annas per *mana* of land.'

In August, Fakir Mohan arrived in Dompara. When he set about his official business, he found that Nidhi Pattanayak and the rebel chiefs would not cooperate with him at all. When he directed the landholders to deposit land revenue, they said that, although five years' taxes were owed by them, they would pay only one year's arrears. The raja was adamant that the land had to be reassessed and the taxes increased. The land-holders objected to the reassessment.

Under such circumstances, Beames came on a tour of Dompara in December. Supplying provisions for the sahib and his retinue was Fakir Mohan's responsibility. He issued a warrant to the cowherds that they bring one maund of ghee and four maunds of milk and curd. Since they grazed their cattle in the forests owned by the raja, they were bound by custom to supply these free of cost. However, after the uprising had taken place, the cowherds had discontinued the supply of milk, ghee and curd to the palace.

It was raining that morning as Fakir Mohan waited for the cowherds to fetch the provisions but no one turned up. After a long wait, a cowman called Sitha Behera approached timidly, carrying a small quantity of milk and ghee. Seeing him, Fakir Mohan flew into a tearing rage. He said to the paiks, 'Tie this man to a log, pour the milk and the ghee on him, and give him a good thrashing.' The paiks promptly carried out the order. Hearing Sitha Behera's cries and watching him receive blows from the heavy cane, the other cowherds got scared, and they soon turned up carrying provisions.

Fakir Mohan called on Beames and apprised him of the situation prevailing in the kingdom. He explained to Beames that the lands should be reassessed and the rate of taxes should be increased in view of the fact that land in Dompara had been assessed twenty long years ago. But Beames said that he had given the subjects his word of honour that taxes would not be increased. This now placed Fakir Mohan in a tight spot for he had decided to increase the rate of taxes in order to placate the raja. He had to do something. A bit of double dealing was called for.

The next morning, Fakir Mohan went to Beames and said, 'The subjects want me to mediate in the dispute between them and the raja. If Your Honour agrees to this, I'll act as the mediator.' Beames said, 'Very good, Babu. Very good. I'll feel very happy if you could do so. But everything should be discussed in my presence.'

It was a cold, rainy and windy day. The subjects were asked to come to Beames's camp in the afternoon. Beames emerged from his tent, covered from head to foot in a blanket. He said in Hindi, 'Dear subjects. I am happy to learn that you want Fakir Mohan Babu to mediate in the dispute between you and the king.' Four to five rebel chieftains shouted, 'If the dewan could settle the dispute, why did you travel all the way from Cuttack in the wind and the rain?' Beames could not make out what they said, and asked Fakir Mohan, 'What are they saying?' Fakir Mohan explained, 'They say that, of course, the dewan will sort out our problems. You have unnecessarily come all the way from Cuttack in this awful weather.'

This made Beames very happy. He said, 'Very good. Very good. The dewan will settle the dispute. He is a capable man and I trust him. *Salaam*, my subjects, and goodbye.'

All of Fakir Mohan's problems were now over. He craftily got Nidhi Pattanayak's nephew Jagabandhu arrested, and, implicating him in a false case, had him jailed for six months. Pathan paiks were sent out to collect tax arrears. For many years now, they had been ill-treated and humiliated by the subjects. Now, backed fully by the dewan, they merrily went around looting and terrorizing villages. A very old pandit had taken the side of the rebels. Two

Pathan paiks held him by the arm and made him run up and down the village path three times at midday. In a big village called Talabasta the Pathans stood guard over the only well there and did not allow the villagers to draw water from it. The villagers could not do their cooking and in the end, had to submit.

By the time Beames left Dompara, Fakir Mohan had the situation fully under his control by applying the principles of punishment and manipulation, since the principles of charity and mercy had already proved utterly ineffective.

Cuttack, January 1877

On 1 January 1877, the title 'Bharateswari', the Empress of India, was conferred on Queen Victoria according to a new law enacted in England. To mark this occasion, durbars were held in Delhi and other places in India.

By coincidence, it was the same day in the month of Pousa, in which Yudhisthir had ascended the throne of Hastinapur. According to the almanac, this day was *chandrabasara*; its astral sign was Pusya, and it was auspicious for the coronation of a monarch.

A grand durbar was arranged in the Barabati fort in Cuttack. Festivities and fairs continued for seven days. To organize all this, a committee headed by Ravenshaw had held several meetings over a month on the second floor of the Cuttack Printing Company building. The highlights of the durbar were the following:

Monday, 1 January: Chief among those who were felicitated at the durbar held in the fort were zamindars such as Radhashyam Narendra, Kalipad Bandopadhyay and Baidyanath Pandit. It had been decided to bestow the title of maharaja and *khilat*, the accoutrements of his investiture, on the raja of Puri. But when his name was called out, it was found that he was not present.

Tuesday: This day was set apart for illuminations and fireworks. Candles illuminated the road leading from Mastan to Chandni Chowk, and oil lamps lit up roads in Ranihat, Cuttack Chandi and the fields around the fort. Government offices and bungalows were also decorated with oil lamps. Fireworks were of three types: English, local and garjati. These were displayed on the sands of the river Katjuri, and the invited guests watched them from the Lalbagh bungalow and its premises. The English fireworks dazzled the spectators with stars of many colours, fiery shapes of flowers, fruits, trees and snakes. Lal Mahtab, a locally made cracker, was a great attraction. Among garjati crackers, the missiles won everyone's admiration.

Wednesday: Wrestling matches and other competitions took place under tents at the durbar. It was great fun to watch the races run by schoolchildren and military sepoys, and the sack races. Spectators shouted encouragement to the bearers in the palanquin race and greeted Bidei Behera and Dadhi Behera, who came first and second respectively, by clapping their hands. Besides all this, there were magic shows, shows put up by snake charmers, wrestling matches, *telingi* music, and circus shows. The Oriya Bazaar circus put up a number of events. Food brought in palm leaf baskets was distributed among children. Lest caste rules and restrictions should create problems, the sweets had been made by Brahmins, and men from the cowherd caste were placed in charge of serving water.

Thursday: On this day, the Europeans called on Commissioner Ravenshaw at his bungalow. The sahibs who had come from Cuttack and elsewhere met Ravenshaw and were entertained by him. The natives had no part in this programme.

Friday: Nearly two hundred native dignitaries including rajas, zamindars and government officials were received and entertained by the commissioner. A native *majlis* was organized in the hall of the durbar. Nautch girls from Ganjam and Calcutta, prostitutes and *gotipua* dancers from Cuttack took part in it.

Saturday: A horse race was held in the Chakkar field in Chauliaganj from 7 a.m. to 9 a.m., and the winners were awarded prizes. In the evening, a meeting of pandits took place in the durbar hall and poems on the title of Bharateswari being bestowed upon Queen Victoria were read out. The poem written by Gobinda Rath was adjudged the best. All the expenses for this meeting were borne by the rajas of Mayurbhanj and Keonjhar.

Sunday: Sweets and blankets were given away to beggars who had assembled in the premises of the collectorate. In the evening, sweets were distributed to police guards.

When the festivities came to an end after seven days, Divyasingh, accompanied by Tarakant Vidyasagar, arrived in Cuttack to receive his title. The letter which had been sent to the raja of Puri had mentioned that the title 'Maharaja', would be bequeathed on him at the durbar, but the raja had to buy the following items of khilat, for five hundred rupees, before the bestowal ceremony:

Choga	154 rupees
Silk pyjama	15 rupees 4 annas
Benarasi pugri	32 rupees
Shawl comforter	30 rupees
Benarasi handkerchief	05 rupees
A sword	15 rupees
A shield	12 rupees
Indau Kalaga	120 rupees
A pearl collar	116 rupees
A bottle of perfume	12 annas
Total	500 rupees

After paying five hundred rupees for the khilat, the raja of Puri wanted to meet Ravenshaw before receiving the title. But

Ravenshaw informed him that he would not see him. On being refused permission to call on the commissioner, Tarakant took Divyasingh to Bichitranand's house and entreated him to arrange a meeting between the raja and the commissioner. Bichitranand went to Ravenshaw and suggested that as Divyasingh's taking offence at the place allotted to him in the order of precedence, and staying away from the durbar was an insult to the other rajas of Orissa, he be asked to apologize to the raja of Keonjhar and the raja of Mayurbhanj. Divyasingh wrote to them apologizing for his act of impropriety. The next day, Divyasingh went to the commissioner's cutcherry, made an offering of one gold mohur and sought permission to meet Ravenshaw. But Ravenshaw again refused to see him and sent word through Bichitranand that the sanad conferring the title on the raja would be sent to Puri at a later date.

Puri, April 1877

The pandits of Benares had informed the raja of Puri well in advance that the festivals of *Baruni Snana* and *Govinda Dwadashi* would fall in the month of February and that he should expect pilgrims in very large numbers. According to the Bengali almanac, Govinda Dwadashi fell on 25 February. However, the Oriya almanacs said nothing on the matter and the raja consulted the pandits of Puri. The pandits of Puri and the Oriya astrologers rejected the Bengali almanac and were firm on the fact that Govinda Dwadashi could never fall on 25 February. The dewan, Tarakant Vidyasagar, supported the Bengali almanac and tried hard to persuade the raja. However, in this instance, the raja took the side of the Oriya pandits.

The pilgrims from northern India respected the opinion of the pandits of Benares and not what the raja thought. For the priests of Puri, this was a wonderful opportunity to make money.

They rented lodging houses, paying large advances, and set out to collect pilgrims. Although no arrangements had been made at the temple for the celebration of Govinda Dwadashi, pilgrims in large numbers assembled in Puri in the last week of February. Puri had never witnessed a crowd like this ever before. Even the *Navakalevar* Festival, which had taken place three years earlier, had not attracted a crowd as large as this.

The pilgrims began assembling in front of the temple on the morning of 21 February. When about twenty thousand pilgrims had gathered, the raja asked the collector to send more policemen and a Hindu deputy magistrate. Unfortunately, both the collector and the superintendent of police of Puri were away on tour. The acting magistrate then sent some policemen to the temple. When the gate was thrown open for the pilgrims, it was found that their number kept growing by the hour and the temple could not accommodate them. A few *Naga* and *Bairagi* mendicants and sanyasis ignored all entreaties and helped themselves to the offerings meant for the deities. On seeing that things were getting out of hand, the servitors closed the temple gate.

On 22 April, the raja again urged the authorities to place hired constables on guard duty near the temple. After this was done, the raja, accompanied by the deputy magistrate Mahanand Gupta and other officials, went to the temple and opened its gate. But when people scrambled and shoved each other in an attempt to enter the temple, the servitors had no option but to close the gate once more. The gate remained shut throughout the day and the pilgrims had to return disappointed.

Collector Armstrong returned to Puri on the morning of 23 April and instructed the raja to construct a barrier in front of the gate to control the crowd, and asked him to tell the priests that they would be responsible for maintenance of order. Executing this order took time, and the pilgrims grew desperately anxious.

When the crowd grew even larger towards evening, Armstrong wrote another letter to the raja and sent a joint magistrate to the spot. The joint magistrate took forty policemen with him and opened the temple doors. But there was such a rush that it was impossible to control the crowd. The joint magistrate himself was thrown down in the melee and he was compelled to close the temple doors. When the raja's men saw that things were getting out of hand, they ran away.

On the morning of 24 April there were pilgrims everywhere, in front of the four gates of the temple, near the Narendra tank, and in all parts of the town. Babu Mahanand Gupta advised the raja to throw the Lion Gate open but the latter refused to do so under the pretext that it could not be opened while offerings for the deities were being prepared inside. When the gate remained shut in the afternoon even after the offerings had been prepared, the pilgrims were restless and annoyed, for they had hoped to have a sighting of Lord Jagannath on that very day.

At about midnight, Armstrong arrived at the Lion Gate on horseback and ordered the gate to be thrown open. The pilgrims tried to rush into the temple in a desperate hurry, all at the same time. There was such a crowd inside the temple, and so many pushed their way into it from outside that two persons died near the Horse Gate, and the temple doors had to be closed yet again.

The incident was repeated on the night of Dola Purnima. Since the temple doors had remained closed all day, the crowd had only increased. Word was sent to the raja repeatedly but he took no steps to open the temple doors. He was busy at the time discussing with the raja of Khallikot the amount the latter should pay to obtain the privilege of being the first to have a darshan of Lord Jagannath. In the meantime the crowd began to swell. The people dragged the superintendent of police from his horse and trampled on him. Armstrong would have suffered the same fate but luckily for him, he was carrying a stout staff in his hand. He wielded it vigorously and forced his way out.

When at last the temple doors were thrown open at midnight, nine persons died in the scramble inside the temple. The doors were shut with great difficulty and the people waiting outside were informed of the incident. As the blood of the victims had desecrated the temple, all the offerings prepared for the deities had to be thrown away. The trouble the pilgrims had gone to, coming all the way to Puri to see the Dwadashi Festival, had led them nowhere.

Armstrong took great pains to persuade people to go home. When the temple doors were opened in the morning, Babu Mahanand Gupta, who had remained shut up inside the temple all night, came out and gave a full account of the events to Armstrong. When news of what had happened was sent to the palace, Divyasingh was so high on opium, he was utterly beyond comprehending anything.

A detailed report on the accidental death of eleven pilgrims reached Ravenshaw after a few days but he did not give it much attention. He had in the meantime been transferred to Calcutta as a member of the board of revenue and was getting ready to bid farewell to Cuttack. Although he had initially planned to spend only a few months in Orissa, Ravenshaw had ended up spending twelve long years in the province. The famine had been a terribly painful experience for him during his tenure of office. After 1866, he had devoted himself to the task of improving the province. In many ways he had become almost like an Oriya, so much so that he would smoke only the Oriya *pikas*. On 21 March, when Ravenshaw finally quit Orissa, the *Dipika* wrote: 'The people of Orissa feel sad at the departure of Mr Ravenshaw. True, he was incompetent as an administrator, but people had grown fond of him for he had spent a long time in the province, and no matter whether he succeeded in his undertaking or not, he wanted to do good to Orissa. He paid particular attention to the spread of education and has left behind such monuments as the college and the medical school.'

After receiving orders from Calcutta, John Beames, then collector of Cuttack, took over as commissioner on 27 March. His first task was to go to Puri and conduct an inquiry into the incident at the temple. Beames met the priests as well as others in Puri and received an account of the incident from them. The raja of Puri submitted a written statement explaining the incident. But when Beames sent for him, Divyasingh only rambled incoherently. In their depositions, the temple servitors lied so that the raja, Divyasingh, would not get into trouble.

On returning to Cuttack, Beames forwarded a long and detailed report on the matter to the government. He said that the incident took place because the raja of Puri had acted irresponsibly and all the blame should be placed on this boy. He further said that the best thing to do was to completely divest the raja of his powers as the superintendent of the temple, but such a step could not be contemplated under the prevailing circumstances. However, Beames directed the raja to form a committee of Hindus which would chalk out a plan for managing such a large assemblage of pilgrims in future. He recommended that until such a plan was submitted by the raja, the title of maharaja and the khilat be withheld.

All the same, Beames knew what the raja of Puri meant to Oriyas. It would not matter to them that the government did not confer on him the title of maharaja. They would also not be much bothered by the opinion of a handful of sahibs. For the people of the province, this stupid boy was not only maharaja, he was also the living deputy of Lord Jagannath.

Balasore, June 1877

The people of Orissa were very happy that Mahatma Beames had succeeded Mahatma Ravenshaw as commissioner. However, the people of Balasore were happier than the others, for Beames had earlier been the collector of Balasore. When news reached Balasore that Beames would visit the district in the month of June, a meeting was called to plan a reception. On 7 June, local gentlemen held a meeting at the Government English School, and proposed that the town be illuminated to receive the esteemed guest and, in his honour, a public library would be set up in Balasore. Now, everyone busied himself with collecting subscriptions for the illumination. Shyamanand Dey set about organizing a special reception for Beames.

Beames arrived on 14 June on a two-week tour of Balasore. The town was lighted up in his honour on 16 June at night. Flowers and glass-shaded lamps adorned the road leading from the collector's bungalow to the centre of the town. Floral gates had been erected and government offices, as well as the houses of the richer residents of the town, had been decorated. At 9 p.m. Beames, accompanied by the collector, set out in a carriage to watch the illumination. He was followed by many rich and distinguished people. After going round the town, the procession reached the new bungalow Shyamanand Dey had got constructed at Podhuapara. There, Beames was received by the raja of Mayurbhanj, several zamindars, the sahibs of Balasore, businessmen and officials. In response to the reception accorded to him, Beames made a speech in Hindi.

> Gentlemen! We are extremely pleased with the reception you have given us. Although we left Balasore four years ago, Balasore has not left us. We had tried to contribute to the well-being of the district but whatever we had done was not very much. We had never expected that we would be accorded such a warm

reception after an interval of four years for the little we did for Balasore. Many gentlemen are present here today. Only a very few among them are unknown to us. Even those whom we do not know feel great affection for us. Their presence here bears evidence of that. Among those whom we know are many whom we look upon as our dear friends, nay, brothers. During our stay in Balasore we have grown very fond of the place. The people of Balasore have shown the same promptness in obeying the orders of the government which they have displayed in carrying out our instructions. There are many in Balasore who, not guided by self-interest, have always devoted themselves to ensuring the well-being of others. We declare openly that, whether Balasore chooses to remember us or not, we shall never forget Balasore. We sincerely want Balasore to stay forever in our heart, and to let us stay in its heart forever.

After the speech, the sahibs and the dignitaries went up to the terrace and watched the fireworks. Later, they were entertained by music and the dance of nautch girls. Beames returned to the collector's bungalow late at night.

On 21 June, another reception in honour of the sahib was held at the residence of Brundaban Chandra Mandal at 5 p.m. On 26 June, the prize-giving ceremony of the Barabati School and the old Hindu Girls School was held in the living room of Madan Mohan Das. Besides Beames and the collector of Balasore, the raja of Nilgiri and some local gentlemen were present at the meeting. The children sang a song which described the importance of learning and the joy of receiving a reward. Then they staged a short play in English on Alexander and the bandit, and on Canute and his courtiers. After the distribution of prizes, Beames addressed the audience, first in Oriya, then in English, praising Madan Mohan Das's efforts. The same night, a reception in Beames's honour was held at Umesh Chandra Mandal's residence. What set this apart was the fact that, here, Beames was honoured according to native customs.

During his stay in Balasore, Beames visited all the offices and schools there. On 28 June, he inspected the St. Joseph School. When he arrived there, the children welcomed him with a song, the opening lines of which were as follows:

We worship your lotus feet
Oh Your Excellency, John Beames,
A great soul, commissioner of Orissa,
You, who adorn the forehead of Orissa
Like a mark of tilak
How fortunate we are,
For you have set foot here today.
The joy of the children knows no bounds
And every voice says, Beames, Beames.

The song went on to say that since Queen Victoria lived in a white island far away, beyond deep seas, the children forget their sorrows by setting their eyes on Beames's face, which was beautiful like the moon. In the song Beames was called the lord of life, the helmsman in the lake of Orissa and so on. All this delighted Beames no end, and he addressed the girls in Oriya. That day, at 5.30 p.m., Beames left Balasore and set off for Cuttack.

Dompara, June 1877

Fakir Mohan had brought the affairs of Dompara entirely under his control and devoted all his attention to collecting the tax arrears for the previous five years. He had, in the meantime, earned the reputation of being a tough administrator, and the pradhans were terribly scared of him. So collecting land revenue proved extremely easy. Eighteen thousand rupees were collected from Talabast alone in a single day. There was no box or chest where so much money could be kept so Fakir Mohan put all of it in a sack and carried it to the palace.

At the time, the raja did not live in the main palace, but chose to live in a house he had got constructed in the palace garden.

Of course, he was glad when Fakir Mohan, carrying the sack full of money, met him, but said that he would have nothing to do with it. When Fakir Mohan insisted, the raja said, 'I wanted the land settled and the taxes increased. This has been done and I am happy. You should keep this money.' Saying this, he went back into his house.

Fakir Mohan now took the sack of money to the queen and asked her to keep it but she too refused to have anything to do with it. At first, Fakir Mohan thought he would keep the money for himself but later felt that it would not be the right thing to do, for the raja paid him a salary and provided for him all the other necessities of life. Therefore, he got some bearers to convey the cash to Cuttack, gave it to one of the raja's moneylenders who lived in Balu Bazaar and collected from him a receipt saying that the raja had repaid his debts.

Fakir Mohan now turned his attention to the settlement work to be completed in four to five months. For Fakir Mohan, this meant a lot of hard work. Every morning, he would set out on his big Kathiawari horse, carrying a double-barrelled gun. It would be evening by the time he came back home after supervising the work of measuring and assessing the land. When it was time to collect the tax, the raja's presence was required, but he was in Calcutta. On receiving Fakir Mohan's letter he promptly returned to Dompara and was very glad that the settlement work had made good progress.

Now the raja stayed on in the palace and his communication with Fakir Mohan improved. The raja and Fakir Mohan were often seen drinking beer and exchanging small talk in the palace garden. The raja even started talking to Fakir Mohan about his private life. One day, he said to Fakir Mohan, 'Please find a good teacher for my son, Prince Brajendra.' Fakir Mohan thought for a while and said, ' The best person for this job in all of Orissa is Pyari Mohan Acharya but I don't know if he will accept the job.'

Pyari Mohan, after giving up his higher studies halfway through, was now busy working for the welfare of the province. He had set up an organization called the Cuttack Young Men's Literary Association, which held discussions from time to time. He had also earned a name for himself as a good orator, both in Oriya and Bengali.

Another achievement to Pyari Mohan's credit was the founding of a school in Cuttack. In 1873 he had set up a private school called the Cuttack Academy with only twelve students. The same year he had also launched a fortnightly called the *Utkal Putra*. In both these endeavours he was greatly assisted by his classmate, Gobinda Rath from Banki. Another classmate of his, Madhusudan Rao, was now in Cuttack but he could not offer him much help because he was a government servant, and Pyari Mohan sometimes criticized the government. All this, however, did not in any way affect their close friendship.

Pyari Mohan and Gobinda Rath together collected whatever money was required for running the school and the newspaper. In 1875, the school was upgraded to a Middle English School and it had sixty students. Pyari Mohan was having great difficulty in mobilizing the funds needed for the school and when he was invited by the raja of Dompara to join as private tutor to the prince, he readily agreed.

Fakir Mohan and Pyari Mohan felt very happy to find themselves together in Dompara. Although Fakir Mohan was eight years older than the latter, who was only twenty-six, they became close friends. However, this happy time was not to last very long. Fakir Mohan received a letter from the commissioner's office appointing him assistant manager in the feudatory state of Dhenkanal. When Fakir Mohan showed the appointment letter to the raja, he expressed his unwillingness to let him go and said that he would increase Fakir Mohan's salary. Finally

Fakir Mohan took him to Beames. The raja insisted that Fakir Mohan stay back in Dompara. Beames took Fakir Mohan aside and said, 'Babu, this raja is a crazy fellow. He can never be relied on. Don't listen to him.'

In the end, it was decided that Fakir Mohan would leave Dompara. The day he took leave, Raja Raghunath was in tears. He gave Fakir Mohan five thousand rupees to construct a house in Cuttack. He also presented him with a Nepali knife, and a pen and an inkpot from his own writing desk.

After Fakir Mohan left, the raja appointed Pyari Mohan in his place as the dewan of Dompara.

Dhenkanal, August 1877

The maharaja of Dhenkanal, Bhagirathi Mahendra Bahadur, had died a few months before Fakir Mohan joined as assistant manager. The maharaja was a huge man, weighing one hundred and forty kilograms. But his immense body had not stopped him from leading a very active life. He was a very good hunter and during his lifetime, he had shot three hundred and eighty Royal Bengal tigers. He had set up schools and hospitals in his kingdom. During the famine in 1866 he had relieved the distress of the destitutes in several ways and was also a member of the Cuttack Relief Committee. For these services, the government had conferred on him the title of maharaja. He was one of the chief patrons of the Cuttack Printing Company and the *Utkal Dipika*. In fact, the large two-storeyed building of the company was the result of his efforts. Two large chairs were always set aside for the maharaja in a room in the upper storey of the office of the printing press in Dargha Bazaar. The maharaja was a man of taste and he had a palace in Dhenkanal which was modelled on the commissioner's residence at Lalbagh.

Bhagirathi suffered from fistula and the only way he could find relief from pain was by taking large doses of opium. To help him get rid of opium addiction, the civil surgeon of Cuttack, Dr Stewart, had prescribed an English painkiller. One night Bhagirathi was in great pain but he had run out of the English medicine and so someone was sent to the dispensary to get this. The messenger roused the Bengali doctor from sleep and asked for the medicine. By mistake, the doctor sent the raja something that was poisonous and when Bhagirathi took it, he was taken severely ill. A messenger rushed to Cuttack on horseback and brought Dr Stewart with him. Dr Stewart's treatment saved Bhagirathi's life, but realizing the terrible mistake he had committed, the Bengali doctor ran away, mortally scared. He never returned and people began to gossip that he had been devoured by a tiger in the jungle.

However, after this mishap, Bhagirathi never fully regained his health. He was operated upon by Dr Stewart in Cuttack when he went there to attend the durbar. He returned to Dhenkanal after the operation, and there, in February 1877, breathed his last.

Fakir Mohan had made the acquaintance of Bhagirathi earlier. When Fakir Mohan was the dewan of Nilgiri, a large meeting of rajas, dewans and zamindars had been held in Bichitranand Das's garden in Tulsipur. This was where Fakir Mohan had first met Bhagirathi and from that day on they were on cordial terms with each other. Once, Fakir Mohan, his arms full of stationeries he had bought for the royal family of Nilgiri, was walking through Buxi Bazaar in Cuttack town. When he saw Bhagirathi's enormous carriage approaching, Fakir Mohan slipped into a shop. However, Bhagirathi had spotted him, and, stopping the carriage in front of the shop, he got him to come out of his hiding place.

When Fakir Mohan came to Dhenkanal, it was being ruled by Dinabandhu, the maharaja's adopted son who was then underage. Babu Banamali Singh was manager, Pyari Mohan Sen the royal tutor, and Bijay Kumar Chakravorty was the assistant surgeon.

In no time, Fakir Mohan had formed a close friendship with all of them. One outcome of the friendship was that, since Banamali and Bijay were fond of alcohol, Fakir Mohan too began to drink regularly.

In August, a few days after Fakir Mohan arrived in Dhenkanal, Commissioner Beames paid a visit to the state in August to inspect its affairs. The day after his arrival there, he went to take a look at the palace. Behind it stood a large gloomy house with a huge courtyard. The maharaja's concubines, sixty in number, lived there. The place lay abandoned, for the maharaja had long since given up visiting his concubines for reasons of health. Beames decided that those concubines who had no children should marry other suitable men and leave the palace. Those with children should stay on, and they would be maintained at the expense of the palace.

The raja had a large army of servants. It was found that for every single task two persons had been employed. This was so because, instead of a salary, a servant received a grant of land. So while one person did chores at the palace, the other went off to his village to manage the landed property. As a result, in place of the twenty-four people needed to carry the raja on a sedan chair, forty-eight had been employed. As many as seventy-two persons waited on the raja's person. For instance, the services of four servants were required for the raja to brush his teeth. One of them would go out and lop off a branch from a tree. Another made twigs of the right size from it. The twigs were carried by yet another servant and laid in the appointed place. The fourth servant's job was to place the twig in the royal hand. Beames removed three out of these four from service.

Six cooks worked in the royal kitchen. Beames dismissed four of them. One of these went to Fakir Mohan and weeping, entreated him to save his job. Fakir Mohan took him to Beames and lavished so much praise on his skills as a cook that Beames not only retained him he even raised his salary from seven rupees to thirty.

A durbar was held before Beames left Dhenkanal. To mark the occasion, roads were cleared and decorated with floral arches, water-filled pitchers and mango leaves. Banners, on which were inscribed 'God save Commissioner Beames' and other such legends, hung from the arches. The durbar was attended by around a hundred persons including officials, bearers, pandits, pradhans and the raja's relatives. Bengali songs were sung and an English orchestra played before the pandit sabha began. The pandits recited slokas and delivered speeches in Sanskrit.

Not to be outdone, Beames concluded the proceedings of the durbar by singing the lines *Lalita lavangalata* from the *Gita Govinda*. Although, in the voice of the sahib the sweet Sanskrit words sounded grotesque and obscure, no one was left in any doubt as to his formidable scholarship.

Beames started for Cuttack from Dhenkanal on 30 August at 7 p.m. After he had travelled a short distance, it began raining hard. Luckily for him, a jamadar from the palace carrying a lantern fitted with red and blue glass shades came to light their way. Beames, riding his palanquin, managed to cover some distance in the light of this lantern but soon had to stop at an overflowing stream. He decided to send someone to Dhenkanal to get an elephant. As he waited inside his palanquin in the driving rain, drinking brandy and smoking his cigar, Beames composed the following poem in French describing his leaving Dhenkanal, and grumbling about the heat and rain, the bad roads and the howling of the jackals.

> Je suis parti de Dhenkanal
> Par un chemin très inégal.
> Un gros orage tropical
> Versait son torrent pluvial.

Et tout autour de Dhenkanal
Hurlaient les loups at les chacals.
Les sentiers de Dhenkanal.

After some time two elephants arrived. On one's back was fastened Beames's palanquin and the other carried the rest of his party. They resumed their journey to Cuttack at midnight.

Cuttack, February 1878

Cuttack had seen many friendly, polite and soft-spoken sahibs who freely mixed with the natives. Nevertheless, the relationship between the sahibs and the natives always remained an unequal one. Native gentlemen were received cordially at the residence of British officers but there was no question of their meeting on an equal footing for the sahibs were rulers after all and the natives, no matter how wealthy, respectable or educated they might be, were no better than ordinary subjects. There was no way they could get together in the sphere of social intercourse. A vernacular textbook had this to say on the rules to be observed by the natives while meeting with a sahib at his residence: 'He should never call on the sahib before 10 a.m. or after 1 p.m. He should greet the sahib twice: once while entering the room and again before taking leave of him. Never try to shake hands with a memsahib unless she herself stretches out her hand. Attention should be paid to the way one is dressed. The native should take care that the clothes and turban etc. he wears are clean.'

Collector Beadon was the first to deviate from these rules. In August 1877 he invited native gentlemen to a get-together which he organized at his own residence. For the first time ever, British officers and native gentlemen were seen here meeting each other as equals. Among those present were several zamindars, four lawyers, all the deputy collectors, munsifs and the senior officials of the education department. Apart from these, five other native gentlemen had been invited, chief among whom was Gourishankar Ray. The party went on till midnight. The entertainment included sitar and piano recitals, games of cards and games of chess. Commissioner Beames entertained everyone, talking in his broken Oriya. However, the natives cavilled at one thing about the party: the invitation cards had not been sent out by Beadon. These had been signed by Deputy Collector Rangalal Bandopadhyay and the text read more like a summons from the court than like a proper invitation.

On 1 January 1878, native gentlemen were invited to the commissioner's residence at Lalbagh on the occasion of Queen Victoria's assuming the title, 'The Empress of India'. In December, Ravenshaw had returned to Orissa and taken over from Beames who had been transferred to Chittagong as commissioner. The people of Orissa were, of course, glad that Ravenshaw had come back; but they were equally unhappy that Beames was leaving them. The party thrown by Ravenshaw on 1 January was a great success.

So far, however, a party involving native gentlemen and the sahibs had never been held at a native gentleman's residence. Many years ago, some sahibs had been invited to zamindar Baidyanath Pandit's residence to watch a circus, and once to Golakchandra Bose's house to watch a wrestling match. But there, the sahibs and the natives had not really interacted freely with each other. To bring this about, Deputy Collector Jagmohan Ray organized a party at his residence on 2 February.

At this gathering were present thirty-five sahibs and an equal number of native gentlemen. The party was in no way less gorgeous than the one held at Lalbagh earlier. The house and the courtyard were tastefully decorated with chandeliers, lanterns and flowers. Refreshments were served in the parlour on the first floor, and the parlour on the ground floor was set apart for games and entertainment. The entertainment included sitar and violin recitals and a dance by nautch girls. Following the British practice, short speeches concluded the party. All the speakers stressed the importance and usefulness of social intercourse between the natives and the sahibs. Babu Rajendra Mishra, a lawyer, made his point by quoting Shakespeare: 'Are we not brothers?'

Everyone enjoyed the get-together thoroughly except one person: Radhanath Ray. He stood apart from all the gentlemen present at the party. He had come to Cuttack a month ago after being promoted to the post of joint inspector of schools. He was now the highest officer in the education department of Orissa and was one of the few Oriyas serving in such an elevated position. Everyone at Jagmohan Ray's party tried to make friends with him but he sat in one corner, glum and quiet. He listened to the music for a while but when the nautch girls danced, he got up and left. A few Englishmen made fun of him, but how could Radhanath have explained to them that his late father Sundar Narayan had been keeping a watch on him, hiding in the darkness of Jagmohan's backyard?

A few days after the party, a rumour went around in Orissa that Commissioner Ravenshaw had recommended Jagmohan for a high position in the administration. It was also insinuated that Jagmohan had thrown the party with this ulterior motive. Ravenshaw was taken to task for having recommended a Bengali instead of an Oriya. In the end, however, the job went to an Oriya, Nandakishore Das. People now praised Ravenshaw and said that Jagmohan had spent so much money in vain: the sahibs helped themselves to the dishes but quietly forgot their promise to give him a big job. It is ultimately *karma* which is all powerful!

eight

Puri, February 1878

On the first of January, a durbar was also held in Puri to mark the completion of one year of Queen Victoria's assuming the title 'The Empress of India.' A temporary structure was erected on the main street of Puri. Two thrones, one meant for the collector and the other for the raja, were placed there. The durbar began after a ceremonial gun salute. A letter of felicitation was read out. The collector made a speech while the people chanted, 'Victory to the Queen'. This was followed by a dance performed by prostitutes who had been brought over from Cuttack and Rambha. The pandits recited slokas invoking god's blessings. In this manner, the durbar went off without a hitch. But the raja did not turn up for the durbar and the throne meant for him lay empty.

As time passed, Divyasingh's condition went from bad to worse. Now he was entirely in the power of the palace servants and drugged himself with opium and bhang. After things went wrong during the Govinda Dwadashi festival, the government had informed Divyasingh that he would receive the title of maharaj a only after he submitted a plan for managing the affairs of the temple. But, in spite of the repeated reminders sent by the collector, the raja did not submit a plan. The papers relating to the conferment of the title lay in the Puri collectorate.

Divyasingh was a great source of worry for Rani Suryamani. She had expected that the boy would change as he grew older. Divyasingh was now twenty-three and two years ago, he had been blessed with a son. But nothing about his nature seemed to have changed. Not having received the benefit of education, and having spent all his time in the gymnasium in the company of servants had completely corrupted his nature and perverted his character. Let alone ordering the affairs of the temple or taking care of his landed property, he even avoided polite company. Almost always high on opium and bhang, he often beat up his servants who complained about him to Suryamani almost daily. The rani would hush the matter up but she was scared that Divyasingh's doings might not remain a secret for long, for he was not in his senses when he assaulted the servants. Sometimes he even broke their heads.

At last Suryamani decided that she would seek the advice of Sibadas Babaji. The previous year, when cholera had broken out in the palace, the queen had sent for Sibadas. Sibadas had made a prediction that, in spite of his medicines, the goddess would claim five lives. In fact, five people had died of cholera and this reinforced the rani's faith in him. When she asked him for a cure for Divyasingh, Sibadas said that his medicines would only work if Divyasingh stopped using opium. Nevertheless, when the rani insisted, Sibadas gave her some ash and asked her to persuade Divyasingh to take it.

Divyasingh, however, refused to take the ash. Divyasingh's servants convinced him that the rani was planning to poison him. He now behaved like someone possessed and was terribly angry with Sibadas who had prescribed the ash for him. Moreover, since Sibadas Babaji used to meet the rani at night, the servants made dirty jokes at their expense and this incensed Divyasingh. One day, Divyasingh ran into Sibadas and asked him, 'Scoundrel

Babaji, what happened to your attempt to cure me?' Sibadas was on his way back after meeting the rani. He retorted, 'You are a telenga, after all. Opium has robbed you of your senses. Who can cure you?'

Sibadas left, having said with this. But his words left Divyasingh seething rage. He got into a palanquin and ordered the bearers to chase Sibadas. Luckily for him, Divyasingh's servants persuaded him to turn back from the Atharnala bridge. They advised him that some other ways of teaching Sibadas a lesson should be found. Divyasingh told his servants, 'I want to teach the bastard a lesson he will never forget.' A detailed plan of action was worked out. The jamadar, Sarjan Upadhyay, and the old priest, Narayan Bahinipati, were given the money needed to buy everything required for the plan.

After all the arrangements were made, it was decided that Sibadas Babaji should be called to the palace on 23 February. In the evening, Bahinipati sent the chaprasi Gopi Singh and the *sejiapat* Maharatha to call on Sibadas. There, they made a mistake and went to another babaji who told them that that the person they were looking for must be Sibadas Babaji who lived in Bhagabanpur. So they went to Sibadas Babaji and asked him to accompany them to the palace, leading him believe that he was to treat a patient there. On the way to the palace, Patita Nayak, Balakrushna Mishra and Nidhi Mishra joined Sibadas. Near Janakadeipur, Nila Behera joined the party.

They stopped for a while on the way and drank some bhang and smoked ganja. It was dark by the time they reached Puri. Maharatha made them wait outside the palace gate and went inside to inform the raja. Gopi Singh's duty for the day had come to an end so he handed his sword to the guard and went home. Maharatha came back and asked Sibadas to go in. Sibadas's four friends stayed outside.

Sibadas was led to the place where Divyasingh practised wrestling. The door was closed behind Sibadas to make sure he could not escape. Inside the gymnasium Divyasingh and nine others waited. The moment his eyes fell on Sibadas, Divyasingh became wild with rage and hit him on the head with a heavy lathi, screaming, 'Kill the bastard.' Now the others encircled Sibadas. Sibadas, who was a strong, well-built person, tried to break free and jump over the boundary wall but he could not for the top of the wall was studded with nails. He then tried to escape by climbing a tree inside the gymnasium but it too, was studded with nails. He banged on the door desperately but it was securely locked.

The servants rained blows on Sibadas with their lathis, and he finally fell. Four people made him lie on his back and pinned him down. Divyasingh urinated on his face. Two scavengers, Bana Naik and Ganesh Naik, took human excreta from a pot and stuffed it into Sibadas's mouth. But Sibadas shook them all off and sat up. However, they hit him repeatedly and again overpowered him.

Now they subjected Sibadas to unspeakable tortures. They inserted an iron wire into his genitals and poured quicklime on them. They pushed a length of pith deep into his rectum and when it could not be pushed any further, they set it on fire. Different parts of Sibadas's body were singed and burnt. Sibadas's screams only egged Divyasingh and his accomplices on to torture him with greater ferocity. When, after long four hours, Sibadas's screams ceased, they thought he had died and dragged his body out of the palace and flung it outside.

Around midnight, Sibadas came to and dragged himself with great difficulty to the Lion Gate of the temple. Hearing his groans, two beat constables came running in. Sibadas was lying on the ground, completely naked. His body was covered with bloody wounds and he was suffering from multiple burn injuries. He was taking out pieces of pith from his body. The constables helped him up and took him to the police station. When they passed Rathagadhapara, Sibadas shouted, 'Nila, Patita. Come quickly to me. I am dying.' His friends were sleeping on the outer veranda of the palace. They rushed in. Nila Behera spread his shawl on the ground and made Sibadas lie down on it. Patita got some water and made Sibadas drink a little. After recording his statement, the police took him to the hospital.

Late at night, the native doctor Nasiram Ghosal was roused from sleep. He came to the hospital and examined Sibadas. His condition was critical. He was administered a dose of purgative which expelled thirty-four pieces of pith from his body. Sibadas was in such pain that it could be kept under control only by giving him a large quantity of opium.

Armstrong received the news in the morning and he immediately rode down to the hospital. He sent for the superintendent of police, Mahanand Gupta, and the deputy magistrate, Nabin Chandra Sen. Although he had been heavily drugged with opium, Sibadas writhed in agony and was in no state to make a statement. Nevertheless, Armstrong sat down to record his declaration. Extreme pain and the opium made Sibadas incoherent. However, he somehow managed to say that Divyasingh and his servants had done this to him.

Armstrong directed the deputy collector to conduct an on-the-spot inquiry. The deputy collector found blood and faeces on the floor of the gymnasium. The place bore marks of a violent scuffle. Sibadas's necklace was found lying under a window in Kapasia lane near the palace. A report mentioning all these facts was submitted to the collector. The police carried out preliminary investigations, collected evidence relating to the crime and reported that Sibadas had been brutally assaulted inside the palace. On the order of the magistrate, Divyasingh and nine servants of his were arrested.

In no time, the news of the raja's arrest spread through the town of Puri and people started saying all manner of things about the incident.

Cuttack, April 1878

Ravenshaw was not satisfied with the police report which Armstrong had sent him on the arrest of the raja of Puri. The whole thing was simply incredible. What could have possibly motivated the raja of Puri to commit such a ghastly deed? It might well be that the babaji was a wicked fellow and had evil intentions. And what had the raja of Puri to say in self-defence? Ravenshaw wrote to Armstrong asking him to explain all these points fully.

On receiving this letter, Armstrong felt terribly cross with Ravenshaw and abused fourteen generations of his ancestors. If Ravenshaw thought Armstrong was crazy, Armstrong himself thought Ravenshaw to be utterly worthless. Both were right, up to a point. It was true that Armstrong was a competent officer; but on occasions when he lost his temper he did things which no person in his right senses would do. It was impossible to make him change his mind once he had decided on a certain course of action. Whenever anything relating to Orissa came up during a discussion, he used to boast, 'I am a pukka Oriya. My name is Bhujabal which is Oriya for Armstrong. Ha. Ha. Ha.'

The point of Ravenshaw's letter was that the investigations had not revealed the full picture. Although Sibadas had made another statement he said nothing new for fear that the ladies of the palace might get dragged into the case. As regards the motive of the crime, he only said that Divyasingh was angry with him because he obeyed the rani, not him. During the inquiry,

Divyasingh kept absolutely quiet about the matter and said that he had no witnesses. One of the accused said that he did not know who assaulted Sibadas. For all he knew, Sibadas might have been beaten up by a drunkard in some brothel.

Sibadas began to get better but soon went down with an attack of tetanus. Divyasingh and the nine servants were taken to the hospital and an identification parade was held. Sibadas succeeded in identifying Divyasingh and each of the nine servants who had attacked him.

Divyasingh was released on bail for two thousand rupees up to 11 March when the case was to be heard. Now that tetanus posed a threat to Sibadas's life, the case of assault changed into a murder case, Divyasingh's bail was cancelled and he was taken into custody. After suffering excruciating pain for two weeks, Sibadas died at midday on 10 March. On 11 March, the case came up for trial in Armstrong's court. The nine servants were Sarjan Upadhyay, Gopi Routra, Daitari Singh, Gopal Das, Narayan Bahinipati, Baji Santra, Arjun Singh, Ganesh Naik and Bana Naik. All of them were employed in the palace.

During the trial, the defence refused to cross-examine the witnesses and said nothing in self-defence. Their actions made it clear that they had planned to do this during the trial at the court of the sessions judge. The dying declaration of the victim left no room for doubt: he had identified the accused, especially Divyasingh, and the jamadar Sarjan Upadhyay and Daitari Singh—these two were tall, hefty fellows from northern India—as well as the seventy-year old bearded priest, Bahinipati. On the basis of this evidence, Armstrong charged them with murder under section 302 and forwarded them to the sessions court.

Armstrong wanted Deputy Magistrate Nabin Chandra Sen to present the case at the sessions court in Cuttack. But Ravenshaw wanted the superintendent of police, Greaves to take charge of this case. This made Armstrong so furious that he called Ravenshaw 'that rogue from Cuttack' and other names. He wrote to Ravenshaw that appointing the prosecutor for the case was the job of the collector, not the commissioner. Finally, the matter was referred to the government and it was decided that both Nabin Chandra and Greaves would be prosecutors.

A few days later, Ravenshaw took leave and left Orissa. Mr Smith joined as commissioner in his place.

On 17 March, Divyasingh was taken from Puri to Cuttack in a palanquin as a custodial prisoner. The police conveyed him to jail in a hired carriage from the bank of the river Katjuri. Fortunately, as the news had not reached people in Cuttack, it did not cause any disturbance. Later, however, the news spread and large crowds collected in front of the jail.

The case came up for hearing before Sessions Judge Dickens on 26 March. Divyasingh was defended by Evans and Handlee. They were regarded as the best lawyers at the time, and they charged a thousand rupees a day. On the prosecution side, there were the government lawyer, Hariballav Basu and the sessions seristadar, Kshetramohan Bose.

Anticipating trouble, Smith had deployed a large number of policemen to guard the court on all sides. The courtroom was packed with people since morning, and many also sat in front of the jail. When the palanquin which carried the raja proceeded from the jail in the direction of the court, hundreds of people followed it shouting, 'Haribol'.

The hearing began at half past eleven. The witnesses who gave evidence on that day included the hospital compounder, the road cess engineer who had drawn a plan of the scene of the crime, the police inspector, Rama Rao, and the chaprasi, Gopi Singh. The next day, the crowd of spectators thinned out. By 31 March, all the witnesses on the prosecution side had given evidence.

On 1 April, Barrister Evans argued in defence of the accused. Present in the court that day were Collector Beadon and several other sahibs. Evans emphasized the high esteem in which the raja of Puri was held in Orissa and argued that it was impossible for an eminent person like him to have committed such a ghastly and despicable deed. His defence rested on the following arguments: the whole case rested on the statements made by Sibadas; however, Sibadas's statements contradicted each other. Religious inhibitions rendered incredible the fact that the raja of Puri could have associated himself with persons belonging to the Hadi caste or that he could have touched human excreta and urine. And no one would ever call someone to his own house and assault him in the presence of witnesses. In any event the defendant was not required to establish who was responsible for what had happened to Sibadas Babaji.

After this, several witnesses were produced by the defence. Their depositions stressed one point: the accused persons were not present at the scene of the crime. Divyasingh said he was fast asleep at the time; Sarjan Upadhyay said he had gone to inquire into the matter relating to Ram Khuntia's adopting a son; Gopi Routra claimed he was doing guard duty at the palace gate; Daitari Singh said he was watching a dance; Gopal Das submitted that he was sleeping at the residence of Hati Sardar; Narayan Bahinipati said that he was down with fever and lying at someone's house when the incident took place; Baji Santra said he was in his village collecting his share of the harvest, Arjun Singh said he was having a meal at the Panditji Mutt, and Ganesh and Bana Nayak claimed that they were away attending the wedding feast of someone belonging to their caste.

On 4 April, Evans again presented his arguments in defence of the accused and expressed the hope that the honourable judge would not follow the example of the mofussil officers who had sentenced the accused on the basis of meagre evidence and advised him to appeal against the verdict at a higher court. He urged the honourable judge to pronounce a verdict after carefully weighing the evidence. Greaves responded to this. However, his response seemed insipid and colourless coming as it did after Evans's powerful address. Greaves simply rehearsed the evidence given against the accused and urged the honourable judge to impose the heaviest of penalties on them.

After the hearing came to an end, the judge sought the views of the assessors, Kalimohan Ghosal and Biharilal Pandit. They withdrew into a room, discussed the case and came back after a while. They expressed their view that the evidence against the accused was not conclusive and they were, therefore, not guilty. Saying that he would pronounce the verdict after a week, the judge adjourned the court.

On 11 March, the court assembled at 11 a.m. The courtroom was crowded to suffocation. The onlookers noticed something odd: the raja of Puri had not been given a chair to sit on. This led to all manner of speculation about the verdict. Judge Dickens read out the name of each of the accused and mentioned the sentence awarded to him. The seristadar translated what he said into Oriya: Divyasingh and four of his servants—Sarjan Upadhyay, Gopi Routra, Gopal Das, and Narayan Bahinipati—were sentenced to deportation for life. The rest were acquitted for lack of evidence. All along, Divyasingh had remained quiet. Now he broke down and wept.

After the police led the convicts away, Judge Dickens got down from his seat, leaving a copy of the verdict on the table for the perusal of the barristers and others. The verdict filled seventeen sheets of foolscap paper on both sides. Everyone praised it for it was extremely well written and well thought out, and it read like a short novel. Knowledgeable people remarked, 'Of course, nothing less could be expected of Charles Dickens's son.'

Puri, May 1878

The verdict caused tremendous stir in Cuttack. People strongly disapproved of Divyasingh's ways and his character but the news of the Gajapati Raja of Puri being sentenced to deportation left them depressed, and soon a wave of sympathy for Divyasingh began to build up.

While the trial was in progress, Nabin Chandra had stayed in Cuttack with his old friend, Rangalal Bandopadhyay. He informed Armstrong about the verdict which made the latter very happy. Armstrong sent a letter to Nabin Chandra by return of post praising him. Nabin Chandra was eager to go back to Puri for he had left his newborn baby there. However, Armstrong was of the opinion that there was a possibility that people loyal to the raja of Puri would attack him on the way and he would do well to wait until the collector made arrangements for safe passage.

In the end, Nabin Chandra set off for Puri, escorted by armed constables. As had been anticipated, a person close to the raja followed him with a party of men. When the constables stopped them, they explained that they too were on their way to Puri; they walked behind the deputy magistrate's palanquin because they thought overtaking him would have amounted to disrespect.

When Nabin Chandra called on Armstrong he embraced him and cordially ushered him in. He gave Nabin Chandra tea and told him that he could counter the argument that the title 'Raja' was a venerable institution. Saying this, he handed Nabin Chandra a piece of paper. He had prepared a note after having consulted several books and records. It contained the following comment on the rajas of Puri:

> The history of Orissa has always been stained with blood. When Raja Prataprudra died, his Commander-in-Chief, Gobinda Bidyadhar, murdered the Raja's two minor sons and ascended the throne. He founded the Bhoi dynasty. Gobinda Bidyadhar's

son, Chakrapratap was poisoned by his son Narasingh, who captured the throne. Mukund Harichandan entered the palace riding a palanquin and disguised as a woman, and assassinated Narasingh. Mukund became king and founded the Chalukya dynasty. He lost his life in a battle with the Muslim invaders of Orissa. Ramachandra, who was the son of Gobinda Bidyadhar's general, murdered the Saura tribal sardar of Khurda and became king. This is how the line of the kings of Khurda began, who are now called the rajas of Puri.

Nabin Chandra went through the note and said, 'You have collected lots of interesting and significant facts but evidence against the character of the accused or that of his ancestors is not admissible in a court of law.' Armstrong felt annoyed and disheartened by his remark. He said, 'I will read the verdict once more and find new arguments at the time of appeal.' It was decided that if the raja of Puri appealed against the verdict, Nabin Chandra would go to Calcutta and prosecute the case for the government.

Reactions to Dickens's verdict were varied. The *Indian Daily News* published from Calcutta praised the verdict saying, 'It will be advisable if the raja does not appeal against the verdict in the high court.' On the other hand, the *Indian Mirror* criticized Judge Dickens for having chosen to ignore the views of the assessors of the case.

Divyasingh appealed against the sentence in the high court. Nabin Chandra went to Calcutta and explained the case to the advocate general, Mr Paul. The raja of Puri was again defended by Barrister Evans who was now assisted by Barristers Branson and Manmohan Ghosh. A full bench consisting of Chief Justice Garth and two other judges heard the appeal. The hearing began on 6 May. The lawyers defending the raja of Puri presented their arguments for four days. Then, Mr Paul countered these and the lawyers argued for a long time.

On 13 May the judges read out their verdict. They upheld the verdict passed by the sessions judge. The appeals of Sarjan Upadhyay and Narayan Bahinipati were rejected. Gopal Das and Gopi Routra were acquitted because, during the identification parade, Sibadas had not been able to identify them properly.

Now, all over Orissa, people talked of nothing but the case involving the raja of Puri. Around this time, a horse belonging to the raja died in Puri and one of his elephants died in Khurda. These incidents convinced people that the raja was going through a dark period in his life which was dominated by the inauspicious planet, Saturn.

When it was time to shift Divyasingh from the jail in Cuttack to Calcutta, it was feared that riots might break out. Therefore, all the arrangements were made in extreme secrecy. On 23 May, at 4 a.m. the police put Divyasingh in a horse carriage and took him to Jobra. From there he was ferried to the lighthouse by steamer. From the lighthouse, Divyasingh was taken to Calcutta in a ship and was kept in the Presidency Jail there until he was deported to the Andamans.

Calcutta, January 1879

The Brahmo Samaj was founded by Raja Ram Mohan Roy in 1828. A few years after his death, the leadership of the Brahmo Samaj passed into the hands of Debendranath Tagore in 1841. Raja Ram had accepted many elements from Christianity but Debendranath was of the view that only elements from Hinduism should constitute the Brahmo faith. Debendranath had connections with Orissa for his father Dwarakanath Tagore owned a zamindari in the province. Dwarakanath had purchased the Pandua zamindari in 1811, paying a sum of ten thousand rupees. He used to visit Orissa from time to time to put in order the affairs of Pandua.

In spreading and propagating Brahmoism, Debendranath was greatly assisted by Keshab Chandra Sen. Sen was not a Brahmin and knew no Sanskrit. Nevertheless, Debendranath's partiality to him enabled him to become an acharya of the Brahmo Samaj at a very young age. Through their efforts, many branches of the Brahmo Samaj were set up all over India and in Burma. In 1864, Debendranath established a branch of the Samaj in Cuttack. Gourishankar Ray and Jagmohan Ray, among others, joined it. With the subscriptions raised by Jaganmohan, a Brahmo temple was built in Oriya Bazaar. For the construction of the temple, a substantial amount was donated by Debendranath himself.

Keshab Chandra and his supporters wanted to introduce the beliefs and practices of Christianity as well as other religions; they mobilized opinion against the institutions of child marriage, polygamy, casteism etc. This led to differences between Keshab Chandra and Debendranath, and, as a result, the Brahmo Samaj split into two in 1868. The faction led by Debendranath was called Calcutta or Adi Brahmo Samaj and Keshab Chandra's faction came to be known as Bharatiya Brahmo Samaj. The split had repercussions in Orissa too. The Brahmo Samaj in Oriya Bazaar came to be redesignated Adi Brahmo Samaj. In 1869 the Utkal Brahmo Samaj was established through the efforts of Professor Haranath Bhattacharya of the Cuttack Zilla School, who was a follower of Keshab Chandra Sen. His students, Pyari Mohan Acharya, Madhu Rao and some others became its members. However, they obtained permission to hold prayer meetings at the Oriya Bazaar Brahmo temple every Sunday.

In 1876, under the leadership of Shibanath Shastri, who was a Sanskrit teacher at the Hare School, Calcutta, Bipin Chandra Pal and a few others created a new institution with the aim of combining the religious and social ideals of Brahmo Samaj with the political ideals of Surendranath Banerjee. Prior to this, Keshab

Chandra's Brahmo Samaj had no distinct political perspective. In 1877, Bipin Chandra formally embraced Brahmoism.

In 1872, largely due to Keshab Chandra's efforts, the Civil Marriage Act had come into force. Under this law, boys could not be married before they were eighteen and girls before they reached the age of fourteen. When, in 1878, Keshab Chandra gave his thirteen-year-old daughter in marriage to the sixteen-year-old son of the raja of Coochbehar, the Brahmo Samaj headed for yet another split. A new samaj called the Sadharan Brahmo Samaj came into existence, with Shibanath Shastri as one of its leaders. A school called the City School was established with the aim of educating the samaj workers. Shibanath Shastri worked as the school secretary.

Bipin Chandra dearly wanted to teach at the City School, but even after two attempts at the F.A. examinations, he had been unsuccessful. Besides, since he had passed out of a mofussil school in Sylhet, it was doubtful that he could control the smart Calcutta boys. For these reasons, he was refused a teaching job at the City School. Around this time, he was requested by Jadumani Ghosh, a Brahmo leader, to join as the headmaster of the Cuttack Academy. Pyari Mohan Acharya had written to Jadumani asking him to find a Brahmo headmaster and two assistant teachers who would be willing to work for a small salary and contribute to the spread of Brahmoism. Bipin Chandra was twenty years old at the time. Although he knew nothing about Cuttack, he readily agreed to take up the job and set off for Cuttack. He was to get thirty rupees a month and free accommodation.

In January, Bipin Chandra and the two assistant teachers left Calcutta, boarding a ship called the Sir John Lawrence. The ship set sail in the morning and reached the mouth of the river Ganga in the evening. They boarded another ship there and after sailing for six hours arrived at the mouth of the river Mahanadi in

Chandbali. From there, one had to travel to Cuttack by steamer. These steamers had no first or second class but in the green boats tugged by these steamers, there were cabins for upper-class passengers. Bipin Chandra was given a cabin in one of these green boats. The room next to his cabin was the kitchen, and the head cook was a south Indian. Cooking had been a passion with Bipin Chandra since childhood. During the twenty-four hours it took him to travel from Chandbali to Cuttack, Bipin Chandra taught himself how to cook south Indian dishes.

Cuttack, March 1879

On reaching Cuttack, Bipin Chandra assumed charge of the Academy. Two other positions there were filled by Brahmos from Calcutta, Brajendranath Sen and Rajchandra Choudhury, who had accompanied him. The two were friends of Bipin Chandra, belonged to Sylhet, and like Bipin Chandra, had failed in their F.A. examination.

In Cuttack, Bipin Chandra made friends with Pyari Mohan. He was deeply impressed by Pyari Mohan's idealism, intrepidity, and eloquence. He also got to know, and befriended, Gourishankar, Radhanath and Madhu. The cultural environment of Cuttack appealed to Bipin Chandra. In those days, meetings were held almost daily in the two-storeyed building of the Cuttack Printing Company. In a way, this building functioned as the town hall of Cuttack. When the title, 'Empress of India' was conferred on Queen Victoria, a plan to construct a Bharateswari Bhavan in Cuttack by raising subscriptions was initiated. A model of the proposed building had also been prepared and it adorned the commissioner's office, but no funds could be mobilized for the building. The need for a meeting hall in the town was met by the Cuttack Printing Company.

Around this time, in Cuttack, many new institutions such as the Debating Club, the Utkal Sabha and the Cuttack Young

Men's Literary Association came into being. They held their meetings in the building of the Cuttack Printing Company and shaped many orators in town. At the time Pyari Mohan was indisputably the best orator in Cuttack and was equally at home in both Oriya and Bengali.

Pyari Mohan gave lectures on subjects ranging from Oriya literature, alcoholism and addiction to other intoxicants, and even the evils of bribe-taking. Whenever he addressed a meeting, the two-storeyed building, including its veranda, was thronged with people. His sonorous voice spilled over on to the road outside the Printing Company's premises and the whole area resounded with the applause of the audience. However, Pyari Mohan's eloquence was flawed in one respect: he often went beyond the bounds of propriety and decorum. The element of obscenity in ancient Oriya literature formed the chief target of his scathing criticism. If Pyari Mohan was the best orator in Cuttack, the worst was Radhanath Ray. Whenever Radhanath stood up to speak, his hands and legs shook and his voice grew so feeble that no one was able to hear what he said. He would quickly get to the end of his speech and sit down.

At the beginning of March, a meeting was convened at the Printing Company to welcome Babu Bhudev Mukherjee. People who were present there included Gourishankar, Pyari Mohan, Radhanath, Madhu and Bipin Chandra. Bhudev, who was school circle inspector, had come to inspect the schools of Orissa. As officer he was responsible for Patna, Bhagalpur and Burdwan divisions as well. Two years previously, he had been awarded C.I.E. and had achieved distinction as the editor of the *Education Gazette*. Since it was his first visit to Orissa, it had been decided that a special reception was called for. It fell to Radhanath and Pyari Mohan to make all the necessary arrangements for this.

Bhudev Mukherjee arrived in Orissa on 15 March, and accompanied by Radhanath, went on a tour of inspection of schools in Puri district. He returned to Cuttack on 22 March, and on 24 March a reception in his honour was held at 8 p.m. in the premises of the Printing Company. The meeting was presided over by Nandakishore Das. Babu Bihari Mishra introduced the distinguished guest and told the audience how, having begun his career as headmaster of a school, Bhudev had risen to such a high position, a position which carried a salary of fifteen hundred rupees a month. He lavished praise on Bhudev and proposed that Bhudev be properly honoured at the meeting for his great qualities and his contribution to the welfare of society.

Seconding the proposal, Pyari Mohan dwelt on Bhudev's generous and noble nature and took this opportunity to emphasize that there were no differences between Bengalis and Oriyas. Bipin Chandra Pal expressed his great pleasure at the way Bengalis and Oriyas had come together to honour Bhudev. Then he spoke on the value of self-education. He claimed that although Bhudev had not received a university education or degrees, he had acquired much learning by self-education.

Expressing gratitude for the speeches made in his honour, Bhudev protested that he did not deserve all the praise. In our country, he said, people made idols of wood or stone and offered them worship and asked for boons. Sometimes, their prayers were answered, not because they worshipped the idols but as a result of their own sincerity and dedication. Similarly, the kind words said by the speakers bore testimony to their own virtues and their nobility.

After Bhudev's speech, perfume, *paans* and garlands were distributed, and rose water was sprinkled all around. The meeting came to an end. In a remarkably short time, the gentle and bearded Bhudev, who looked like a sage, had endeared himself to everyone. The day after he would turn fifty-four. On that day, he took Radhanath with him and set out for an inspection of the schools in Balasore.

Balasore, April 1879

Bhudev and Radhanath were seated in Baikunthanath Dey's garden. It was evening and everything was quiet. There was no one around. Together, they had inspected several schools and concluded official business for the day. Radhanath, who was a man of few words, sat gazing at the stars. When they had spent a long time without exchanging even a word, Bhudev said, 'Why do you lose yourself gazing at the stars? Doing such a thing all the time is not good. This brings your insignificance to the surface and your identity gets dissolved; you become apathetic to your worldly duties. Contemplation of the infinite suits only yogis!'

Bhudev always gave Radhanath such advice. When he had first arrived in Orissa, his opinion of Radhanath was not a favourable one for some people had prejudiced Bhudev against Radhanath. But after he met Radhanath and got to know him well, he grew very fond of him. Radhanath presented him with two of his published collections of poems in Bengali, and showed him the manuscript of a collection of poems entitled *Lekhabali* written in Bengali. This manuscript contained poems in which mythical women such as Janaki, Subhadra and Devyani pleaded with their husbands. There was in it one poem in which figured non-mythical characters called Kumarnath and Kamalkamini. They were supposed to belong to Remuna in Balasore and Kamal was Kumar's maternal uncle's daughter. The poems were of a very high quality and were free from the immaturity which characterized poems in the earlier collection, *Kabitabali*. However, these poems were heavily charged with eroticism. Bhudev went through the poems avidly, and of the poem 'Kamalakamini', he observed that the depiction of erotic experience between cousins exceeded the limits of propriety. In his view, this excessive concern with eroticism was detrimental to moral health and should therefore be discouraged.

Whatever Bhudev said was worth remembering. The arguments he entered into while inspecting schools were full of wisdom and erudition. When he visited the Cuttack Academy, Pyari Mohan could not remain present on account of illness. He was represented by his Brahmo friend Jadumani Ghosh, who came from Calcutta. Bipin Chandra Pal was, of course, present in the school. In the course of discussion, the topic of the relative merits of Brahmoism and Hinduism came up and the arguments soon grew heated. The discussion would have got out of hand had Bhudev not clinched it by saying, 'If Brahmoism had stayed at the point to which Maharshi Debendranath had brought it, I, too, would have presented myself to the world as a Brahmo.' Such an admission, coming as it did from an orthodox Hindu like Bhudev, indicated his deep faith in monotheism.

During their journey, Bhudev and Radhanath talked passionately about literature and their discussions ranged from Goethe, Shakespeare, Kalidas and Bhavabhuti to Upendra Bhanja and Michael Madhusudan. Radhanath introduced Bhudev to ancient Oriya literature by reciting to him lines from Upendra Bhanja's 'Labanyabati' and 'Baidehisa Bilasa'. Listening to the lines from 'Baidehisa Bilasa', such as 'badana puriachhi hasa harase' (the face is filled with joyous laugher), Bhudev commented, 'It is surprising that Bengalis call Orissa a land of porters.'

Bhudev gave Radhanath much useful advice on how to write. After reading the manuscript of *Lekhabali* he said, 'Why dissipate your time and energy writing about old worn out themes? I have gone through your manuscript and I will, of course, publish it in the *Education Gazette* but I hope you will try to create something new. For instance, you have painted a portrait of Subhadra but no matter how hard you try, you can never excel Vyasa in the portrayal of this character. Do something original. Orissa is a beautiful province. Nothing is a fitter subject for poetry than its enchanting natural scenery. In reality, Orissa is the ideal midwife for the birth of a poet. Wherever you cast your eyes in Orissa, you will find new material.'

On hearing this, Radhanath replied with characteristic humility, 'Inventing incidents and characters is beyond someone like me.'

On their way from Cuttack to Balasore they passed through the kingdom of Darpani. Radhanath recounted to Bhudev a legend associated with the place: The raja of this kingdom held a mirror *(darpan)* before the emperors of the Ganga dynasty when they got their hair groomed. There was a beautiful tank by a rest-house for pilgrims at the foot of a hill near the road leading to Puri. Once the child of a wealthy north Indian pilgrim suddenly disappeared while playing near this tank. All attempts to trace him proved futile.

Bhudev interrupted, 'But I have heard another story relating to this place: Once the son of the emperor of Utkal came here on a hunting expedition. The princess of if this place fell in love with him at first sight. She secretly placed her portrait and a love letter in a mirror. When her father held this mirror before the prince, the portrait and the letter fell out leaving the former acutely embarrassed and upset. He came home and took his daughter severely to task. Heartbroken, the princess threw herself into the tank and killed herself.'

Radhanath understood that the story had been invented by Bhudev himself and that he had made it up from what Radhanath had just said to him. This was in fact a lesson for Radhanath. He decided, at that very moment, that he would try to adapt existing legends to contemporary tastes.

Before leaving Balasore, Bhudev sent the following report on Radhanath to the higher authorities:

Baboo Radhanath Ray should be placed in independent charge of all schools in Orissa; his salary should be increased and his post should be upgraded. I am convinced that he is in every way equipped to manage on his own a whole circle. I wholeheartedly agree with sahibs such as Beames and Norman, who are of the view that Radhanath is highly learned, extremely intelligent, and very sincere. I therefore recommend that, according to section 13 of the government resolution, Radhanath be placed in the highest grade of the junior education service and he be left in independent charge of the Orissa division.

Bhudev wrote a little poem addressing Radhanath which expressed his deep affection for the latter more eloquently than the above recommendation. This poem was published anonymously in the 23 May issue of the *Education Gazette*. The opening lines of the poem are as follows:

Radhanath, you are Orissa's pride
Gentle, humble, calm and generous
You have mastered several tongues
And studied so many texts
Wandering in the garden of verse
You are a cuckoo singing sweetly
For ever your heart overflows
With feelings tender and heavenly.

Khandapara, August 1879

Although the writing of *Siddhanta Darpan* had been completed ten years earlier, no arrangements for its publication could be made. Every day, Samanta Chandrasekhar would take down the palm leaf bundles, dust and wipe them, and put them back. Aged only forty-four, he nevertheless looked upon himself as a very old man. His financial worries were compounded by his illness. The stomach ache caused by attacks of indigestion and gripes was becoming increasingly unbearable.

Siddhanta Darpan had not been printed yet and no one had read it, yet the book had become well known in all of Orissa.

Samanta Chandrasekhar had also earned fame as a great astrologer. Whoever had any doubts relating to astrology now approached him for help. In time, a few wanted to become his disciples. His first student was Rudra Narayan Jyotirbhusan Bhattacharya from village Nandipur in Midnapore. He lived for two years in Chandrasekhar's house in Khandapara and studied the *Siddhanta Darpan*. He translated the book into Bengali and on returning to Midnapore, brought out an almanac called the *Rudra Panjika*. However, this was replete with errors because he had not fully mastered astrological calculations. So Chandrasekhar stopped publishing the almanac after a year.

When the raja of Manjusha came to hear of Chandrasekhar's knowledge of astrology, he sent a pandit from his court to receive training from him. Thus Ballabh Vidyabhushan and Sirdhar Praharaj came to Khandapara. However, neither was able to master the intricacies of *Siddhanta Darpan*. Chandrasekhar's more successful disciples included Gadadhar Vidyabhusan from Manjusha, Damodar Vanibhushan from Talcher, and Sadashiv Khadiratna from Panchagada in Khurda. All these disciples helped spread Chandrasekhar's fame.

In 1878, Pandit Rudranarayan got a book titled *Sukshma Panjika* printed by the Puri Printing Company and circulated it. In eight slokas and the commentaries thereof, Chandrasekhar was eulogized as a great astronomer in the tradition of the greatest astronomers since the Satya Yug, who had established his findings after personal observation of the sky in the 4978th year of the Kali Yug.

A few years earlier, pandits in Puri had come to the decision that only *Druksiddha Panjika*, which had strictly followed *Siddhanta Darpan*, was reliable and that all temple rituals would be observed in accordance with its calculations.

However, in spite of all this, *Siddhanta Darpan* could not find a publisher. Naturally, Chandrasekhar felt terribly disheartened. He occasionally went to Cuttack and found out from Gourishankar how much money would be needed to get his book printed. The sum which Gourishankar mentioned was beyond Chandrasekhar's wildest imaginings. Through the *Dipika* Gourishankar had urged rajas and wealthy gentlemen in Orissa to extend financial help for the publication of *Siddhanta Darpan*; but, like earlier appeals made by the *Dipika*, this too had fallen on deaf ears.

The 12 July 1879 issue of the *Dipika* carried the following news item:

> An American Professor, through his calculations, has predicted that Jupiter, Saturn, Uranus and Neptune (the last two planets were not known to native astrologers in the past; so they do not have native names. These two planets have been discovered only recently) will come closest to the sun in the course of their revolutions in 1880. The professor predicts that terrible calamities will befall the earth during the period from 1880 to 1887. The Asian continent will lose all traces of human life. Europe will suffer a more or less similar fate and in America, human beings numbering a crore and a half will perish. Epidemics will be accompanied by cyclonic storms and tidal waves. Mountains will tumble down, and, as compasses will fail to work properly, thousands of sailors out at sea will lose their lives. Animals, birds and fish will die. The few who will survive the epidemics will be destroyed by famine and civil war. During the last two years of this period, fire will rage everywhere. Let Indian astrologers find out if this prediction is based on accurate calculations, and how the planets could be propitiated.

This terrifying news published in the *Dipika* made Chandrasekhar open his books, and he was soon absorbed in all kinds of calculations. He forgot to eat or drink and spent all his time doing calculations. The work occupied Chandrasekhar for several days. He finished his calculations on 4 August and on that very day he sent Gourishankar a letter which was meant for publication in the *Dipika*. According to his calculations, the American professor's prediction was wrong and that for the four planets to reach that kind of position it would take eleven lakh years.

Cuttack, October 1879

On 13 September, the following advertisement appeared below one for the sale of castor oil made by the inmates of the lunatic asylum Cuttack.

The History of Orissa
By
Sri Pyari Mohan Acharya
Price: One rupee only

Available for sale at the Cuttack Printing Company Press

Pyari Mohan had been working on this book for a long time. Four years earlier, Radhanath Ray, the joint inspector of schools in Orissa, had issued an advertisement that if someone wrote a history of Orissa in Oriya, and if it was approved by the joint inspector, the author would receive three hundred rupees as reward. Radhanath advised Pyari Mohan to revise the manuscript in a few places and get it published. Ravenshaw, too, asked Pyari Mohan to consult old records at the office of the commissioner and collect relevant historical facts. Pyari Mohan went to the commissioner's office and sifted through the records and documents. *The History of Orissa* was the outcome of these efforts. The book was long in getting published on account of his illness and problems at the printing press. In his preface Pyari Mohan wrote:

> I must gratefully acknowledge my indebtedness to many books and records from which I have collected facts for my book. These include accounts of Orissa authored by Hunter, Stirling, Sutton, Toynbee and Mitra, census records, histories of India

written by Elphinstone, Marshman, Blogman, some Islamic sources, records of the Asiatic Society, a few books in Sanskrit, Bengali and Oriya such as Manu, *Chaitanya Charitamrita*, *Dardhyata Bhakti*, and a few documents, old and recent, from the Commissioner's office.

When the book came out, it was warmly received by everyone, for it was the first of its kind. The book also greatly enhanced Pyari Mohan 's standing in society. For someone like him, who was only twenty-eight, this was the third major achievement. He had already received recognition for the publication of the magazine the *Utkal Putra* and for his founding of the Cuttack Academy.

The publication of *The History of Orissa* was soon followed by a crisis in the Cuttack Academy caused by Bipin Chandra Pal's leaving the school. The circumstances under which he gave up his job were not happy ones and these left Pyari Mohan sad and embarrassed.

Before leaving for Calcutta for the puja holidays, Bipin Chandra had drawn up a list of students who had been selected to appear for the entrance examination. A test had been conducted at the school and six students had been chosen. Bipin Chandra had filled up and signed their application forms, and had left these with Pyari Mohan, who was to send these on to the registrar of the university along with the examination fees. The entrance examination was to be held in November.

Among those students who had failed the school test there was one who had tried hard to persuade Bipin Chandra to let him through. But Bipin Chandra had refused to oblige. When he came back after the puja vacation, he discovered that Pyari Mohan had thrown away the applications signed by him and put his own signature on new forms and that the boy, whom Bipin Chandra had rejected, had been selected to appear for the entrance examination. Of course, Pyari Mohan, as rector of the school, was within his rights to do so. However, since he had left the school in Bipin Chandra's charge, he should not have interfered with Bipin Chandra's decision and curtailed his authority. In protest, Bipin Chandra resigned from the Cuttack Academy.

When he left Orissa, Bipin Chandra resolved that from now on, he would devote all his time to serving the country. He had spent less than a year in Cuttack, but he realized that this had been for him a period of apprenticeship. Cuttack had given him his first opportunity to take part in public life. The building of the Cuttack Printing Company was the place where he had honed his oratorial skills and his first mentor had been none other than Pyari Mohan.

Puri, March 1881

On 1 March, a group of strange looking people arrived at the gate of the Jagannath temple. The entrance was not yet crowded and only a few pilgrims were on their way into the temple. The reason why members of this group drew attention to themselves was that, covered in dust and dirt, they looked like snake charmers; the men wore nothing except a small loin cloth and the women were almost naked. They were carrying a pot of cooked rice in their hand from which they had been eating, and morsels of food clung to their fingers. As the temple was out of bounds for people belonging to the lower castes, a servitor tried to shut the Lion Gate to them.

The party, consisting of thirteen men and three women, threw the servitor down, shouting 'Alekh, Alekh,' and forced their way into the temple. However, at the request of the servitor, they did not carry the pot of rice into the temple but left it by the Aruna Pillar. Two hundred pilgrims also entered the temple along with them. When the group found the doors of the *bhoga mandap* locked, they forced it open and went into the Jagamohan. By this time, four hundred pilgrims had surrounded them to watch the fun.

They tried to force their way into the sanctum of the deities, but its doors were tightly shut and in spite of all their efforts, they could not succeed in opening them or in breaking into the sanctum. Then they came out of the temple and tried to find out if they could enter the sanctum through some other opening. By now, nearly a thousand people had gathered to watch. A slight scuffle had also broken out.

One of the persons in the group, who was shouting the most loudly, now climbed on to someone's shoulders to see if he could break into the sanctum, but he crashed and fell on a stone in front of Agniswar Mahadev. He lost consciousness and was carried outside by his companions. He could not be revived and died an hour later.

The police were informed. The assistant superintendent of police, Clark, came to the Aruna Pillar. The dead man lay there, surrounded by his companions. A crowd of nearly a thousand people stood encircling them. Since the temple was out of bounds for Clark, Sub-inspector Krupasindhu Mohanty went inside to conduct an inquiry. The body was sent for a post-mortem and fifteen members of the group were arrested, charged with breach of peace and other offences.

It was learnt from them that the dead man was the leader of the party and that his name was Dasaram. They had set out from Sambalpur about a week ago in obedience to their guru's orders. The guru had instructed them to desecrate the Jagannath temple by scattering left over food there, and to take the three idols to the main street of Puri and burn them down. Alekh himself, their deity, had allegedly appeared to the guru in a dream and had set him this task.

They further revealed that another party was on its way to

Puri from Sambalpur. Clark immediately sent policemen to find out if such a party was indeed approaching Puri. He also informed Armstrong about the incident. Armstrong, being the kind of man he was, was expected to rush to the spot on horseback as soon as he heard. So Clark sent word to him that there would be no point in his coming to the Aruna Pillar as the dead body had already been conveyed to the hospital and the rest of the party were now in the lock-up.

That day, around evening, at Satyabadi, the police arrested another party which was on its way to Puri. This group included six men, eleven women and eleven small children. This group, too, intended to carry out their guru's order to desecrate the temple and to set the idols on fire.

At night, all the offerings which had been prepared inside the temple that day were thrown away, and, since someone had died inside the temple, it was purified by performing suitable rites. In his report, the civil surgeon B.B. Gupta said that Dasaram's death was caused by his fall, with a full stomach, on the stone.

Clark and Krupasindhu finished their inquiry and filed a case in the cutcherry of the deputy magistrate, Kamalnath Ghosh. Two different charges had been brought against the accused: the first group was booked under sections 147 and 297 of the penal code for illegal entry and breach of peace; the second group was booked as vagrants under section 94 of the Civil Code.

On 7 March, the magistrate pronounced his judgment on the second case after hearing the depositions made by the temple servitors, the civil surgeon and police officials. Referring to the case (Her Majesty versus seventeen defendants including Maya, Bhaja, Jeera, Heera), the magistrate observed that the defendants could not be penalized under section 94 for they were no different from the hundreds of wandering beggars who came to Puri in search of livelihood; they were in rags, and their extreme poverty could not lead one to suspect that they were engaged in committing crimes in order to make a living. However, four of them had confessed that they were going to Puri with the intention of taking out the images from the temple and setting them alight. This proved that they had taken part in a riot according to section 143. In view of this, the magistrate sentenced Maya, Bhaja, Jeera and Heera to seven days' rigorous imprisonment and acquitted the others.

The verdict on the first case (Jagua Singh versus fifteen defendants including Dhani, Situ, Bhagat, Mayaram) was given on 14 March. It was established during the trial that the defendants had travelled to Puri under Dasaram's leadership to burn down the images of the deities. Such was their faith in the guru that some of them claimed to have heard his voice from the skies. Sixteen of them had left the children and a few others, and come to the temple. When they tried to force their way into the temple, Dasaram fell on a stone slab in the scuffle and died. So deep-rooted was their faith that they were convinced that the guru had taken Dasaram to himself. They complained that they had been roughed up by the temple guards but the servitors said that they had beaten them lightly only to force them to leave the temple premises. After the witnesses gave their evidence, the magistrate pronounced all fifteen defendants guilty as charged and sentenced every one of them to two months' rigorous imprisonment under section 147, and to one month's rigorous imprisonment under section 297.

Commissioner Smith reported the attack on Lord Jagannath to the government. The government, upset by this unusual incident, ordered the commissioner of Chhatisgarh to investigate the activities of the religious sect thoroughly and send a report.

Calcutta, August 1881

When eleven pilgrims had died in a stampede inside the Puri temple four years earlier, the government had directed the raja of Puri to form a committee which would formulate rules and regulations for the proper management of temple affairs. It was decided that unless the raja did what the government had asked him to do, he would not receive the sanad and the khilat of maharaja. The mishap had occurred in February 1877, during the *Govinda Dwadashi* festival. When the raja took no steps to form the committee even after a long delay, Armstrong wrote him a stiff letter. In August, the raja set up a committee, the members of which included Mahant Madan Mohan Das, Mahant Radhacharan Das, Adhikari Rasbehari Das, Ramachandra Rajguru, Nilambar Bahinipati, Gobinda Santara and a few others. This committee framed the rules and sent them to the collector, who, in turn, forwarded them to the commissioner.

Many people raised objections to these rules. To sort the matter out, Armstrong called a meeting of the general public in Puri. Here, many expressed their support for the rules framed by the raja's committee. After discussions, it was decided that a new committee be constituted taking a few of the gentlemen present as members. This committee would frame new rules for the management of the temple. Members of this committee included the deputy collectors Nabin Chandra Sen and Mahanand Gupta, Munsif Jagat Ballav Majumdar, zamindar Loknath Ray, headmaster Ramdas Chakravorty, Mahant Narayan Das, and Pandit Tarakant Vidyasagar.

Shortly afterwards, Divyasingh got embroiled in the murder case and was deported. His son Mukunda was then only two years old. Queen Suryamani was, therefore, placed in charge of the temple and its landed property.

In spite of all this, the new committee went ahead with holding meetings in order to frame the rules for the management of the temple. But the members on this committee failed to reach a consensus on any issue whatsoever and, in the end, submitted to Armstrong two sets of rules. After going through these, Armstrong slightly modified the set of rules framed by Mahant Narayan Das and Tarakant Vidyasagar and forwarded it to the commissioner. These rules had provided for the convenience and safety of the pilgrims.

Before these rules were framed, Ravenshaw had sent the government a proposal suggesting that the management of the temple be withdrawn from the raja and placed in the hands of a committee. However, the proposal had been turned down because the law department was of the opinion that such a step could not be taken in view of a law passed in 1840.

When Armstrong forwarded a new set of rules, the law department was again consulted. They advised that it would not be right for the government to frame rules for the management of the temple. But, if the raja happened to be a minor, the government could appoint a manager. However, this would entail an amendment of the 1840 Act. The government now sought the views of the board on this matter.

In February 1879, Dampier, a member of the board, came to Orissa and discussed the matter with Commissioner Smith, Collector Armstrong, and several local gentlemen. On returning to Calcutta, he expressed the view that when the raja was a minor and unfit to rule, the government should have the power to form a committee and entrust it with the task of ordering the affairs of the temple. A new law should be passed for this purpose.

The government accepted this view, but it took a lot of time to decide how to translate it into practice. On the one hand, there was no need to pass a new law; the government could appoint a committee according to section 539 of the Civil Procedure Code. To reach a decision on the matter, a meeting was held on 22 August 1881 at the board office. Among those present were member of the board Reynolds, the advocate general G.C. Paul, the legal remembrancer T.T. Allen, and the standing counsellor, W.C. Bonnerjee. Paul was of the opinion that section 539 was not applicable to Jagannath temple, for it applied only to charitable trusts. Allen, too, shared Paul's view. Bonnerjee, on the other hand, contended that even if the temple were treated as a trust, no court of law would allow the appointment of anyone as manager in place of the raja as long as the 1840 law was in force.

Everyone agreed with Bonnerjee. A lot of discussion followed but in the end, no decision regarding the introduction of changes in the administration of the temple could be arrived at. The Puri temple continued to be run in a chaotic and disorganized manner by Queen Suryamani, who had never ever stepped out of the palace.

Cuttack, November 1881

Reports on the members of the Alekh sect now began reaching the government from different places. Besides the commissioner of Chhatisgarh, the tehsildar of Banki, Balaram Bose, the tehsildar of Angul, Bichand Charan Pattanayak, and the manager of Dhenkanal, Banamali Singh, had submitted their reports. Having studied all these, the judicial department issued a resolution on 21 October. This contained an account of the attack on Lord Jagannath as well as facts about the sect.

The followers of this sect, who wear the *kumbhipata* bark and are called the *kumbhipatuas*, believed in Alekh Swami who had come from the Himalayas in 1864 to Banki and had initiated sixty-four disciples. From there, Alekh Swami had gone to Dhenkanal and his cult had then spread to Sambalpur. The central tenets of this cult consisted in a belief in one supreme being, truthfulness and obedience to the guru. Members of the Alekh cult did not accept idol worship; they did not take medicines; they ate only during daytime, and cared little for personal hygiene. Anyone who violated these norms was expelled from the sect. The tehsildar of Angul persuaded the criminally inclined *Panas* tribe to join this sect and thus brought the crime rate down.

Bhima Kandha of Sonepur was the leader of the kumbhipatua sect. Though born blind, he had memorized the Ramayan and the Mahabharat by listening to these epics being recited. He himself composed songs. The kumbhipatuas held Bhima in great reverence. Although they regarded Bhima's relationship with one of his female disciples with suspicion, they did not question his authority on this account. When the woman became pregnant, Bhima predicted that she would give birth to the great warrior Arjun, who would destroy all unbelievers. Everyone took him at his word. But, in the end, the woman was delivered of a girl. Bhima now claimed that he had been told in a dream a few days earlier that this girl would kill the unbelievers with the power of her maya. But, when the baby girl died a few days later, Bhima explained that she, who was a goddess after all, had left the world, for she found it overburdened with iniquities.

After this incident, some of Bhima's followers left him and formed another sect. Nevertheless, many chose to remain with Bhima who got a platform constructed and sat on it with the woman by his side every day in the morning. His followers offered worship to them and drank the milk in which they had washed their feet.

The kumbhipatuas who had gone to Puri were from Chandrapur. Their leader, Dasaram, was confident that when they burned the idol of Jagannath, the Hindus would lose faith in their religion and embrace the Alekh cult.

As soon as the resolution came out in the *Calcutta Gazette*, Gourishankar published its Oriya translation in the *Dipika*. A few days later, when Bichand Pattanayak came to Cuttack, Gourishankar discussed the Alekh sect with him at the

Cuttack Printing Company. Bichand warned that although the kumbhipatuas were not at the moment being troublesome, they might create problems for the government in future. He predicted that one could never rule out the recurrence of incidents like the attack on Lord Jagannath in the years to come. Gourishankar said, 'I sounded a note of caution long ago.'

Bichand protested, 'This cannot be true, for no one had studied this sect before I did. It was I who persuaded the Panas to embrace the kumbhipatua cult, and I had sent a report to the government regarding my initiative.' On hearing this, Gourishankar rolled out a reed mat on the floor and set about scanning old issues of the *Dipika*. In fact, the 1 June 1867 issue of the *Dipika* had carried a piece on the Mahima religion. About ten years earlier, in the 26 August 1871 issue of the *Dipika*, a letter on the fruit-eating kumbhipatuas of Dhenkanal and other garjats had been published. Gourishankar continued his search and located a piece on Mahima Babaji which had come out in the 6th September 1873 issue of the *Dipika*. He read it out: 'They do not recognize the Vedas or other holy scriptures. Nor do they offer worship to any deity. Their religion has no Vedas, nor any other written scripture. They recognize only Mahima and no one else. They refuse to have anything to do with rajas, Brahmins, barbers, gardeners and prostitutes.'

Gourishankar went on to read aloud the comments he had made on this at the time: 'We have nothing to say on religious matters but we would like to know why followers of this sect regard the raja as an enemy of religion, and what they mean by the word 'raja'. If by this is meant a raja of a garjat, we have nothing to say. But if it refers to the British Government, we have difficulties with it. The authorities should make the members of the sect explain fully what they have in mind. It is likely that they might be portraying the British as enemies of religion and, in the process, diminishing people's loyalty to the Government. This may eventually lead to rebellion.'

Bichand conceded defeat, and their discussion came to an end. However, Gourishankar decided that he should call on Madhusudan Das and talk to him about this matter.

Two months earlier, Madhusudan had appeared in Cuttack just as suddenly as he had vanished from Balasore fifteen years ago. However, he had undergone many changes in the meantime: he had converted to Christianity during his stay in Calcutta. In 1873 he had married Soudamini Chattopadhyay, a Bengali Christian who had been his classmate at Bethune College, and was one year older than he. While in Calcutta, he had taken up different jobs: he had been a lecturer at Srirampur College, the headmaster of Garden Reach High School, a private tutor to Asutosh Mukherjee and so on. In 1878 he had taken a degree in law and set up practice at the Alipore Court. That very year his wife passed away. Now, back in Cuttack, he had taken up residence in Dagarpara and had set up his chambers in a rented house in Beharibag. He combined legal practice with active participation in public meetings in Cuttack. Though aged only thirty-three, he was reckoned a famous man in Orissa for he was its first M.A. and the first Oriya lawyer. If someone said 'Madhu Babu', it referred only to Madhusudan Das.

Gourishankar was ten years Madhu Babu's senior. Nevertheless, the two happened to be very good friends, and they made a point of meeting each other at regular intervals. A noticeable change had come over Madhu Babu since he returned from Calcutta: he spoke only in Bangla, and everyone had to talk to him in Bangla. However, this was nothing unusual in Orissa at the time, because educated Oriyas, especially those who had embraced Brahmoism, conversed in Bangla and used it in their correspondence. Even Fakir Mohan and Madhu Rao were no exceptions.

After his discussion with Bichand Pattanayak, Gourishankar chanced to meet Madhu Babu. The latter had, in the meantime, read the resolution relating to the kumbhipatuas. When Gourishankar narrated to him what had passed between him and Bichand regarding this subject, Madhubabu said, 'Before any of you knew anything about Mahima, I had heard of him and seen him.'

Madhubabu's father, Choudhury Raghunath Das used to be the raja of Patia's vakil, and his work sometimes took him to Patia. In 1874, after passing his entrance examination, Madhusudan had accompanied his father to Patia and there he had seen Mahima Gosain. On the day of Dola Purnima, Mahima Gosain had come to Patia and delivered a discourse there. Madhusudan had listened to him with rapt attention, and the quality of Mahima's character and his piety had deeply impressed him.

When Gourishankar raised the question of treason, and such matters, Madhubabu said, 'Had Mahima Gosain been born in a province like Bombay Presidency, Punjab or Bengal, he would have become as famous and esteemed as Dayanand Saraswati or Ram Mohan Roy. Pity, he was born in Orissa.'

Mayurbhanj, December 1881

Radhanath distinguished himself during the four years he served as joint inspector of schools in Cuttack. People in Orissa accorded him a pride of place among the literati. He had received warm appreciation from the educated section of society for the textbooks he had written. Once, while visiting Mayurbhanj on official business, he had had occasion to make the acquaintance of the raja, Krushna Chandra Bhanj. The raja and Radhanath sometimes happened to meet at Shyamanand Dey's residence in Balasore, too. Although Krushna Chandra was the same age as Radhanath, the latter gave Krushna Chandra the respect due to a father, for he was a royal personage. Accordingly, Radhanath, affectionately treated Krushna Chandra's eleven-year-old son, Sri

Ramachandra as his younger brother. Radhanath advised the raja on the management of the educational system in Mayurbhanj. His advice was also sought on which magazines should be procured from London, and which books the royal library should buy.

Ramachandra respectfully treated Radhanath as his elder brother and maintained a regular correspondence with him. In his letters he talked about matters such as his private tutor, his health, horse-riding, and the books he had read. Radhanath's replies to his letters solemnly advised him to be truthful, to follow the path of virtue, and suggested to him a list of books he should read.

In 1881, Krushna Chandra wrote to the commissioner requesting him to appoint Babu Nandakishore Das, who was then assistant superintendent of the garjat mahal, as dewan of Mayurbhanj. In his view, Nandakishore would be an ideal choice for the post. The raja was willing to pay him a salary of six hundred rupees per month. However, Nandakishore thought he would not gain financially if he accepted the job, so he declined the offer.

Krushna Chandra's health was indifferent, and he thought he might die soon. He, therefore, wanted to groom Ramachandra as a worthy successor. He felt that his problem would be solved if he could persuade Radhanath to become his dewan, who could then also teach Ramachandra. Krushna Chandra wrote to Radhanath asking him to join as the dewan of Mayurbhanj. He wrote to Shyamanand Dey to persuade Radhanath to accept the job. He requested Commissioner Smith to loan Radhanath out to his kingdom. When no clear response to the offer came from Radhanath, Krushna Chandra wrote him the following letter:

Dear Sir,

We are in receipt of the two letters you wrote us. We have written to Sri Raja Shyamanand Dey, too. We will get in touch with you when we receive a reply from him. You will certainly realize that my house belongs to you, and that you will feel absolutely at home here. If you would kindly come over here, we would feel that you have been the means of saving our life. You know very well what illness we are suffering from at the moment. When we exert ourselves our condition changes for the worse. We now leave Ramachandra's upbringing in your hands. He is your younger brother. You will take whatever measures are necessary for ordering the affairs of the kingdom. We are confident that you would agree to come to Mayurbhanj. We vest you with all our powers. Do accept our request.

Sri Maharaja Krushna Chandra Bhanj

When Radhanath received the letter, he thought of what he would gain and what he would lose if he accepted this offer. He was now placed in a grade which fetched him four hundred rupees a month. In the near future he expected to be promoted to grade one. Krushna Chandra was willing to give him six hundred rupees a month. In addition to this, he would be given rent-free accommodation and travelling allowance. Radhanath now made inquiries about the government officials who had taken up service under rajas of feudatory states. The deputy inspector of schools of Cuttack, Pyari Mohan Sen, received a monthly salary of one hundred rupees before he took a job under the raja of Dhenkanal, who gave him one hundred and eighty rupees a month. When he went back to government service, Pyari Mohan discovered that he had been deprived of his annual increments and that he had been transferred out of Cuttack. He had thus ended up a loser. But, on the other hand, the tehsildar of Angul had gained by choosing to serve in Dhenkanal. He had been getting a monthly salary of two hundred rupees from the government. The raja of Dhenkanal gave him the same salary but he also gave him twenty-three thousand rupees in cash and appointed him *behera pradhan*, which was a supervisory post which brought him another fifteen thousand rupees. However, Radhanath thought that it would look extremely odd if he took the rather undignified job of behera pradhan along with that of dewan.

Radhanath consulted many people including Madhu Rao, Shyamanand Dey, the director of education, and a few others. Before arriving at a decision, Radhanath wrote a letter to Krushna Chandra, which said:

Revered Majesty,

I received your letter today. The letter reflects the kindness and charity which fill your royal heart. I always regard Your Majesty as my father and Sriman Ramachandra as my younger brother. I pray to god to bless Ramachandra so that he has a long life and establishes himself as a ruler as famous as you are, or earn even greater fame than Your Majesty has won.

At present, I am placed in the 400 rupees grade. Although Your Majesty offers me 600 rupees I feel diffident about taking up the job. Why? There are several deep seated reasons for this, which I'll explain to Your Majesty when I present myself in person to you; I feel unable to state them in writing. Your Majesty may ask, 'Why? You will retain your government job, and should you feel like giving up your job at Mayurbhanj for some reason, you could always return to your earlier job. What, then, is your problem?' There are several answers to this question but all these cannot be given in this letter. However, I can mention one here: suppose I revert to my earlier job after working at Mayurbhanj for six months or a year. I shall find then that I have been transferred from Cuttack to some far-off station like Bihar, Dacca and Chatagram, and also that another person has been appointed on a permanent basis to my present post. Besides, I will also be deprived of the benefit of my annual increments.

In the garjats everything is deeply personalized. Just as someone could rise very high in a short time as a result of royal favour, he can come to harm if he for some reason incurs royal displeasure. Serving under the government, however, minimizes these opportunities as well as the risks. One's career, therefore, becomes less precarious.

If the reasons stated above are in any way offensive to Your Majesty, I hope, generous as you are, you would forgive my lapses. I know very well that Your Majesty counts me as one of your dependents and as one of the members of Your Majesty's family, and by the grace of god the bond that ties me to Your Majesty would never be dissolved. However, if I have the good fortune of ever taking up the job in Mayurbhanj, a new relationship between Your Majesty and myself would be established, and this, in the best interests of both of us, should supersede the earlier one obtaining between us.

I have worked for long years in one department and risen as high as it is possible to do in this department in Orissa. I sincerely want to work in other departments, do other kinds of jobs, and, by god's grace, establish myself by giving a good account of myself. But I will be able to translate this dream into reality only through your generosity. I wonder if Your Majesty considers me deserving of his kindness; but all I can say is that, if hard work and sincerity qualify one for receiving royal favour, I will never fail to be worthy of it.

Since I am at present a class two officer in the education department, I am entitled to annual increments, of which I will be deprived if I choose to leave the department. If, unfortunately for me, I have to come back to my earlier post, I have to begin with my old scale of pay. Taking all these things into consideration, I feel that I do not stand to gain should I decide to go to Mayurhanj. I leave it to Your Majesty to understand why I would be unwilling to take up the job offered to me under these circumstances.

I am a native of Balasore and so I look upon Mayurbhanj as my chief place of shelter. I am willing to live as a subject of the Mayurbhanj state under favourable circumstances. Mayurbhanj is blessed for it has Your Majesty as its ruler. If the Almighty gives Sriman Ramachandra a long life, his reign will be even more glorious than the present one. It is another matter whether I am able to contribute to its glory or not; but I will always continue to wish Mayurbhanj well.

The Commissioner wants me to convey to him my views regarding this matter at the earliest. However, arriving at a decision on a serious subject like this takes time.

Your obedient servant,
Radhanath Ray

Radhanath was expecting that on receiving this letter, Krushna Chandra would, on his own, offer him a higher salary or make arrangements for enabling him to earn more money from other sources. But no such offer came. His friends, for their part, did not openly dissuade him from going to the garjat, but they dwelt on the problems he might face there. The director of education, Mr Croft, made it clear to him in a letter that since there was no chance of his getting promoted to class one in the near future, he was free to go to Mayurbhanj, if he so wished. While he was being assailed by these uncertainties, Radhanath received a letter from the assistant superintendent of garjat asking him to let him know if he would go to Mayurbhanj or not. He was supposed to have communicated his decision ten days earlier.

Radhanath received this letter during his tour of Puri. He cursed Krushna Chandra and his own luck. Peeved, he replied to the letter, saying, 'During my visit to Mayurbhanj I had met the Maharaja, discussed the matter with him, and had requested that I be given a month or two to make up my mind. However, if the matter is so urgent that it cannot admit of any further delay, I regret that I am not in a position to say that I would accept the job.'

Krushna Chandra, on his sickbed, was very sad to learn that Radhanath had expressed his unwillingness to come to Mayurbhanj.

Cuttack, December 1881

Pyari Mohan received a lot of praise when *The History of Orissa* was published. However, he also came to be vilified by a few. Since he attacked superstitions in Hinduism in his public lectures, he was labelled anti-Hindu. The vilification campaign rose to such a pitch that Pyari Mohan had no option but to publish the following letter in the *Dipika*:

> I have come to know that a few persons are trying to convince others that I habitually revile Hindus and Hinduism. I challenge these gentlemen to say in which of my lectures, or in which portions of these lectures, I have said things derogatory to Hindus or Hinduism. I humbly request the editor and others who have attended my lectures to clarify if I have ever made disrespectful remarks about any religion, or if I have said things which would have hurt the sentiments of the practitioners of any religion.
>
> Yours,   Cuttack
> Pyari Mohan Acharya   28 December 1880

Pyari Mohan's *The History of Orissa* became the target of another concerted attack which was led by Kalipada Banerjee of Cuttack. He wrote against the book in Calcutta based newspapers and published an article under the title 'Jagannathi Number One'. He focused on what he regarded as a major error in Pyari Mohan's account of Kalapahad's invasion of Orissa. Here is what Pyari Mohan had written on the subject:

> After Kalapahad conquered Puri, he set about desecrating and vandalizing Hindu gods and goddesses. Lord Jagannath's servitors took his image away and buried it in Parikud, which lay on the shore of the Chilka lake. But wicked Kalapahad found out about this, and went to Parikud, dug out the image and conveyed it on an elephant to the banks of the river Ganga. There he flung the image into a funeral pyre. But the Oriyas, deeply devoted to

the Lord as they are, did not let the idol burn to ashes. A man called Bisara Mohanty took the image out of the pyre, salvaged its holy navel and carried it back to Orissa. The raja of Kujang received the navel and installed it in a temple.

Kalipada argued that Pyari Mohan's statement about Lord Jagannath having been burnt in a funeral pyre would cause devotees to lose all their respect for the images in Puri temple; and pilgrims would stop coming to Puri and refuse to eat the mahaprasad of the temple.

When Kalipada's letter came out in the *Daily News* published from Calcutta, it triggered a heated controversy in Orissa. In Pyari Mohan's defence, it was said that he had relied on the *Madala Panji* and Sutton's *History of Orissa* for his account of Kalapahad's attack. Since Sutton's *History* had been earlier prescribed as a school textbook, there was no reason why someone should find Pyari Mohan's account objectionable. It was further argued that the falling of stones from the Puri temple had had no influence on the flow of pilgrims to Puri. Even the arrest and deportation of the raja of Puri had not led to any disturbance in the temple. Why should then a portion in Pyari Mohan's *The History of Orissa* cause any trouble?

Kalipada did not rest content with writing letters to newspapers and distributing pamphlets. He sent a petition to the collector drawing his attention to the matter. He pointed out another error in Pyari Mohan's *History*: the book contained a statement that although the government had promised to introduce Permanent Settlement in Orissa in 1813 they had deprived the people of the province of this benefit. In Kalipada's view, this amounted to insulting the government by calling them deceivers.

The collector sought the opinion of the education committee on the matter. The committee held a meeting on 7 April and consulted the members. The deputy inspector of schools, Uma

Prasad De, and a couple of members took Kalipada's side, but other members of the committee found nothing objectionable in Pyari Mohan's statement. The interpretation of the words 'funeral pyre' led to a lot of arguments. While Kali Babu and his supporters insisted that they meant fire in which dead bodies were burnt, the others argued that the words meant any fire made by burning pieces of wood. Similarly, many in the committee were of the view that 'deprive' could not be made to mean 'deceive'. In the end, the committee came to the conclusion that Pyari Mohan's book contained nothing objectionable at all.

Upset that his efforts had come to nothing, Kalipada now published another letter bearing the title 'Jagannathi Number Two'. In this he wrote that in 1867, students of Baideswar school had refused to attend class when they were taught the portion in Sutton's *History of Orissa* relating to the desecration of the image of Lord Jagannath. In the end, the school was closed down. The letter also carried an account of what had transpired at the meeting of the education committee, and a virulent attack on Pyari Mohan's book.

This letter was quickly followed by yet another under the title 'Jagannathi Number Three'. The letter reproduced the correspondence regarding the book between the collector and other authorities. Among these, one was of special significance: it was written by Uma Prasad De and he had said, 'The author of the book pours scorn on the religious sentiments of Hindus by spreading lies about Lord Jagannath just as he openly ridicules Hindus in public meetings attended by immature young persons.'

Although the book had received a reward from the government, these controversies led to its being withdrawn from schools on Collector Pawsy's order. This came as a painful blow to Pyari Mohan.

Before the dust of this controversy settled, another serious problem occupied Pyari Mohan's attention. The problem related to a case registered against the tehsildar of Banki. Pyari Mohan's close friend, Gobinda Rath, had accused the tehsildar of Banki of having taken bribes, and he had requested the commissioner to transfer the said tehsildar from Banki. After teaching for a few days at the Cuttack Academy, Gobinda Rath had returned to Banki and devoted himself full time to writing and social work. He had now taken this extreme step in response to the intensity of public opinion against the tehsildar in Banki.

When this case came up for trial, Pyari Mohan was manager, Dompara. To boost Gobinda Rath's morale, he wrote to him.

My dear Rath,

The task you have set yourself demands a lot of caution. Make sure the witnesses depose properly in the court. They can never be wholly relied on to tell the truth. That the Commissioner has declined to transfer the tehsildar gives me cause for apprehension. Be careful. Virtue will certainly triumph in the end. Bear this in mind and keep trying. Leave the rest to the Almighty.

Send the news to all Bengali and Oriya newspapers. Wire the *Mirror* and the *Statesman* that people of Banki have petitioned the Commissioner against the tyranny of the deputy magistrate there, and that the petitioners have requested the Commissioner to remove the said official from Banki for the duration of the trial, but the Commissioner has refused to do so and had summoned witnesses etc.

Consult Madhu and send the news by telegram. Wire the news after evening so that you could send thirty-six words for one rupee.

Write back giving me all the news.

Yours,   20 August 1880
Pyari Mohan

When newspapers carried stories on Banki, the commissioner sent his seristadar Balaram Bose to take over charge from the tehsildar of Banki, Srinath Babu. The *Balasore Sambad Bahika* published the following satirical poem on the incident;

> Listen, O Pariksha
> The strange tale of Gobinda.
> No one's power is absolute.
> The demon Ravana has been removed
> But his followers roam the land
> Looting people.
> But no one dares oppose them.
> They take money
> But everyone stands awed and scared.
> The Lord who lays the wicked low
> Took the form of Gobinda,
> Who displayed great courage.
> A copy of *Haribansa* in hand
> He went to the law court
> To kill one of these demons.

On 23 December, Pyari Mohan arrived in Cuttack from Dompara. He had high fever. Madhu Rao came rushing to his residence. When Pyari Mohan saw him, he said, 'I am going to die.' Madhu protested, 'But how can you say so. When we were children, we had resolved that we'd all die on the same day. We have so much work to do.'

Pyari Mohan suffered for a few more days from the fever and on 29 December at 9 a.m. breathed his last. He was only thirty at the time of his death. Condoling his death, people praised the three great monuments he had left behind: the magazine, *Utkal Putra*, The Cuttack Academy, and *The History of Orissa*. But people forgot to add to this list two living monuments left behind by Pyari Mohan: his friends Gobinda Rath and Madhu Rao.

nine

Puri, December 1882

There was no news of Divyasingh after he was transferred from Cuttack jail to Calcutta jail. Once, news arrived that he had been given the work of a composer at the printing press of the Presidency Jail in Calcutta. The last thing people heard of him was that he had been sent to the Andamans on a ship called the Sahara on 4 September 1878. His legs had to be fettered during the voyage for he behaved like a mad man. When the ship reached the island, he cried inconsolably, and had to be kept in a special cell.

As for Queen Suryamani, she was relieved that Divyasingh was deported, and she hoped the palace would now be a quiet place. She did nothing about getting Divyasingh's punishment mitigated. However, Divyasingh's father, the raja of Khemandi, petitioned the British Parliament, praying to them to set his son free. He went to great expense and hired a lawyer for this purpose but his efforts came to nothing in the end.

Now Suryamani made it her chief concern to ensure that Divyasingh's son would inherit all the property and the privileges. On behalf of the underaged boy, she wrote to the government requesting that the pension which the then raja of Puri had received be given her in the interest of Divyasingh's wife Niladri and their son Jagannath Jenamani. Her lawyer argued before the district judge that Divyasingh's deportation had disgraced him so thoroughly that he should be divested of all his rights and his property should pass on to his son. The district judge accepted her petition and passed the following order:

Jagannath Jenamani, a resident of Khundheibent Sahi in Puri district is a minor. Until he reaches the age of discretion, that is, till the year 1897, Suryamani Pata Mahadei is placed, by this court's order of the 12th of this month, in charge of the property of the above-mentioned person according to section 7 of the statute number 40 of the year 1858. However, exercising the powers vested in this court by section 21 of the same statute, the court will have the right to invalidate this certificate. You have been vested with the following powers:

You are required to take stock of the property of the underage person. You are also required to collect the income from his estate and settle all dues owed by the estate. You will have to conduct all court cases relating to the property.

You are required to be careful while carrying out the task with which you have been entrusted. You shall neither sell nor mortgage any part of the minor Jenamani's property. Moreover, you shall not give anyone *pata* valid for more than five years without taking this court's permission. You are required to maintain proper records of income and expenditure and keep all necessary documents. This must be borne in mind

27 August 1879

Queen Suryamani appointed Ramprasad Singh, who was the commissioner's seristadar, to order the affairs of the zamindari and the temple. While everything seemed to be in order, news arrived that a plan to enact a new law, on the strength of which the affairs of the temple would be managed by a committee, was being contemplated in Calcutta. Suryamani called Ramprasad and discussed the matter with him. They decided that they could get the problem out of the way by declaring Jagannath Jenamani the raja of Puri. For this purpose, the following royal decree was issued: 'The *parichha* of the temple of Lord Jagannath and other servitors are hereby informed that the coronation of Jagannath Jenamani will take place on Monday the 20th day of Magha. You are all required, as custom demands, to present yourselves before His Majesty.'

On 1 May 1882, Jagannath Jenamani ascended the throne, assuming a new name: Sri Mukunda Dev. Such a step did not find favour with many for Divyasingh was still alive. The *Dipika* had this to say of the coronation:

> How would it have mattered if the throne would have lain empty for a few more days? Although the Raja has been deported for life, the possibility of his coming back under some circumstances can never be ruled out. The rules of the prison and a pardon from the Empress of India may bring about his release. He has a long life before him, and in view of his youth, it cannot be said that his crime is beyond pardon. Again, one should not forget that his son is but a mere child, and will remain a minor for quite some time, and that his affairs will be managed by others. Under circumstances like these, one wonders why he should be placed on the throne now. One gets the impression that this step is calculated to rob the jailed Raja of whatever sympathy people still feel for him.

Heedless of the criticism her action invited, Suryamani turned her attention to the law that was going to be enacted in Calcutta. Adverse circumstances had made her worldly-wise and had sharpened her survival instinct. She was now well equipped to face problems with courage. She set about mobilizing popular opinion against the proposed law. On 8 July, Madhab Panda, along with four hundred and fifty people, wrote to the commissioner saying that the proposal to set up a committee which would manage the affairs of the Puri temple scared them. The raja of Puri had always overseen the affairs of the temple and for this reason, all the rajas in India had held him in high esteem. If the management of the temple passed into the hands of a committee, they argued, the affairs of the temple would be thrown into disarray.

On 18 July, Suryamani herself submitted a long petition to the lieutenant governor. With the help of quotations from the *Madala Panji*, she stated that in the Satya Yug, Raja Indradyumna the constructed the temple for Lord Jagannath and there offered worship to the Lord. Later, in the *Treta* and the *Dwapar* ages, other rajas had worshipped Lord Jagannath in the temple. However, the temple collapsed during the Kali Yug, and Raja Anangabhima Dev had got a new temple built and ordered its affairs. Thus, for generations, royal families had been managing the temple. After the deportation of Divyasingh, Suryamani herself was looking after the administration of the temple on behalf of her grandson. Taking the management of the temple out of the hands of the royal family would, therefore, not only amount to an insult to Hinduism, it would also constitute a slight to the royal family, and throw the affairs of the temple into disorder. Although her son had been deported, he was still alive, and he had a son. It would be unfair to deprive Divyasingh's son of his inheritance.

Not content with having done this, Suryamani persuaded sanyasis and the mahants of mutts to send petitions to the government. A petition submitted on 19 July reiterated the claim that since the Satya Yug the right to manage the temple had been vested the raja. It pleaded in its concluding part that the management of the temple be left in the care of the Puri royal family, and the proposal to set up a committee be cancelled.

On 22 July, the Brahmins of Puri and those from the sixteen sasanas too sent a petition. In it they argued that although the affairs of the temple in Bhubaneswar and Satyabadi were being managed by committees, these temples occupied a position which was much inferior to that of Puri, and that, in any case, the committees were not doing a good job. Then, with the help of texts such as *Niladri Mohoday* and *Kshetra Mahatamya*, they established that worship to Lord Jagannath could not be offered in the absence of the raja of Puri. Entrusting any other body with the management of the affairs of Puri temple would amount to an insult to the Hindu community. On receiving these petitions, the government thought better of forming the committee.

With a view to establishing the authority of the raja of Puri fully, Suryamani now decided to name regnal years after Mukunda's name. On the occasion of Sunia, Mukunda, a minor, marched to the palace in Balisahi with great pomp and proclaimed the beginning of a new regnal era under his name. From this Sunia began the third regnal year of Mukunda Dev, for, according to convention, the second regnal year began at the time of the ceremony. Three hundred rupees were collected by way of *salami*. However, this step was disapproved of by many, for Mukunda's father, Divyasingh, was still alive. Some people irreverently referred to the regnal year as the year of *mahalia* Mukunda Dev.

In December, Suryamani got Jagannath Jenamani's name changed to Raja Mukunda Dev in all official records by sending in an application to the district judge.

Cuttack, September 1883

The lawsuit which Gourishankar had filed against the Cuttack municipality demanding that he be repaid a sum of three rupees thirteen annas and three paise took a year and a half to be settled.

Cuttack collector R.H. Pawsy was then chairman, Cuttack municipality. In 1880, when the revision of municipality taxes had taken place, Pawsy sahib had raised the tax on Gourishankar from nine to twelve rupees. This was done in view of the fact that

Gourishankar's brother, Harishankar, had, in the meantime, taken up a job that earned him a salary of thirty rupees a month.

In 1882, the vice-chairman of the municipality doubled this amount and sent Gourishankar a notice demanding payment of six rupees towards taxes due for three months. But since taxes had not been revised at the time, Gourishankar petitioned against this notice. He was informed by the authorities that his monthly income had exceeded two hundred rupees. He himself was earning one hundred rupees a month as editor of the *Utkal Dipika* and as secretary, the Cuttack Printing Company. His younger brother, who lived with him, received a monthly salary of thirty rupees. Another brother of his had recently landed a government job carrying a monthly salary of thirty-two rupees. In view of this, higher taxes had been levied on him. In June 1882, Gourishankar filed a review petition challenging this decision, but Collector Pawsy refused to reconsider the order.

According to Gourishankar's own calculations, he was to pay three rupees towards taxes for three months but he received a notice asking him to deposit six rupees instead. When he did not pay this amount, one of his palanquins was auctioned off by the authorities. Gourishankar had to spend a sum of six rupees thirteen annas and three paise to get it back. The thirteen annas and three paise were realized from him to meet the expenses incurred for the issue of the warrant.

Gourishankar approached the munsif court seeking justice and filed a case against Pawsy, who was chairman of the municipality, to recover three rupees thirteen annas and three paise. In January 1883, the munsif, Harikrishna Chatterjee, dismissed the case on the ground that the case lay beyond his jurisdiction.

Around this time, Pawsy sahib took leave for twenty months. A meeting was convened to bid Pawsy farewell. On the same day Gourishankar lost his case in the munsif court. The function was held at the parlour of Biharilal Pandit's two-storeyed house, and

Madhusudan Das was its chief organizer. At the farewell dinner were present, Commissioner Smith, District Judge Organ, the new collector, Jones, all the sahibs in Cuttack and other distinguished people. After the dinner Madhu Babu paid a tribute to Pawsy, and Pawsy, on his part, made a short speech in response to this.

The sahibs sang 'He's a jolly good fellow,' and when the band played 'Auld lang syne', all stood up, holding hands, and danced. Then they all came out on to the veranda and watched the fireworks. In the meantime, the tables were removed from the parlour and arrangements for the majlis were made. The sahibs sat beside native gentlemen. A performance by *gotipuas* was followed by dances by three troupes of nautch girls. It was 2 a.m. by the time the merry-making came to an end. The next day, at 10 a.m. on 30 January, Pawsy sahib boarded a steamer from the Jobra pier. Many people were present there, and their eyes were moist.

Needless to say, the most distinguished resident of Cuttack, Gourishankar, was present at all these events. On Pawsy's departure from Orissa, he had this to say in the *Dipika*: 'We pray to god that He grant the sahib a safe voyage to England. May god bless him with good health during his stay in England and bring him back safely to this country after his furlough comes to an end. May his prosperity continue to bring us joy.'

Gourishankar now appealed to the court of the District Judge J.B. Organ against the earlier verdict. His lawyers were Bipin Behari Mitra and Jagneswar Chandra; the municipality was represented by the government lawyer, Hariballav Bose and Barrister Wilkins. Again, Gourishankar filed another case in the munsif court, praying that the sum of seven rupees and two annas, which had been collected from him at a later date, be refunded to him, and that he be paid twenty rupees by way of compensation.

After the lawyers argued the case in the district judge's court, Morgan pronounced his verdict, expressing dissatisfaction with the position taken by the munsif and ruled that Gourishankar was entitled to a refund, and that he should be paid the expenses he had incurred at the munsif and the district judge courts. On 18 August, Gourishankar published the following letter discussing the performance of the municipality signed by a resident of Banka Bazaar:

> The Municipality collects taxes from us in advance. If someone fails to pay up, his clothes and utensils get auctioned off. No one complains, for all this is done in public interest. With the money collected in this manner roads with drains on either side have been laid all over the town. A few days ago, the main roads have been lit up by lamps, and carts fitted with tin and wooden containers to carry garbage and dirty water have been provided.
>
> As soon as day breaks, sweepers convey garbage and dirty water from one end of the town to the other, their carts loudly creaking all the time. But rather than benefit from all this, we suffer miserably: The sweepers collect filth in their tin chests and pour it out on the road in front of our houses twenty days out of thirty in a month. One day, when I came out hearing a loud noise, I found filthy water gushing out like mountain streams from the tin containers on the cart. The sweepers were dancing with joy. When we protested, they simply went away with their carts. The flood of filthy water laps at our doorsteps; worms force their way into our houses; and the stink makes the nose want to quit the face.

A few days after this, in September, Munsif Harikrishna Chatterjee gave his verdict in Gourishankar's case. This time, too, the verdict went in Gourishankar's favour. At the end of it, the munsif stated: 'In my opinion, Gourishankar Ray is entitled to compensation for the loss he has suffered on account of the wrongful and devious action of the defendant. The small amount he has demanded as compensation for the loss of social standing and the pains he had to take in order to assert his rights, I grant him. He will also be paid court expenses. Interest at six per cent will also be charged on this amount from today.

Puri, September 1883

Although Queen Suryamani had got Jagannath Jenamani crowned as Raja Mukunda Dev by obtaining an order from the district judge, and become the custodian of his property, this arrangement was not accepted by the collector of Puri, Mr Grant. He wrote to the commissioner saying that as long as Divyasingh remained alive, the property could not pass into the hands of Mukunda, or, for that matter, anyone else. Again, as the title of maharaja had been withheld from Divyasingh, it would not be proper to call Mukunda a raja. If someone were to be appointed the custodian of the royal property, he or she should be chosen by Divyasingh.

The government responded to this saying that the title of raja could not be conferred on Divyasingh's minor son as long as the former remained alive. However, the government's letter mentioned that should Divyasingh's family want to lay claim to this title in view of the fact that he was serving a life sentence in the Andamans, they might send in another application.

In the meantime, K.G. Gupta had succeeded Grant as collector, Puri. He informed Suryamani that if she had anything to say in this matter she should submit a written statement supported by documentary evidence. In response to this, Suryamani sent a lengthy petition.

The petition of Suryamani Patmahadei of Kundhaibentsai Rajbati Town of Pooree Orissa Division Showeth:-

That your petitioner has been called upon in your Perwana No. 329 Dt. 26th June, 83 to produce evidence before you in support of the petition praying that her grandson's name and title of Raja Mukund Deb be confirmed by Government. She therefore begs leave to state as follows:-

1. That the Rajah of her (Bhoi) family having ascended the throne of Gajapati dynasty are well-known to be hereditary Raja. This fact is admitted by Orissa histories and will be manifest from the genealogy of her family. In Sakabda 1503 Raja Ramachandra Deb the founder of the Bhoi Dynasty ascended the throne and from that time till Sakabda 1736 i.e. till the beginning of the British Supremacy, the Rajas of the said Bhoi family were independent Rajas of Khurda and had to be titled as Maharaja and the era called Ankas had to be reckoned from the date of their reign. Again, from Sakabda 1737 i.e. from the accession of the British Raja in 1803 till her son Dibyasinga Deb's transportation for life in 1878 though the title of Rajas was used in some of the official letters and Maharaja in some, yet the general public were addressing the Rajas of his family as Maharajas and they are still addressing them as such. Again in the almanac of this country and also in the horoscope of the people the name of the Maharaja and his Anka are as a rule entered. Hence there is no doubt that the Rajas of his family were hereditarily called as Maharajas from time immemorial. Even under the British Government though they were addressed as Rajas in official papers yet they were designated by the public as Maharajas. The ancient *Madlapanji*, the almanac of the country, the histories of Orissa by Sutton, Hunter, Pyari Mohan Acharya and Shibchandra, the copy books of old documents in the Registration office, the documents filed herewith and the settlement papers fully bear testimony to the foregoing facts i.e. the title of Raja was hereditary in their family. Besides the statement which was prepared in your office with reference to Government circular dated 20th June, 1869 containing the names of titled chiefs of this district will show that the title of Raja was hereditary in his family.

2. The Parwana No. 577 issued by the Collector of Pooree dated 16th July 77 shows that Government was pleased to grant

her son Dibyasinga Deb a Sanad confirming his Maharaja title and that Sanad was however withheld for a short time only. You will see that they who hold the title of Raja are invested by Government with the title of Maharaja. There is no instance of titling one as Maharaja if he be not a Raja in the first instance. If the Government had not accepted the hereditary title of Raja of her family then how could it grant the title of Maharaja to her son?

3. In the district of Pooree the Brahmins of 16 Sasans and 32 villages come to Pooree on Pousha and Gamha Purnima days to celebrate the ceremony of yearly coronation of the Maharajas of her family and present them with golden sacred threads according to the dictates of the shastras.

4 There has been a practice from time immemorial that in every fourth generation the name of the Raja should recur. This will be borne out by the genealogy of her family, the old *Madlapanji* and the almanacs of the country. Accordingly, her grandson, being fourth in generation, has assumed the name of Mukund Deb.

5. According to the dictates of the shastras some of the Nitis and Sebas of Sri Jagannath Deb should be performed by the Raja himself or in his absence by his representative called Mudirath nominated by the Raja. If the gadi be vacant it will be difficult to appoint the next Mudirath. Consequently the religious usage of the nation will have to be interfered with. She was therefore compelled to pass her grandson to the *Gadi* under the name and title of Raja Mukund Deb according to the custom of her family. The shastras, Narad's *Pancharatna*, *Suta Samhita, Bamdev Samhita* quoted in *Niladri Mahoday* are authorities on the subject. These facts may also be proved from the testimony of respectable Mohaunts, Sebaks and Rajas, Zemidars. If necessary they will be produced as witness. That in raising her grandson to the gadi she has not disobeyed the orders of Government. This has been done simply to maintain her family usage and to observe the dictates of shastras. If the

title be not granted she will unnecessarily be much disgraced in the eyes of the public.

On receiving this petition, Collector K.G. Gupta conveyed to the government his view that existing customs demanded that a raja was needed for the rituals of the temple to be conducted properly. Conferring on Mukunda the title of raja would, therefore, be a generous gesture, and it would also please the Hindus.

Suryamani now had to sort out a small but vexing problem. Out of the 2500 rupees which the raja of Puri received as pension, 115 rupees went to Divyasingh's grandfather, Padmanabh Ray. When Padmanabh died, problems regarding his queens who survived him cropped up. Padmanabh had two queens: Srimati and Chandramani. After Padmanabh's death, Suryamani gave only fifteen rupees to these widows. When they complained to the collector, K.G. Gupta, he ordered that Srimati and her son Bhagirathi be paid seventy rupees and the rest should go to Chandramani. Suryamani wrote to the collector saying that Bhagirathi was not Srimati's son; he was Padmanabh's illegitimate child. When the matter was referred to the commissioner he ordered that until it was established that Bhagirathi was an illegitimate child, Srimati should receive seventy rupees and Chandramani, forty-five. The collector, Puri, was directed to deduct this amount from Suryamani's pension if she refused to pay this amount to the widows.

Suryamani now had no option but to keep quiet, for her more pressing problem was how to get the title of raja conferred on Mukunda.

Dhenkanal, September 1883

Fakir Mohan had spent more than six years in Dhenkanal. Nowhere else had he stayed so long. Yet, his stay in Dhenkanal was not an entirely agreeable experience. For most of this period, he was worried and unhappy. In Dhenkanal, he was also not in the best of health. One important reason why he did not keep well was his addiction to alcohol.

When Fakir Mohan had first arrived in Dhenkanal, he had made friends with the manager, Banamali Singh, the tutor of the prince, Pyari Mohan Sen, and the assistant surgeon, Bijay Chakravorty. Of these, Pyari Mohan did not touch alcohol, Banamali drank moderately. Bijay was a drunkard and carried alcohol with him wherever he went. At that time almost everyone in Dhenkanal from kittens to devotees of Lord Mahadev had got into the habit of drinking. Drinking had become a part of daily life. Servants used to buy alcohol in bottles for the men of their masters' families along with other provisions. *Sundhi* distillers had set up liquor shops in different parts of the town and gentlemen frequented these places in the evening.

A few months after Fakir Mohan came to Dhenkanal, the tehsildar of Angul, Bichand Pattanayak, sent word that he was proceeding on leave and would go home by way of Dhenkanal. Fakir Mohan now busied himself with organizing a reception for Bichand. Awnings were put up in a mango orchard in village Baulapur which lies on the bank of the river Brahmani, and arrangements for cooking were made. Banamali, Pyari Mohan, Bijay and Fakir Mohan arrived in Baulapur at 9 a.m. riding two elephants. Shortly afterwards Bichand's boat came ashore and he disembarked carrying a carton of liquor bottles. After everyone freshened up, the party began. Bichhand had brought with him English brandy of excellent quality. A bottle was opened and its contents poured into glasses. Fakir Mohan was going to dilute it with water but Bichand stopped him saying, 'We have met after such a long time. We must drink it neat.'

Banamali drank a little and stopped. But the rest of the party finished the bottle before food was served. At three in the afternoon, having had their lunch, they got into Bichand's boat and sailed six miles down the river to another village where they set up camp for the night. Drinking went on through the night, too. Fakir Mohan became unwell for he had drunk heavily. Next day, in the morning, Bichand sailed to his village, and Fakir Mohan and his friends came back to Dhenkanal.

Fakir Mohan's health now steadily deteriorated. He was suffering from headache, indigestion, sleeplessness and piles. He started drinking two ounces of country liquor on the pretext of taking medicine. This led to further deterioration of his health and he was bedridden most of the time.

Fakir Mohan used to get all kinds of Ayurvedic medicines such as *tailapaka*, *dhatu jaran maran*, *kasturi*, *makardhwaj* tablets made at home and would distribute them to poor people free of cost. He sent for a *sundhi* and got him to prepare *mrutasanjibani sura*, an intoxicating drink. This he imbibed daily under the pretext of taking a medicine.

In the middle of all these troubles, a terrible thing happened to Fakir Mohan: his six-month-old son died. His young wife, Krishna Kumari, unable to bear her grief, took to bed. To give her solace, Fakir Mohan began translating into Oriya Valmiki's Ramayan which he had borrowed from the maharaja's library, and read the translation out to her. As time went on, Krishna Kumari was absorbed in listening to the Ramayan and slowly overcame her grief. Every evening, she would lay two seats and wait for Fakir Mohan to read the Ramayan to her. After he finished rendering the first canto, he got it printed in 1880 and distributed it free of cost. Although Beames had left Orissa two years earlier, Fakir Mohan dedicated the book to him. It was printed at the Cuttack Printing Company. Of the book, Gourishankar said in the *Dipika*, 'Since there is no dearth of Oriya translations of the Ramayan, the general public would benefit if Fakir Mohan devoted himself to some other task.' But Fakir Mohan went on translating the Ramayan undeterred. By the time he had finished rendering the Ayodhya canto, his wife had completely recovered and he was blessed with a son.

At about this time, Fakir Mohan got into trouble on the professional front. John Beames had had to revert to his post as collector after serving as commissioner, when Ravenshaw came back after the expiry of his leave. Beames had hoped that he would be appointed commissioner when Ravenshaw left Orissa. But Smith replaced Ravenshaw as commissioner. A few days after this, Beames got transferred and left Orissa in August 1878. As Beames was Fakir Mohan's patron and chief source of support, Fakir Mohan felt helpless and vulnerable. Smith, for his part, looked with suspicion upon anyone who had been given a job by Beames.

Even after Beames's departure, Fakir Mohan, Radhanath and a few others still expected that he might come back to Orissa. But their hopes were dashed when they received the following letter from Beames, who was now posted in Chittagong:

My dear Radhanath,

It was a great blow to me to leave Orissa, and a still greater one when I found that I was not allowed to return there on Mr Ravenshaw's transfer. Someone, I know not who, told Sir Eden on the occasion of his visit to Cuttack that I was very unpopular in Orissa; and that is I suppose the reason why I am not allowed to return to that place. I dislike Chittagong extremely. I have never been in so bad a place in my life. I am always sick here. I have no society, and the natives are detestable people—the lowest class of Bengali Musalmans—full of treachery and litigiousness. I shall never cease to take a deep and sincere interest in all that concerns Orissa; and I shall always try to get back there. Some day perhaps I may be successful. At present I am sick both in body and spirit and dare not look forward to any further success or happiness in this world. Should I ever again come into favour and be able to see you or any of my old friends, I shall always gladly do so. At present I am, so to speak, 'bhrashta—an outcaste.' I am sorry Kailas has behaved so badly. I was thinking of getting him a berth here, but I cannot of course do so now.

Please remember me to all my friends in Orissa.

Yours sincerely,   Chittagong
John Beames   10 October 1878

The letter which Beames wrote to Radhanath on 2 May 1879 caused even greater disappointment to his friends in Orissa. In this, Beames said that he had given up all hopes of ever returning to Orissa. He was even contemplating going back to England after four years. These were the words with which he closed his letter: 'The memories of the happy days I had spent in Orissa bring me joy, and I feel happy when I think of my kind and affectionate friends there. I hope that you achieve the success which I have not been abl. to attain.'

Smith's suspicion towards anyone loyal to Beames was only one of the many problems which beset Fakir Mohan. When Beames had visited Dhenkanal, Fakir Mohan had saved the job of a cook by pleading for him before the sahib. Later, Fakir Mohan helped this cook rise to the position of a muktar. Once Fakir Mohan had dismissed the case of one of this muktar's clients. So he turned violently against Fakir Mohan and began intriguing against him.

Taking advantage of Fakir Mohan's illness, his *peshkar*, his subordinate, too, started making mischief. He crossed out Fakir Mohan's judgments, changed them and took bribes. About this time, Nandakishore Das came to Dhenkanal on a tour of inspection. He found that every case register had been tampered with. Fakir Mohan sat through the night and tried to prepare new registers but the task seemed impossible for it involved hundreds of registers. If Nandakishore had stated the facts in his report, Fakir Mohan would certainly have lost his job. But Nandakishore did not mention in his report the alterations made in the registers; he only observed that in the office of the assistant manager, Fakir Mohan, many records were found in a damaged condition.

Having gone through Nandakishore's report, Commissioner Smith himself came to conduct an inquiry. It now seemed unlikely that Fakir Mohan could escape this time for the alterations made in the registers were evidence of Fakir Mohan's incompetence and worthlessness. Seeing no other way out, Fakir Mohan at last took a desperate step: he asked the peshkar to make a hole in the thatched roof of his office, tore all the records and put them in a corner of the room, and poured water on them. Smith came and saw this; he could easily sense that this had been done deliberately. But since he had no hard evidence, he granted funds for the purchase of an almirah. Before going back to Cuttack, he said to Fakir Mohan, 'Baboo, remember you survived because you are in a garjat.'

Now anonymous letters began arriving which accused Fakir Mohan of corruption. Nandakishore Das investigated the matter and reported to the commissioner that the charges were baseless and that Fakir Mohan was an honest person. But Smith said, 'I don't trust that man at all.'

At last, oppressed by all these troubles, physical as well as mental, Fakir Mohan took six months' leave and went off to Balasore. The manager, Banamali Singh, now turned against him. The judgment which Fakir Mohan had given regarding a dispute in village Baulapur was inquired into. It was alleged that Fakir Mohan had given two different judgments in the case. Banamali Singh investigated the matter and reported that Fakir Mohan had written out his judgment long after he had tried the case; he had also claimed that he had conducted an on-the-spot inquiry without actually having gone to the place. While at Balasore, Fakir Mohan received a letter from the commissioner asking him to explain his action.

Fakir Mohan was now forty years old and he was ill and bedridden. He was secretly advised by Nandakishore Das that, under the circumstances, the best thing for him to do was to resign. Acting on this advice, Fakir Mohan sent in his letter of resignation from Balasore.

Puri, August, 1884

The commissioner forwarded K.G. Gupta's report regarding the conferment of the title 'raja' on underage Mukunda Dev to the government. The lieutenant governor wrote to the government of India suggesting that the government should not go into the matter of whether the title was a hereditary one or not; they should give the title to Mukunda Dev on the basis of personal merit. The government of India accepted the view of the commissioner and the collector that conferring the title on Mukunda Dev would be perceived as a generous gesture and it would please Hindus in general and the people of Orissa in particular. In April 1885, a sanad came to the commissioner. It said:

Sanad

Simla, the 29th March, 1884

To
Jagannath Jenamani, Puri.

I hereby confer upon you the title of 'Raja' as a personal distinction.

Ripon
Viceroy and Governor General

The government had directed the commissioner to pass on the sanad to Mukunda Dev. They also wanted to know if it would be in order to present him with khilat. Queen Suryamani was now informed that Mukunda had been granted the title 'raja', and that he would receive it in a durbar on payment of nazrana. By this time, F. Jones had succeeded K.G. Gupta as collector, Puri. He received the following letter from Suryamani:

From
Ranee Suryamani Patmahadei, Pooree

To
F. Jones Esquire,
Collector-Magistrate, Pooree.

Sir,

In acknowledging receipt of your letter dated 15th May, 84 I am very glad to learn that the Government of India has been pleased to confer on my grandson the title of Rajah as a personal distinction. The Commissioner of Orissa Division desires to know what amount of nuzzer in gold mohurs I am willing to present to Government. In reply I have the honour to state that with a view to circumstances I am at present willing to present to Government a nuzzer of Rs 1500/- in gold mohurs.

2. I am told that a durbar will be held at Cuttack for the purpose and my grandson will have to attend it to receive the said title from the Commissioner of Orissa. As he is a boy only 7 years old and is very much attached to me and is not yet familiar with Hakims (Government Officers) he is unable to attend the Durbar. I would therefore request the favour of your making proper arrangements to have the title conferred on him by the Commissioner or by yourself in your Bungalow.

Suryamani Patmahadei   Pooree
                                                        10 June 1884

At long last, the sanad was sent to Puri, and Mukunda, accompanied by his muktar, collected the piece of paper from Jones.

Having won her battle to get Mukunda his royal title, Suryamani now proceeded to serve a notice on the government under section 426 of the Civil Code demanding that she be refunded the amount which was being deducted from the pension of the raja of Puri and paid to the widow of Padmanabh and his illegitimate son, Bhagirathi.

Duspalla, September 1884

Fakir Mohan remained jobless for a year after leaving Dhenkanal. However, the translation of all the seven cantos of the Ramayan, which he had begun while in Dhenkanal, was completed in Balasore. Baikunthanath Dey provided the financial support for those cantos which had remained to be printed. His father, Shyamananda Dey, gave him a reward of seven hundred and fifty rupees for this translation. With this money Fakir Mohan cleared all his outstanding debts. Commissioner Smith had left Orissa by this time. So Fakir Mohan went to Cuttack and approached Nandakishore Das for help. Luckily for him the post of dewan at Duspalla was lying vacant at that time.

Accompanied by a servant, Fakir Mohan took a boat from Gadagadia ghat and sailed for Duspalla. Nine days later, the boat arrived at Belpada. Madhuban, the capital of Duspalla, lay at a distance of fourteen miles from here. When the boat reached Belapada Fakir Mohan found himself in a miserable condition. The boat was small and he had to spend nine long days in a cramped cabin on it. As a storm had broken out on the eighth day of the journey the boat has to be moored at an island in the river and Fakir Mohan had had nothing to eat the whole day. Although he had no energy left to disembark, he jumped off the boat with a flourish to impress the people who had come to receive him. Unfortunately for him the ground was slippery and he fell.

However, some spectators picked him up, fed him, put him in a palanquin and sent him to Duspalla. As he could not reach Madhuban before nightfall, he had to spend the night in a village which lay four miles from the fort. He reached the fort the next day in the morning. A house had already been arranged for him there. It was crammed with provisions sent from the royal store. Whenever a guest arrived in the state, the royal storekeeper was required to send him the necessary provisions including twigs to brush his teeth to last him as long as he stayed. After a wash Fakir Mohan proceeded to call upon his majesty.

The raja of Duspalla, Chaitanya Deo Bhanj, was a tall sturdy man who sported a long beard. He had a strange temperament. A few years ago, when Beames was the commissioner of Orissa, the raja had found himself in a tight spot. He had abducted the wife of one of his subjects and had forcibly kept her in his palace. When her husband protested the raja threw him out of the kingdom and his men looted his house and took it into their possession.

While wandering in the neighbouring area, hungry and miserable, the man was persuaded by some people to go to the raja and ask him to restore his wife to him. At the raja's court, the sepoys tied him up, gave him a thrashing and branded him with a hot iron. When he fell unconscious they threw him on the banks of a river. At night, his relatives took him to Cuttack in a boat, put him into a hospital and brought the matter to the notice of Beames, the commissioner-in-charge.

At first Beames refused to credit that the incident had taken place. But, when the man came from the hospital and showed to Beames the marks on his body left by the hot iron, Beames instantly ordered the removal of the raja from office. This order was conveyed to Duspalla through the superintendent of police,

Cuttack. Initially, the raja refused to meet the superintendent Then he met him and said that the woman's husband was telling a lie and that he would meet the commissioner and explain everything to him personally.

When Chaitanya Deo Bhanj came to Cuttack, he was tried in the court of Beames and was found guilty on the basis of testimony provided by witnesses. It became clear that the king was an oppressive man. Beames detained the raja in Cuttack and sent a dewan to Duspalla to set its affairs in order. He wrote to the government suggesting that the king be removed and the kingdom be placed under a British officer until the raja's son, who was a minor, came of age.

On hearing of this Chaitanya went into the chamber of Beamse and threw himself at his feet. This man was of dark complexion, fat, tall, well-built and resembled an animal, he now looked even more grotesque. He took off his turban, pulled Beames's feet and tried to place them on his head. He wailed and made such a nuisance of himself that Beames's servant threw him out. He was so scared that he immediately left for Duspalla and released the woman from the palace. He gave her husband a lot of money and granted him a plot of land with the arrangement that he would never ever have to pay any rent for it.

Although the government shared Beames's view in relation to this matter, there were doubts as to whether the government could legitimately dethrone a feudatory chief. At this time Ravenshaw, the commissioner of Orrisa, was on leave and in Calcutta. When his opinion on this matter was sought he was of the view that the chief should not be dethroned. It was therefore decided that Chaitanya would not be deposed but the dewan whom Beames had sent there would control the affairs of the kingdom.

Fakir Mohan was aware of the incident mentioned above. He also knew that so far no dewan had found it easy to work with the raja. Many dewans had been posted to Duspalla but none of them had lasted long. Nandakishore Das had warned Fakir Mohan about this. But Fakir Mohan desperately needed a job and was determined to keep the raja in good humour.

When Fakir Mohan arrived at the palace he found the raja and his courtiers waiting for him. The raja sat on a raised platform reclining against a pillow. On his left on the floor was seated the record-keeper, the store-keeper and others. Behind them stood ten or more servants. A number of record-keepers had come from villages to see the new dewan. To the raja's right a seat had been laid for Fakir Mohan.

Fakir Mohan saluted the king and occupied his seat. But the raja said nothing to him, looked him over several times and kept making signals to people standing behind him with the thumb of his right hand. This went on for about twenty minutes. Then the raja asked, 'Dewan Babu, how much ghee do you take with your rice every day?' Fakir Mohan said, 'About a *tola*, Your Majesty'. The raja turned to look at his courtiers, winked at them and said to Fakir Mohan, 'No, no, this won't do. You must have half a seer of ghee with your rice every day. Store-keeper! See to it that two seers of ghee are sent to the dewan's residence.'

After a while, the raja said to the dewan, 'Do you think I am an illiterate person? Let me show you how well I can write?' Before the raja finished saying this, he breathlessly set about a scribbling. After two sheets of paper were covered with his writing the raja held them up and proudly displayed them to everyone, saying, 'See how well I have written out the royal order. Could my uncle, when he was the raja, ever write like this?' The courtiers, for fear of being whipped, fined and jailed, exclaimed in a chorus 'No, Your Majesty, never'. The raja again asked, 'Can the raja of Nuagarh, raja of Khandapara or any other raja write like me?' This time, before the couriers could make any reply, the raja raised his hand and said, moving his thumb from side to side, 'They never can. They never can'. When the pieces of paper passed to Fakir Mohan, he found that nothing except the words 'Sri Chaitanya Deo Bhanj, fort Duspalla, Joromo' were written on them again and again in a peculiar hand.

This was how Fakir Mohan's first meeting with the raja came to an end. Later, he learnt from others that the raja looked upon himself as a very handsome, knowledgeable and virtuous person. He was convinced that only fat people were handsome and wise. For this reason, he had arranged for ghee to be sent to the residence of Fakir Mohan, who happened to be lean and thin. He was unlettered but he could somehow manage to sign his own name. Long practice had enabled him to write his name, Chaitanya Deo and other things quite fast on paper.

Fakir Mohan realized that he wouldn't be able to get along with such a man for long.

Cuttack, September 1885

Radhanath Ray was now the most powerful official in the education department in Orissa. He had also come to occupy a place of great importance in Oriya society. However, some people had recently started spreading rumours about him. They were led by one Dinanath Bandopadhyay who lived in Cuttack. Dinanath looked upon himself as the custodian of Orissa's conscience and raised his voice in protest whenever he thought someone had been doing something unjust. Letters from Dinanath filled many pages in the *Dipika* and other magazines.

Dinanath first launched an attack against Radhanath by publishing a letter in the *Dipika* on 25 October 1880. The attack focused on the following: an award of 300 rupees which had been announced for writing a book in Oriya. The book was to be submitted at the office of the commissioner within a period of six months. It so happened that Radhanath's dearest friend, Madhu Rao, won this award for his book *Prabandhamala*. Dinanath alleged that Madhu could submit the book in six months' time because he had been informed about the award beforehand; that others found it difficult to write their books at such short notice. Moreover, many of the essays included in the book were written jointly by Radhanath and Madhu and had been published in a magazine called *Utkal Darpan* four to five years earlier. And what was most objectionable was the fact that, before choosing this book for the award in his capacity as joint director, Radhanath had praised this book in the pages of the *Balasore Sambad Bahika*.

The controversy over this book continued for two long years. The *Dipika* had this to say of the book: 'The language used in this book is not pure Oriya. Like many other Oriya books published in recent years, its language is heavily influenced by Bangla.' This remark led to a lively exchange of letters in the *Dipika*. Someone writing under a pseudonym defended Radhanath and commented that Dinanath was wasting everyone's time. Dinanath responded by sending a long reply to this which he closed by saying, 'We are not going to reply to any anonymous letter hereafter.' At last, Madhusudan wrote to the *Dipika* clarifying certain things. Dinanath's response was an even longer letter. He now claimed that Radhanath got books written by himself approved as school textbooks.

In July1883 Radhanath's patron and well wisher, Bhudev Mukherjee, retired from service. Radhanath now felt helpless and vulnerable. He passed through a period of financial hardship and regretted his earlier decision not to accept the job offered to him by the raja of Mayurbhanj. His health too gave way.

As time went by, the voices criticizing Radhanath grew shriller. It was alleged that during the selection of textbooks, he was partial to books published by the Utkal Press which was owned by Baikunthanath Dey. Earlier, there used to be a committee for selecting textbooks; this was no longer in existence in Radhanath's time. Radhanath selected the textbooks himself and, although he prepared a long list, since he happened to be the highest official in the education department, teachers had no option but to buy books which were recommended by him; in other words, books brought out by the Utkal Press. It was further alleged that several books published by this press, which did not bear the name of any author, were actually written by Radhanath himself, or by his brother, Sitanath Ray, who was an employee of the press. Some even suggested that Radhanath persuaded many authors to get their books printed at Dey's press or sell the copyright of their books to Dey. It was pointed out that Radhanath never forgot to single out Baikunthanath for praise in the annual reports of the education department.

Madhusudan got dragged into this controversy. As deputy inspector of schools, he was a junior colleague of Radhanath. Their close friendship was well known to everyone and the fact that together they had written a collection of poems entitled *Kabitabali* was equally well known. The magazine *Balasore Sambad Bahika*, which used to support Radhanath earlier, now turned against him. One Gobind Chandra Pattnayak, who was an employee in the education department, edited it. Angered by his criticism, Radhanath withdrew the permission he had given him to edit this magazine.

Dinanath now threatened that unless the education department changed its ways, his Anti-drinking and Anti-bribery Association would feel obliged to take the matter to the higher authorities just as it had done in the case of the Public Works Department in order to curb its excesses. In a letter to the *Dipika*, he wrote: 'To hear such terrible things about a sacred institution like the Education Department is unbearable, and this is a matter of great shame for a civilized society.'

Madhusudan's book *Chhandamala* gave rise to yet another controversy. Some claimed that Madhusudan had exerted pressure on schools to buy this book. Joint Inspector Radhanath Ray was asked to investigate the matter. Many voiced their fear that the inquiry would not be an impartial one. Not only was Madhusudan a very close friend of Radhanath's, he often remained present during the inquiry. The procedures followed in the inquiry also came under fire. One day, Radhanath called some teachers to the Cuttack Normal School and asked them, 'Has Madhu forced you to buy his book?' The teachers said, 'No, we bought the books on our own and sold them to the students.' No other reply should have been expected from them, for no teacher would have dared speak against his superior officer.

Gourishankar, too, mounted a severe attack on Radhanath and Madhusudan in the *Dipika*. In his opinion, for someone to enter the textbook business in collaboration with his junior colleague was a despicable thing to do. *Sanskarak o Sebak*, a magazine which had taken Radhanath's side in this controversy, wrote: 'People regard Radhanath much superior to Gourishankar in matters relating to scholarship, courtesy and patriotism.'

Thus the whole controversy descended to the level of slander and mud-slinging. The above remark amused Gourishankar greatly for, eighteen years ago, in a poem included in *Kabitabali*, Radhanath had compared him with the great warrior Arjun, and had described how he was fighting the forces of darkness in Orissa wielding a powerful weapon like the *Utkal Dipika*!

Radhanath was now passing through a time of severe mental stress. Many of his friends had by this time turned against him. Magazines carried articles criticizing him. To add to his woes, municipality sweepers killed his pet dog. Acute asthma too caused him extreme discomfort. However, in the middle of all this, his long poem, 'Kedar Gouri,' priced at one paisa, had been published by the Utkal Press and this gave him immense pleasure. In this poem, following Bhudev Mukherjee's advice, he had blended fact with fiction.

Balasore, August 1886

The criticism against Radhanath's role in selecting Oriya textbooks grew more intense. Another book which aroused a lot of public disapproval was *Pratham Patha*. Jagannath Rao, who was Madhusudan Rao's younger brother, had written it. Unfortunately for Jagannath, he worked as head clerk in Radhanath Ray's office. This book was attacked on several counts: faulty spelling, factual errors, grammatical mistakes and so on. A sentence from this book was quoted to prove that this book had been written to flatter Englishmen. It went like this: 'The dogs in our country are not as big and as good as their counterparts in England.' Word went round that, as Jagannath had worked in Radhanath's office, he had managed to find out what kind of books were required by schools and so was able to write such books and get thousands of copies sold. Of the book the *Dipika* had this to say: 'On page 21 one comes across the saying, "It is better not to earn anything than to earn money through unfair means." This is a wonderful ideal; however, the author himself is the farthest from it.'

The next act in the drama involving Oriya textbooks was staged in Balasore. Schoolchildren in this district had been given books such as *Bichitra Ramayan, Chautisa* and *Na Poi*. These had been published by the Cuttack Printing Company. Baikunthanath Dey got some passages from these books translated into English and sent them to the government complaining that these books were obscene and therefore should not be placed in the hands of children. He drew attention to the following lines in *Bichitra Ramayan*: The hermit made love to the beautiful woman (page 10); they made love following the rules prescribed in the treatise on love, her friends encircled her and asked her how she made love; on her full and round breasts were seen marks left by nails, and so on (page 17). When the government sought the opinion of the joint inspector, Radhanath informed them that he was in agreement with Baikunthanath. As a result, the government stopped buying these books.

Some pointed out that Baikunthanath's *Pratham Siksha*, which had been prescribed as a school textbook, and the second edition of which was in the press, also contained a piece which could be considered obscene. When Baikunthanath brought out the fourth edition of this book, he took care not to include the piece containing those lines.

Radhanath's critics now targeted his long poem, 'Kedar Gouri'. In the introduction to this poem, Radhanath had claimed that he had based it on Puranic sources. But the story concerning Kedar and Gouri was nowhere to be found in *Shiva Purana* or *Ekamra Purana*, or *Kapila Samhita*, which carried descriptions of the holy place, Bhubaneswar. On the other hand, the story was unmistakably based on the legend of Pyramus and Thisbe. Since Radhanath claimed the authority of Puranic sources for his poem, it was demanded that he tell his critics from which Purana he had borrowed his material. Radhanath chose to keep quiet.

To make matters worse, the textbook selection committee, of which Radhanath was president, decided to prescribe Sitanath Ray's *Pathamala*, which cost four annas, for lower primary schools in the place of *Bodhoday* by Ishwar Chandra Vidyasagar which cost two annas. This decision came under fire, too, for Sitanath happened to be Radhanath's younger brother.

Authors used to submit their manuscripts to this committee and make arrangements for getting them printed if the committee approved them. In one instance, however, Chaturbhuj Pattanayak, a crony of Radhanath's, first had his book *Swasthyasadhan* printed and then submitted it to the committee. In the introduction to his book, he mentioned that he had decided to place a printed book in the hands of the esteemed members of the committee for he felt that they might find it difficult to go through a manuscript. The introduction also informed the readers that the deputy inspector, Madhusudan Rao, had gone through the text thoroughly and revised it. This gave rise to suspicions that Chaturbhuj knew for sure that the committee would approve his book and therefore he had his book printed. But what took one's breath away was the fact that the publisher of this book was Chaturbhuj's two-year-old son, Nirmala Chandra Pattanayak!

Another issue which came up during the controversy surrounding the book related to Chaturbhuj's intention to spread Brahmoism. There were now two well known champions of Brahmoism in Orissa: Madhusudan Rao and Chaturbhuj Pattanayak. Although the book *Swasthyasadhan* dealt with matters relating to hygiene, it also contained views which were critical of Hinduism. For instance, in one place, it said that a stone idol would not grow thin if it were not fed and that a stone idol did not do any work. In another, it was mentioned that, when men and women married very young, their children were born very weak and were prone to diseases, and that unless this practice was abolished, the country would never prosper. Critics of the book also pointed out that it contained material unfit for reading by the young. For instance, it mentioned that prostitutes lured people away from the paths of virtue, and made them fall prey to venereal diseases.

All these attacks left Radhanath terribly depressed. During a tour of Balasore, he talked to Baikunthanath about the worries oppressing him. Baikunthanath comforted him and reassured him saying that he would get articles published in magazines supporting Radhanath. While they were talking, Fakir Mohan came in and joined them. He had come to Balasore on leave, and he felt very pleased to find Radhanath with Baikunthanath. However, Radhanath did not stay long; he left shortly afterwards, saying he was not feeling well.

Fakir Mohan was now dewan of the raja of Pallahada. Since he did not get on well with the raja of Duspalla, Commissioner Metcalfe had got him out of Duspalla in the beginning of 1886. After sitting idle in Cuttack for a few days, he was sent to Pallahada as dewan. Here, his relations with the raja were cordial, and what was more, he had not much to do. He spent time playing dice and translating the Mahabharat. Whenever he had nothing to do, he took leave and came over to Balasore.

One reason why Radhanath avoided Fakir Mohan was that the latter loved making jokes while he himself was of a serious disposition. A few years ago, Fakir Mohan had widely circulated in Balasore an embarrassing incident involving Radhanath and everyone there continued to have fun repeating the story. The incident had a basis in fact; however, it was exaggerated in Fakir Mohan's narration.

Once Fakir Mohan and Radhanath happened to travel together to Cuttack by steamer. After dark, the steamer entered the river Dhamra; just then, a terrible storm of wind and rain blew. The gale buffeted the little steamer and almost sank it. Radhanath gave up all hopes of surviving this ordeal. Since the cold made him shiver, he covered his body with a part of his dhoti. He hurriedly tied a large lump of opium in the end of his dhoti and listlessly waited for the steamer to go down. He started whenever a noise came from any direction. Now and then he cast vacant looks at Fakir Mohan. At that moment, he made one feel that he believed he would somehow escape this crisis by covering himself with his dhoti, the lump of opium in hand.

Radhanath returned to Cuttack but the mental stress continued. Only the thought that his poem 'Chandrabhaga' was going to be published by Dey's Utkal Press a year after 'Kedar Gouri' had come out gave him some comfort.

Bamanda, October 1886

At thirty-five, Basudev Sudhal Dev had ruled Bamanda for just seventeen years, but had managed to achieve a great deal. His fame had spread throughout Orissa. These days, an advertisement carrying the heading Bamanda regularly appeared in the front page of the *Dipika*. A book written by Sudhal Dev, titled *Alankar Bodhoday*, had established his reputation as a writer. The annual report of the government lavished high praise on him as a ruler. However, he had had to endure much before he found himself in this position.

Basudev had to face his first problem soon after he ascended the throne. Since Brajasundar's own son Brindavan was born of a maidservant, he had chosen as his heir his brother Harihar's son, Basudev. Brindavan protested against putting Basudev on the throne, and he received support from Basudev's uncle, Devadurlabh. Devadurlabh took Brindavan with him and went to meet the commissioner in Sambalpur. Luckily for Basudev, the commissioner was already aware of Brajasundar's decision and had met Basudev during an earlier trip to Bamanda. He therefore rejected Brindavan's petition.

Shortly after this, another problem surfaced. The political agent had directed Basudev to remain under the supervision of his father, Harihar, until he came of age. However, Basudev was more loyal to the late Brajasundar, who had adopted him, than to his own father. This was something Harihar did not appreciate at all. When the question of Basudev's marriage came up, he decided that, in accordance with the wishes of the late

Brajasundar, he would marry the princess of Kalahandi, Giriraj Kumari. Harihar was opposed to this match. But Basudev went on to marry the princess of Kalahandi, paying no heed to Harihar's reservations.

In this way, the differences between father and son grew sharper. Harihar was a tyrant and he used to oppress the subjects. This alienated Basudev from his father even more. Things came to a head when Harihar ordered one of the royal servants to loot the house of a tenant who had not been able to pay the taxes. The tenant approached Basudev, who did not cancel his father's order, but he promised the tenant that he would pay him four times the amount he would lose as a result of the looting. When word of this reached Harihar, he told his cronies that it would be impossible for him to show his face in Bamanda after this incident. In fact, the next morning, he disappeared from Bamanda.

Two years after his marriage, his queen, Giriraj Kumari, died after giving birth to a son. Grief stricken, Basudev decided that he would go on a long pilgrimage. He left his baby son in the care of his mother, and, accompanied by a few servants, he first went to Sambalpur. There he called on the political agent, and after that, travelled first to Sonepur, then to Cuttack by boat. All arrangements for his stay in Cuttack had been made by Gourishankar. He was put up in a house in Jobra and was shown round the city. Basudev visited the Cuttack Printing Company and the Mission Press. He attended the prayer meeting of Christians at Cuttack Church. The sights he saw included the stone embankment on the river Katjuri, the racecourse at Chakarpadia, the Station Club inside Barabati fort, and the Gadgadia ghat. He shopped in Buxi Bazaar.

From Cuttack, Basudev went to Chandbali by canal and from there he travelled to Calcutta where he spent one full month. During this time he had a darshan of the goddess Kali at Kalighat and visited the conference hall of the Asiatic Society, the Museum and the Botanical Garden, the paper mill at Serampur, and saw flying shuttles at work. He also called upon Ishwar Chandra Vidyasagar.

He left for Benares. Here he went to the observatory and acquainted himself with the methods of teaching astrology. He took a dip in the river Ganga at the Manikarnika ghat. He went to the temples of Lord Visweswar and the goddess Annapurna. He offered oblations and fed the Brahmins. From Benares, Basudev went to Ayodhya and there he took a holy dip in the river Gomti. The sights he saw there included the palace of the Nawab of Lucknow, Canning College, and the Imambara. In Kanpur, he visited a number of factories. In Delhi, he visited the Qutab Minar, the Red Fort, and Jantar Mantar. He went to Agra, where he saw the Taj Mahal. He went on a pilgrimage to Mathura and Vrindavan. In Prayag, he performed religious rites and distributed gifts to the poor. There he paid a visit to the Albert Park and Mayo College. In Gaya, he went to Bodhgaya and offered oblations to the spirits of his ancestors. In Baidyanath, he participated in a religious discourse and finally returned to Bamanda by way of Singhbhumi.

All through this journey, Basudev was looking for his father but he was nowhere to be found. After arriving in Bamanda, he learnt that his father was in Sambalpur and that he was ill. Basudev went there and brought his father back to Bamanda.

Basudev had turned his back on worldly life and had gone on a pilgrimage after his wife's death but on his return, he wanted to set up home once more. A matchmaker and a Brahmin priest went to different places looking for a bride for him. In time, Basudev married two daughters of the zamindar of Rerua. A few days later, on his way back from Calcutta, he married another woman in Kharsuan and brought her over to Bamanda. With these three wives, Basudev had eleven daughters and eight sons.

After settling down, Basudev turned his attention to the affairs of his estate. He divided his estate into three parts and appointed a magistrate for each. He replaced the durbar with a nine-member council. He founded charitable hospitals in Deogarh and Kuchinda, and had a road from Bamanda to Deogarh constructed. He wrote to Vidyasagar requesting him to find a good teacher, and on his advice, brought Bijaya Chandra Majumdar over to Bamanda. He set up an English school. He also established a laboratory on the model of the observatory he had seen in Benares. He invited pandits from Kasi and Mithila and engaged them in research in ancient methods. He invited Professor Jogesh Chandra Ray from the Cuttack College and sought his advice on how to run the laboratory. He set up a printing press in Deogarh which was called Jagannath Ballabh.

One evening, Basudev was discussing the affairs of the estate with an old teacher, Ganeswar Pattanayak. After all his achievements were enumerated, Basudev asked, 'Sir, what else can be done for Bamanda?' Ganeswar thought for a while and said, 'It would be nice if Radhanath Ray could be persuaded to set foot in Bamanda.' The most famous person in Orissa had not yet visited Bamanda, for Bamanda did not come under Radhanath's jurisdiction.

Basudev readily agreed to this proposal and a letter of invitation was immediately sent to Radhanath. Radhanath was delighted to get the letter, but he was also a little put off for he would have to take leave if he were to visit Bamanda. However, he took leave and left Cuttack for Bamanda on elephant back in October 1886. On the way, he remembered that it would be proper on his part to take the raja a gift. This might bring him a reward. So he set to work on composing a poem. The poem had five stanzas and it began like this:

Fie, flatterer fie, fie
Your life—hateful, crawling:
Fie your calling fie fie
The earnings from that calling.

Radhanath did not like what he had written, but he thought it would do. He had no idea that arrangements on such a grand scale had been made to receive him in Bamanda. As soon as his elephant arrived in Deogarh, he was welcomed with an eleven-gun salute. Basudev himself came and ceremonially received the poet. He showed him round different places of interest. Unattended by any servants, Basudev and Radhanath visited a garden which the raja had created. Many varieties of native and foreign species had been planted there. One day, they went to see the waterfall at Pradhanpat. On other days, they went to see the old capital of the kingdom, Purunagarh, the hospital, the printing press, the library of Sanskrit texts, etc. Radhanath had originally planned to spend only three days in Bamanda; but he ended up spending a week there. During this time he read out his five-stanza poem on sycophancy at a gathering of writers and received from the raja an award of five hundred rupees.

At last, carrying the five hundred rupees which sycophancy had earned him, Radhanath returned to Cuttack. He wrote an essay on Bamanda under the pseudonym, 'The Traveller', and sent it to a magazine called *Nabasambad*. In this, he lavished praise on Basudev Sudhal Dev in the hope that his friendship with the raja would prove useful some day in future. He then devoted himself wholeheartedly to writing *Nandikeshwari*.

ten

Puri, December 1886

The raja of Puri had been informed by the government two years earlier that he would be given a sanad at a special durbar. But, at that time, Queen Suryamani wrote to say that Mukunda Dev was too young to be able to attend the durbar. The collector, Puri, therefore, sent for Mukunda and personally handed the sanad to him. However, when the lieutnant governor, Sir Rivers Thomson, held a durbar in Cuttack in November 1885, Suryamani decided that Mukunda should go there and receive the royal khilat. At the durbar, eight-year-old Mukunda, dressed in full regalia, became the centre of attraction. The number of people who thronged to see Mukunda going to and returning from the durbar far exceeded those who flocked to see the other rajas, or even the lieutnant governor himself.

Honouring the raja of Puri in this way was part of the authorities' plan to humour the people of Orissa; at the same time, they were also looking for ways of ensuring the smooth functioning of the Jagannath temple during the period of Mukunda's minority and the sentence of deportation that Divyasingh was serving. A meeting of government lawyers was convened in Calcutta, where they expressed the view that no steps in this regard could be taken under the Civil Code for this code was not applicable to religious trusts. The government, therefore, amended article 539 of the Code and brought religious trusts under its jurisdiction, and by amending Act Ten of 1840, made arrangements for appointing more trustees for the temple. The government then decided that, as suggested earlier by Collector K.G. Gupta, the affairs of the temple would be managed by a committee headed by the raja of Puri, and a salaried manager would run the temple administration. It was also decided that an application would be made to the civil court seeking its permission to carry this arrangement into effect.

Before the application was sent to the court, the commissioner asked his seristadar, Ramprasad Singh, to inquire into the affairs of the temple and submit a report to him. When Ramprasad went to the temple and asked the *deulakaran* to give him a list of jewels and other assets of the temple, Queen Suryamani instructed the temple servitors not to let Ramprasad see any records or accounts of the temple.

Receiving no cooperation from the temple servitors, Ramprasad approached the queen's dewan, Anandachandra Mukherjee and her *bisoi*, Dinabandhu Routra. They demanded that Ramprasad show them the written order authorizing him to inspect the temple records. Ramprasad had received no such written order, so he went back to Cuttack and submitted a report to the commissioner, mentioning the difficulties he had faced in the course of the inquiry.

Commissioner Metcalfe went through this report and consulted the government pleader, Hariballav Basu. It was decided that the matter would be taken to the law courts and that a case would be filed by the collector, Puri, in the district judge's court. Accordingly, on 15 December 1886, the collector of Puri, J.H. Savage, filed a case in the court of the district judge. The defendants in the case included Raja Divyasingh Dev, Queen Suryamani Patamahadei, Queen Niladri, Deulakaran

Ramachandra Samantra, the storekeeper Jogi Mekap and a few others. The following demands were made:

That the jewellery mentioned in the petition and the other gold and silver ornaments of the temple which were not needed during the daily worship of the deity be deposited in court or kept under safe custody elsewhere. If necessary, a receiver be appointed for its safe-keeping and maintenance. That the defendants give a complete and accurate account of all the jewellery, gold and silver, money and moveable property in their possession. That, the defendant, Suryamani give complete and accurate account of all the landed property belonging to the temple which she controlled. That Suryamani account for all the revenue, profit, income and dues which she received from the landed property, and the gifts made to the deity. That she account for whatever she had earned since the day she took charge of the temple affairs and whatever she had spent from this income.

The court was also requested to appoint new trustees as per article two of the 1840 Act and to place the management of the temple in their hands. The trustees should look after all moveable and immoveable assets of the temple. An appropriate plan should be drawn up for the proper management of these.

In this court case, the collector was represented by lawyers Hariballav Basu and Lalbehari Ghosh. The defendants' lawyers were Ramashankar Ray and Madhusudan Das. The collector requested the court to appoint a receiver and a tehsildar who would ensure that temple property was not misused during the trial. The court accepted this request and appointed the mahant of Emar Mutt as honorary receiver and Ramprasad Singh as tehsildar. The latter was to receive a monthly salary of one hundred rupees. The nazir of the district court was instructed to go to the temple and prepare a list of jewels and other valuables.

The case created quite a sensation in Puri. Court officials sealed the rooms where the records and the valuables of the temple were kept. Police now guarded the four entrances of the temple. Guards were also posted in front of the queen's cutcherry.

Queen Suryamani refused to hand over the keys to the record room and the treasury of the temple, saying that she had received no orders from the court to this effect. She also wrote to the collector protesting against the posting of guards in front of her palace; this, in her view, amounted to an insult to her. After this, the collector withdrew the guards.

The nazir now got the temple storehouse opened through a court order and made an inventory of the pieces of silk and cotton cloth it contained. The palace, the residence of the deulakaran and that of the tadhaukaran were raided and records relating to the temple were seized. These were placed in the custody of the receiver. The fate of the temple was now left to be decided by the court.

Cuttack, January 1887

The problems relating to the management of Jagannath temple caused some anxiety among the people in Orissa. The government took the matter to the law court on 15 December. Before this, on 5 December, while the government was contemplating legal action, Gourishankar convened a special meeting of the Utkal Sabha on the first floor of the Cuttack Printing Company building to discuss the affairs of the temple. Although the meeting was organized at a very short notice, more than a hundred people attended it. Prominent among its organizers were Baidyanath Pandit, Ramashankar Ray, Golakchandra Bose, Gobinda Rath, Kapileswar Vidyabhushan and Yajneswar Chandra. Three resolutions were passed at this meeting:

First, the government's move to file a case was unwarranted since the general public was unaware of any lapses in temple management. Second, the government would offend the sensibilities of Hindus if it took the extreme step of removing the raja of Puri from the office of the superintendent of the temple. Third, as the income from land allotted to the temple had become inadequate on account of the rise in the prices of goods, the raja had to spend a certain amount from his own pocket to manage the affairs of the temple. If he were removed from office, the government would have to incur heavier expenses; alternatively, it might have to discontinue some of the rituals at the temple.

These resolutions were forwarded to the government. In the *Dipika*, Gourishankar wrote: 'We earnestly request the Government that they should abandon the idea of taking the management of the temple from the Raja's hands; it would be better if they brought about improvement in the affairs of the temple by executing some of the good plans suggested by the raja.'

After the collector of Puri filed the case, the Bhagavat Bhaktipradayini Sabha held a large public meeting on 26 December. A meeting on such a scale had never before been organized in Cuttack. The meeting was presided over by Yajneswar Chandra, a lawyer. Speakers described how temple affairs had been mismanaged after receivers were appointed to conduct them. They pointed out that Muslim constables guarding the temple did their cooking near the temple and Hindu constables wearing belts made of cowhide wandered about the temple premises. Speakers condemned the action of the government referring to slokas in scriptural texts such as *Niladri Mahoday* and passed a number of resolutions amid cries of 'Haribol'. The resolutions touched upon the following:

The rites of worship at the Jagannath temple cannot be performed without the raja's participation. No lapses in the management of the temple have occurred, which would warrant legal action on the part of the government. Raiding the temple and the store house before serving notice on the raja was an unjust step on the part of the government.

A resolution expressing sympathy for the queen was sent to her by the sabha. Resolutions demanding the withdrawal of the court case were also communicated to the government. All Hindus in India were requested to unite and take lawful steps to protect their religion. Gourishankar wrote in the *Dipika*: We ask, in the name of Queen Victoria, the Empress of India, is this the principle which governs British rule in India?

This controversy now reminded people of the raja of Puri who was then serving a sentence of deportation. On 5 January 1887 a petition bearing the signatures of 1500 rajas, zamindars and men of substance was sent to the lieutnant governor, entreating him to grant a pardon to Divyasingh Dev in Queen Victoria's jubilee year. A few days later, the raja of Bamanda made a similar request to the lieutenant governor in another petition.

Prayer to His Excellency the Governor General of India

Traditionally, the Emperor and kings in India set a few prisoners free on certain special occasions and permit a few deported prisoners to return home. Following this time-honoured practice, our revered Victoria freed a large number of prisoners and allowed a number of deportees to come back home when she assumed the title the Empress of India. We are extremely glad that we are now celebrating the Golden Jubilee of the glorious reign of the Empress of India. Needless to say, the joy of every Indian celebrating this occasion will know no bounds if our Governor General graciously orders the release of the former Raja of Pooree.

Srijukta Raja Sudhal Dev   Killa Bamanda

However, all these letters, petitions and prayers did not make the government relent.

Puri, January 1887

As there were protests against the deployment of Muslim policemen around the Puri temple, they were replaced by Hindu policemen. These policemen used to enter the temple premises wearing shoes and belts; now they were forbidden to do so. On 5 January 1887, a clerk sent by the receiver spread out his handkerchief on the jewelled throne of the deities and leaned against it. The temple priests took serious exception to this and insisted that the temple had been desecrated. Arrangements were made to purify the temple through a *mahasnana*.

While all this controversy surrounding the temple was raging, a society called the Sri Sri Jagannath Sanatan Dharmarakshini Sabha was founded at the Bada Akhada Mutt in Puri. A meeting was convened on 16 January to discuss if the decision of the government to take over the management of the affairs of the temple posed a threat to the Hindu religion. The meeting was held at six in the evening and was attended by around three thousand people. The deliberations continued for a full five hours.

Babu Haradhan Ray led saying that according to the scriptures, there were certain temple rituals which could be performed by none other than the raja himself or by a Brahmin belonging to the *agnihotri* sect on behalf of the raja. If the government took over the management of the temple, these rituals could not be performed; as a result, some of these would have to be discontinued. This would amount to interference in the religious life of the Hindus. To substantiate this point he read out a sloka from *Niladri Mahoday*:

> *Tato bandapanante cha raja puspanjali trayam*
> *Pratikshepati bhaktyacha tatah karpura varti bhih*

Speakers who followed him dwelt on how temple rituals had not been observed properly and how Hindu religion was being

J.P. DAS

dishonoured after receivers had been appointed to order the affairs of the temple. They mentioned the following examples:

Although the Hindu constables no longer wore belts and shoes when they guarded the temple, they kept their unwashed and soiled clothes inside the temple premises. They climbed on to the holy platform in front of the storehouse, the seat of Lord Lokanath, which was out of bounds for the general public. Shudras were not supposed to enter the Changada room but the assistant receiver sat there. On the day the store frequently house had been raided, government officials had entered it wearing socks on their feet. So on and on.

The resolutions passed at the meeting were translated into different languages and were sent to all Hindu rajas and maharajas, journalists and eminent persons, soliciting their support and sympathy. Copies of the resolutions were also communicated to the lieutnant governor and the governor general who were requested to withdraw the court case and to allow the raja of Puri to assume charge of the temple.

Two more meetings were held by the same society, on 23 January and on 30 January, where it was said that the people of Orissa felt too upset to celebrate the golden jubilee of the reign of the empress of India on account of the litigation relating to the temple. If the government granted the deported raja of Puri freedom and withdrew the court case involving the temple, the people of Orissa would feel overjoyed and would participate in the jubilee celebrations with reverence and gratitude.

One day, a deputy collector, a Brahmo, while inside the temple, refused to accept prasad offered to him by a servitor. This led to the demand that the temple ought to be purified because the gentleman in question was not a Hindu since he had refused to accept prasad. Some even mentioned that during Maratha rule, shoes were not permitted inside the town of Puri, and that Muslims, when they came into town, would never stay inside it; they would stay near Harinighat jail. It was noted with dismay that under the British, Hindus roamed the streets of Puri wearing shoes and chewing paan; emboldened by the example of the constables, they now went near the seats of deities wearing shoes. The mahant of Radhaballav Mutt had allowed two Kabuli Muslims to take up residence inside the mutt premises and had employed them to collect land revenue.

Around this time, the following song came to be widely circulated:

> Hindu religion has gone to dogs. See what's going on inside the Puri temple.
>
> Pathans now guard its four gates like incarnations of Yama, the god of death.
>
> To get in, you must tell them the names of three generations of your ancestors.
>
> Wearing their cowhide belts they cook their food in the Lion Gate police station.
>
> The aroma of meat wafts into the temple spelling doom for purity and religion.
>
> It has been decreed that the *firang* will now serve Lord Jagannath.
>
> They will check if the mahaprasad is good or bad.
>
> Kaliyug has come, for the temple is going to become a hotel.
>
> The end of dharma will come, for the deities have lost their power.
>
> All you Hindus, now pray to the Queen with folded hands.
>
> If she takes pity on you, your holy city will be saved.

Cuttack, February 1887

Arrangements began for celebrating the golden jubilee of the reign of Queen Victoria on a grand scale. Yet, whenever discussions were held on how to organize the celebrations, some voiced the view that people, in spite of their intense loyalty to the great queen, felt unable to participate wholeheartedly in the festivities on account of their deep unease over matters relating to the Jagannath temple. Nevertheless, even the Sri Sri Jagannath Sanatan Dharmarakshini Sabha convened a meeting to discuss the celebration of the jubilee, and it was decided at the meeting that although Queen Suryamani had given them some money for illuminations, they would, nevertheless, mobilize more funds for the ceremony.

To mark the occasion, the Utkal Sabha prepared a letter of felicitation which read as follows:

> We are delighted and we feel immensely grateful that the Almighty has enabled the reign of Queen Victoria to continue for more than fifty years. We fervently pray to the Lord to let her rule for many more years. Like her subjects living in other parts of her empire, we too strongly believe that no ruler could be more generous or benevolent than our beloved Queen. On this auspicious occasion, we offer her our sincere best wishes as a small token of our deep appreciation for her long, just, impartial, and glorious rule. We remain unflinchingly loyal to her throne.

The jubilee celebrations commenced on 16 February. Two days before this, a piece of good news had arrived by cable from Calcutta. The high court had ordered the receivers appointed by the court and their subordinate employees to refrain from interfering in the affairs of the temple until further orders. The credit for getting the court to issue such an order went entirely to Queen Suryamani's lawyer Madhu Babu.

On 16 February, in the morning, twenty-one guns were fired in the premises of the collectorate to formally announce the beginning of the jubilee celebrations. However, not many had assembled there to see the parade and the gun salute. A large crowd had gathered in front of the gate of the town jail. On that morning 132 male and eleven female prisoners were set free. Only sixty-nine convicts, who were serving out sentences for having committed crimes like murder, remained in the jail. Every released convict received from the jubilee committee a length of cloth, two *annas* and a photograph of Queen Victoria.

In the morning, people prayed in temples, mosques, mutts and churches in Cuttack for the queen's well being. At eleven, beggars thronged the premises of the collectorate. The physically handicapped among them were given a piece of cloth, the others received two annas each. At midday, sixty-five *sankirtan* teams started from different parts of the town and toured the town singing and playing musical instruments. At five, they assembled in the premises of the collectorate and sang and played music there. Illuminations were organized in the evening. The jubilee committee had made arrangements for the roads to be lit up with lamps. All government buildings had been illuminated. Two large gates had been put up in Mian Mastan and Balu Bazaar, which carried banners saying GOD SAVE THE QUEEN and similar slogans. The Cuttack Printing Company had been decorated with special care and it looked gorgeous.

At eight in the evening, the dance of nautch girls was held under an awning put up in front of the cutcherry of the collector. Four teams of nautch girls from Cuttack and one from Bankuda entertained people well into the morning. The sahibs left at about ten but the native gentlemen sat and enjoyed the show all night long. Elsewhere, in Chandni Chowk, Adalat Pokhari, Buxi Buzaar, Ranihat and Telenga Bazaar, people spent the night watching the Krishna Lila.

On the morning of 17 February all students in Cuttack, from those studying in primary schools to those going to college, assembled in front of Ravenshaw College and from there went around town in a procession. While going through the town they sang a song celebrating the jubilee which had been composed by Radhanath Ray.

Sing, all together, in happiness bound
Let the country fill with joyous sound.
Like a mother's lap is her empire's sway
Here let subjects trouble-free stay.
Ma Victoria has the world's respect gained
In this world she has fifty years reigned.
Though she didn't carry us in her womb
Verily she is our very own dearest mom.

In the afternoon of the same day, teams of wrestlers came from different parts of the town to the cutcherry premises and displayed their feats there. At night, a play was staged in the fort for the sahibs; another was put up at Kalipada Banerjee's residence for the benefit of native gentlemen. This marked the end of the two-day long jubilee celebration in Cuttack.

People had hoped that the prisoners who had received a pardon on the occasion of the jubilee would include the raja of Puri. But, to their great disappointment, they learnt that although 23,305 prisoners including 330 doing time in the Andamans were released on this occasion, the raja of Puri was not considered worthy of mercy in view of the seriousness of the crime he had committed.

Puri, June 1887

Before the jubilee, the Calcutta High Court had issued an interim order to the effect that the receivers would not interfere in the management of the temple. In March they pronounced a final verdict on the matter and rescinded the earlier order issued by the district judge of Cuttack relating to the appointment of receivers in the temple. In the higher court's view, the collector of Puri had filed a case because he felt that the managers of the temple were not discharging their duties properly, and that it was necessary to constitute a committee which would order the affairs of the temple. But scrutiny of the records submitted to the court revealed no evidence of misappropriation or misuse of temple funds. In view of this, whatever might be the purpose behind the case, the appointment of receivers was totally unwarranted.

The verdict made everyone, especially the people of the town of Puri, very happy. Mahant Raghunandan Ramanuj Das resigned from his job as receiver. On 27 March 1887, the Sri Sri Jagannath Sanatan Dharmarakshini Sabha held a meeting and gave the mahant the following tongue-in-cheek advice: 'The mahant has gone into great expense during his receivership; now he should make offerings to Lord Jagannath and distribute gifts to poor Brahmins and Vaishnavas to express his gratitude to the lord for having relieved him of this burden.'

The problem was that although the government had the welfare of the people in mind, they had failed to understand what the people really wanted. No matter how incompetent the raja of Puri might be, the people of Orissa did not want the management of the temple to be taken out of his hands. This was made clear in a letter Madhu Babu wrote in the *Dipika* under the pseudonym, 'A Lunatic'. In this he said that he collected discarded scraps of paper as a matter of habit. On one of these he had come across a picture which showed the raja of Puri praying to Lord Jagannath; a policeman held his left hand, and a huge crowd attacked the policeman in an attempt to save the raja.

In Calcutta, the *Statesman* expressed satisfaction over the verdict of the High Court and held the lieutnant governor Sir Rivers Thompson wholly responsible for the affair since he had ordered the matter to be taken to the court of law without having investigated it deeply. Thompson left in April and Sir Stewart

Bailey replaced him as lieutnant governor. As soon as he assumed office, he turned his attention to the court case relating to the Puri temple and called Madhusudan Das and Commissioner Metcalfe to Calcutta for a discussion.

The discussion was held on 16 April in the office of the secretary of Bengal province, H. Nolan. At this meeting, Metcalfe made it absolutely clear that the government had no intention of taking the management of the temple from Queen Suryamani's hands or interfering in the affairs of the temple. He added that the government was not aware of the appointment of receivers and the raid on temple property until the queen filed an appeal in the Supreme Court. Nolan said that the provincial government wanted an amicable settlement of the matter; however, the final decision would rest with the government of India.

After the discussion with Nolan, Madhu Babu published a letter in the *Statesman* on 20 April, informing the general public that the government wanted an amicable settlement of the temple issue. The letter upset the lieutnant governor for he felt that although Madhu Babu had written the letter with the best of intentions, he should have kept the matter secret.

Madhu Babu came back to Orissa after succeeding in his mission and went to meet Queen Suryamani. The queen now felt quite relieved because she had gone through a great deal of trouble on account of the litigation. She could also never forget the humiliation of having been compelled on one occasion to go to the court to file an affidavit. The news made the people of Orissa very happy, too. They said that Madhu Babu had justified his name Madhusudan, which meant 'the one who had slain the demon Madhu', by saving the honour of the raja of Puri in this hour of crisis.

The government of India agreed to reach an amicable settlement of the case relating to the temple. The lieutnant governor sent the terms of the settlement to the queen in June. Important among these were the following: the management of the temple would be placed in the hands of Raja Mukunda Dev. During the period of his minority, the queen would act as his guardian and appoint a manager. Should she wish to dismiss the manager, she must inform the court a week in advance and appoint another manager immediately.

The court case relating to the temple was nearing a settlement but the Sri Sri Jagannath Sanatan Dharmarakshini Sabha, which had come into being in response to it, did not go out of business. It had become a permanent institution. Its members met every Monday evening at the Bada Akhada Mutt and discussed various issues after a recital of scriptures and prayer to the Lord. Issues other than those concerning the temple came to be discussed too: issues such as the government order to inoculate people forcibly, the levy of a latrine tax, the performance of the chairman of the municipality, etc. The society now functioned as an alert guardian of the town of Puri.

In the middle of all this rejoicing over the amicable settlement, people forgot to pay any attention to the news that in the Andamans, Divyasingh had lost his mind and that he had been shut up in a lunatic asylum.

Cuttack, October 1887

The Utkal Brahmo Samaj had been established on 1 July 1869. Every year, on this day, the Brahmos organized an annual function in Cuttack. In 1887, the Brahmos in Cuttack planned to celebrate the foundation day on a grand scale. It was decided that the celebrations would begin on 26 June and last for eight days. The chief organizer of the function was Madhusudan Rao. Sadhucharan Ray, who taught at Academy School, assisted him. Every day, Madhusudan Rao led prayer sessions at the Brahmo temple. On 2 July a *sankirtan* team toured differrent parts of the city singing devotional songs and returned to Madhusudan's residence. At the Chaudhury Bazaar square, Madhusudan delivered lectures both in English and in Oriya. On 3 July, the function was concluded with a lecture on Ram Mohan Roy which was organized at the Cuttack Printing Company.

Three non-Brahmo Hindu boys participated in the function. They were three brothers—Biswanath Kar, Lokanath Kar and Bholanath Kar—who came from Mulabasant village. Lokanath was a student of the Medical School and the other two were studying at the Academy. The three sometimes visited Sadhucharan Ray at his residence, and occasionally went to the Brahmo temple to listen to Madhusudan's lectures. Lokanath came to Sadhucharan Ray's residence every Saturday and returned to the Medical School on Monday in the morning.

Needless to say, the brothers gradually got drawn towards Brahmoism. They gave up Brahminical rituals and took off their sacred threads and wore them around their necks. When they went to their village, their parents were upset by their strange ways. All three were married. Their behaviour disturbed their in-laws, too.When they left their village for Cuttack, everyone advised them against associating themselves with Brahmos.

A few days after the annual function had come to an end, the following advertisement appeared in the magazine *Nabasambad*:

> Lokanath Kar and Raghunath Singh, students of the Cuttack Medical School, and Harekrushna Mohanty from Birol village have publicly expressed their desire to embrace Brahmoism. They will be initiated on the Sunday of 10 July 1887 at the Brahmo temple at Ganga Mandir.

Lokanath was initiated on 10 July. His two brothers discarded their sacred threads soon after. This created quite a sensation throughout Orissa. His uncle, Madhab Chandra Kar, who was childless, had adopted Lokanath. Madhab taught in a school in Baragarh. When the news of Lokanath embracing Brahmoism reached him, he wrote a long letter to the *Dipika*. He gave vent to his grief, addressing eminent Oriyas:

> I receive a salary of 25 rupees. Enduring great hardships at home, I have spent everything I have earned for these boys in the hope that they would look after us when we got old. Now I find myself adrift in an ocean of grief. If you could suggest a way out, I would humbly follow it. I feel dazed and the world has grown dark for us. By becoming Brahmos, these boys, who could have taken up government jobs, have plunged fourteen persons—their grandfathers and grandmothers, their wives, fathers-in-law and mothers-in-law, I myself and my wife—in an ocean of worries. You may say that their in-laws will not be affected by their action. But you must accept that eight persons have no hope of escaping this ocean of misery. Kindly help us find a solution to our problem.

Although Gourishankar was himself a Brahmo, the *Dipika* published an article condemning the conversion. A rejoinder to this appeared in *Nabasambad* which was edited by Sadhucharan Ray. A reply to this was published in the *Dipika*.

On 20 July the Bhagavat Bhaktipradayini Sabha of Cuttack held a meeting at Gopaljiu Mutt. Since the festival of *Nandotsav* fell on this date, the members organized a sankirtan and afterwards listened to the recital of the chapter on the birth of Lord Srikrishna from the Srimad Bhagavat Gita. Then they went on to discuss Lokanath's becoming a Brahmo, although this topic had not been included in their agenda. Anyway, the matter was discussed and the following resolutions were passed:

> First: This Association feels extremely sad and apprehensive on learning that an underage Brahmin student of the Medical School has embraced Brahmoism and that two underage students

of the Academy School have discarded their sacred threads with the intention of becoming Brahmos. It is the view of the Association that educational development of this backward province will receive a setback unless religious conversion is legally prohibited.

Second: People believe that the Deputy Inspector of Schools, who is a Brahmo, has initiated one of the above-mentioned boys into the Brahmo order and that a teacher of the Academy School is actively encouraging two boys studying at this school to discard their sacred threads. In view of this, the Association feels that the principle of religious tolerance promoted by the government has been violated in this instance and that suitable action is called for.

Third: The Association resolves that a petition bearing signatures of people be sent to the Government through the Commissioner, and copies of the same be forwarded to the Director of Schools, the District Magistrate, Cuttack, and the President, District Board.

Members who took a leading role in getting these resolutions passed included Ramashankar Ray, Gobinda Rath and Kapileswar Nanda Sharma. Pandit Markandeya Mohapatra of Puri expressed the view that it was not proper to discuss a matter which had not been included in the agenda. But no one paid him any attention.

The issue of conversion certainly exercised people but they now expressed their deep unease over the propriety of officers in the education department and teachers engaging themselves in proseletyzing activities. Even someone like Lalitmohan Chakravorty, who had become a Brahmo when very young in spite of the opposition of his parents, criticized Madhusudan and Sadhucharan.

While this controversy was going on, another incident in October fuelled it further. Joint Inspector Radhanath Ray appointed Bijaychandra Majumdar as second teacher in Puri Zilla

School without advertising this post. Bijaychandra was then living in Calcutta after having spent a few years in Bamanda. There was another reason why this appointment created controversy: it was rumoured that Bijaychandra was going to marry Madhusudan Rao's daughter.

Puri, December 1887

After the receiver was withdrawn from the Puri temple and the status quo restored, the efforts to settle the lawsuit which the government had brought against the raja of Puri also slackened. The Sri Sri Sanatan Dharmarakshini Sabha now concentrated on discussing such matters as the use of tinned ghee in the temple, the need for curbing theft inside the temple premises and the necessity for lighting the temple for the convenience of devotees.

On 25 August 1887, Divyasingh died of tuberculosis in the Andamans. This news reached Orissa in November. Queen Suryamani performed the funeral rites on 21 November. A thousand Brahmins were fed mahaprasad twelve days after the funeral. They were given one anna each as dakshina. The next day, the mahants and sadhus of all the mutts of Puri were invited to a feast.

A regnal year in the name of Mukunda Dev had been declared earlier but since his father Divyasingh was still alive, no one had recognized it. Now every one accepted the regnal year named after Mukunda Dev. The magazine, *Oriya*, which had been launched from Balasore since October for the benefit of pilgrims to Puri, bore '35th regnal year of Divyasingh Dev' on the cover of its first issue. On the cover of its second issue now was written, '9th regnal year of Mukunda Dev.'

After the funeral rites of Divyasingh had been performed, Madhu Babu came to Puri to discuss with Queen Suryamani the draft of the application for the settlement of the lawsuit. He went inside the palace and talked to the queen, who spoke to him from behind a door. It was decided that the proposals to be sent to the government would include the following:

The seristadar of Cuttack judge court, Harekrushna Das, would be appointed the queen's manager. The arrangements made for the management of the temple would remain in force till Mukunda came of age. The manager would oversee the management of temple affairs and take care of the land, which had been allotted to the temple. According to the Act of 1860, the power of conducting the affairs of the temple would remain vested with Raja Mukunda Dev; but, during his minority, Queen Suryamani would exercise it. Steps would have to be taken to increase the tax levied on temple lands.

Before taking his leave, Madhu Babu wanted to meet Raja Mukunda Dev. The raja was ten years old but, like his father, he took no interest in studies and spent all his time with the servants. He spent hours with the birds and animals kept as pets in the palace. Among these, his favourites were a herd of pigs. When Madhu Babu went to meet him, he found him in the pigsty. Madhu Babu asked Mukunda a number of times to come out, but Mukunda refused to oblige him. In the end, Madhu Babu had to go back to Cuttack without being able to see the person for whom he was taking so much trouble. The application from the queen was submitted to the commissioner on 9 December.

A few days after this, Madhu Babu and Gourishankar went to Madras to attend the third session of the Indian National Congress as the representatives of the Utkal Sabha.

Cuttack, June 1888

Radhanath's long poem 'Chandrabhaga' was published in September 1886. A year later, in November 1887, his long poem, 'Nandhikeshwari,' got published. This Radhanath dedicated to the raja of Bamanda, Basudev Sudhal Dev. In the dedication Radhanath mentioned that the hero of this poem was one of the raja's ancestors. But this was clearly an overstatement for the central character of the poem, Chora Ganga Dev, had little to do with the real, historical Chora Ganga Dev. The poem was based on meagre historical material, a few foreign poems, and Radhanath's own poetic imagination. He had devoted a lot of his energy to writing this poem and was hoping that it would appeal to his readers. But the readers were put off by the incident involving the princess of Orissa who betrayed her father in order to win the love of an enemy of her country. While some described the poem as a jewel adorning the neck of the muse of Utkal, others expressed the view that the love depicted in the poem was selfish, indistinguishable from lust, and that it flouted all rules of decorum and propriety. In view of the perversion and bad taste which seemed to overwhelm Oriya literature, poems like 'Nandikeshwari' should be discouraged. Such attacks thoroughly disheartened Radhanath and he wondered if he should continue writing in Oriya at all.

The controversies surrounding certain decisions of the education department also continued to bother Radhanath. After the dust over the appointment of Bijaychandra Majumdar settled, Radhanath got embroiled in a dispute involving Barabati School in Balasore. Baikunthanath Dey and Bhagaban Chandra Das quarrelled over the management of the school. Radhanath took Baikunthanath's side and wrote an article in the *Oriya* under a pseudonym supporting Baikunthanath's cause. He also tried to win other people to Baikunthanath's side by showing them relevant records. This, on the part of a highly placed official like him, was extremely improper. Commenting on the issue, the *Dipika* had this to say: 'How long can the cat go on drinking milk closing its eyes and pretending that no one sees it?'

Now another allegation was brought against Radhanath: that he was indulging in nepotism while selecting examiners. Ignoring the claims of many deserving teachers, he selected his own supporters such as Sadhu Charan Ray and Biswanath Kar, his clerk Jagannath Rao, who was Madhu Rao's younger brother, and Bijaychandra Majumdar, who was Madhu Rao's prospective son-in-law. Many complained that Radhanath and Madhusudan were joining hands and engaging in corrupt practices in the education department. Their critics jokingly called them the governor general and the lieutnant governor of the education department.

The critics of Madhu Rao's role in propagating Brahmoism also targeted Radhanath, for he had not taken any action against Madhu Rao. The collector, in response to the petition regarding Lokanath embracing Brahmoism, which the Bhagavat Bhaktipradayini Sabha, Cuttack, had sent, declared Madhu Rao's missionary activities improper. In February, the government sent the following order:

> The Government hereby endorses the order passed earlier by the Collector, Cuttack, to the effect that Madhusudan Rao, as long as he remains Deputy Inspector of Schools, is forbidden to act as a priest or teacher of the Brahmo faith.

In May, the *Balasore Sambad Bahika* wrote: 'Whenever Joint Inspector Radhanath Babu finds a position lying vacant, he ignores the claims of native Oriyas and loses no time in giving it to a fellow Bengali or a distant relative. Again, he is not above adopting subterfuges to get this done. Let alone a sub-inspector's job, even the job of inspecting pandit, which in the fitness of things should go to native Oriyas, goes to distantly related brothers-in-law of Radhanath Babu.'

In June, Basanti, Madhu Rao's eldest daughter got married to Bijay Chandra Majumdar. Now it became clear that the criticism levelled earlier at Madhusudan was not entirely baseless.

Oppressed by all manner of worries like these, Radhanath now concentrated on writing a long poem titled 'Usha'. He knew that only poetry could give him comfort.

Puri, December 1888

On 26 July, the government informed the commissioner of Cuttack that the collector of Puri and the queen should now submit the agreement relating to the lawsuit concerning the temple to the district judge. Before Madhu Babu could send word of this to the queen, he received a letter from her. In it she wrote that on 31 July, during the Car Festival, a crow had flown in and perched on the right arm of Lord Jagannath. This, the queen wrote, was a bad omen; she sought Madhu Babu's opinion on what was to be done about this. The lawsuit involving the temple had already taken a lot of Madhu Babu's time, and the case had gone on for a very long time. Suppressing his feelings of annoyance, Madhu Babu wrote to the queen saying that the only way the evil omen could be countered was by signing the deed of agreement.

On receiving the letter from the commissioner, the collector got the petition drafted. Puri now had a new collector. When the litigation had begun, Savage was acting collector in Puri. He was succeeded by Jones who committed suicide by slitting his throat with a razor. In his place had come Taylor who was earlier sub-divisional officer, Khurda.

The gist of the draft agreement was as follows:

The plaintiff, the Collector, Puri, and the defendant, Suryamani Patamahadei, defendant number two Mukunda Dev and defendant number three Niladri Dei respectfully beg to inform you that they have amicably settled the above-mentioned case and have reached the following agreement. They pray to you to extend your kind approval to the same.

Mukunda Dev will remain in charge of the management of the temple. However, during his minority, his grandmother, Suryamani Patamahadei, will order the affairs of the temple. She will appoint an able manager. If the queen removes the manager, she must appoint another immediately, or else the court will take steps to appoint one. It will be the manager's duty to see to it that the servitors do their job properly, and that no inconvenience is caused to the devotees when they go to the temple, and that the mahaprasad is not unsafe etc.

This agreement, signed by the collector and the queen, was submitted to the court on 3 October. The case came up for hearing at the court of Judge Bragan in December. Pleaders Hariballav Ghosh and Lal Behari Ghosh represented the plaintiff and the defendants were represented by Madhusudan Das and Ramashankar Ray. The district judge accepted the petition. At last, in this manner, the lawsuit involving the temple which had gone on for such a long time, came to an end.

eleven

Twenty-two years previously, Commissioner Ravenshaw had put Dhanurjay Narayan Bhanja on the throne of Keonjhar. And yet, even after the lapse of so many years, Dhanurjay had not been able to win the affections of the Bhuyans. Moreover, he had made matters worse by becoming a tyrant after ascending the throne.

Forced labour was the chief cause of disaffection for the Bhuyans. Whenever the raja or his cronies happened to pass through Bhuyan settlements, they made the Bhuyans serve them and bring them provisions for free. On occasions, the raja made them carry loads and go to places outside the kingdom. They had to thatch the raja's house and give him goats on festive occasions. However, they received no payment for these services.

Sometimes, cronies of the raja called Bhuyans living in far-off villages for forced labour. The Bhuyans had to stay away from home for a long time and as a result they had to neglect their land and suffer losses. On the occasion of the raja's marriage, about five years ago, they were made to carry loads all the way to Patna and had to spend more than a month away from home. Moreover, in the previous year, the raja had resettled the land belonging to the Bhuyans and had increased the tax per plough and per household. All these rendered the Bhuyans miserable and feelings of resentment kept smouldering in their hearts.

In 1891, Dhanurjay decided that he would irrigate the fields in Nijagarh with water from the Machkandana mountain stream. This involved digging a canal by cutting rocks in a hill and the project was accomplished with forced labour. Bhuyan labourers were not given food, nor wages. They broke stones with the help of crowbars from morning till evening. They were given a two-hour break during which they cooked the rice they had brought from home. If a poor Bhuyan had no rice, he had to work on an empty stomach. If someone slackened even slightly, he was whipped.

When the oppression became unbearable, the Bhuyans convened a panchayat. On being informed of this, Dhanurjay sent his assistant manager, who took a number of soldiers with him, to them. The assistant manager caught about seventy Bhuyans, of whom ten were hanged. Among the captured Bhuyans, there was one called Gopal Nayak.

Gopal Nayak's younger brother, Dharanidhar was working at the time as a surveyor in Singbhum. He happened to be the most educated member of the Bhuyan community. Dhanurjay made him work for him for a year and a half without giving him a salary. Dharanidhar ran off to Mayurbhanj and worked for a few years there. When a dispute over the boundary between Keonjhar and Singbhum arose, Dhanurjay recalled him and got him to work for him in Singbhum.

On hearing that his elder brother had been arrested, Dharanidhar came back to Keonjhar and when he saw how the Bhuyans had been treated, he chose to lead the uprising. He wrote to the commissioner in Cuttack and the government in Bengal complaining against the raja's tyranny. Since nothing came of it, he convened a panchayat, which was attended by Bhuyans, Juangs and other victims of the raja's oppression. On receiving intelligence of this, Dhanurjay came there with his assistant manager and soldiers and took many of them prisoner. However, Dharanidhar managed to give them the slip.

Now the Bhuyans determined to rise in rebellion. On 2 May, about a thousand Bhuyans and Kondhs went to Chamakpur and tied up the constables and paiks stationed there and looted the village. After this, they looted a number of villages such as Kalikaprasad and Nayapat and compelled the paiks and sardars of Kendujhar to swear allegiance to them. They also blocked the road to Keonjhar by posting armed guards on it. Scared by all this, Dhanurjay left the palace and escaped to Anandpur, which lay fifty miles away.

The manager of Keonjhar, Fakir Mohan Senapati, was at that time stationed in Anandpur. He had left his job as dewan, Pallahada, long ago. He had had very little to do in Pallahada. Translating the Mahabharat and playing dice were not enough to occupy him. He had faced another inconvenience while there. He was used to eating a lot of paan, but in Pallahada paan was not available. Feeling utterly fed up, Fakir Mohan gave up his job and returned to Balasore. Soon he was out of money, but managed to land the post of manager, Keonjhar, through the good offices of Nandakishore Das.

Before Dhanurjay reached Anandpur, Fakir Mohan had received news of the uprising through a letter sent by the raja through a runner. Two days after the letter came, Dhanurjay himself arrived in Anandpur at nine at night. He had set out from Keonjhar fort in the morning, accompanied by a few trusted men on three elephants. Fakir Mohan made arrangements for putting Dhanurjay up in Anandpur and set off for Cuttack the next morning to meet the commissioner and inform him about the uprising. He spent the night at Kantajhari and the next day he left his elephant at the Dulidiha Lock in the river Brahmani, and boarded a steamer. He reached Cuttack at nine in the morning the day after.

Fakir Mohan first called upon the assistant commissioner, Nandakishore Das. The same day he met the commissioner, G. Toynbee. Toynbee had heard of Dhanurjay's misrule and he shouted at Fakir Mohan. With great difficulty, Fakir Mohan got him to order the superintendent of police of Balasore to proceed to Keonjhar with a hundred constables to help Dhanurjay.

On his way back Fakir Mohan ran into Dhanurjay at Tangi. It was decided that having come so far Dhanurjay should not go back without meeting the commissioner. Since Dhanurjay had left in a great hurry, he had not brought decent clothes. So a tailor was sent for and a dress was made which Dhanurjay could wear when he went to meet the commissioner the next morning.

Toynbee told Dhanurjay off and made it clear that he would do nothing to help him. But when Dhanurjay said that his family needed protection and that he was willing to bear all the expenses, Toynbee relented. It was decided that the deputy commissioner of Chaibasa would be asked to put down the uprising and that soldiers and policemen would be placed at his disposal. A cable bearing this message was sent to the government. Fakir Mohan and Dhanurjay returned to Anandpur after receiving Toynbee's assurance.

Meanwhile, the rebels, who now numbered about twenty thousand, looted many villages and, on 12 May, attacked the fort. However, the paiks in the fort repulsed their attack. The rebels, on their part, succeeded in blocking all roads. They also held a number of paik prisoner in Indrachhatra and Raisuan hills. Many paiks and zamindars deserted the raja and came over to the rebels' side.

Dhanurjay and Fakir Mohan started recruiting paiks in the Anandpur area. With great difficulty they managed to find only three hundred decrepit old men, many of whom suffered from night blindness. The guns they carried were rusty and their swords were no good. It was settled that Dhanurjay would stay in Anandpur and that Fakir Mohan would lead this army of paiks to Keonjhar. Accordingly, on 13 May, Fakir Mohan left Anandpur, accompanied by two hundred and fifty paiks, four constables, and three elephants.

The next day, when they reached the Basantpur pass, the rebels encircled them and disarmed the paiks. The rebels took Fakir Mohan to Raisuan and brought him before Dharanidhar. Everyone now recognized Dharanidhar as the chief and he was certainly the undisputed leader of the uprising. Word had got round that Dharani was Queen Victoria's adopted son and that the queen had sent him to rule Keonjhar. The rebels were so angry with the tyrannical officials of the raja that they would have summarily executed Fakir Mohan. But Fakir Mohan saved himself by saying that he now acknowledged Dharanidhar, not Dhanurjay, as the raja of Keonjhar and offered to serve him as his manager. He even went so far as to ask for a salary. It was decided that he would be granted seven acres of rent-free land for his services.

Fakir Mohan now actively set to work to get Dharanidhar captured and to bring Dhanurjay back to the fort. Dharanidhar enjoyed absolute power in the area and, claiming that he was the tikayat of Keonjhar, he issued parwanas to every part of the kingdom and made people send provisions to him. In the meantime the rebels had released convicts from the jail and looted the royal treasury.

Appreciating the gravity of the situation, the deputy commissioner of Chaibasa, Dawson, asked the government to send troops from Calcutta. On 21 May, leading a group of soldiers and policemen, he set off from Chakradharpur and reached Jayantigarh the following day. From Anandpur, the Guys, the superintendent of police of Balasore, accompanied by Dhanurjay, proceeded towards Keonjhar. Dawson received news that the rebels had captured the royal armoury and were planning to attack the fort with cannons. He sent the sub-inspector, Sasibhusan Ray, to ascertain the real position, but the rebels captured Ray and took him to Dharanidhar.

Fakir Mohan and Sasibhusan put their heads together and worked out a plan. They convinced Dharanidhar that if he went and met the British officer, the latter would place him on the throne. At this moment news came that British troops were approaching Raisuan. Fakir Mohan made Dharanidhar put on strange-looking royal finery and ride an elephant, and sent him to meet Dawson. Dharanidhar met Dawson on the way and when he got down from the elephant the British soldiers surrounded him and took him prisoner.

Dawson's soldiers burnt down Dharanidhar's camp and set Fakir Mohan and the other prisoners free. They seized his arms and ammunition, arrested all his men and marched towards the fort. Guys and Dhanurjay arrived there the same day. Some rebels were captured; others escaped into the jungle. Dhanurjay was escorted to the fort.

Commissioner Toynbee came to Keonjhar on 16 June to hear the grievances of the subjects. His investigations convinced him that there would be fresh trouble if Dhanurjay continued to rule Keonjhar. So he decided that Dhanurjay should be sent to Cuttack, and an Englishman called H.P. Wylie would become manager of Keonjhar.

Dharanidhar was tried in Cuttack and was sentenced to seven years' rigorous imprisonment under articles 125, 127 and 340 of the Indian penal code.

Anandpur, March 1892

All this, however, did not bring an end to the problems in Keonjhar. Dhanurjay appealed to the commissioner to restore him to the throne. Madhusudan Das defended him. However, Toynbee rejected the raja's petition. Madhusudan appealed against this decision and petitioned the lieutenant governor. In his petition, Madhusudan argued that there was no evidence at all that Dhanurjay was a tyrant. The lieutnant governor, Sir Charles Eliot decided that he would go to Keonjhar and investigate the matter personally.

Eliot set off for Cuttack in February. On the way, at Bhadrak, about two hundred people from Keonjhar met him and gave him a petition in which they had listed their grievances. After arriving in Cuttack, he discussed the Keonjhar issue with Toynbee, Wylie and Dhanurjay. In the meantime, some people from Keonjhar also arrived in Cuttack. Toynbee and Wylie were of the opinion that the raja should not be reinstated. However, after discussing the matter with everyone concerned, Eliot said that Dhanurjay would be allowed to return to Keonjhar but at the same time, a political agent would also be sent there. Nandakishore Das was appointed the political agent and was vested with substantial powers. Wylie was to leave Keonjhar. Fakir Mohan was to be relieved of his duties since he had become extremely unpopular among the subjects; Babu Durgadas Mukherjee would replace him.

Fakir Mohan called upon the lieutenant governor at the dak bungalow in Bhadrak when the latter was on his way back to Calcutta. The lieutenant governor merely said, 'When did you come? Is everything all right?' and went off to inspect the jail. Fakir Mohan realized that he had lost his job.

The lieutnant governor returned to Calcutta. Wylie did not go to Keonjhar but went back to Baripada from Cuttack. The nineteen elephants he had brought with him from Keonjhar, he left in Fakir Mohan's care.

Fakir Mohan now proceeded to Anandpur to hand over charge and return the elephants. His mind was now oppressed by all kinds of worries, for he was again going to be without a job. However, as he rode his elephant, he found solace in pieces of paper and a pencil. He thought he should prepare a list of all the writers and other distinguished persons of the province. Then he thought that a mere list would not appeal to readers; he should, therefore, list the special qualities and achievements of these persons. He began by writing 'Om' at the top of a piece of paper and invoking the goddess Sarala: 'I pray to you, mother, who resides in Jhankada, and who plays on a veena and blesses us with knowledge etc.' By the time he reached Anandpur, he had finished half of the task. As soon as he got down from the elephant he gave whatever he had written to the press with the instructions that it should be set in type and printed. He gave this work the title *Utkala Bhramanam*, for this work contained descriptions of various places in the province. He finished writing at about ten at night. The book came out from the press the next evening.

Around this time Dhanurjay, Nandakishore and Madhu Babu arrived in Anandpur. They all looked triumphant. But Fakir Mohan was terribly depressed. He had been told that day that his pet dog, of which he was extremely fond, had died. This had given him more pain than even the prospect of losing his job. He handed over the charge of the office and the treasury to another person in the presence of Nandakishore. After this he presented everyone with a copy of *Utkala Bhramanam*. Laying aside his work, Madhu Babu started reading the book. Of him it said the following:

Come Mr M.S, let me shake your hand
You have brought glory to our motherland, etc.

Nandakishore, too, liked what the book had said of him:

You, Nandakishore, possess virtues numerous
To describe them all would be preposterous, etc.

Dhanurjay went through the book carefully. It bore mention of rajas of Duspalla, Talcher, Bamanda, Mayurbhanj etc., but nowhere did it mention the raja of Keonjhar.

That night, Fakir Mohan left Anandpur on an elephant. He carried with him a bundle containing five hundred copies of *Utkala Bhramanam*. He had decided that he would distribute them when he reached Balasore. The distant future did not worry him at the moment. He was to reach Basantia which lay on the border of Keonjhar estate. Dhanurjay had instructed the mahout to leave Fakir Mohan there and come back. Now Fakir Mohan wondered what arrangements he would make to go from there to Balasore.

Cuttack, June 1892

Like others, Radhanath, too, received a copy of *Utkala Bhramanam* by post. This booklet had become a talking point among the literati in the province. Everyone who was someone in Orissa found himself mentioned in it. Even Ravenshaw and Beames, who had left Orissa, had found a place in the booklet. What it said of him pleased Radhanath immensely. The first two lines of the portion dealing with him went like this:

Blessed you are, Radhanath, verily blessed
Throughout the land your fame has spread

Radhanath had gone through a rather bad time over the last few years. In March 1890, Pandit Gobinda Rath had sent a letter to the Sudder Board containing allegations against Radhanath. Rath had complained that, as the highest official in the education department, Radhanath had used his clout to get textbooks written by his friends and relatives approved, paying no attention to their deficiencies or price. The board had forwarded this petiton to the director, and Inspector Brahmamohan Mallik had come to Orissa to investigate the matter. Mallik inquired into the allegations made by Pandit Rath and gave a clean chit to Radhanath in his report. However, Pandit Rath was not satisfied with this report and demanded that another inquiry into the matter be instituted. But his protests went unheeded.

Like his official decisions, Radhanath's poetry, too, came to be subjected to hostile criticism. Of his long poem, 'Kedar Gouri', one wrote: "The complexity of the poem will defeat any living commentator for its author Radhanath is none other than an incarnation of Shakespeare.' Of 'Nandikeshwari' it was said that it revealed a perverted imagination and that the poet had constructed unreadable, ugly, despicable and repulsive narratives.

In 1890, Radhanath's son, Sashibhusan, who was then fifteen, suffered an attack of epilepsy. As time passed his illness so disabled him that he had to give up his studies and stay at home. This came as a blow to Radhanath and added to his woes.

However, in the middle of all these worries, Radhanath wrote a long poem titled 'Parvati' and sent it to Basudev Sudhal Dev for publication in *Sambalpur Hitaishini*. The poem had been written by Sashibhusan's sickbed. The intense pain his son suffered so upset Radhanath that he could not complete the poem. Basudev revised the text of the poem in places and got the unfinished poem printed at the Jagannath Ballav Press in 1891. The *Dipika* had this to say of 'Parvati': 'We can't imagine what prompted Radhanath Babu to choose this revolting episode from the history of this land of heroes, which is rich in edifying incidents. All we can say here is that by narrating such an ugly episode, Radhanath has defiled his pen.'

However, one letter brought him a little comfort; it had been written by the raja of Mayurbhanj, Sri Ramachandra Dev. It said:

My dear Sir,

Let me offer you my congratulations on the publication of your work 'Parvati', a copy of which you so kindly sent me. I admire it very much. Gobind Babu told me a month ago that you would be paying us a visit in August. We should indeed be very glad if you could come sometime this year during your tours.

I am very busy just now with state affairs and my studies, and I am getting gradually into the right mould.

With my compliments.

Yours sincerely,   Baripada,
Sri Ramachandra Bhanja Deo   30 September 1891

P.S. I hope your son is all right.

The letter left Radhanath a little dissatisfied for he well knew that Sri Ramachandra must not have gone through the book and the letter was no more than a polite gesture. Sri Ramachandra had received education in the English medium and he had little affection for Oriya. Like his other letters, this too, was written in English. All the same, Radhanath entertained hopes of receiving financial assistance from the raja at some future date.

His thoughts now turned to Basudev Sudhal Dev. True, the raja had got his book printed, but he had not given Radhanath any money. Moreover, he had sent Radhanath only ten to twelve copies of the book, which he had given away. He was now left with no copies of the book. What pained Radhanath was the fact that these two rajas, who called themselves his friends, never extended to him any financial support.

Of course, Sri Ramachandra often requested him to contribute to the *Utkala Prabha*, a literary magazine which was published from Baripada. Awards were given to poems and essays published in this magazine, and writers such as Gobinda Chandra Mohapatra and Biswanath Kar had received awards for their contributions on more than one occasion. Radhanath had expressed his unwillingness to write for the *Utkala Prabha* because, as a government official, he was not allowed to accept any award. In any case, his long poem 'Chilika' was published in this magazine and he received one hundred rupees as reward.

Radhanath now decided that he would set to work on writing an epic in blank verse, which would be based on the episode of the last journey of the Pandavas in the Mahabharat. Since he had often in the past been accused of borrowing heavily from Bangla and foreign literature, he chose to begin his epic with a prayer to the goddess Sarala: 'O Goddess whose abode is a lotus flower, tell me what the king of Kurus did etc.' He had hoped that he would receive financial help from the rajas of Mayurbhanj and Bamanda for his epic. He therefore invoked the raja of Mayurbhanj, although the context of the poem did not warrant it, at the beginning of the fifth canto: 'O, you are the young tree which embodies the hopes of Utkal etc.' Elsewhere in the canto he also wrote: 'It is at your command, O warrior, that I am writing this epic.' Portions of the fifth canto of the epic got published in the *Utkala Prabha* and earned the poet a cash award. But hopes of getting anything more from Ramachandra, whom Radhanath had praised to the sky in his poem, remained unfulfilled.

Radhanath now decided to lavish praise on the raja of Bamanda in the next canto of his epic poem. Before proceeding to describe Yudhisthira's attainment of enlightenment, Radhanath addressed the following words to Basudev Sudhal Dev: 'O, you lord of the roaring waterfall, you who adorn the head of Utkala like a jewel, your presence has vested your fort with an aura of sanctity.' But this prayer too fell on deaf ears, and there was no sign of any financial reward coming from Bamanda.

Radhanath had gone on a tour of Balasore in April 1892. He and his family had to return in a bullock cart since steamer services from Bhadrak were stopped during the summer months. Radhanath set to work on the seventh canto of *Mahayatra* in spite of the acute discomfort caused by the heat and the difficult ride. His heart was also full of resentment against the rajas of Mayurbhanj and Bamanda. He finished writing the canto within a week after reaching Cuttack. After this he laid aside the incomplete epic.

Just at this time, an offer of financial assistance arrived from an unexpected quarter. Radhanath received a letter from the raja of Athamallik, a small kingdom, which said:

Dear Sir,

No words could ever adequately describe how much good your writings have done to Orissa. Deep darkness had covered Orissa's sky since the death of great poets like Upendra Bhanja and Abhimanyu. However, fortunately for us, you, like the full moon, have started dispelling this darkness and have brought us glory.

We keep ourselves informed about you by talking to our manager, Damodar Babu. We are extremely glad to learn that you are at present engaged in writing an epic in blank verse. We shall give you a cash award of three hundred rupees to enable you to finish this great work early. May I hasten to add that this trifling sum of money is as nothing compared to the value of your verbal wizardry. All we want to do is to pray to you to finish this great work, which is of so much value to our motherland. We hope you would be so kind as to forgive us.

Yours obediently,   Athamallik
Maharaja of Athamallik Fort,   16 May 1892
Sri Mahendra Dev

The thought that there was at least one raja in Orissa who appreciated his worth and who was able to express himself with such grace and elegance pleased Radhanath a great deal.

Another piece of good news arrived a few days later: the post of inspector of schools was to be created specially for Orissa, and Radhanath took up this post on 21 June 1892. This was a moment of happiness in Radhanath's otherwise drab and desolate life.

Puri, August 1893

The Asiatic Society of Calcutta now decided to act on its earlier plan of shifting the Navagraha pata from Konark to Calcutta. They wrote to the Public Works Department, and in 1892 the department offered three alternative courses of action to the government: conveying the slab on rails to the sea beach and shipping it from there to Calcutta which would cost 24,952 rupees; taking it to the Telikud rivulet on iron rails and sending it to Calcutta in a boat constructed specially for this purpose which would cost 5200 rupees; unnecessary portions of the pata could be hewn off and then the cost of sending it to Calcutta through Telikuda by boat would come to 750 rupees.

Needless to say, the third alternative was accepted as it involved the least expense. A part of the slab, two and a half feet thick, was hewn off from the back of the pata which was four feet thick.

When news of this reached Puri, the Sri Sri Jagannath Sanatan Dharmarakshini Sabha called an urgent meeting. After much discussion, members concluded that shifting the pata would amount to an insult to Hindu religion. They prayed to the government to institute an inquiry into the matter and rescind its order to shift the pata. However, the *Dipika* observed: 'We understand that the government has taken the decision to shift this precious work of art in order to preserve it; no other intention motivates their action. If Hindus are offering worship to these idols and have made necessary arrangements for their preservation, these should by no means be transferred to some other place. If, on the other hand, Hindus have neglected to take care of this wonderful ancient piece of sculpture and have left it exposed to the elements, the government, by taking steps to preserve it, is doing nothing wrong; in fact, it can be said that they are doing us a favour. It would therefore be unfair to oppose the government in this instance.'

Another proposal was put forward in a letter to the *Dipika*: 'If the Hindus do not come forward to provide funds for the preservation of the Navagraha idols at Konark, steps should be taken to bring them over to Puri and keep them somewhere inside the temple premises. In this way, proper care could be taken of the idols. Since the repairs are now being carried out in the temple, it would be convenient to shift the idols there at this time. It is true, more expenses will be involved in conveying the idols from Konark to Puri. But it would be all right if money is made available from temple funds for this purpose since the idols are considered sacred by the Hindus.'

Around this time an incident occurred which greatly upset the residents of Puri. The Cuttack superintendent of police came to Puri, where he took pictures of the Jagannath Temple with his camera; he went from there to Konark and got the Navagraha idols photographed. To people this amounted to an act of disrespect.

Soon after, a photographer working with the department of archaeology came to Puri to take pictures of the temple. Earlier, photographers used to place their cameras at Mangu Mutt or the Lion Gate to take pictures. But this photographer went into the temple and took pictures of the Kalarahat Gate and even of the deities seated on the jewelled throne. The Sri Sri Jagannath Sanatan Dharmarakshini Sabha launched an agitation, wrote to the temple superintendent urging him to take necessary action, and sent a petition to the government regarding the matter.

On receiving the petition, the lieutenant governor consulted the Hindu trustees of the Asiatic Society and sought their opinion on whether the Navagraha idols should be shifted to Calcutta. At this time, Mr Beglar, an engineer who formerly worked for the archaeology department, wrote to the government expressing the view that transferring the idols to the Calcutta museum would in no way serve the interests of archaeology; on the other hand, removing them from an ancient and sacred site would be viewed as a cruel and unfeeling act on the part of the government. He suggested that by renovating the temple at Konark, the government would preserve a glorious piece of ancient architecture.

On hearing from the lieutnant governor, the Asiatic Society appointed a three-member committee to investigate the matter. The members appointed to this were Mahendra Lal Sirkar, Mahesh Chandra Narayaratna, and Haraprasad Shastri. The committee decided that Mahesh Chandra should go to Konark and take stock of the situation there. In February, he travelled to Konark with his family and held a consultation with pandits in Puri. He learnt that whatever might have been the case in the past, a lot of people now worshipped the Navagraha idols. Removing them from their present site would therefore hurt the sentiments of Hindus.

This the Asiatic Society duly conveyed this to the lieutnant governor. The government finally decided not to transfer the Navagraha idols to Calcutta and instructed the archaeology department not to touch them in future. The department was further instructed to put the stone slab where it had lain earlier.

The archaeology department carried out the government's orders and built a thatched roof over the idols. This pleased the pandits of Puri. However, shortly afterwards, the government decided to take a few statues from Konark to the Calcutta Museum. The pandits voiced their protest against this decision, but, this time, the government paid them no heed at all. Thirteen statues from the temple of Konark were conveyed to Calcutta.

Cuttack, March 1894

The lane that ran past the Kali temple in Cuttack was known as the Mahal lane for Nilamani Haldar's palace had once stood in this part of the town. After Haldar's house crumbled, people came to call this place Nilamaani Padia or Nilamani Field. Madhusudan Rao had built his house in one part of the field. A building with a thatched roof which housed the Cuttack Town School occupied another part of the field. In the course of time, the school building collapsed and the school was shifted elsewhere. Madhusudan now persuaded Radhanath to purchase this plot of land and construct a house there. On 1 December 1892, Radhanath got confirmed in his post as inspector of schools, Orissa. A few months later, he left his rented house in Sheikh Bazaar and came to stay in his own house. The lane came to be known as Kaligali.

At the beginning of 1892, Radhanath was drawn into yet another controversy. This time, ranged against him was the great medieval Oriya poet, Upendra Bhanja, no less. The books that Pyari Mohan Sen, deputy inspector of schools, had bought for distribution as prizes among primary school students included a few poems by Upendra Bhanja. Lala Ramanarayan Ray, a teacher from the Cuttack Girls' School, took serious exception to this and published a trenchant attack in the *Utkala Prabha* which was published out of Mayurbhanj. He contended that it would not be right to place the poems of Upendra Bhanja, whose hallmark was their eroticism, in the hands of young children. The *Dipika* countered this by saying, 'In view of the literary worth of Bhanja's work, there was nothing wrong in giving these away as prizes to school children.' This position was not a disinterested one, for the Cuttack Printing Company had published several works by Bhanja, complete with annotations. Moreover, since these books did not sell in large numbers, ways had to be found to dispose of them.

This, in time, swelled into a full-scale conflict between ancient and modern literature, and later, between the late Upendra Bhanja and Radhanath Ray. People lost no time in taking sides. Since the

Utkala Prabha expressed its unwillingness to get involved in this controversy, critics of Bhanja and supporters of Radhanath chose Sudhal Dev's *Sambalpur Hitaishini* as their mouthpiece. Many in Orissa suspected that Ramanarayan had deliberately started this controversy for he was a junior colleague of Radhanath's.

As it became increasingly difficult to use the pages of the *Dipika* for this debate, the Cuttack Printing Company brought out in August 1893 an irregular magazine called *Indradhanu* to continue its attack on Radhanath and champion the cause of Bhanja. Patrons of this magazine included Gourishankar Ray and Gopal Ballabh Das. A month after the publication of this magazine, a magazine called *Bijuli* was launched in Bamanda, Deogarh, to support Radhanath's cause. It received support from Ramanarayan Ray, Basudev Sudhal Dev, Biswanath Kar and others. While *Indradhanu* was priced at two paisa, *Bijuli* was distributed free of cost.

These two magazines reached different parts of Orissa and split the Oriya literati. Once an essay signed by a Gopabandhu Das appeared in the *Indradhanu*. In this, Radhanath had been caricatured thus: a piteously thin man who thinks he is a pandit but who is no better than a jackal treated like a lion in the untouchables' quarters. Word reached Radhanath that the writer of this piece was a student of the Puri Zilla School. He immediately set out for Puri to inspect the school. There he received an anonymous letter saying that the second master of the Zilla School had revised Gopabandhu's piece. At the Zilla School, Radhanath first proceeded to investigate into the allegation that the headmaster and other teachers took bribes from their students in the form of coconuts and pickles, and also into the matter of the insulting things the additional master, Maguni Das, had said about the native doctor of Puri. After this, Radhanath took the headmaster with him and asked the teachers if they read, wrote in, or subscribed to, the *Indradhanu*. All the teachers replied in the negative. Then Radhanath went into Gopabandhu's class and put the same question to the students. The students said that they had never heard of any magazine called the *Indradhanu*. Finally Radhanath asked Gopabandhu point blank if he was the author of the article caricaturing him in the *Indradhanu*. Gopabandhu told him bluntly that he had not written it. Radhanath came out of the classroom after instructing the headmaster to make further inquiries into the matter.

The next day, the headmaster conducted the inquiry in a way which he knew would please Radhanath. In Gopabandhu's absence, he collected statements from his classmates and reported to the inspector that none other than Gopabandhu was the author of the said piece and that the boy was now feigning ignorance. The headmaster recommended Gopabandhu's expulsion from the school. On learning of this, several eminent persons in Puri called upon Radhanath and urged him to change his mind. In the end, it was decided that Gopabandhu would be deprived of seven days' scholarship money for having told a lie and he would not be given the prize he was to receive for his performance in the previous year's examination.

Radhanath came back to Cuttack on 2 February 1894. Throughout his return journey, his mind unceasingly dwelt on the year-long controversy surrounding him and Upendra Bhanja. After he arrived in his Kaligali residence, he decided to put an end to the controversy by writing a letter to the *Indradhanu*. He thought the matter over for two long days and drafted the following letter:

To
The Esteemed Editor
Indradhanu

Sir,

1. Since Ramanarayan babu has attacked Bhanja's poetry, some have assumed that his criticism rests on the foundation of my own views. This assumption is utterly unfounded.

2. Ramanarayan babu has been writing since his adolescence, he has also been discussing Oriya literature for long. His knowledge of ancient Oriya literature is in no way inferior to mine. There is no need for him to learn anything from me.

3. As a friend, I have gone through some of his pieces, but I have never tried to influence his views. In my opinion any attempt to influence him would amount to unwarranted interference. Moreover, Ramanarayan babu, or any other writer in his place, would never brook such interference. I clearly remember that when I had once asked him to omit parts of some pieces written by him because I did not agree with views expressed there, he had refused to oblige me. His views may be wrong, but whatever he writes embodies his own views, not borrowed ones. Had he written his pieces in the light of my views, the occasion for this controversy would not have arisen in the first place.

4. It is not fair to hold me responsible for the views of Ramanarayan babu or anyone else. I should be held responsible only for views expressed in my own writings.

5. My knowledge of literature is extremely limited and the time at my disposal is very short. I have neither the ability nor the time to engage in a debate on this matter. In this connection, I must admit that I have not gone through all the works of Bhanja. Those who have read them thoroughly are qualified to discuss and evaluate them. I, for one, do not have the right to enter into such a discussion.

6. Those who suppose that adverse criticism by Ramanarayan babu, or anyone else for that matter, could diminish the fame of a poet of Bhanja's stature or of any other true poet are

mistaken. It is not given to criticism to bestow immortality on or withdraw it from a poet. I do not remember Ramanarayan babu having arrogated to himself this power anywhere in his writings.

7. Only the very stupid or a most hotheaded person would suppose that adverse criticism could dislodge Bhanja from the exalted place he occupies in the history of literature. A few contributors to *Indradhanu* count me such a stupid or hotheaded person. It would be futile to try to counter their views.

8. I revere Bhanja as one of my literary mentors since my childhood. Evidence that I have not merely paid him lip service, but that I have paid real tributes to him is easily available in my own poetry. Few in Orissa have followed in Bhanja's footsteps more devotedly than I have done.

9. Whatever works of Bhanja I have gone through have convinced me that he was an extraordinarily gifted poet. Not to speak of poets in modern times, but even in the ancient period, one comes across few equals of Bhanja in Orissa. Some poets did excel him in one or two areas of artistry, but none ever surpassed him when the totality of poetic achievement is taken into consideration.

10. I have the feeling that, in places, Ramanarayan babu has levelled unjustified criticism at Bhanja's poetry. In particular, the criticism of Bhanja's eroticism has far exceeded the limits of propriety. In my opinion, only twenty to thirty stanzas in the poems of Bhanja may be deemed unacceptable. I am well aware that noted western literary critics regard this kind of writing with extreme disfavour. Under their influence, many Bengali critics, too, express their hostility to eroticism in poetry. Sanskrit aestheticians recommend that erotic feelings should not be expressed in explicit terms and that these should be conveyed obliquely, through suggestions. On the other hand, the actual practice of several European and Sanskrit poets would provide justification for much of Bhanja's poetic practice. These conflicting views place me in a dilemma and I feel unable to make up my mind. In

any case, I am of the opinion that, in view of Bhanja's great poetic achievement, respectfully rejecting a few lines charged with extreme eroticism would not be a bad thing to do.

11. I am not used to countering baseless allegations. It has been my experience in the past that several charges brought against me have always proved unfounded. I had therefore chosen to keep quiet throughout the present controversy.

I have written this in order to honour the sentiments of some genuine well-wishers of mine.

Yours obediently,   Cuttack
Radhanath Ray   5 February 1894

After he finished writing this, Radhanath wondered if he should send it to the *Indradhanu*. For one thing, the *Indradhanu* might not publish the letter; for another, it was an irregular publication. While going on a tour of Balasore in March, Radhanath gave the letter to the editor of *Nabasambad* for publication. It came out in the 14 March issue of the magazine and put an end to the Bhanja-Radhanath controversy.

Mayurbhanj, April 1894

Having got his letter published in *Nabasambad*, Radhanath now wanted to resume his literary activities. His repeated attempts at composing the eighth canto of *Mahayatra* had failed utterly. For days on end, he kept reciting the last few lines from the seventh canto, in the hope that they would provide him with the inspiration to write on: 'In a moment the sublime scene vanished from Yudhisthir's view as he stood near Sahya mountain.' But powerfully evocative words like these or the lofty emotions they conveyed refused to rush into his mind. Feeling thoroughly fed up, he at last laid aside the notebook in which he was writing the eighth canto and decided that he would translate something before resuming the writing of the long poem. Long ago, while going through Tulsi Das's *Ramcharitmanas*, he had delighted in the description of the seasonal cycle in the Kiskindhya canto. He now took out a new notebook, wrote *Tulasi Stabaka* (Leaves of Tulsi) on its cover, and located his own copy of the *Ramcharitmanas*.

Another thought had crossed his mind in the meantime: he considered publishing his collected works. He had paid a second visit to Bamanda in November 1893 and on his way back, met the poet Gangadhar Meher in Sambalpur. They now formed something like a mutual admiration society and exchanged letters regularly. Gangadhar convinced him that the time had now come for putting his writings together and publishing them in the form of his collected works. However, such a project would involve a lot of expense. After a lot of discussion about locating possible sources of funds, it was concluded that only two rajas were in a position to finance such an ambitious venture. Experience convinced Radhanath that there was little hope of receiving any financial assistance from Basudev and his son Sachchidanand, although they had given him royal treatment when he had visited Bamanda. So he made up his mind to write to the raja of Mayurbhanj to ask for help.

Sri Ramachandra had ascended the throne of Mayurbhanj in August 1892. Although he had come of age before this, the affairs of Mayurbhanj were managed by Wylie who had made his residence in Baripada. When Sri Ramachandra took over he had a great problem on his hands, for Wylie had left the royal treasury empty. Earlier, Sri Ramachandra had made a mention of this in one of his letters to Radhanath.

Encouraged by Gangadhar, Radhanath was going to write to Sri Ramachandra to ask for help when he came across a letter written by Sriramachandra's grandmother which was published in the 7 April issue of the *Dipika*. The letter said:

To
The Esteemed Editor,
The Utkal Dipika

Sir,

I shall remain obliged to you forever if you would find space for the following in your world-famous magazine. This deserves the attention of the general public.

The government took the management of Mayurbhanj into its own hands after the death of my son, Maharaja Krushna chandra Bhanja and it sent my grandson, Sri Ramachandra Bhanja to Cuttack for his studies. I had opposed this move. The former Commissioner, Lamini Sahib, assured me that the government was sending the young prince to Cuttack for his higher studies and that it had no intention of making him lose his caste or religion. In fact, the government, he said, would take every care to prevent such a thing from happening.

I again raised objections when Baboo Gobinda Chandra Mohapatra was appointed the tutor and guardian of the prince. The government once more reassured me saying what Wylie Sahib had said earlier. I lodged hundreds of complaints when a wicked sahib called Mr Kiddel was appointed the prince's tutor, for I feared that the company of such an evil person would expose the young prince to the danger of losing his caste and his religion.

Readers! You can find out for yourself whether I am saying the truth by looking into this tutor's actions. Mr Kiddel, an enemy of our religion, took my grandson on a tour of Darjeeling and Ceylon, and is now trying to make him desert his own religion by using a young woman as bait.

Readers! Do you know who this young woman is? She is none other than the daughter of the famous Brahmo, Mahatma Keshub Chandra Sen. The two wicked tutors, Mr Kiddel and Baboo Gobinda Chandra Mohapatra have conspired in league with the Raja of Coochbehar to get my grandson married to Keshub Chandra Sen's daughter. It is rumoured that they will receive a reward of one lakh rupees for their services. On 13 April, Mr Kiddel took the raja to meet the Lieutenant Governor. Again, please note that Kiddel has persuaded my darling grandson to move away from me and stay in a pukka house half a kilometre away from the palace at Belgadia. Now, no one can meet the prince without Kiddel's permission. Kept in isolation, tempted with false hopes and scared with threats, the prince is always being prompted to give up his religion, his caste and his virtues. Some might feel like asking how the tutors are going to benefit from their actions. All I have to say in reply to this is that their chief object is to execute their wicked scheme by instilling in the prince feelings of animosity towards me. They harass people who seek to give the prince sage counsel and thus silence them. I think that the government is unaware of these goings on. I am not surprised at this. The tyranny of these two tutors has so scared people that they dare not write a letter describing my grievances to the government.

Readers, please tell me if these tutors are teachers or *patels?* I wonder if the government intends to destroy my family through these poisonous snakes. If this really is what the government wants to do, it should first kill me before carrying its design into effect.

My son is dead. The pain of losing him I thought I would overcome by seeing my grandson live in happiness. How terribly disappointed I have been in my hopes! I curse the day I was born. My life is a cursed one.

Readers will easily understand why I am sending this appeal to the government. I entreat them to give my grandson wise advice, and save him from the clutches of his wicked counsellor, and persuade him to stay with me in my palace, where he can order the affairs of his kingdom on the advice of people experienced in statecraft. If he does so, the danger which threatens Sanatan Hindu religion will disappear and the glory of the government will endure forever.

Sri Rama Dei   Baripada
Queen Mother, Mayurbhanj   2 April 1894

Radhanath called Sashibhusan and gave him this letter to read. He asked him to collect more information about the situation by writing a letter to the raja. Sashibhusan had given up his studies on account of poor health and had made up his mind to devote his entire life to serving his famous father. He sat down to write a letter to Sri Ramachandra Bhanj.

Khandapara, August 1894

Samanta Chandrasekhar, now aged fifty-nine, was convinced that he would not live long, and that *Siddhanta Darpan* was not going to be published before his death. Since the time he was twenty-three years old, he had noted down whatever he observed while gazing at the stars, and he had set to work on writing *Siddhanta Darpan* when he was twenty-six. The book had been eight years in the writing and was completed in 1869. For twenty-five years the manuscript had lain waiting for a publisher.

These twenty-five years were a time full of worries and unhappiness. Ailments like dyspepsia and colic always kept tormenting him. He had to support a family of eight—he had five sons and a daughter—on an annual income of only five hundred rupees and sixty *bharanas* of rice. He used to receive an annuity of fifty rupees from the raja of Manjusha for having measured the height of Mahendra hill. But after the raja died, his son reduced the annual grant to thirty rupees.

The attitude of his nephew, Natabar Singh, the raja of Khandapara, also added to his woes. In the beginning, the fact that his uncle pored over sheaves of palm leaves and that people mockingly called him the court astrologer was not at all to Natabar's liking. Later, when Chandrasekhar achieved great fame as an astrologer, Natabar grew even more hostile towards him.

True, *Siddhanta Darpan* did not find a publisher, but Chandrasekhar's fame kept spreading throughout Orissa by word of mouth. In 1876, pandits in Puri had convened a meeting to decide which almanac should be followed for observing rites at Jagannath temple. The meeting had been attended by many Hindu astrologers and pandits and they reached the conclusion that the almanac based on calculations in *Siddhanta Darpan* was accurate. In 1888, the *Mukti Mandap* in the Puri temple had permitted Chandrasekhar to bring out a short almanac in Oriya. He convinced every one of his abilities by correctly predicting the time of solar and lunar eclipses. He also kept up a correspondence with astrologers living in other parts of India and cleared their doubts. He knew no language other than Oriya and Sanskrit. So, whenever he received letters in Bengali or in Devanagari script, he got them read to him by his disciples, and wrote out his replies in Sanskrit.

Among government officers, it was K.G. Gupta, collector, Puri, who had first recognized Chandrasekhar's scholarship and had written to the government recommending him for a title. Many years later, in 1893, Chandrasekhar received the following letter from the government:

To

Pandit Chandrasekhar Singh Harichandan Mohapatra,

I hereby confer on you the title 'Mahamohopadhyay' in recognition of your personal achievement.

Viceroy and Governor General   Lansdowne
                                                  3 June 1893

No one outside the Brahmin caste had ever before been awarded the title Mahamohopadhyay by the government. The news made everyone in Orissa happy, except Raja Natabar Singh, who was reported to have said, 'Uncle may lick this scrap of paper if he likes'. A few days later Chandrasekhar received the following letter from Calcutta:

Dear Sir,

The Lieutenant Governor will hold a durbar on Tuesday, 20 March in the reception room of Belvedere to hand over the titles conferred on you and other gentlemen. I request you to kindly remain present at Belvedere, if possible, at 4.45 p.m. on that day.

Kindly let me know if you would be able to attend the function.

Yours faithfully,   Calcutta
Under Secretary,   8 March 1894
Department of Political Affairs

P.S.: The persons who are to receive the titles will walk past the gate of Alipore Jail and enter the room from the western side climbing a flight of stone steps.

Chandrasekhar felt he was too old to undertake a journey to Calcutta by road. And he would lose his caste if he sailed to Calcutta. So he wrote back expressing his inability to attend the durbar.

On 1 January 1894, the government conferred the title Rai Bahadur on Radhanath Ray's brother-in-law Gobind Ballabh Ray, who was zamindar of Kaupur. Since Chandrasekhar could not go to the durbar held in Calcutta, it was decided that the commissioner, Orissa division, would hold a special durbar in Cuttack and confer the titles on Chandrasekhar and Gobind Ballabh Ray. The durbar was to be held on 29 August at the Barabati fort, and a letter informing Chandrasekhar of this was duly sent to him.

Chandrasekhar consulted the almanac and chose an auspicious moment to start his journey to Cuttack. He sailed down the Mahanadi to Cuttack in a boat, accompanied by his son, Chakradhar. The boat reached Cuttack two days later. Chandrasekhar performed puja and went to sleep in the boat, for his almanac told him that it was the 28th of August. The sound of cannon shots woke him up. Fearing that his calculations might have been wrong, he turned the palm leaves of his almanac again and reassured himself that it was indeed 28th of August. He now saw someone proceeding on horseback, followed by a royal retinue. He threw a cotton towel over his shoulder and followed the procession. He was informed that the raja of Athgarh was on his way to the durbar. When the procession reached the fort, it was found that the decorated pandal was empty, for the durbar was over by that time. But this did not dampen the enthusiasm of the raja. His followers blew their trumpets at the gate of the fort for quite a while before going away. Chandrasekhar enquired after the commissioner and was told that he was at the club.

The chaprasi at the club refused to permit a rustic old man like Chandrasekhar to enter the club premises. Chandrasekhar persuaded him with great difficulty to let him in by blessing him and reciting a lot of Sanskrit slokas. After the durbar, the commisssioner, Cook sahib, was having tea with his wife on the veranda. Chandrasekhar had a very hard time convincing Mr Cook that he was none other than Mahamohopadhyay Chandrasekhar Singh Harichandan Samant Mohapatra of Khandapara, and that he had missed the durbar. Mr Cook was going out for a game of tennis. So he said to Chandrasekhar in Hindi, 'Come and see me at my residence at eight tomorrow in the morning.'

From here Chandrasekhar made his way to the residence of the assistant superintendent, Sudam Charan Naik. Sudam Charan gave Chandrasekhar a piece of his mind. He felt even more annoyed when Chandrasekhar tried to convince him that it was the 28th of the month, not the 29th. Anyway, in the end, it was settled that they would call on the commissioner the next morning.

When they met the commissioner, Sudam Charan described Chandraskehar's many accomplishments and how he had devised several ingenious instruments. Cook sahib led them to the back of his residence, walked with them along the embankment of the river Katjuri and pointed at the Saptasajya range of mountains. He turned to Sudama Charan and asked, 'Can your pandit measure the height of this mountain with the help of his instrument?' When Sudam Charan asked Chandrasekhar to do so, he said that he had left his instruments in the boat. It was then settled that Chakradhar would go and get the instruments from the boat, and Chandrasekhar would finish his calculations by the time the sahib returned from his office for lunch.

Unfortunately for Chandrasekhar, his son brought over all his instruments except the one he most needed at that time. However, this did not upset Chandrasekhar. He set about designing a measuring instrument by borrowing two pieces of wood from a carpenter who was working at the sahib's residence. He now walked into an open space and looked at the mountain range. He took out a piece of chalk and busied himself with making all kinds of calculations on the floor. According to his calculations, the height of the mountain was 1178 cubits and 16 fingers.

Commissioner Cook had got the height of the mountain from official records. Chandrasekhar's calculations were not hundred per cent correct but they came very close to the actual height of the mountain. Pleased by this, Cook went and shook hands with Chandrasekhar and said that he would hold a special durbar, where he would be awarded the title four days later. The news made Sudam Charan very happy and he took Chandrasekhar to his own residence. After arriving there, Chandrasekhar said, 'First, I must take a bath. I have to purify myself for I have just touched a *mlechha*.'

Cuttack, September 1894

After Radhanath translated two descriptions of rainy and autumn seasons from the Kiskindhya canto in *Ramacharitmanas*, he lost interest in this kind of work. The raja of Athamallik, Mahendra Deo, had offered financial help to enable Radhanath to finish writing *Mahayatra*. But he could not see his way to completing this work so he decided that he would get the translations printed and dedicate them to Mahendra Deo. A slim volume entitled *Tulasi Stabaka* appeared in July 1894. On the dedication page, Radhanath wrote the following:

> Humbly dedicated to Maharaj Mahendra Deo Bahadur, the ruler of Athamallik, who is blessed with every virtue.

Your Majesty,

The day on which I received the encouraging and sympathetic letter concerning my composition of *Mahayatra* is a memorable one in my life. Until then I was under the impression that love of language, appreciation of literature and connoisseurship had deserted Orissa and taken shelter in the remote kingdom of Bamanda, ruled by the descendant of the Gangas, Sri Sudhal Dev. On the day I just mentioned I had to change my earlier opinion. I had resolved to finish writing *Mahayatra* and dedicate it to Your Majesty, but hopes of putting the resolution into practice have receded. It is foolish on someone's part to offer worship to Saraswati, the goddess of learning, if one has been denied good health, peace of mind and leisure.

Expressing my gratitude and devotion to Your Highness is my bounden duty. A bunch of beautiful flowers gathered from the garden would have been a fitting tribute to your glorious name. However, as I feel unequal to such a task, I venture to make a present of a bunch of unremarkable Tulsi flowers to Your Majesty. I shall feel greatly honoured if Your Highness condescends to accept it.

A humble servant of Your Majesty,   Cuttack
Sri Radhanath Ray   27 July 1894

A few days later, Gobind Ballabh Ray came to Cuttack to receive his title and stayed with Radhanath, his brother-in-law. In public, Radhanath expressed his happiness over the conferment of the title on Gobind Ballabh. But, the practice of honouring rajas and zamindars who extended little support to the cause of literature, left him very displeased. After he returned from the durbar, Radhanath made up his mind to write a poem on this subject. He took out a new notebook and wrote *Vaiyasiki Vani* on its cover, for the words of wisdom and criticism he was going to write would seem appropriate if they came from the sage Vyasadeva's mouth—thus spoke Vyasa. The first few lines of the poem referred to the Barabati fort: 'Hallowed by memories of Utkal's past glory, Barabati stands grandly decorated today.'

When the writing of the poem had made a little progress, Radhanath received an invitation to attend the second durbar which was being held specially to honour Chandrasekhar. Radhanath was a great admirer of Chandrasekhar and made a point of calling on him whenever he went to Khandapara on tour. He therefore arrived at the durbar on 3 September before anyone else did.

Arrangements for this durbar had been made at the commissioner's office, and in scale, it was much smaller compared to the earlier one. At 9.30 a.m. sharp, Cook sahib came to the marquee, received the guard of honour, and went inside. The guests stood up. After the commissioner and the others took their seats, the seristadar presented Chandrasekhar to the commisssioner. Chandrasekhar withdrew his hands for fear that the sahib might again shake hands with him and pollute him. But the sahib only asked him how he was doing and gave instructions that he be robed with the khilat. When Chandrasekhar came out wearing the ceremonial robes he looked extremely funny. Radhanath now added two more lines to the poem he had started composing: 'Why do you adorn this meeting hall. O flower of Utkal, Chandrasekhar.' To these he added another line, 'Does this garland of honour suit you?' At this time, Gobind Ballabh Ray nudged him and remarked, 'The darbar held on Wednesday was a grander event than this.' Radhanath said nothing in reply because he was looking for a line which would rhyme with the one he had just composed.

The commissioner delivered a speech in English which was translated into Oriya by his assistant Babu Gopal Ballabh Das: 'Mahamohopadhyay Chandrasekhar Singh Harichandan Mohapatra Samant! The sanad which the viceroy and governor general of India have awarded you in recognition of your many accomplishments, we have now great pleasure in handing to you on this occasion. You belong to a royal dynasty. But, unlike other royals who choose to live a life of pleasure and worldly pursuits, you have devoted yourself to studies relating to Sanskrit and science, especially astrology, and have fulfilled your life by achieving great fame. Without taking the help of modern European instruments you have been able to calculate with great accuracy the movements of stars using methods you have ingeniously devised yourself. We hope that you will enjoy a long life and your countrymen will emulate your great example.'

After the durbar came to an end, everyone congratulated Chandrasekhar. Gourishankar reminded him that a meeting to felicitate him was going to be held the same evening at the Cuttack Printing Company. Radhanath walked up to Chandrasekhar, and recited in spite of himself. 'Can coins be minted from pure gold?' This rhymed with the line he had composed earlier.

The meeting began at 8 p.m. in the Cuttack Printing Company building which had been decorated with leaves, flowers and floral arches. Chandrasekhar was seated on a high chair. Two welcome songs were sung. The first went like this: Come, friends and embrace Pathani Samant on this happy occasion. The other began thus: Come friends, let us offer floral tributes as a mark of reverence to the learned Chandrasekhar.

Pandit Markandeya Mahapatra delivered a speech in Sanskrit recalling the great achievements of the guest. After this, Chandrasekhar was requested to make a speech. He recited a few slokas from the *Siddhanta Darpan*, which sought to prove that the earth was stationary and that the sun went round it. He came to a sloka which said the following: 'O, you who believe that the earth moves round the sun, you are all extremely clever, and you have defeated many pandits with your arguments. If you think you have proved that the sun is stationary and the earth goes round it, now listen to me and be quiet.'

He then went on to read out slokas which argued that the earth was static and rounded off his speech by reciting a sloka which he had composed that morning. Translated into English it read thus: 'The English astrologers who claim that the earth is in motion are like elephants, and this, my essay, is like a lion which will subdue them.'

Barapali, March 1895

Gangadhar Meher felt quite aggrieved for he received little financial gain from his writings. His poem 'Indumati', which he had dedicated to the raja of Mayurbhanj and published in the *Utkala Prabha*, brought him only twenty-five rupees. No other help had been extended to him by Sri Ramachandra. Gangadhar sent his next poem 'Utkal Lakshmi' to the *Utkala Prabha*, but it was rejected. So Gangadhar sent it off to the *Sambalpur Hitaishini* and was thus deprived of the prize money he would have received if the *Utkala Prabha* had published it. Finally Gangadhar wrote a long letter to his dear friend, Radhanath, listing all his grievances. He requested Radhanath to get *Indumati* approved as a textbook.

Radhanath was again passing through a period of mental agony when this letter arrived. After *Tulasi Stabaka* came out, his detractors alleged that many of the couplets in the book contained attacks on his critics. For example, one couplet read thus: 'Mountains endure torrential rain/ Just as good persons endure evil words from the wicked.' However, if his detractors had done their homework they would have found that these were but the literal translation of a line from *Ramacharitmanas*. Radhanath's detractors were by this time in no mood to listen to reason. Radhanath wrote a long letter to Gangadhar full of grievances relating to his life as a writer.

Sri Hari Saranam

My dear Sir,

Please accept my sincere apologies for the delay in replying to your letter of 2nd March.

The *Utkala Prabha* has reappeared, it is true, but Gobinda Chandra Mohapatra seems to regard it as his personal property. The maharaja is possessed of many virtues, but love of literature cannot be counted as one of them. Like you, I too, had mistaken him for the future Vikramark of Utkal. But, to my dismay, I discovered that he is utterly indifferent to his mother tongue. He does provide the *Utkala Prabha* with financial support, but he has nothing to do with founding it. Its real founder is the former headmaster of Baripada, Chaitanya babu, who is now resident in Keonjhar. Gobinda babu is a Sanskrit scholar; he has also a good command of Oriya, but he has no love for his mother tongue, nor is he an unselfish person like Chaitanya babu. The Maharaja always speaks English. In all likelihood, he also thinks and dreams in English. Worshipping sahibs and hunting are his chief diversions.

In Europe, kings and men of property are great patrons of art and learning. If we had a couple of such kings and wealthy men in Orissa, our poor Oriya language would have established itself in the world as a language to reckon with. It is a pity we can't find a single such person in Orissa. Relatively speaking, the Raja of Bamanda deserves more credit; but, considered objectively, what he has done or is doing for Oriya language or literature is negligible.

If a person like you had taken birth in Europe, he would have received a monthly pension of at least 200 rupees.

Family worries, problems relating to my job, and the utter indifference displayed towards art in our land have compelled me to give up literary pursuits. Acquiring true knowledge of literature takes time. In Orissa, people think nothing of comparing Upendra Bhanja with a poet of Kalidas's stature. They blithely compare the Himalayas with a mountain like Kapilas. In such a land, knowledge of literature is difficult to acquire. I have loved literature since my childhood. But it was much later in life that I realized what great literature is. Unfortunately I had to give up my literary pursuit just when this knowledge dawned upon me. I am now forty-six, and fast sliding into old age. That I'll be able to do anything worthwhile is a thought I now no longer dare entertain. However, I always remain keen that worthy sons of our motherland like you should prosper.

God willing, I may go to Barapali from Calcutta by way of Sambalpur. If we could spend two or three months together, we would both benefit much from each other's company.

Send me three copies of *Indumati* and a letter of application. I will submit these with my recommendations to the school book committee. The pity is, most of the members of this committee are utterly devoid of knowledge of literature. They are selected not on the basis of their abilities, but their social position. For this reason, often strange and undesirable decisions get taken.

Your affectionately,   Cuttack
Sri Radhanath Ray   18 March 1895

Radhanath's letter deepened Gangadhar's despair. He, too, like Radhanath, was becoming increasingly disillusioned with the rajas and zamindars of Orissa. He had worked for the zamindar of Barapali, first as an *amin*, then as *malmoharir*, and received a salary for his services. But he received no financial support or encouragement from the zamindar for his literary activities. When the prince of Barapali, Mahendra Singh, married Sri Ramachandra Bhanja's sister, Gangadhar had gone to Baripada and made the acquaintance of the maharaja. But, apart from the twenty-five rupees he had received for 'Indumati', he got no further help from the raja of Mayurbhanj. He had been told that the new raja of Bolangir, Maddal Ganjan Singdeo, was a worthy ruler; but the raja had not done anything for the cause of literature yet.

In his *Vaiyasiki Vani* Radhanath had written the following lines about Chandrasekhar, showing the rulers of Orissa in an unfavourable light:

> There is a king like Sri Ramachandra
> Who, though young in years,
> Is possessed of knowledge the old boast of.
> There is a king like Basudev, a great patron of learning.
> And yet they let a tree of knowledge
> Like you wither.
> What an irony of fate!

One day, Radhanath asked Sashibhusan to write a letter to the maharaja of Mayurbhanj saying that he should at least send some timber Radhanath needed for constructing his house. No response to this letter came, for Sri Ramachandra was then too busy trying to sort out a serious personal problem. A few days earlier, he had attracted a lot of criticism throughout Orissa for marrying the daughter of Keshab Chandra Sen, the famous Brahmo. Everyone was of the view that the rajas of Orissa should never marry outside Hindu royal families. Newspapers wrote that a ruler, who orders the affairs of hundreds of thousands of people, and who is looked up to as an ideal, should not ignore considerations of caste, lineage, family, and let only love shape the course of his actions. If he does so, could he discipline court officials or other members of the royal family if they consorted with prostitutes or women of low caste? The raja's Santhal subjects expressed their disapproval of the royal match through this ingenious and colourful analogy: 'Black ants walk in one column, red ants in another. A black ant never leaves its column and join that of the red ants, nor does a red ant stray from its column and get into that of the black ants. Why, then, should the raja leave his column and join another's?'

twelve

Khandapara, March 1895

Chandrasekhar spent his days looking at the sanad and the nights gazing at the stars. In spite of all the publicity given to him by magazines and newspapers and the efforts made by well-wishers such as Gourishankar and Radhanath, his *Siddhanta Darpan*, written twenty-five years ago, had not found a publisher yet. In 1887, Gourishankar had published the following appeal in the *Dipika*: 'We appeal to the rajas, zamindars and men of means in Orissa that one of them should bring glory to himself and to his motherland by taking steps to get this treatise printed. A better opportunity than this for earning fame and merit rarely comes one's way. The rajas of Talcher and Bamanda have won the gratitude of the people of Orissa by publishing and distributing religious texts free of cost. But one who publishes this treatise will do something that would benefit India. If some wealthy person decides to undertake the publication of *Siddhanta Darpan*, he may please write to us. We will do our best to get the book printed at a reasonable cost.'

This appeal fell on deaf ears. Bowed down by old age and illness, sixty-year-old Chandrasekhar passed his days in Khandapara, turning over the palm leaves of *Siddhanta Darpan*, and feeling more and more despondent. One day, he received a letter from Radhanath saying that he should go to Cuttack and meet Professor Jogesh Chandra Ray who taught science at the Cuttack College. Professor Ray would do something about getting *Siddhanta Darpan* published.

Though Jogesh Chandra Ray was a professor of science, he was deeply interested in literature and history. His articles on matters relating to the Vedas and the Puranas were published in *Pradip* and *Dasi*, magazines edited by Ramanand Chattopadhyay. Besides Oriya, Bengali and English, he had command over Sanskrit, Marathi and Gujarati. He tirelessly endeavoured to establish the origins of the Vedas. This was why he had come to be interested in astrology and in Chandrasekhar and the *Siddhanta Darpan*.

On receiving Radhanath's letter, Chandrasekhar set off immediately for Cuttack, taking his son Chakradhar with him. Arriving in Cuttack, they went straight to Radhanath's residence in Kaligali, but by that time Radhanath had already left for his office. Sashibhusan put Chandrasekhar up in a rented house in Chandni Chowk, and in the evening, sent him to Jogesh Chandra's residence. As Jogesh Chandra was not at home, Chandrasekhar sat on the road in front of his house waiting for him. After a time, Jogesh Chandra returned home accompanied by a few colleagues. He felt very sorry to see Chandrasekhar sitting on the road outside his residence. He took him inside. Chandrasekhar chose to sit on the floor of Jogesh Chandra's drawing room. He opened his cloth bag and began taking out palm leaf *pothis*.

Jogesh Chandra's friends could hardly believe that this shabby old man sitting in front of a scatter of palm leaves was a famous astrologer. He might have acquired knowledge of Sanskrit and written a few slokas but it seemed unlikely that he knew anything about stars and planets. They called Chandrasekhar outside. It had already grown dark, and stars glittered in a clear, cloudless sky. In the western sky Venus and Mars lay six degrees apart. Hemachandra, a friend of Jogesh Chandra, now asked

Chandrasekhar, 'Can you measure the distance between Mars and Venus?'

On hearing this, Chandrasekhar let out a piteous shriek and rolled on the ground, clutching at his belly. Wondering if the question he had asked was offensive, Hemachandra looked up at Chakradhar, who reassured him, saying, 'There is nothing to worry about. Since father is a colic patient, he has these attacks sometimes. He'll be all right after some time.' As a matter of fact, Chandrasekhar sat up a little while later, took a little snuff, and brought out a measuring instrument from his bag. He gazed up at the sky. Then he made a few calculations with the help of a piece of chalk on the veranda of Jogesh Chandra's house. The result of his calculations came very close to the actual distance between the two planets.

Jogesh Chandra had brought a telescope to his house for he wanted to show it to Chandrasekhar. At first, Chandraskehar could not figure out what this strange looking thing was. Jogesh Chandra explained to him how to use it. Chandrasekhar took one look at the sky through the telescope and began dancing with joy. The celestial bodies at which he had been gazing with his naked eye now seemed so close, almost at hand. Gazing at these kept him absorbed for quite a while. After taking a look at all the stars familiar to him, he turned to Jogesh Chandra and asked, 'What is the magnifying power of this instrument?' Jogesh Chandra asked him, 'What do you think?' Chandrasekhar took another look at the moon through the telescope and made some mental calculations. Then he said, 'A hundred times, approximately'. This was the correct answer.

Now, they all came back into the sitting room and discussed what was to be done about publishing *Siddhanta Darpan*. Chandrasekhar's heart, however, was not in this discussion; heavenly bodies in their new aspect now floated before his eyes.

If only someone gave him a telescope; if only he had come by the instrument earlier! Seeing the bundles of palm leaf, Jogesh Chandra said, 'The contents of these must be copied on paper. Then the text has to be rewritten in the Devanagari script so as to make it accessible to pandits all over India.'

It was settled that Chandrasekhar would first get the whole book copied on paper in Oriya script. Then arrangements would be made to copy the text in Bangla and Devanagari script in Cuttack. After all this was done, steps would be taken to arrange funds and to send it to a press. It was estimated that about a thousand rupees would be needed to get the treatise printed. Sudam Charan Naik, assistant superintendent of the garjat mahals, would be entrusted with the task of persuading some raja to provide the financial support.

No more discussion on astrology could be held with Chandrasekhar that day. It was settled that they would all meet the next evening. When they met, Jogesh Chandra said that the astrologers of Bengal would never change their views regarding auspicious days and movements. Chandrasekhar explained that almanacs based on old methods of measurement of the movements of the moon could never achieve accuracy. Therefore, what was needed was more sophisticated methods of measurement. Earlier, pandits accepted older almanacs for general use but there was now a need for a more accurate almanac for the observarance of important rites such as marriages, thread ceremonies and yajnas. To Jogesh Chandra's remark that this was a matter of debate, Chandrasekhar replied by quoting a sloka, '*Pratyakshanub havamnalumpati vacha yuktiryatah*,' which meant: arguments are no match for direct observation of facts.

The discussion then turned to the question of whether the earth was stationary or in motion. Jogesh Chandra tried to persuade him to change his view for all the scientists in the world were convinced that the earth moved round the sun. Chandrasekhar said that he would be able to furnish several proofs of the fact that the earth was stationary. An omniscient person had also confirmed his belief in this truth. Jogesh Chandra managed to gather from Chandrasekhar the following details about this omniscient person: One day, a Brahmin called Chakrapani Mishra had come to Chandrasekhar. He claimed omniscience. To test his powers, Chandrasekhar held a few kernels of *bara* berries in his fist and asked Mishra to tell him what he was holding. Chakrapani first said seeds, then seeds having a rough surface, and finally, seeds of bara berries, thereby dispelling all of Chandrasekhar's doubts regarding his omniscience. Chandrasekhar now said to him that a doubt kept entering his mind and requested him to remove it. Chandrasekhar had not told him about the controversy about whether the earth moved round the sun or vice versa, which was then bothering him. Chakrapani Mishra meditated for a while and revealed that Chandrasekhar's doubts concerned two large bodies. He went on to say that one of these was radiant and the other was without radiance. Finally the omniscient Brahmin declared that the earth was stationary and the sun went round it.

This settled the question once and for all for Chandrasekhar; he had now no doubt at all that the earth was static. Jogesh Chandra wanted to know where this great man lived. Chandrasekhar said that a few days after his visit to Khandapara, Chakrapani Mishra had climbed the Tarini mountain to satisfy his curiosity about heaven. He had fallen from there and died.

Jogesh Chandra could not decide whether to be amused or annoyed by the story. However, one thing became absolutely clear: Chandrasekhar would never change his mind. So Jogesh Chandra bid him goodbye after asking him to arrange to copy the contents of the palm leaf bundles on paper. The next day, Chandrasekhar called on Radhanath before leaving for Khandapara where he set Pandit Ghanasyam Mishra to copy out the manuscript on paper.

Puri, May 1895

The application for the out-of-court settlement of the case relating to the Puri temple had been granted in December 1888; but nevertheless, problems continued to beset the management of temple affairs. A small incident which had taken place on 6 February caused a great deal of trouble. A Hindu inspector from Puri municipality had gone into the temple premises carrying a measuring tape. Unfortunately, the tape was kept in a leather case. This gave the pandas a pretext to declare that the temple had been defiled. All the food that had been cooked in the temple that day was thrown away and rites of purification were performed. The cooks suffered big losses as a result and, in protest, they refused to cook for two days. In consequence, the pilgrims were put to a lot of hardship. The Sri Sri Jagannath Sanatan Dharmarakshini Sabha called a special meeting to discuss the matter and passed the following resolution:

> Last Wednesday, after worship was offered to Lord Jagannath in the morning, a municipality employee brought a measuring tape in a leather case into the temple premises and took the measurements of the place meant for *padhiaries*. On account of this, a lot of provisions stored in the temple pantry got desecrated and a rite of purification of the Lord had to be performed in the evening. Our esteemed Queen met the expenses involved in this rite. On Wednesday and Thursday only *kotha* offering was made to the deities, and *chhatra* and other kinds of offerings could not be prepared. As a result, one found it difficult to buy flattened rice even when one was willing to pay one rupee for five seers. Brahmins, Vaishnavas, and destitutes living on charity faced a great deal of hardship during these two days. This is a very regrettable matter and has caused damage to our religion.

When a copy of this resolution reached Queen Suryamani, she sent word to Madhu Babu. After Madhu Babu had won the case relating to the temple the year before, the queen made a point of consulting him on every matter. Madhu Babu, on was very keen that the affairs of the temple be managed properly. As the queen kept bringing temple matters to his attention all the time, Madhu Babu met with Commissioner J.A. Hopkins and it was decided that the seristadar of Cuttack judge court would be appointed the queen's manager and sent to Puri immediately. On 19 February, Harekrushna Das left for Puri in a palanquin.

When he arrived in Puri, Harekrushna Das realized that he had been asked to do the impossible. He was not able to meet with the queen because she was always in purdah. The temple priests and servitors cared for no one in the world. The minor raja, Mukunda Dev was now no longer under the queen's control; he kept himself surrounded by his servants. Pandit Kapileswar Mishra had been appointed his tutor but Mukunda was not interested in his studies. In the midst of all these worries, Harekrushna's chief comfort lay in being able to live in Puri and having a daily darshan of Lord Jagannath. Unfortunately, he fell ill in October. As a devotee of Lord Jagannath he refused to take any medicine except the water with which the Lord's feet had been washed. He died a few days later.

Krushnachandra Mohanty was now appointed manager of the temple. In February 1892, the collector of Puri, D.B. Allen, informed the commissioner that, physically and mentally, Mukunda was in a bad way and his tutor was not able to discipline him at all. Mukunda, Allen said, should therefore be placed under the Court of Wards. However, Commissioner Toynbee did not agree, for he thought it was unlikely that Mukunda, now sixteen, would improve by being placed under the Court of Wards.

A few days later, on 6 March 1892, a godown in Puri caught fire. The fire spread to the palace of the raja of Puri. All houses with thatched roofs in the palace premises were reduced to ashes. The door and the window frames of *pukka* structures caught fire and a lot of property was destroyed. Women in the palace ran into the Madhuban garden. Mukunda escaped into the main street of Puri wearing nothing but a towel. Some people entered the palace and tried to put out the fire, but Mukunda drove them away. Many birds and animals died in this fire and a lot of damage was caused to the palace.

The *navakalebar* festival was to be held in 1893, for the year had two Asadh months in its calendar. The festival had been celebrated in 1855, and, before this, in 1874. People eagerly looked forward to this festival, for it was going to be celebrated after such a long interval. But Queen Suryamani did not want to celebrate it for it meant a lot of expense for her. Besides, word had gone round Puri that if the festival were held, within a year, one Brahmin, one carpenter, and one member of the royal family would die.

When the queen took no steps for celebrating navakalebar, pandits, saints, sanyasis and temple servitors held a meeting inside the palace premises. Suryamani informed them through her dewan that the festival could not be celebrated because a key servitor, Pati Mahapatra, was ill with smallpox. People present at the meeting suggested that another Brahmin should perform the rites associated with the search for the trees from which idols of the deities were to be made. Pati Mahapatra would have recovered from his illness by the time the other rites were to be performed.

However, the queen took no decision regarding the matter. So, the servitors of *chhatisa niyog* wrote to her to say that Pati Mahapatra was now fully recovered and that she should fix a day on which appropriate rites would be performed. This letter, too, went unanswered. Bisoi, who was the link between the queen and the world outside, was too busy building a pukka house after his house burnt down in the palace fire. Whenever anyone asked him for information, he said he had heard nothing from the rani. The Sri Sri Jagannath Sanatan Dharmarakshini Sabha had no option but to forward another resolution to her: 'If the Rani refused to act even after she had got a list of rites submitted to her in writing by the servitors, it would hurt the sentiments of Hindus all over India and cause damage to the Sanatan Hindu religion. We, therefore, pray to Her Majesty to take necessary steps for celebrating the navakalebar festival.'

In the end, after much fuss, all that the queen agreed to permit was the change of the attire of the deities. However, since pilgrims coming from outside were unaware of what was going on, they came to Puri in large numbers to witness navakalebar and they filled up the town.

This incident made Suryamani extremely unpopular. Mukunda showed no signs of improvement either. In 1894, Kapileswar Mishra retired from his job, and no other home tutor for Mukunda was appointed. In this way, a stupid, unlettered, friendless Mukunda, who had known little affection, waited to be put on the throne.

In May 1895, two people, Upendra Das and Lakshminarayan Mohanty sought the permission of the government to file a lawsuit against Mukunda under Article 539 of the Civil Code. Had this case been admitted, many deficiencies in the temple administration would have come to light and attempts might have been made to reform it. But when an inquiry was initiated, Upendra said that he had not filed any such lawsuit and Lakshminarayan was found to be a poor and mischievous person. The two had wanted only to frighten Mukunda into paying them some money. The case had no merit and it would have meant a lot of expense for the temple. So the government refused permission to these two persons to file the lawsuit.

Khandapara, January 1896

Sudam Charan Nayak persuaded the raja of Athamallik, Mahendra Deo, to grant one thousand rupees for the printing of *Siddhanta Darpan*. Once this promise was made, work on copying the text on paper and writing it in Devanagari script went on in full swing. After college hours, Jogesh Chandra was devoting all his energy to this work. Once every week, a messenger carrying bundles of paper came to Cuttack from Khandapara. Jogesh Chandra sent Chandrasekhar long letters seeking clarification for doubts encountered while going through them. In addition, Jogesh Chandra contacted printing presses in Calcutta to find out about the cost of printing the book.

While the work of getting the *Siddhanta Darpan* ready for publication was progressing, problems concerning the printing of the almanac arose. The Cuttack Printing Company had started bringing out *Utkal Panjika* in 1867. This was based on the principles enunciated in the *Siddhanta Darpan*. Since Chandrasekhar was not in a position to prepare the almanac all by himself, it had been arranged that his disciple, Harihar Khadiratna of Khurda, would prepare it and Chandrasekhar would revise it. After this arrangement had gone on for some years Harihar died and it fell to his son Sadashiv to continue the work.

For his services, Harihar used to receive one hundred rupees a year from the Cuttack Printing Company, but Chandrasekhar got nothing. Later, when Chandrasekhar objected to this arrangement, the Printing Company gave him thirty rupees a year. A few years later, Chandrasekhar met Gourishankar and demanded that as the author of the almanac, he should be entitled to half of the profits made from the sale of the almanac. Gourishankar placed the matter before the board of trustees of the company who acceded to Chandrasekhar's demand. Chandrasekhar now received about three hundred rupees per year from the company.

This arrangement worked for a few years. Then Sadashiv Khadiratna contracted an eye infection and Chandrasekhar got his disciple, Rajaballabh Mishra, a school teacher in Khandapara, to do the job. The most difficult task for someone preparing an almanac is the accurate prediction of the time of solar and lunar eclipses. Chandrasekhar had not taught Rajaballabh this skill. For, had he done so, Rajaballabh could have published an almanac on his own.

Sadashiv Khadiratna, after Chandrasekhar replaced him with Rajaballabh, got another almanac published by the Arunoday Press, employing methods he had learnt from Chandrasekhar himself.

A third almanac also appeared in the market. It was brought out by Sitanath Ray's press in Balasore. On its cover was mentioned that it was based on methods enunciated in Chandrasekhar's *Siddhanta Darpan*. It was published by Nimai Charan Ghosh, a teacher at Kaupur school. He had never met Chandrasekhar and it was very unlikely that he had ever gone through *Siddhanta Darpan*. In fact, without Rajaballabh Mishra's knowledge, his nephew, Harihar Nanda, had copied all his calculations and sent them to Sitanath Ray. In his press, a list of auspicious days and moments was kept ready; other things were taken from the almanac published by the Cuttack Printing Company and added to this list. In places the almanac was slightly altered to give the impression that it was the work of another person.

Confusion resulted when three different almanacs appeared in the market in 1896. Chandrasekhar published a letter in which he pointed out errors in the almanac brought out by the Arunoday Press. At the close of the letter, he had this to say of

Khadiratna: 'Khadiratna knows nothing about solar eclipses. He can predict the timing of a lunar eclipse with a certain degree of accuracy but there will still be a margin of error in his prediction. A solar eclipse is a difficult matter and predicting it demands great powers of logic. Though I have taught him the skills for forecasting it, he has completely forgotten them. The observance of various rites at Jagannath temple and the needs of the general public demand an error free and reliable almanac. Needless to say, publishing an almanac which is full of errors is an act of impiety. I close by saying that if a learned person disrespects his teacher, he may succeed in this world, but he will be punished after death; if someone without learning betrays his teacher he will be made to suffer in this world and the next.'

The Cuttack Printing Company also issued the following warning to its customers: 'The popularity of our almanac has prompted another press in the city to bring out an almanac which is sold at four annas a copy. But this almanac is much shorter than the one published by us, is costlier, and its calculations are far from accurate. Our patrons are advised not to buy this almanac mistaking it for the one published by our company. The author of the almanac published by us is the famous astrologer of Orissa, Mahamohopadhyay Sri Chandrasekhar Singh Samant. Our patrons will not be shortchanged if they take care to make sure that his name is printed on the cover of the almanac.'

Puri, May 1897

In January 1897, on Madhu Babu's advice, Mukunda, who had been ill for a long time, was brought over to Cuttack for treatment,. He was put up in a rented house and the civil surgeon began treating him. Mukunda had cooks and servants to attend to him in this rented house, but from time to time, he had mahaprasad brought over from Puri for him. One day, a servant called Ballabh

Subudhi arrived from Puri carrying mahaprasad and pickles. He handed the cook a small packet saying that it had been sent by the temple *chamukaran*, Hari Subudhi, with instructions that the cook should put some of the powder from the packet into Mukunda's paan. Luckily, the cook told Mukunda of this. Madhu Babu was duly informed, and the police were alerted. A warrant for the arrest of Hari Subudhi was issued by the magistrate, and Subudhi was placed in judicial custody in Cuttack. The joint magistrate got the depositions of Mukunda, Ballabh Subudhi, and the cook recorded. The powder contained in the packet was sent to Calcutta for forensic examination.

The report said that the powder was not poisonous. Moreover, there was no reason why Hari Subudhi would want to kill Mukunda, and he swore that he had not sent the packet. So in the end, he was let off. But the whole incident remained enveloped in mystery. The upshot was that Mukunda grew exceedingly suspicious in matters relating to food. He also grew more resentful of Suryamani. He was now convinced that the queen had designs on his life, and if the packet did not have poison in it, it had certainly carried something on which a spell had been laid.

On February 1897, Mukunda reached the age of twenty-one. According to the agreement reached in 1888, Suryamani was to remain in charge of the estate and the management of temple affairs until Mukunda came of age. Now she was relieved of her responsibilities. She had been shouldering these responsibilities since her husband, Raja Birakeshari, had died thirty-eight years ago. If one disregarded the three years during which Divyasingh had been raja of Puri, Suryamani had been the raja of Puri, for all practical purposes, for thirty-five long years. Mukunda now ascended the throne and relegated Suryamani to the women's quarters in the palace.

People could not help comparing Mukunda with his father, Divyasingh. Divyasingh had been a robust, well built man whereas

Mukunda was thin, short and sickly. While Divyasingh was stupid and short-tempered, Mukunda was an utterly ignorant person but of a pious and quiet disposition. He sported a beard, wore his hair long and did not clip his fingernails, for he was scared of being shaven by a barber. He used to wear red silk dresses, observed all religious rites and was a vegetarian. Only on the occasion of Durga Puja would he eat non-vegetarian food offered up to the goddess.

Mukunda was very fond of birds and animals and had a large number of pets. In one part of the palace were kept birds such as parrots, mynas, gobara birds and pigeons; in another, he kept animals such as deer, rabbits and wild mice. However, of all animals, it was pigs on whom Mukunda chose to lavish his affection. He had an area inside the palace premises fenced off and reared a number of pigs there. He looked after them personally and gave a name to each. However, he never touched these pigs for fear of getting defiled. He employed servants to take care of the animals who were fed under his close personal supervision. He called these pigs 'boars' and objected vehemently if anyone referred to them as pigs. He fed the cows and buffaloes kept in the palace with his own hands. For most of the day, he would remain busy looking after birds and animals.

Mukunda was afraid of appearing in public and spent most of his time behind closed doors. Whenever he went out in a palanquin, all the slits and openings in the palanquin were covered with curtains to prevent people from seeing him. Whatever time he could spare after tending to his birds and animals he whiled away gazing out at the road from the window of his room. If he saw a beggar or a poor man passing by, he would call him in and give him food. A few beggars, who were acquainted with his disposition, made a habit of walking up and down the road that ran below his window.

After he became raja, Mukunda one day decided that he would go out and give alms to beggars outside the palace. Small change and cowries were brought from the bazaar in exchange for coins of larger denomination. Cowries had long become obsolete but people used this worthless currency as gifts on religious occasions. On the appointed day, Mukunda got up early in the morning, bathed and went out to do his pious deed for the day. Servants carrying two baskets loaded with loose change followed him. Beggars and lepers were sitting on either side of the road leading to the temple. Mukunda, concealed by curtains in his palanquin, flung coins towards them. A fight broke out among the lepers and the beggars as they scrambled for them. Mukunda enjoyed this unprecedented sight. However, soon the fighting stopped and the beggars and the lepers went back to where they had been sitting. The palanquin bearers now raised the palanquin from the ground. Just then, a beggar woman rushed towards the palanquin, screaming, and threw a few coins and cowries into it, shouting, 'Here, take back your money and go back to the hole from where you have come.' This made the beggars burst into laughter. The palanquin bearers hurried him back to the palace. Mukunda now ordered them, 'Go and bring that beggar woman before me.'

The beggar woman in question was called Khandi. She had come to Puri only recently but her sharp tongue had made all the beggars in the town fear her. Her real name was Sadhabi, and she had been born into a farmer's family in Suanla. She had been given the name Khandi because one of her hands was deformed. She always kept this hand covered with the border of her saree. She had married a Kapil Jena when she was a little child. When Kapil died she married one Jagu Baral of Dasipara village and became mother of a son called Madan and two daughters, Pata and Rupei. After Jagu Baral passed away, Khandi got her son

Madan employed as a servant in someone's house in Gopalpur village and she herself went to live there. She prepared cowdung cakes which she brought to Puri daily to sell. But she could not support herself with this work and began begging.

After getting to learn all about Khandi from his servants, Mukunda provided for her and got her to work at the husking paddle in the palace. He also put her and her daughters up in a hut near the pigsty. In a very short time, Khandi acquired a formidable reputation as a shrew in the palace. Before complaints against her could reach Mukunda, she would flood him with allegations against her accusers. She would not hesitate to abuse Mukunda if he did not act on her complaints. As a matter of fact, Mukunda was now beginning to fear Khandi. In no time, the name 'Khandi' was known to everyone in the palace, and the people of Puri.

One day, at midday, when Mukunda was visiting his pigsty, Khandi called to him, 'Hey Prince, come here.' Mukunda entered her hut which was dark inside. Khandi, who lay on the floor, sat up. She was in a good mood today and talked nicely to Mukunda. Encouraged by this cordial reception, Mukunda, exchanged a few pleasantries with her. Finally, Mukunda mustered courage and asked, 'Tell me, why are you called Khandi? Which part of your body is deformed?'

This made Khandi explode. Her face went red. She cast off the saree she was wearing and stood stark naked before Mukunda, trembling in fury. She shouted, 'Take a good took, you black-faced raja, and find out for yourself where I am deformed.'

Cuttack, August 1897

Radhanath's poem, 'Yayati Keshari', came out in 1895. This was dedicated to the prince of Bamanda, Sachidanand Dev, as a token of Radhanath's second visit to his kingdom. The next year, his unfinished epic, *Mahayatra*, which he had written long ago, was published with support from the queen of Kanika. It carried a foreword by Madhu Rao. Radhanath had intended to dedicate this book to the queen of Kanika, but she, as its publisher, dedicated it to the then commissioner of Cuttack, Ramesh Chandra Dutta.

Immediately after its publication, *Mahayatra* came under fire. The praise Radhanath had lavished upon the raja of Mayurbhanj and the raja of Bamanda was singled out for trenchant criticism. Previously, in his long poem, 'Chilika', Radhanath had praised these rajas extravagantly. He had done so in the hope that the arrival of these two great men on the scene would signal the end of a dark night for Oriya language and culture. Now his critics thought his mention of these two rajas in a poem based on episodes of the Mahabharat was not only unwarranted, it amounted to blasphemy.

To add to Radhanath's woes, around this time, a book titled *A Critique of Mahayatra* came out. However, he was comforted in this hour of crisis by none other than one of the rajas he had praised in superlative terms in his poetry: Sri Ramachandra Bhanj. In a letter addressed to Radhanath's son, Sashibhusan, he wrote:

Dear Sashi Babu,

I have received your letter. Sorry for the delay in replying to it earlier, which was caused by the pressure of work. I will send the timber when the rains start. If you could ask Rasik Babu to get the trees felled and the wood seasoned, things will become a lot easier. I am so occupied at the moment, I cannot pay full attention to this task and delay would result. Please let me know if Rasik Babu can get this done.

I recently came across a book called *A Critique of Mahayatra*. Thank god critics belong to a rare minority in the world. Their nature is diseased and they are congenitally incapable of discovering anything good, generous or beautiful in life. In fact, they are disciples of Satan. From beginning to end, the book spouts poisonous fumes of intolerance. The writer of the book has found an outlet for his pent up feelings of resentment against your father. I send you my regards. Please convey my regards to your father.

Yours affectionately,
Sri Ramachandra Bhanjadeo

Baripada,
Mayurbhanj,
11 May 1897

Queen Victoria's diamond jubilee was celebrated in June 1897. Radhanath received a letter from Calcutta informing him that the title Rai Bahadur would be conferred on him. He would receive the ceremonial robe and the sanad at a durbar to be held at the Belvedere Palace. The news put Radhanath, who had written a poem attacking the institution of durbar a few years ago, in a painful dilemma. Sashibhusan was in Puri at the time. To him Radhanath wrote: 'Oh, how I wish I had the liberty to refuse this honour! But being a government servant, I can never do such a thing'. He somehow avoided having to go Calcutta for he did not have the courage to face the durbar which he had ridiculed earlier. One afternoon, he quietly went to the commissioner and received the sanad from him. It stated that the title Rai Bahadur was conferred upon him in recognition of his personal achievements. The piece of paper had been signed in Simla in June by the governor general, Lord Elgin.

Messages felicitating Radhanath now came pouring in from everywhere. Men of distinction in Cuttack called on him to offer their congratulations. Magazines carried poems greeting him. These were even worse than the poem Radhanadh himself had written in honour of Queen Victoria years ago. Meetings were held in different parts of Orissa to felicitate Radhanath. A meeting on the grandest scale was organized in Bamanda. Since Basudev was indisposed at the time, the prince, Sachidanand presided over it. A long and detailed report on the deliberations at this meeting was sent to Radhanath, who responded by writing an almost equally long letter. In this, after expressing his gratefulness to those present at the meeting, the kingdom of Bamanda, and its raja, Radhanath said:'If I have contributed anything to the improvement of Oriya literature, the credit must go to the most esteemed ruler of Bamanda, Maharaja Sudhal Dev. I was greatly devoted to Oriya literature since my childhood, and I began a deep study of it at that tender age. However, for different reasons, especially since I received no encouragement from anyone I soon lost all interest in my literary pursuits. For about ten years, my attitude to literature was one of utter indifference. Had I had the good fortune of making the acquaintance of a great lover of learning like Maharaja Sudhal Dev, the best years of my life would not have been wasted. Maharaja Sudhal Dev, on his own, wrote a letter encouraging me and revived my nearly extinct interest in literature. He also invited me to visit Deogarh. In obedience to his order, I travelled there and got an opportunity to meet the maharaja. This meeting was a turning point in my life as writer.'

Radhanath kept being felicitated in this manner for over two months. While the whole of Orissa enthusiastically congratulated Radhanath, Gourishankar Ray and the *Utkal Dipika* did not bother to honour the poet in any way.

Puri, August 1897

One day, when Mukunda was about to have his meal, Khandi came rushing in and shouted, 'Don't touch that food. It is poisoned.' Mukunda got up and threw the dishes into the courtyard. The next day, a crow was seen lying dead there, and Mukunda was left in no doubt that people in the palace were conspiring to kill him. At the same time, he came to believe that except Khandi, he could not trust anyone in the palace.

A few days later, thieves broke into Khandi's hut and stole her belongings. People in the palace thought the whole thing had been stage managed. But Mukund filed a report at the police station and gave Khandi a place to stay near his own residence. Mukunda now spent a lot of time with Khandi and occupied himself with sorting out Khandi's problems. He had to settle quarrels between Khandi's daughters, Pata and Rupei, spend time warning servants who had been rude to Khandi and fining the cook who had not put enough salt in the food he had served to Khandi. Apart from these, at times, some bigger problems had to be attended to.

One morning, an old man came to the palace gate and said that he wanted to go inside. When the gatekeeper refused to let him in, he sat down and set up a howl. He said that he was Khandi's third husband whom she had married after the death of Jagu Baral, her second husband. The matter was brought to Mukunda's notice and he asked Khandi about it. Khandi said, 'How could that decrepit old man be my husband?' The palace guards threw the old man out and told him that they would kill him if he ever set foot in Puri.

The incident persuaded Mukunda that Khandi should get married again. A groom was found for her: Dasarathi Jena, who was a servant in the palace. That he was much younger than Khandi was overlooked. The marriage was celebrated in style in the palace premises. Mukunda worked very hard to make all necessary arrangements for the wedding and granted Dasarathi a month's leave. Shortly afterwards, Khandi came to Mukunda and requested that Dasarathi should be given a decent job. As superintendent of the temple, Mukunda gave Dasarathi the job of temple constable.

Khandi had by now become a talking point in Puri. However, in spite of having received so many benefits, she could not stop complaining. Every day she brought some new complaint to Mukunda and leaving whatever work he had in hand, he would promptly get down to solving her problem. One day, Khandi came to Mukunda and said, sniffling, 'These wicked boys tease me by calling me Khandi.' Mukunda comforted her saying, 'From now on, everyone will call you "Pata's mother".' The very same day, public criers announced throughout the town of Puri that Khandi would be addressed as Patama. Street urchins now joked: 'Pigs should not be called pigs but boars and Khandi should not be called Khandi but Patamaa. Adults composed and sang obscene songs about her.

These developments upset Suryamani extremely and she sent word to Madhu Babu. But at the time Madhu Babu was in England, undergoing medical treatment. So, Suryamani's messenger met Baidyanath Pandit and Gokulanand Choudhury. In March 1891, Madhu Babu, Baidyanath and Gokulanand had been empowered through a power of attorney to order the affairs of the temple. Now that Mukunda was mismanaging temple affairs, Suryamani wanted Baidyanath and Gokulanand to intervene. But they were sceptical about the validity of this power of attorney after Mukunda had come of age and ascended the throne. So they sent word to Suryamani that she must wait until Madhu Babu returned from England.

Cuttack, October 1897

After leaving Keonjhar, Fakir Mohan spent a few days in Balasore with no work on his hands. He had become well known as the writer of a textbook on the history of India, and the translator of the Mahabharat, the Ramayan and the Gita. But now he achieved even greater fame as the author of *Utkal Bhramanam*.

To have one's name mentioned in this book amounted to being acknowledged as someone who really counted in Orissa. Those who did not figure in it hoped they would find a place in its second edition.

Fakir Mohan had also become famous throughout Orissa as an administrator in the princely states. But this role had earned him as much fame as notoriety. People criticized him for having tyrannized over subjects as an agent of the rajas, and for having sided with the rajas in their disputes with their subjects, and so on. Someone had written the following about him:

> Schemer, knave, phony, traitor
> Such other sinner there is none,
> Wrecker of homes and instigator,
> Fake, fraud, forger all in one.
> He with his canny cunning fraught
> Too clever by half to be ever caught.

Fakir Mohan was now fifty. He had decided not to take up another job but financial hardship drove him to look for one. He went to Dompara as dewan for the second time. A few months after he went there, his second wife, Krishna Kumari, died. At the time his son was thirteen years old and his daughter, eleven. Fakir Mohan took them to Madhusudan Rao who was then superintendent, the Cuttack Normal School. He lived in a house in the school premises. Madhusudan agreed to let the children stay with him.

The children's expenses worked out to thirty-five rupees a month. Fakir Mohan gave Madhusudan maintenance expenses for the children for three months and went off to Dompara. His children spent a year with Madhusudan. Later, Fakir Mohan rented a pukka house in Cuttack and put them up there.

Fakir Mohan gave up his job in Dompara in 1896. He purchased a plot of land in Dhuanpatria Sahi in Cuttack and got a house constructed there. Around this time, he found himself in financial straits and dealt in timber and sold window and door frames to make a living.

After he came to live in Cuttack, Fakir Mohan's relationship with writers such as Radhanath and Madhusudan grew closer. In 1897, Biswanath Kar set up a press in Cuttack and brought out a literary magazine called the *Utkal Sahitya*. He persuaded writers to contribute to his magazine, and repeatedly urged Fakir Mohan to contribute a short story to the *Utkal Sahitya*. Fakir Mohan wanted to send a poem instead but Biswanath was of the view that Fakir Mohan should set down his rich and varied experiences in prose. One day, Biswanath showed Fakir Mohan a letter he had addressed to Gangadhar, which said, 'Why don't you send an essay? Now you will be told off. Polite words won't do any more.'

Goaded by Biswanath in this manner, Fakir Mohan now set to work. He had recently gone to Kendrapara and spent a few days with his son-in-law Gagan Behari Choudhury who was munsif there. The zamindari of Kendrapara was now in the hands of the descendants of Radhesyam Narendra. While in Kendrapara, Fakir Mohan learnt how the zamindar had dispossessed a weaver of a parcel of land to get his cutcherry building constructed there. During his career as an administrator in feudatory states, he had seen how zamindars oppressed their poor subjects. He decided that he would write about an oppressive, wicked landlord. He wrote 'Om' at the head of a sheet of paper and began thus:

Ramachandra Mangaraj was a mofussil zemindar; also a moneylender. His transactions in lending rice far exceeded those in moneylending. It is said that for eight miles around, no other moneylender could thrive. The man was very pious indeed. There are twenty-four ekadasis in a year. Had there been forty, we have no doubt that he would have observed them all. On the day of ekadasi, he took nothing except tulsi leaves and water ...

Once he had put pen to paper, he found that he wrote on, as if driven. He finished six pages at a stretch. Then he thought that he would send the story to the *Utkal Sahitya* in instalments and bring it to a close after four to five instalments. That evening, he took whatever he had written to Madhu Rao and sought his opinion. Madhu liked it so much that he read it through at one go and praised it lavishly. Fakir Mohan, however, was diffident because he was writing a story for the first time in his life. He, therefore, decided to publish it under a pseudonym. Madhusudan found him one.

The October 1897 issue of the *Utkal Sahitya* carried the first chapter of *Chha Mana Atha Guntha* written by an author called Dhurjati.

Khandapara, December 1897

Too many problems now retarded the progress of the work of editing the *Siddhanta Darpan*. The portions which Rajaballabh Mishra copied out from the palm leaf manuscript and brought over to Jogesh Chandra contained quite a few errors. Sometimes the slokas did not make sense, at other times calculations could not be made according to them. Jogesh Chandra wrote long letters seeking clarifications and waited until Chandrasekhar sent corrections or revisions. On occasion, Chandrasekhar himself travelled all the way to Cuttack to explain them to Jogesh Chandra. On other occasions, work on the *Siddhanta Darpan* had to be discontinued when replies to Jogesh Chandra's queries failed to arrive. Jogesh Chandra meanwhile received reminders from the Indian Depository Press in Calcutta. In the beginning, Jogesh Chandra had undertaken the task with great enthusiasm but now he cursed himself for having taken up this work. On one occasion, he wrote a stiff letter to Chandrasekhar when he received no reply to his repeated queries. This prompted a quick reply from the astrologer.

Dear Sir,

It is but natural that you would feel very upset when you did not receive a reply to three letters you had written me. The day after I arrived back in Khandapara, a granddaughter was born. She died forty days later. I am afflicted with ailments such as dropsy, and flow of blood into my right eye. Casting horoscopes, propitiating planets, performing a rite meant to lengthen the life-span of the queen of Talcher, my daily chores, settling disputes among my tenants never allowed me even a moment's respite.

Since my mind has begun wandering, I am answering only those questions which I could handle without straining myself too much. As I am not familiar with Devanagari script, I have entrusted my son and Rajaballabh Mishra with the task of copying out the text. In spite of their ill health, they have been able to finish the first half of the text and are now engaged in copying out the second half. Please send me the last three parts of the text. We cannot provide an errata. Please let me know what you did about the photograph. As for your question, all I can say is that the earlier part of my text explains the position of stars like Ashwini.

Old age is blunting my intellect. I am no longer in a position to revise or edit my book. The Lord Almighty wants my fame to spread through your agency. Or else, why should no one ever have come forward to help me until now? The example you have asked for I will send to you in four days' time. Rajaballabh Mishra will visit Cuttack sometime next week. He will take other examples. Nothing to add at the moment.

Yours,
Sri Chandrasekhar Singh Harichandan Mahapatra Samant

However, Chandrasekhar did not send the example as promised, nor did Rajaballabh Mishra go to Cuttack, with the result that work on the publication of *Siddhanta Darpan* suffered further delay. This added to Jogesh Chandra's worries and annoyance.

The publication of the annual almanac too ran into difficulties. Gourishankar had told Chandrasekhar that the quality of Rajaballabh Mishra's work was not as good as that of Khadiratna. This, Chandrasekhar passed on to Rajaballabh Mishra. From that day, Rajaballabh nursed a grievance against Chandrasekhar. When a suitable opportunity presented itself, he told Chandrasekhar that Gourishankar had insulted him by describing the almanac as 'Printing Company's almanac' instead of 'Samanta Chandrasekhar's almanac'. In doing so, Rajaballabh insinuated that Gourishankar looked upon Chandrasekhar as one of his employees. On Rajaballabh's instigation, Chandrasekhar demanded seventy-five per cent of the profit accruing from the sale of the almanac. Gourishankar flatly refused to oblige him.

After this, Rajaballabh made Chandrasekhar enter into an arrangement with Sitanath Ray. It was decided that an almanac prepared by Chandrasekhar would be brought out by the Ray Press. Chandrasekhar was to receive a sum of three hundred rupees in the first year and from the following year, he would receive three-fourths of the profit made on the almanac. As part of this arrangement, Chandrasekhar prepared almanacs for Sitanath for two years.

Gourishankar now had no option but to seek Khadiratna's help. Though one of Khadiratna's eyes was completely damaged, he set to work on preparing an almanac which came to be published by the Cuttack Printing Company.

The fact that two almanacs were available in the market created quite a lot of confusion. Pandits debated the relative merits of the two almanacs. The Mukti Mandap in Puri and Sadharma Prakashini Sabha of Sasan Damodarpur took part in this debate. Pandits in Puri celebrated the Mahastami and Prathamastami pujas on the basis of the Printing Company almanac. Khadiratna wrote a letter to the *Dipika* pointing out all kinds of errors in the almanac brought out by the Ray Press.

As a result, the sale of the company almanac far exceeded that of the one brought out by the Ray Press.

Cuttack, December 1897

In April Madhu Babu set off for England to undergo treatment for appendicitis. Gourishankar repeatedly urged him to make a point of meeting Ravenshaw while there. Ravenshaw had of course, been popular as commissioner of the Orissa division. But he came to enjoy even greater popularity after he retired and left for England. None of his successors had spent as long a time as him in Orissa, nor had they made any efforts to get close to the people of the province. Besides, people gave Ravenshaw credit for all the good things that happened in Orissa after the great famine, which included the founding of a college, a girls' high school, the survey school, the medical school and the port at Chandbali. However, there was a special reason behind Gourishankar pressing Madhu Babu to call upon Ravenshaw while in England: he was feeling guilty for having published, not once but twice, the news of Ravenshaw's death.

Ravenshaw had left Orissa in April 1878 and joined as commissioner, Burdwan. About six months after this, the *Indian Mirror* which was published from Calcutta carried the news of Ravenshaw's death. The *Dipika*, too, published this news, but at the same time expressed scepticism about its veracity, because some other newspapers in Calcutta had reported the passing away of H.I., not T.E. Ravenshaw. It suggested that the deceased Ravenshaw might be some other person.

However, on 31 August, the *Dipika* published the news of Ravenshaw's death in a black-bordered box. In this, the great deeds of 'our dearest friend Mahatma Ravenshaw' were listed and prayers were offered up to the Almighty to let the soul of the departed rest in peace. However, soon after this news was published, word came from Ravenshaw's daughter who lived in Calcutta that her father was very much alive. Tendering an apology for his mistake, Gourishankar wrote in the *Dipika*, 'It is believed that if the death of someone is announced while he is still alive, the span of his life is extended. We sincerely hope this will come true in the sahib's case.'

Madhu Babu did not know Ravenshaw personally. However, while in England, he went to call on him at the insistence of Gourishankar and others. Ravenshaw resided in Sussex at the time. When Madhu Babu got down at the Three Bridges station, he found Ravenshaw waiting for him. As Madhu Babu was the only coloured person at the station, Ravenshaw went up to him and introduced himself. He took Madhu Babu to his residence in his horse-drawn coach. Although Ravenshaw had left Orissa some twenty years earlier, he was still able to speak broken Oriya. He sat Madhu Babu down beside him and, offering him a *bidi*, said, 'Here, smoke an Oriya pika.' He too, lighted a bidi and said that he had not been able to give up the habit of smoking Oriya pikas. Then he took Madhu Babu around his house and showed him various things from Orissa such as filigree works from Cuttack, pipes, a knife and a machete, elephant tusks he had received as presents from the raja of Dhenkanal, and tribal weapons from Keonjhar. After this, he led Madhu Babu to his tool room and boasted that he could do all kinds of things from repairing a clock to making a chair with his tools.

Ravenshaw asked after all the important people in Orissa and enquired in particular about Keonjhar and Nayagarh. Madhu Babu talked to him about the affairs of these kingdoms at length as he happened to be their lawyer. On learning that Orissa was in the grip of another famine, Ravenshaw had written to the government saying that he was willing to go back to Orissa and work there. But the government did not want to engage people from outside. Thus, old Ravenshaw's wish to revisit Orissa could not be fulfilled. When Madhu Babu took leave of Ravenshaw, the latter asked him to pay his respects to all his old friends in Orissa.

The *Utkal Dipika* published a letter from Madhu Babu giving an account of his meeting with Ravenshaw and requested the rajas and zamindars of Orissa to donate a sum of a thousand or fifteen hundred rupees to make it possible for Ravenshaw to revisit Orissa. On reading this, Babu Radhacharan Das of Balasore wired the *Dipika* suggesting that funds for this purpose be raised and said that he was willing to contribute to this fund. The raja of Keonjhar informed that he would donate four hundred rupees. Not to be outdone, the raja of Mayurbhanj offered five hundred rupees to the proposed fund. But, like many other initiatives undertaken in Cuttack earlier, this too, led nowhere, and the plan to invite Ravenshaw to Orissa never took off.

Madhu Babu returned to Orissa in November. Meetings were organized to felicitate him. His fame now spread throughout Orissa as he was the first Oriya to have made a trip to England. He had gone there to undergo medical treatment, not to study law; but everyone in Orissa now called him Madhu barrister.

Madhu Babu now turned his attention to his unfinished tasks. The most important of these concerned the Jagannath temple. After he left for England, Baidyanath Pandit and Gokulanand Choudhury had fallen out with each other and neglected the affairs of the temple. It was even alleged that Baidyanath Pandit had misappropriated four thousand rupees from the temple funds. As a result of all this, Mukunda went on managing, or more accurately, mismanaging the affairs of the temple.

Madhu Babu went to Puri and found that the affairs of the estate and the temple were in a state of complete disarray. He was also told everything about Khandi. Ordinarily he would have given Mukunda some advice, but the young raja was not well, mentally as well as physically. Madhu Babu consulted Queen

Suryamani and it was decided that he would take Mukunda to Calcutta for medical treatment.

Puri, October 1898

Mukunda's health showed no signs of improvement in Calcutta. Madhu Babu therefore brought him back to Puri. Back in the palace, Mukunda once more devoted himself to looking after Khandi. He had made her fourth husband, Dasarathi, a constable in the temple. Dasarathi never went to work but he never forgot to come on pay day and collect his salary. This had led to his suspension from service. When it was decided that he would be dismissed, he panicked and resigned in December 1897. Khandi now went and shouted at Mukunda who gave Dasarathi another job in the temple. According to custom, after a servitor was appointed by the raja, the rite of winding a saree around his head had to be performed before he was initiated into temple service. When Dasarathi wanted this rite to be performed, he was beaten up by the other servitors and chased away for he had married a beggar woman and had thus lost his caste. For this reason, he could never be a temple servitor. When word of this reached Mukunda, he said, 'They did not let Dasarathi enter the temple? Fine. I'll make him a *saantra*.' A few days later, Dasarathi became Dasarathi Singh Samantray on the strength of a royal decree. But even this did not satisfy Khandi. So, to placate her, a title was conferred on her son, too, and he came to be known as Madan Chhotray or Madan Singh.

Mukunda now set about looking for grooms for Khandi's two daughters. The marriage of her elder daughter, Pata, was arranged with the son of Kalu Samartha, a temple servitor. The wedding was celebrated with great pomp and ceremony inside the palace. However, this led to Kalu's getting excommunicated from his caste and he was stopped from entering the temple. A great deal of trouble followed and a case was lodged with the police.

Khandi's younger daughter, Rupa, was married to a carter called Jogi Rout. Since there was going to be trouble if Mukunda appointed him a temple servitor, alternative arrangements were made for settling Jogi in life. A title was conferred on him and he was called Sri Jogesh Chandra Routroy and made the tehsildar of Delang.

Khandi now turned her attention to the temple funds. The raja of Puri was entitled to a share of whatever offerings were made by the pilgrims in the form of money or gold. Some gifts were also given directly to the raja himself. Now all these were diverted to Khandi. Moreover, precious ornaments and stones from the temple treasury were brought to Khandi's house under the pretext of repairing them. These, Khandi kept and sent imitation ornaments to the treasury.

Everyone held Madhu Babu responsible for the mismanagement of the affairs of the temple for he was after all the raja's lawyer and guardian. This upset Madhu Babu and he decided that he would convene a meeting of the Utkal Sabha to discuss the affairs of the temple. The following notice appeared in the *Dipika* on 30 April :

> The affairs of the Jagannath temple at Puri are being managed very badly. An open meeting of the Utkal Sabha will be held on Monday 2 May at 6 p.m. at the Cuttack Printing Company, where ways of improving matters will be discussed. All are requested to attend the meeting.

Sri Madhusudan Das, President   26 April 1898
Sri Gourishankar Ray, Secretary

Unfortunately for the organizers, offices were closed that day on account of a Muslim festival and many people had gone off to their villages. Only twenty or twenty-five persons were present at the meeting. Madhu Babu began by explaining at length why he, who happened to be a Christian, got involved in matters concerning the temple. Pointing out that caste distinctions did not exist at the temple, he said that he had exerted himself to protect the royal family in Puri. After this, he gave several instances of how Raja Mukunda Dev was squandering away temple property. Madhu Babu's speech was followed by one given by Raja Baidyanath Pandit who said that the matter of protecting the temple and improving the quality of its management concerned everyone. He further said that he had spent money from his own pocket when he had managed the affairs of the temple.

After a lot of debate it was settled that a plan would be worked out after inquiring into the manner in which temple affairs were being managed at the moment, and after discussing a future course of action with the temple servitors and important people of Puri and the government. It was proposed that a committee would be set up with Raja Baidyanath Pandit, Babu Biharilal Pandit, Babu Madhusudan Das, Babu Khosal Chand, Babu Gourishankar Ray and Babu Ramashankar Ray as its members. The members would submit their report which would be discussed at a meeting of the Utkal Sabha and appropriate decisions would be taken and acted upon.

A few days after this meeting, the *Chandan* festival was held in Puri. On account of mismanagement of temple affairs, certain key rites could not be performed on most days during the festival. To address this problem, the mahants, zamindars, government officials and temple servitors convened a public meeting inside the temple premises which was presided over by the raja of Puri. At this meeting it was decided that to ensure the smooth conduct of temple affairs, a committee consisting of gentlemen from the locality be set up and that the raja of Puri would be president of this committee.

The two committees achieved nothing at all and the situation in the temple went from bad to worse. Everyone now expected old Madhusudan to find a solution to the problem. Madhu Babu had established himself as a brilliant lawyer and, though aged only fifty, he had come to be known as the grand old man of Orissa. In the end, to justify the faith people had reposed in him, Madhu Babu used his lawyer's mind to find a way out of the mess. Four days before the court closed for the Dussehra vacation, Madhu Babu filed a lawsuit in the court of the sub-judge in Cuttack, demanding that he be repaid the sum of fourteen thousand rupees he had spent on the raja's education and medical treatment. He prayed for permission to attach the raja's property and permission was granted to him by the sub-judge. Losing no time, Madhu Babu, accompanied by two court peons, went to Puri and got the palace searched. However, the peons did not search Mukunda's palace; instead, they searched Khandi's residence which lay inside the palace premises. The search yielded ten thousand rupees buried under the floor, pearl and gold necklaces and precious jewellery kept concealed in pots filled with chaff, and in other places.

Soon after this raid, the court was closed for the puja holidays. Mukunda and Khandi went to meet Madhu Babu who told them off and warned Mukunda that if he did not obey him, he would get the palace searched. When the courts opened after the vacation, Mukunda submitted a letter saying that Madhu Babu's demand was a legitimate one and that the seized ornaments should be given to him to settle his dues. Moreover, he signed a bond to the effect that he would from now on act according to Madhu Babu's instructions. A retired British officer, Mr Price, would be appointed manager of the raja's property and the property of the temple. The manager would receive a monthly salary of eight hundred rupees. The raja would not interfere in the manager's work. Madhu Babu would inspect the accounts and supervise the work of the manager. The raja would receive from the manager a thousand rupees a month to meet his personal expenses. This arrangement would remain in force for a year.

At long last a neat solution to the problem had been found. However, it created little enthusiasm among people in Puri for another problem had kept them occupied. A herd of monkeys had made life pure misery for people in the town. The municipal authorities tried to drive them away by shooting down a few. Some people sent a petition complaining that this hurt their religious sentiments. On 29 September, the municipal authorities called a meeting to deliberate on this matter. Pandits were consulted and they opined that there was nothing wrong in killing monkeys to drive them off. Now the people of Puri waited for municipal authorities to take the necessary action.

Cuttack, November 1898

It was midday. Four villagers kept loitering in front of the gate of the law court, waiting for an opportunity to slip in. Hoping to make a little money, a lawyer's assistant walked up to them and asked them what they wanted. These rustics had left their village before daybreak and had walked all the way to Cuttack. They had no work at the court, they had come only to watch the lawsuit involving one Ramachandra Mangaraj. It was gathered from what they said that a case had been filed against Ramachandra Mangaraj, the zamindar of Fatepur Gobindpur, who was charged with the murder of a weaver woman and with having taken away by force her cow and household articles. He had been arrested and thrown into jail. He was to be tried in court that day.

When the lawyer's assistant made too many inquiries, the cleverer one among the villagers took out a sheaf of papers from his cloth bag. These were various numbers of the *Utkal Sahitya*. The clever villager was the son of the village schoolmaster and he knew how to read and write. It was he who had told his friends of the case, about which he had read in the *Utkal Sahitya*. The lawyer's assistant leafed through the magazine and his eyes fell on a piece entitled 'Police Inquiry'. He started reading it. He liked it so much he sat himself down on the ground and was soon absorbed in reading the piece. It dealt with a very serious incident. From the depositions made by the witnesses it was clear that the accused, Ramachandra Mangaraj, was a wicked person, a murderer. After he finished reading this piece, he went through another which featured the lawyer, Ram Ram Lala. Now he rose to his feet and burst out laughing. Handing the printed pages back to the villagers, he said, 'You idiots, you are really stupid rustics. Or else would you have come all the way from your village to watch the trial of Ramachandra Mangaraj? You should have known that there is no one called Ramachandra Mangaraj.' The villagers now turned to look at their friend. He had received a little education all right, but he was utterly foolish. He said, 'How could printed books tell a lie? Do you want us to believe that Champa, Bhagia, and Saria do not exist?' The lawyer's assistant explained, 'You idiots, what you read was but a story. Someone called Dhurjati has written it, cooking everything up.'

When he saw that his words left the villagers terribly disappointed, the lawyer's assistant said, 'All right, you have taken so much trouble to be able to watch that trial. Come with me. A hardened criminal has been brought to the court today. Watch his trial before going back to your village. This case is no less interesting.'

The court was very crowded that day. The accused, Prabhudayal Bhagat, who had absconded, had been caught after twenty long years. Looking at this man who was dressed like a wandering mendicant, one would find it hard to believe that he was a seasoned crook. This is what the police records said about the accused:

On 22 May, 1879, road cess amounting to 4798 rupees and eight annas, which had been collected from the moffussil, was kept at the residence of the nazir, Natabar Das, as the court had been closed for the day. The money got stolen that night and Natabar Das was taken into police custody. Inquiries revealed that the three persons who conspired to steal the money were: Natabar Das's brother-in-law Raghab Mohanty, a wicked man called Prabhudayal Bhagat, and Natabar Das's mistress, Chitrakala. The daroga of the sadar police station, Nilamani Balabantra, arrested Raghab and Chitrakala; however, Prabhudayal gave him the slip. A warrant was issued in his name but he could not be caught. The case was tried. Natabar Das got acquitted on the condition that the money would be realized from him. Raghab was sentenced to one year in jail and Chitrakala received a five-year jail sentence. The real culprit, Prabhudayal, remained at large.

After twenty years, the police had caught him at Lalita Das Babaji Mutt in Puri. The four villagers were glad that they saw Prabhudayal in the dock, even if they could not see Ramachandra Mangaraj. When the court closed for the day, they made their way back to their village.

Khandapara, August 1899

Choosing Sitanath Ray as his publisher and parting with Gourishankar cost Chandrasekhar dearly. Sitanath did not pay him the amount he had promised. Chandrasekhar wrote to Jogesh Chandra about the matter; Jogesh Chandra talked to Radhanath; and Radhanath assured him that he would ask his brother to sort out this problem. But Chandrasekhar did not receive any money.

The work of the printing of *Siddhanta Darpan* had not been completed even four years after it had begun. Chandrasekhar himself, who kept revising the slokas and sending long errata, delayed the progress of the printing. This annoyed Jogesh Chandra no end and he looked forward to the time when the book would get published and cease to bother him. He had written an introduction to the book and all that remained to be done was to send Chandrasekhar's photograph and the complete errata.

But Chandrasekhar constantly pressed Jogesh Chandra to get *Siddhanta Darpan* and the almanac prepared by him registered to stop others from basing almanacs on his treatise and selling them in the market. Chandrasekhar also wanted Jogesh Chandra to help him patch up with Gourishankar. With this in mind he wrote to Jogesh Chandra:

> Taking advantage of my misfortune, Khadiratna prepared an almanac for Gourishankar Babu, basing it on calculations made with the help of his one eye. As a result, two almanacs came into the market. The resources of the Printing Company far exceed those of the Ray Press. The Printing Company will print twelve thousand copies of the almanac. The Ray Press is barely able to print six thousand copies.'
>
> It would be acutely embarrassing to go back to Gourishankar Babu uninvited. Be so kind as to act as mediator, go to Gourishankar Babu and tell him that people are confused by the availability of two almanacs in the market. He should therefore, invite me once more and ensure that only one almanac is available in the market. Ten per cent of the profit should be given to the author. One per cent of the profit should go to Khadiratna as his pension and nine per cent should be my share. If you could get me a letter of invitation to this effect, I would prepare an almanac for Gourishankar Babu. Of the nine per cent, I will give three to my pupils and support myself with the remaining six. Kindly keep the matter a secret from others. When I sever my connections with the Ray Press, it will automatically become public knowledge.
>
> You had written last year that after *Siddhanta Darpan* and the almanac based on this got registered, no one except my pupils would have the legal right to publish it. Acting on this belief, I let Sitanath Babu publish my almanac. But I now find that he can't print a large number of copies.

Anyway, I sincerely hope that you would spare no pains to accomplish the task I have set you. You are master of the art of persuasion. What more can I say? *Vyasah kenopadisyate. Kkimadhikam vijnabaresu sahrudaya siromanisu.*

Yours,
Sri Chandrasekhar Singh Samant

Khandapara
22 June1899

P.S.: I want you to accomplish this task before the full moon night of the month of Shravan. While getting *Siddhanta Darpan* registered, include a clause making it clear that no one can publish almanacs based on its calculations without taking permission from me or my son. I want this done because Sadashiv Khadiratna, though he was a disciple of mine, has got an almanac printed, going against my wishes and is making me suffer losses. Moreover, Khadiratna does not call upon me when he visits Khandapara; I therefore count him as my enemy.

A few days later, Chandrasekhar came to Cuttack and got himself photographed by Bhagirathi Sathia at Sathia's residence in Alam Chand Bazaar. The photograph showed him wearing a shawl and holding a number of palm leaf pothis in his hand. About two months after this, printed copies of the *Siddhanta Darpan*, written by Sri Chandrasekhar Singh, edited by Jogesh Chandra Ray and dedicated to Sri Mahendra Dev, Maharaja of Athmallik, arrived in Cuttack. The sight of the book made Chandrasekhar dance with joy. Jogesh Chandra heaved a sigh of relief.

To wash his hands clean of Chandrasekhar, Jogesh Chandra wrote to him that no action could be taken against Khadiratna as legal experts were of the opinion that a gift made by a teacher to his student should not be taken back. But Chandrasekhar was not one to leave him alone and in peace for he was convinced that the Almighty had created Jogesh Chandra for the sole purpose of advancing his interests. So, not letting the matter rest, he wrote to Jogesh Chandra again, explaining with the help of examples the nature of the teacher–pupil relationship:

Yajnabalkya had studied the Vedas under the tutelage of the Sun god. A lapse on his part angered the Sun who said, 'Return the knowledge you have gained from me.' Yajnabalkya now vomited out the mantras of the Yajurveda. These the rishis deemed unclean so they took the form of 'tittiri' birds and swallowed the mantras. This is an ancient tale. From that day, the *taittariaya* branch came to be established. The poet Murari, in his play, has referred to this incident, when he praises Yajnabalkya's conduct while describing Vishwamitra's message to Janaka.

This was followed by slokas quoted from the play *Anargha Raghav*. Feeling thoroughly fed up, Jogesh Chandra stopped reading the letter and laid it aside.

thirteen

Cuttack, January 1900

Radhanath passed through a period of mental and physical stress after the title Rai Bahadur was conferred on him. He had hoped that he would receive some help from Basudev Sudhal Dev after his second visit to Bamanda. Although he had written a sycophantic letter lavishing praise on Basudev to his son, Prince Sachidananda no rewards came. Now he wrote to Gangadhar, to whom he had grown close of late, expressing his deep sense of disappointment:

Sri Hari Saranam

Confidential

My dear Sir,

I have paid a terrible price for devoting myself to literary pursuits. If I had concentrated on writing textbooks, my financial condition would have improved so much that I would have been able to devote all my energies to literature at this time of my life. Had there been patrons of literature among the Rajas of Orissa, I would have taken retirement long ago and spent all my time trying to contribute to the development of Oriya literature under their patronage. I never got the opportunity to do even one hundredth of what I had aspired to do for Oriya literature. It is impossible to find even one Raja in all of Orissa who genuinely loves Oriya literature. Of course, the raja of Bamanda deserves praise; but he is no more than a glowworm shining in the darkness of a moonless night. My friendship with the raja of Bamanda has not benefited me in the least; it has in fact worked to my disadvantage. Since you are a very intimate and trusted friend of mine, I can unburden my heart to you.

Yours,   12 November 1898
Radhanath Ray

A few days later, the long poem, *Mahayatra*, which he had written three years ago, got Radhanath into trouble. In 1896, the queen mother of Kanika published the first seven cantos of the unfinished poem. Now Radhanath's enemies sent a petition to the government claiming that the fifth canto of the poem contained lines which expressed anti-British sentiments. They cited the following lines in support of their allegation:

The yavanas, coming from a far-off place,
Will suck the life-blood of India

His enemies further alleged that Radhanath had also attacked the British, calling them yavanas in a poem titled 'Sivaji's Exhortation', which was included in his collection *Kabitabali*:

The wicked yavana became the undisputed ruler
And kshatriyas grew powerless and insignificant
Our motherland ceased to belong to us
Shouldn't we hang our heads in shame?

In July 1899 Radhanath received a confidential letter from the government asking him to remove the objectionable portions from *Mahayatra* and bring out a second edition. Radhanath agreed to do so and wrote a letter to the government expressing his apologies. Although the government had not said anything about the poem 'Sivaji's Exhortation', Radhanath removed it from the second edition of *Kabitabali*.

All these worries led Radhanath to decide that he would give up literary pursuits. One evening in December, when Radhanath and other members of his family were warming themselves by a fire, Radhanath flung five unpublished cantos of *Mahayatra* and the scheme of eighteen cantos into the flames. He broke into tears. When Sashibhusan came to him, he pretended that the smoke had brought tears to his eyes.

A few days after this incident, Radhanath went to Calcutta accompanied by his wife to attend a meeting of the education department. While there, on 2 January, he was informed that he had been transferred to the Burdwan division. He was asked to hand over charge while in Calcutta and to proceed from there to Burdwan. Radhanath therefore did not return to Cuttack but went straight to Hooghly. He was convinced that *Mahayatra* was responsible for his getting transferred out of Orissa. A few of his friends suggested that he appeal against this transfer order but Radhanath did not act on their advice. He wrote the following letter to Sashibhusan:

Sashi,

I had never ever dreamed that I would receive a transfer order so unexpectedly. Three officials have received similar orders at the same time. I therefore do not think it would be proper to protest against this order.

I am worried since your mother accompanied me to Calcutta. She is not to blame, for no one can predict the future.

I have written to Braja Babu asking him to give a permanent advance to Raghu Babu. I have enclosed the Director's telegram.

On receiving this letter collect carefully all the printed reports belonging to the office and all my old diaries and give all these to Braja Babu.

Return all the books I had borrowed from the Balasore and Puri zilla schools and the Cuttack Normal School. Send them through a trusted person or by post, and get the headmasters to acknowledge receipt of these through reply cards.

A calling bell belonging to the office is in our residence. Hand this over to Braja Babu. The reports, bags and blankets I have with me now I will send back through your mother or Lokanath.

I shall ask Haranath to escort your mother to Cuttack. I may also take a week's casual leave and take her to Cuttack myself.

Give my best wishes to everyone at the office. They have all expressed their confidence in me and stood by me in my hour of crisis. Convey to them my sincere and heartfelt thanks. Tell chaprasi Bhagaban Jena I will remain indebted to him all my life. He had bade me a tearful farewell. Tell him that I am writing these lines with tears in my eyes.

The conference will begin tomorrow. I'll write to you again when I find the time. I had decided to meet all my friends and well-wishers personally before leaving Cuttack. But I could not do so on account of this strange and sudden transfer order.

Radhanath   7 January 1900

Puri, December 1900

In November 1900, J.C. Price joined as manager and took charge of the raja's private property and the property of the temple. However, Mukunda kept three villages under his own management. The legal document which was drawn up to transfer powers to Price mentioned that three villages, namely, Kudiari, Kusumati and Chanaghara, belonging to the temple, would remain under Mukunda's jurisdiction. A few months later, Mukunda made these villages over to Khandi who started collecting land revenue and rice from the villagers.

By this time Khandi had acquired so much clout that not only was she a talking point in the town of Puri, but a file in her name had also been opened at the collector's office bearing the caption, 'The Khandi, or the Maimed Woman'. The file contained several pieces of important information on Khandi.

Mukunda had sold several plots of land to Khandi and the members of her family at throwaway prices. For instance, Khandi's son, Madan Singh, got an orchard in Khundheibent Sahi measuring five *manas* for only 990 rupees; Khandi got a piece of homestead land in Dolamandap Sahi measuring seven manas for only 1500 rupees; Madan Singh was granted a *patta* authorizing him to collect revenue from Batagan *mouza* for ten years. For this he had to pay the paltry sum of 1056 rupees. He was also granted a patta for life appointing him sabarakar for Saantrapur mouza. It was doubtful whether Mukunda had taken any money at all from them.

These transactions in land apart, a few police cases were registered against Khandi in 1900. They were as follows:

1. Police case no. 1173, section 352, involving Raghuni Sahu and Khandi and another person. Raghuni Sahu had supplied quicklime to Khandi, when she constructed a house. When he asked her to pay 359 rupees towards the cost of the quicklime, Khandi got him beaten up. The case was dismissed as Raghuni failed to appear during the trial.
2. Case no. 1175, section 342 and 352. Pankaj Mahapatra versus Khandi and others. Khandi had assaulted Pankaj and had kept him unlawfully confined.
3. Case no. 1264, section 342. Natabar Jena and others. Natabar's younger brother had married Khandi's daughter. Khandi had promised that she would give him 500 rupees and ten manas of land as dowry. But she gave him only 180 rupees and refused to give the balance. She assaulted Natabar and tied him up when he went to ask for it. However, the case was dismissed for want of evidence.

The appointment of a Christian as the raja's manager too, led to controversy. Some were of the opinion that this amounted to an attack on Hinduism. But others expressed themselves in favour of the appointment as Mr Price worked efficiently and had brought about visible improvements in the affairs of the temple. In any case, the protest against the appointment of a sahib as manager did not assume the proportions of the one organized against the killing of monkeys.

At the end of the year it was announced that the viceroy, Lord Curzon, would pay a visit to Orissa to see the Puri and Lingaraj temples. Government functionaries now set about making the necessary arrangements relating to the viceregal visit. The lieutenant governor himself came to inspect the arrangements. As the viceroy was coming especially to see the temple at Puri, in the fitness of things, it should have fallen to the raja of Puri to organize a reception in the viceroy's honour. But, as everyone was aware of Mukunda's condition, they requested Madhu Babu to take this responsibility upon himself. So Madhu Babu came to Puri more than once to supervise the arrangements being made for the reception of the viceroy.

In the meantime, travelling to Puri had become much easier than before. A railway link connecting it to Khurda Road station was established in 1897. Around this time, Cuttack was also connected to Vizag by rail. About two years after this, a railway link connected Kharagpur to Cuttack. All this made life a lot easier for pilgrims bound for Puri.

On 16 December, when a special train carrying the viceroy arrived at the railway station in Puri, the town wore a completely different look. A beautiful dais had been erected where the viceroy was to be ceremonially received. The road running from it to the beach and the road leading from there to the temple were decorated with flags, flowers and floral arches. An awning was put up in front of the temple where guests were to be seated and entertained. Here, filigree works made at Madhu Babu's factory were displayed. A silver casket containing a speech welcoming the viceroy written on a palm leaf was also on display.

As soon as Lord Curzon arrived, he was driven in a horse-drawn buggy to the temple. He saw the Aruna Pillar and had a view of the temple from the Lion Gate. Then he was taken to the roof of Radhaballabh Mutt from where he saw as much of the inside of the temple as he could. He came to the dais after riding around the temple in the buggy. There, Madhu Babu, Mukunda, and other rajas and maharajas were waiting to receive him. A priest read out the following lines welcoming the viceroy:

> This I humbly and reverentially offer this to the lotus hands of the possessor of all virtues, the most honourable Baron Curzon of Kedleston, KG, GCSI, GCIE, PC the Lord of India.
>
> *Dwaramutkal Desasya Jagannathasya Mandiram*
> *Aitihasika Tattwasya Jnapaknch Visesatah.*

After dwelling on the glory of Lord Jagannath, it was mentioned that when the British first came to Orissa a raja named Mukunda was reigning in Puri. Now, Lord Curzon was visiting Puri when another Mukunda was the raja. This, the speaker observed, was a happy coincidence indeed. An account of how the priests of Puri temple had invited the British general leading the invading army to protect the temple was also provided.

The priest concluded by saying, '*Bayam Hi Shrimatah Rajabhaktah Ajnanubartinah Shrimadgunagrambimugdha Prajah.*' As it happened to be a Sunday, Curzon did not give a formal reply. Saying only, 'Thank you,' he went off to see Gundicha temple and from there he went to the circuit house. The same day, in the afternoon, at half past three, the viceroy left Puri for Bhubaneswar by train.

Hooghly, January 1901

Work overwhelmed Radhanath after he came to Hooghly. Burdwan was a large division in the education department which comprised as many as six districts. The inspector had to visit 132 schools in one year. For this reason, Radhanath had to remain on tour for most of the year. When the controversy relating to *Mahayatra* erupted, he had decided to give up literary pursuits altogether but it was not easy to do so. Literary magazines in Orissa kept pressing him to contribute articles, and poets and writers sent him their work for his comments. One day, he was pleasantly surprised to receive a poem and a letter from Fakir Mohan by post. The letter said:

> Dear brother Radhanath Babu,
>
> Please have a look at this poem. I don't feel satisfied with it. The language and the style leave a lot to be desired. I would treasure it if it is revised and retouched by you.
>
> Yours,
> Fakir Mohan Senapati.

The poem that accompanied this letter bore the title, 'Birahi Haladibasant'. When he went through the poem, Radhanath was reminded of the incident which took place when he had taken leave, gone to Cuttack from Hooghly and spent some time at Fakir Mohan's residence in Bakharabad. Fakir Mohan had turned fifty-seven and had just come back from Kendrapara, having worked there as manager for about nine months. He had made up his mind that he would never seek employment again and that he would lead a life of retirement in Cuttack. At this time he had written a number of poems which he wanted to bring together in a collection entitled *Abasar Basare*. The day on which Radhanath had gone to pay him a visit, Fakir Mohan took him into his garden. There they came upon a dead haladibasant bird lying on the ground. Fakir Mohan told Radhanath that every day, precisely at nine in the morning, two haladibasant birds used to come and fly about in his garden. One day, one of the two died and its partner would not touch food or water. It now lay dead at their feet. Fakir Mohan's poem chose this incident for its theme. A line in it said, 'My friend saw it with his own eyes'. In a footnote he explained this, saying: 'My childhood friend Radhanath Ray Bahadur was a witness to this incident.'

Laying his other engagements aside, Radhanath set about revising the poem. As he did not like the closing lines of the poem, he crossed them out and wrote new ones in their place. He revised a few other lines, copied out the revised version of the poem by hand, and sent it on to Fakir Mohan the very same day. He now resolved that he would again devote himself to writing poetry.

But he found that no matter how hard he tried, he could not write even one line. The mental stress caused by the controversy surrounding *Mahayatra*, by getting transferred out of Orissa, the pressure of work in Burdwan and his ill health had combined to rob him of his zest for life. Moreover, the climate of Hooghly was not good for his health. On occasions, Radhanath toyed with the idea of leaving his job and devoting himself entirely to literary pursuits. Many years ago, he had written in his long poem, 'Chilika', 'I had hoped to spend the last part of my life on your western shore'. It now seemed that hope remained only a hope. There was no possibility of receiving any financial help from the raja of Mayurbhanj or the raja of Bamanda.

That day, in the morning, Radhanath was feeling uncomfortable on account of an attack of asthma. He was also feeling feverish as he had taken a smallpox vaccine the previous day. Even talking took effort and he experienced difficulty breathing. But he had to go to office that day. He usually preferred to walk to office but that day he went there in a horse-drawn buggy.

Radhanath's style of working at his office was a peculiar one. On arriving at the office, he would take off his shoes and and his shirt and put them away. He would not use the office room or work at his desk sitting on a chair. He chose instead to work sitting on a reed mat in a room adjoining his office. As he did not like tables and chairs, he placed the official papers on his knees and did his official work seated in this manner. Only when a sahib paid him a visit would he put on his shirt and occupy his chair. People coming to see him sat on another reed mat spread near his and talked to him. His Bengali subordinates did office work sitting on chairs but they had to sit on the reed mat when they came to meet him. At first, the strange ways of this half-Oriya inspector amused them, but in no time his gentleness, his simplicity and his good qualities inspired feelings of respect and loyalty in them.

Radhanath used to fall ill frequently in his childhood and to find relief from pain he had picked up the habit of taking opium. He was never without a small silver box containing opium. Taking snuff was the only other bad habit he had acquired. That day, he had taken out a quantity of opium and was kneading it in his palm into a ball, although he had already had a dose of opium in the morning. He was in no mood to do any office work. He thought he would have stayed home and tried to write a few lines of a poem if he had had no office work to do that morning.

Now his chaprasi Anand stood before him. Radhanath took a good look at him. Looking at this plump and pot-bellied man, no one would be able to imagine that he was the same skinny child whom Sundar Narayan had brought home during the famine. Anand informed him that a lady had come to see him. Radhanath hurriedly swallowed the ball of opium and asked Anand to let her in. He straightened his back and sat up. Luckily for him, he was wearing his shirt as the weather was a little chilly and also because he was feeling unwell. The fever and the effect of opium made everything seem unreal to him.

The lady came in, greeted him with folded hands and sat down on the reed mat. She was about twenty-three years old, and her name was Nagendrabala Saraswati. She was then staying in Sukhadia village in the Hooghly district. Her husband was the sub-registrar of Jamalpur. She was an extraordinarily talented woman. Although young, she already had two books of poems to her credit: *Marmagatha* (Song of the Heart) and *Premagatha* (Saga of Love). Moreover, a year ago, her book titled *Naridharma* (Duties of Women) had been published. This book had found great favour with conservative Bengalis for they thought it contained many pieces of good advice for women. For instance, it advised women to avoid talking too much to any man other than their husbands; it also forbade women to converse alone with a man. Nagendrabala was going to bring out another collection of poems, titled *Amiyagatha*, which she had named after her daughter, Amiya. She had come to Radhanath to request him to contribute a foreword to this book.

She handed the manuscript to Radhanath who was soon completely absorbed in reading it. The poems moved him deeply as they were permeated by feelings of profound sadness and grief. It seemed as if the poems reflected the present state of Radhanath's mind. They led him back into some forgotten recesses of his memory. When he came back to his senses he found the mysterious and beautiful woman sitting before him.

He said, 'These are beautiful poems.'

Nagendrabala said, 'You don't know me. But I know you for I have read everything you have written.'

'But I write in Oriya', Radhanath said.

'I taught myself Oriya to be able to read your works. I have read every one of your poems. You are my literary mentor,' said Nagendrabala.

'Do you know that disciples have to pay *dakshina* to their mentors?' Radhanath asked playfully.

Nagendrabala came closer, touched his feet and said, 'I do. I am willing to give whatever dakshina you want from me.'

Radhanath said, 'All right. I accept you as my disciple. But you were wrong when you said I didn't know you. After I went through your poems I felt that I have long known you.'

This made Nagendrabala smile, and she said, 'I know. My relationship with you spans several births. Before I was born you had written: Touching the lotus feet of Nagendrabala will bring fulfilment to my life.'

Her words again sent Radhanath back into the past. These lines occurred in his poem 'Meghaduta', which he had composed twenty-seven years ago. At that time he was a young man of twenty-five. Now he was fifty-two and he had gone through so much during this time. And yet he had never in his life experienced a day like this. He felt as if his poetic self, his life, his past, his present and his future had found fulfilment. It seemed to him as if he had floated into a timeless, ethereal world of bliss. It was like a dream. But Radhanath also felt that the ghost of his father, Sundar Narayan had cast a shadow across this world.

Radhanath opened his eyes and looked about. There was no one in the room. Nagendrabala had left a long while ago.

Puri, September 1901

The file on Khandi, which was maintained at the collectorate, grew thicker day by day. It now contained information on how the raja of Puri had transferred more landed property to the members of Khandi's family. For instance, the raja had granted Khandi's son, Madan Singh, a daily allowance of three rupees and ten annas which he himself used to receive from the temple; fifty-eight acres of land belonging to the temple in Ramachandrapur, Kapileswar and Balibaruni villages were transferred on a permanent basis to Madan; the Delang mahal was placed under the management of Khandi's son-in-law, Jogi Rout, on a permanent basis in exchange for a paltry sum of 2500 rupees. Thirty-three acres of land in

Lembai pragana were sold off to Jogi Rout's son Naran Rout in exchange for only seventy rupees; thirty-three acres of land in Machhapada were leased out to Madan in exchange for seventy rupees; Naran Rout obtained the sarbarakari of five villages in Delang on payment of 3298 rupees; he got the sarbarakari of another sixteen villages of Delang by paying 3337 rupees.

The number of police cases against Khandi had also multiplied. The most serious case concerned Khandi's fourth husband, Dasarathi. He sat idle at home after losing his job as constable. Khandi now pestered Mukunda to find him another job. The temple was being repaired at the time. In May 1901, Mukunda appointed Dasarathi as head engineer whose job was to supervise the repair work. But the temple priests did not let him enter the temple premises as he had lost his caste by marrying a beggar woman. Trouble ensued when Dasarathi tried to force his way into the temple, and a case was registered with the police.

Mukunda's greatest worry was how to get people of Khandi's caste to accept her back into their fold. After exerting himself vigorously and going to a lot of expense, he managed to persuade the *chasas* of Kapileswar, Samagar and Batagaon villages to accept her as one of them. The upshot was chasas of fifty-six villages excommunicated the chasas belonging to these three villages. In the end, the chasas of Batagan performed rites of expiation and got accepted back into the community.

Lawsuits were frequently filed against Mukunda for he took loans from many people which he did not repay. His creditors, however, soon found out ingenious ways of recovering their money. Whenever they got a decree from the court they got Khandi's property raided for they knew that Mukunda was bankrupt.

That year, a serious problem relating to the celebration of the Car Festival arose. According to the Oriya almanac, the festival was to begin from 18 June. However, according to the Bengali almanac, it was to start from 17 July, that is, about a month later.

Since the raja of Puri did not bother to take any decision on this matter, temple priests followed the almanac that suited them and brought pilgrims to Puri according to their convenience. Just twenty days before the festival, Mukunda decided that the festival would be held according to the Oriya almanac. But by this time the priests had made their own arrangements.

The day before the festival, an untoward incident took place inside the temple premises. Madhu Babu's daughter, Shoilabala Das, used to come to Puri now and then and stay at her residence there. That day, in the morning, Shoilabala, while taking a stroll along the main street with Mrs Sen, the civil surgeon's wife, and two other ladies, came to the Lion Gate. A temple priest recognized them and invited them to go inside the temple. Shoilabala expressed her reluctance to enter the temple premises. When the temple priest kept pressing her to accompany him, she asked, 'Do you know who I am?' The priest said, 'Who does not know Madhu Babu's daughter? I am asking you to come inside because you are his daughter.'

The temple was very crowded that day on account of the *Netrotsav* festival. A few priests led Shoilabala and her friends through the crowd holding their hands near the deities. When consecrated water was passed round, Shoilabala and a Brahmo lady came away and stood near the Mukti Mandap.

Now a Vaishnav who happened to be there recognized Shoilabala and shouted, 'What! Madhu Babu's daughter has stepped into the temple. The temple has been defiled.' Hearing him shout, the priest who had got Shoilabala into the temple came hurrying out. The Vaishnav slapped him. Others who were present there set upon the priest and started beating him. Another priest came and urged Shoilabala to deny that she was Madhu Babu's daughter and say that she was a member of the civil surgeon's family. But Shoilabala flatly refused to do so.

The temple premises turned into a veritable battlefield, and the collector and the superintendent of police had to be informed. They arrived at the temple gate on horseback and found that a lot of people had gathered there, too, and were shouting. Collector Garret feared that the people might kill Shoilabala. He sent Hindu policemen into the temple premises. With great difficulty, they managed to bring Shoilabala and her friends out of the temple.

A cable was sent to Madhu Babu immediately. He arrived the next day, accompanied by the commisssioner. Newspapers in Calcutta carried exaggerated accounts of the incident. For instance, the *Bengali Mirror* said that the Christian ladies had entered the temple with the intention of ridiculing Hindu gods, and that Hindus found it difficult to perform acts of worship because heathens had entered their temples. So on and on.

Since the temple had become desecrated, purificatory rites were performed. The offerings were thrown away and the observance of rites of worship got delayed. Madhu Babu was very cross with Shoilabala and went to the palace and apologized to the raja on her behalf. The priests who had taken Shoilabala into the temple were fined. A long and detailed account of the incident appeared in the *Dipika* but it omitted to mention Madhu Babu and Shoilabala by name, out of courtesy. They were referred to as a Christian lady and her father.

All went smoothly during the Car Festival. However, pilgrims kept arriving in Puri for a month after the festival was over, for, according to the Bengali almanac, the festival was to be celebrated on 17 July.

Mukunda now dismissed Price and appointed Rasbehari Nayak as manager, giving him a monthly salary of two hundred rupees. Rasbehari had been thrown out of his government job a few days earlier for it was believed he had lost his mind.

In the meantime, Mukunda's own condition had deteriorated further. When he had to interact with people outside the palace, he behaved properly and talked sense. But the moment he set foot in the palace, he metamorphosed into a very different person. His sole aim in life was to find ways of keeping Khandi in good humour. As time passed, he stopped stirring out of the palace and spent all his time hiding in a room. Finding that he had no interest at all in matters concerning the temple and his estate, his employees, Gopinath Pattanayak and Birabhadra Kanungo, ordered the affairs of the temple in ways that suited them. One day, they convinced Mukunda that there was no need for him to bother about the temple and his zamindari, and that he should get someone else to manage them.

On 6 September 1901, Mukunda issued pattas in favour of three persons: Jagabandhu Pattanayak, Chintamani Pattanayak and Birabhadra Kanungo. In one of these it was recorded that in order to bring about improvement in the management of the temple, these people would remain in charge of all activities relating to *amruta manohi*. They would earn 22,000 rupees a year. Out of this, they would keep 2200 rupees for themselves and spend a certain amount on offerings for the deities and give the balance to Mukunda. However, if the expenditure exceeded the income, the deficit would be met by Mukunda. In the second patta it was mentioned that these three persons were authorized to collect land revenue from the estate attached to the temple. They would be allowed to keep ten per cent of the amount collected for their own expenses and spend a certain amount on offerings made to the deities. The balance they would give to Mukunda. In discharging their duties, they would enjoy all the powers and privileges to which the raja himself was entitled. The raja would not interfere in their work in any way. This arrangement would remain in force for a period of two years.

After all the parties to the deal put their signatures on the pattas, Jagabandhu Pattanayak, who was a sub-registrar and who also happened to be one of the signatories, got them registered at his cutcherry. In this way, Mukunda auctioned off the temple to these three crooks.

Hooghly, March 1902

In February 1901, Radhanath took three months' leave and came to Cuttack. In March, Sashibhusan got married. He was now twenty-five years old. He had had an attack of epilepsy when he was sixteen and had been dogged by ill health ever since. He had become a close companion of his father and accompanied him whenever he went on tour. He had also started writing and had published a book *Dakshinatya Bhraman* (A Tour of the South). However, he was known to people in Orissa as Radhanath Ray's son and companion.

In May, Radhanath got his second son Rajanibhusan married and went back to Hooghly. There he devoted himself to writing the foreword to Nagendrabala's collection of poems. He liked the poems and he wrote a brief account of her life and a foreword which was full of praise for her work. The book now went to the press.

These days Nagendrabala came to his office as well as to his residence from time to time. She was a soft-spoken, gentle and friendly person, and in no time she earned the affections of Radhanath's wife, Parasmani. The element of formality had disappeared from their relationship. She now gave him advice regarding his personal life. She asked him to do his office work sitting on a chair. She would not allow Radhanath to sit in his office without wearing a shirt. She also advised Radhanath on what he should wear, on the length of his moustache and on his hairstyle.

Nagendrabala fascinated and frightened Radhanath at the same time. She had come to occupy a special place in his life. She now enjoyed unrestricted access to his office and his residence. To strangers Radhanath now introduced her as the glory of Bengali poetry and his dear disciple.

Nagendrabala was genuinely devoted to Radhanath. She had read everything Radhanath had written and was intimately acquainted with every line of his poetry. A photograph of Radhanath adorned her house. She had got it from Cuttack. At the time, photographs of Kabibar Ray, Radhanath Ray, Bahadur Mahoday were available from the Cuttack Printing Company at two annas per piece. Nagendrabala had kept all Radhanath's books neatly stacked near his photograph. Once Radhanath had paid a visit to Nagendrabala's residence and was amazed to see his own photograph being worshipped there.

On several occasions, Nagendrabala's behaviour scared and worried Radhanath. One day, while discussing a poem at Radhanath's residence, Nagendrabala suddenly moved closer and sat next to Radhanath. Radhanath felt awkward and moved away a little. Nagendrabala said, 'You have written so much about women but it seems you know nothing about them. Tell me, how many women do you know intimately?'

They said nothing to each other after this, but the question kept haunting Radhanath for many days. Another day, Nagendrabala said to Radhanath, 'From now on I will address you as *tume* not as *apana*. Would you mind if I did so?' The question embarrassed Radhanath and he said that she was his disciple and was like his daughter. At this Nagendrabala gave an inscrutable smile and said, 'You are right.' From that day, she addressed Radhanath as tume whenever she was alone with him and as apana when others happened to be around.

When the printing of *Amiyagatha* began, Nagendrabala started coming to Radhanath's residence as she pleased. She now needed Radhanath's help in correcting the proofs, replacing some words with more appropriate ones at the last moment, and other such matters. Parasmani was in Cuttack at the time and Radhanath was staying alone. While *Amiyagatha* was getting printed Radhanath went on tour less frequently and devoted more time to the printing of this book. He certainly liked discussing poetry with Nagendrabala and enjoyed her company, but at the same time, her behaviour worried and disturbed him.

One Sunday afternoon, Nagendrabala arrived bringing a printed copy of *Amiyagatha*. She touched Radhanath's feet and handed the book to him. Radhanath took the book and started re-reading the poems in it. He said, 'The poems are really very good.' Nagendrabala took the book from his hand and said, 'I am glad that you liked my book.' Radhanath said, 'I mean what I said. Your poems are really very beautiful. You should now write another book.' Nagendrabala said, 'I will certainly write another book. You should also write a book. Don't you realize you haven't written anything for a long time?'

'I am not in a state of mind which is congenial to writing. There is no question of finishing *Mahayatra* now. I thought I could have at least finished *Parvati*. But what can I do? I am unable to think up anything new.'

Nagendrabala said, 'You must write. Leave *Parvati* aside and start writing something new. If you can't find characters such as Usha or Nandikeswari and if your mind can't come up with anything new, look at me. I am sitting right in front of you. You should write a long poem about me.' When Radhanath said nothing in reply she lost her temper and said, 'All these years you have written only fiction about women and love. After all, what do you know about women? Have you ever understood the heart of a woman?'

Radhanath kept quiet. Nagendrabala continued, 'All right. I'll make you understand what a woman really wants, what lies in her heart.' Saying this, she moved very close to Radhanath, held him in her arms and said, 'A long time ago, I had promised that I would give you guru dakshina. I will give it to you today.'

Radhanath shrank back and protested, 'No, no. I don't want any guru dakshina.' But Nagendrabala said, as she locked the door from inside, 'I don't want to remain in anyone's debt. You have to accept guru dakshina from me.'

Later when Nagendrabala came back to the sitting room after washing up, she found Radhanath sitting there, looking very sad and miserable. She asked, 'What's the matter with you?' When she did not receive any reply from Radhanath, she edged closer to him. But Radhanath tried to push her away. Nagendrabala put on her slippers and went out of the room. While leaving, she said, 'Well, then. This is our last meeting.'

She kept her word and did not come back. Four days passed. On the fifth, Radhanath sent her a letter through a servant asking her to come back to him.

Cuttack, July 1907

In February 1903, aged fifty-five, Radhanath retired from service and returned to Cuttack. His four-year stay in Hooghly had not been a very happy one. The fact that he had not been able to do any writing during this period caused him much pain. Only the Bengali poems he had written earlier were collected under the title *Lekhabali*. A book of quotations from Kalidas bearing the title *Kalidas Suktayah* was published during this period. The collected works of Radhanath Ray also got published with financial assistance from the raja of Khariar. On the first page of this was printed a poem titled 'Bhutaler Swarg'. It was written by Nagendrabala and it contained the following lines:

> What I have seen has no parallel on the earth
> In the middle of a world animated by greed
> I have seen a holy deity, a picture of heaven on earth:
> Radhanath Ray
> O you, the great artist
> You are my mentor

I am your disciple
At your touch base metal turns into gold
I want a glimpse of your heaven
Nagendrabala, who craves your affection.

Radhanath's relationship with Nagendrabala was one of the sources of his unhappiness during his stay in Hooghly. He could not leave her, nor could he make her his own. On one occasion, Nagendrabala had come to Cuttack and spent some time at Dhabaleswar. She wrote a poem on Dhabaleswar and Radhanath got it published in the form of a booklet from Calcutta. The booklet was dedicated to the 'most revered Srijukta Parasmani Dasi, whom I look upon as my mother, the spouse of the most esteemed poet Ray Radhanath Ray'. Radhanath had sent copies of this booklet to all his friends.

After he returned to Orissa, Radhanath got busy with various meetings and functions. The first annual function of the Utkal Sahitya Samaj was held on 29 December 1903 at the Town Victoria School in Cuttack. Radhanath wrote out an address for this occasion; but, as his voice was not audible enough, it was read out by Pandit Mrutyunjay Banibhushan. The conference of Utkal Sammilani was held in the Idgah field the next day. Radhanath composed a song to be sung on this occasion which opened with the line: 'O sons of Utkal, lay down your lives for your motherland.' The song in Sanskrit he had written addressing Mother India was also sung at this conference. Its opening line was: *Sarvesham no janani Bharat dharani kalpalateyam.*

Radhanath took ill a few days after this and he suffered acute mental depression. It seemed to him that his illness was the punishment for some sin he had committed. To relax he began taking sitar lessons in the evening. He also hired a Sanskrit pandit with whom he discussed classics morning and evening. He took to writing 'Madhusudan' on a piece of paper a thousand times every morning. He spent hours bathing in the waters of the river

Katjuri. But his physical and mental condition showed no signs of improvement. During this difficult time in his life his only source of comfort was his son, Sashibhusan. Radhanath would not part with him even for a moment. Sashibhusan, too, stayed close to his father, like his shadow.

Radhanath was convinced that his sinful relationship with Nagendrabala was responsible for all his sufferings. He now wrote a poem titled 'Satiprati Satidrohira Ukti' (The Unfaithful Husband to his Chaste Wife) addressing Parasmani. It opened thus: 'As a young man and as an adult, I always wanted to follow the path of virtue. I was determined that I would remain loyal to my wife and never be unfaithful to her.' The poem then went on to narrate how fate drew him into the web of a seductress when he left home and went to some place elsewhere. In the poem he described Nagendrabala as an evil seductress and explained that he could not escape the trap she had set for him, as he was physically and mentally weak at the time.

After this, Radhanath sought to give expression to his feeling of contrition in an autobiographical piece. He began this narrative thus: 'Words will never be able to describe the pain and agony that rack my body. It feels as if midday heat flows like a liquid through my veins. A searing pain stabs my ribs and my thighs. Thoughts of putting an end to my life daily cross my mind. This, after all, is the wage of sin. All my bodily organs now rebel against me. My belly, my chest, my legs and hands and eyes torture me. It is as if they all silently accuse me saying: You are a sinner; you have forfeited your right to live; we are no longer willing to do your bidding.

'The sound of a clock striking hurts me. I find playing sitar an agony. I wince when my eyes fall on pictures of virtuous beings such as Rama, Sita, Satyaban and Savitri. Alas! What a man I used to be and what I have turned into. Such a shameful incident took place in the last part of my life.

'What a pity. Even now people describe me as a saintly person. Wherever I have gone I have been presented as this kind of a person. As a matter of fact, for most of my life, I deserved this appellation. It was during the three years which I spent in Hooghly that my character got tainted. How many people suffer such a terrible fate in the evening of their lives?'

Radhanath filled page after page writing in this vein. But this did not bring him peace of mind either. Days passed into months and months into years, but his misery did not abate. In 1906, Nagendrabala passed away, aged only twenty-eight. Even this news did not mitigate Radhanath's suffering in any way.

In the end, he told Sashibhusan that he would be able to expiate his sin and obtain relief from his agony only through a public confession. Sashibhusan tried to dissuade his father from taking such an extreme step. Radhanath went and talked to his close friend Madhu Rao, who lived nearby, about his decision. He also went to the Utkal Sahitya Press and talked to Biswanath Kar. He shared his problem with Baikunthanath De when he came to Cuttack. He even sought Gourishankar's advice. They all, in one voice, urged him to desist from taking such a step.

Undeterred by their entreaties, Radhanath set about writing out the confessional statement which said:

> I humbly pray to the person who would receive this confession to show it to his acquaintances. This is what a great sinner like me has to submit before the public.
>
> I am a great sinner. With folded hands I request you to hate my sin but not the sinner. No one except the Almighty is my accuser, and I am the accused.
>
> For fifty-two years of my life I had remained pure and untainted. When I was aged fifty-three I came to be acquainted with a certain gifted lady in another place. Her extraordinary talent and her writing style drew me towards her and we became friends. I did not know at the time that all these gifts concealed a devious character. I lost control over myself under the influence

of her tainted character. From time to time my conscience did rebuke me, but so powerful was the spell cast by that seductress that it would not let me hear the voice of my conscience.

I have deviated from the path of virtue and yet I go about the business of life as if I were a virtuous man. This I find unbearable. I have brought disgrace upon humanity, to the Education Department, and my conduct has been unbecoming of an old man. A sin so terrible has rarely been committed. My life is approaching its end. All my life I had stuck to the path of virtue, but I committed this sin just when I stood on the threshold of the world beyond life.

Having written page after page in this vein, he concluded the statement by saying:

I once again entreat you all with folded hands to give me your blessings so that I become worthy of the dust your feet.

I humbly request the esteemed editors to take pity on me and publish this confession in their newspapers.

I am aware that people would call me mad because I have confessed my sin in public. But my heart tells me that I have done what I did in obedience to the wish of the Almighty. I had no other option but to do His bidding. I know that many incidents like the one I have narrated happen in the world. Even so, I cannot exercise self-restraint.

Shri Radhanath Ray   Cuttack
                                                   25 July 1907

As desired by his father, Sashibhusan got a thousand copies of the confession in Bengali and another thousand copies in Oriya printed at the Cuttack Printing Company and sent these to all the newspapers and magazines in Bengal and Orissa and to many distinguished persons. He then went back to his father and informed him that the statement had been sent to all the places Radhanath had wanted it to reach. Radhanath took the piece of paper from his hand, and, as he read it, broke down and cried, remembering Nagendrabala.